# The Definition Of Equal

E S Carpenter

Published by Quesylis P H

# Chapter One
## Exemplification

Stephanie finally released him from the tender embrace; still unsteady from the intensity of the moment, then held out her trembling hand and breathed deep as she studied the ring. She wiped the last tears and met Jake's eyes. "You really want to marry me?"

Her glassy eyes caught his attention and momentarily mesmerized him, but his need to confirm his love and ease her doubt brought him back from the momentary bliss. "Yes, I want to marry you. Why did you think for a second I didn't for a second?" He squinted. "Was that english?"

He hugged her tight and their mouths softly sealed together as they stood and kissed in front of the bedroom closet; her toes barely touching the floor. When the kiss ended she asked again, but this time with a big smile. "You really want to marry me?"

He chuckled and shook his head in amazement. He knew she needed additional qualifications. She had always needed additional qualifications. He loved the idea she loved him so much she didn't believe he could love her as much, but her unpretentiousness and fragility were exactly why he loved her and exactly why he loved the thought of being with her for the rest of his life.

And he needed exactly what she provided. He craved her constant requalifying insecurity, and he had full intentions of spending the rest of his life reassuring her. He had just as strong a need to show her his words were gold, as she had need to hear the confirmations.

He slid his fingers through the back of her hair, then met her mouth with his, and kissed her with all his heart. He could feel her soul attached to his, like he felt her tender embrace.

"Jacob?"

"What sweetheart?"

"Can we make love?"

He chuckled, then lifted her in his arms. "Oh sweetheart, I appreciate you asking, but I already decided that's what's next."

Her arms slid around his neck as she gazed softly into his eyes. "Really?" And the response tickled him, as it always did.

He laughed at her requalification. "God, I love you. If you had any idea how much I love you..." The sentence faded without ending. There were no words to express the love he had for her.

He lowered her feet to the floor, took her hand and led her to the side of their bed. She sat in front of him and slipped her slippers off; still admiring the ring as she slid her fingers around the band, then casually looked at him. "When did you buy me this?"

He finished pulling his shirt over his head, revealing the telltale grin her question raised. It sounded innocent enough, but he knew her; and it wasn't. She was still qualifying his intentions, and it tickled him to his core. "Long enough ago, I'm done paying for it."

Her eyes widened and her response softened. "You wanted to marry me for a while?"

He inhaled deeply as her words confirmed his heartfelt intention. "Yeah. I've been planning on marrying you for a while. Is that okay?"

She jumped up, eagerly wrapped her arms around his neck and answered with a long deep kiss. She tried to kiss him more passionately than ever …but failed. She had often kissed him as deeply as she could. He registered her intent though, savoring her heartfelt attempt.

He knew the answer to the next question, but he loved this game they played. "Would you have said yes a while back?"

Her reply was instant. "What do you think?"

He leaned back and laughed. They had been together long enough, to know her need to qualify his love, but he also knew he wasn't allowed to qualify hers. The one thing she demanded was his acknowledgement of her complete love for him. He wasn't allowed to have the doubts she couldn't dismiss no matter how hard she tried. That, she demanded.

"Why are you grinning?"

"Oh, I'm just thinking you're gorgeous and you're going to be my wife." He shook his head, conscious of the ongoing and uncontrollable grin on his face. Quirks like this were the things he fell in love with.

He reached for the bottom of her blouse, then lifted it and she raised her arms in satisfied pleasure. He slipped it over her head and tossed it on the old wood chair in the corner, tenderly wrapped his arms around her and with her snugly against him, plopped on the bed behind them.

"Jake!"

He laughed as they bounced, then rolled on top of her and kissed her softly. She hugged his neck and sighed as the kiss ended, then each quickly struggled to remove the rest of their clothes and hurry under their covers. And as they snuggled together, he slid his hands behind her back and unclasped the only garment she hadn't removed, then slipped it off her shoulders like he was happily unwrapping a present.

He tossed the delicate undergarment toward the chair and it fluttered to the floor a few feet short, then turned to her, admiring her beautiful chest. She didn't have much, but her breasts were magnificent and silky soft. And her nipples were full and even softer ...until they reacted to his touch. He adored her breasts. The memory of his first caress held such emotional depth, he could recall the event in an instant. It broke their fear of a relationship and the memory's intensity was as strong as if it happened moments ago.

He tenderly embraced her and gently cuddled her. There was something astounding about holding her when they were naked. Her entire body was so different than his.

He squeezed her playfully. "And will you promise to be okay if a girl touches me or you see me laughing with one? I'll always be leaving them with the intentions of meeting you. I promise."

She smirked in embarrassment at the thought of the reaction which caused the current scene, and then smiled at the result. She knew her reaction was childish, especially for where they were now, but where they were sure was worth the fears and tears the incident caused.

"I'll try. But do you know how many times I watched a girl come up to us and take you away? I watched it all through high school and I'm sick and tired of it." He knew she was now only playing, but her words were a quiet revelation and he took a breath. He wanted to ask her if she had been in love with him that long. Had she? He didn't know if he should ask.

"Now you have proof on your finger no girl can take me away, not that they ever could. And you can waive it to whomever you have to." He knew she wouldn't, but he wanted her to know she had his approval if she felt the need.

They spent the next hour lovingly worshipping each other and she offered the last thought as she snuggled tight to him before shutting her eyes for the night. "That was the first time we made love as an engaged couple."

His entire heart and soul seemed to respond to the statement and he breathed deep and held her tenderly. He kissed her forehead, "Sleep tight sweetheart." and they passed out in each other's arms.

Jake's efforts to shut off the morning phone alarm woke her and she immediately reached for her ring, making sure it had weathered the night, then rolled on top of him. "How did you know what size to get me?"

He held out his pinky finger and looked at the second digit as if she could see where his eyes focused. "I used the middle of my pinky finger, and asked all three salespeople what they thought." His eyes met hers. "I got lucky?" A slight smile appeared on his face. "What can I say?"

She caressed his face and kissed him. He didn't understand she wasn't looking for an answer. She had his ring. She stared at it as she sat on the edge of the bed, next to him. "I have to call everyone today."

His grin reappeared as the depth of her statement registered. "I know." He exhaled slowly. Every feminine nuance tickled him to his core. He rose and headed toward the bathroom to start their morning pre-school ritual. She followed, staring at her finger. "I need to get my nails done. I can't show people this without my nails done."

"Of course not."

"Are you making fun of me?"

He ignored her question and pulled the shower curtain back so she could step in. She faced him after reaching for one of the two soaps they kept on the tub. "I'm going to be Stephanie Harrison."

"We can be the Blair-Harrisons if you want."

"Nope. I want to be Stephanie Harrison. My mom took my father's name. My grandmother took my grandfather's name. Girls take their guy's name. You called me Stephanie Harrison once and my heart beat fast for an hour, and I still haven't stopped thinking about it. And I'm finally going to be Stephanie Harrison."

His face glowed from the inner tickling her argument produced. "I have no rebuttal for that."

She wiped the water from her eyes and squinted at him. "Well I'm old-fashioned."

He snickered. "Whatever you say…"

He watched her glance at the ring fifty times during the walk to their first class and realized how her actions touched his heart. She did so many amazingly loving things. They kissed before heading their separate way toward their first class and he glanced back a few moments later and caught her looking at the ring. He hadn't stopped smiling this morning.

She tried to pay attention during her first class. She tried to listen to the lecture, taking notes more out of routine than attention, but she couldn't focus on anything but the ring. She kept staring and touching, whether with the opposite hand or the thumb of the hand it was on.

She never moved so fast out the door of an ending class in her life and immediately reached for her phone. She pressed a few buttons and paused. "Mom!"

"Hi sweetheart."

"Jake and I are engaged!"

"Fantastic!"

Her voice turned apologetic. "I know I should have waited until I could tell you in person, but I couldn't wait till weekend. I had to tell you." Her excitement rose. "He gave me the ring last night."

"Where at?" Genna knew he was trying to think of a clever way to give it to her. All four parents and her grandmother knew his intentions. The only person in their immediate family who didn't know was Vicky. Jake thought she'd enjoy telling him, so he left that task for her.

"In our apartment."

"Really."

Stephie stared at the ring. "He told me he tried to think of something clever, but I really needed it." She paused. "Why? Did you know he was going to ask me?"

"Well, yeah. We all knew. He asked your father's permission."

"He asked dad's permission?" She paused for a moment. "How perfect is he?" She wasn't asking her mother, but she said the sentence into the phone just the same.

"He's pretty special." Genna's answer soothed Stephie.

"Yeah." She sighed. "Yeah, he is."

She started up the steps toward the cafeteria doors. "Okay mom, I have to go. I'm between classes, but I'll call you soon. Love you."

"I love you too sweetheart. Have a great day."

"You too mom." She dropped her phone in her purse as she headed into the cafeteria, toward their second period table. She saw him come in the door on the opposite side of the room and waited to give him a kiss. "Hi fiancé."

He shook his head in playful amazement as they sat across from each other. "You're too funny."

"Thank you honey." She hadn't made one move to take a book from her book bag and it caught his attention. "What?"

Her face brightened. "I don't feel like studying."

He stopped setting his books up, and rested his arms on the table. "Okay. What do you feel like doing?"

She sat straight. "Well, we have things to discuss."

"Like what?" He removed an apple from his backpack, took a bite, then handed it to her.

She hopped in her seat. "Like when we're getting married and what kind of wedding we should have."

He reached back into his backpack and pulled out two sodas. "You're such a girl."

Her voice rose. "I wish." She thought for a moment as she continued examining her ring. "Oh how I wish."

His eyes narrowed. "Why at the times you should feel most like a girl, do you seem to feel just the opposite?"

She leaned closer. "Because those are the times I wish more than anything, I was more girl than I am."

He cracked the tabs on both cans. "Sometimes I think you're more a girl to me than you are to you."

"No. Those are the times I wish I was more a girl *for* you, than *for* me."

"And I want you to be exactly who you are. I know you wish you were a cis girl, but I love that you're you." He stared into her eyes, confirming his resolute certainty.

She stared at her finger and sighed. "Did you show either of our mother's the ring?"

"No," He sat and stared at her as she examined her finger and refocused on the joy of her continued reaction. "I figured you would want to."

She looked at him curiously. "Who helped you pick it out?"

"Nobody, but I asked your grandmother where to go."

Her eyes widened. "You asked my father permission to marry me?"

His head shifted back. "How'd you know?"

"Mom just told me. I called and told her we were engaged as soon as my class ended." She folded her hands on the table and studied his eyes. "So when do you want to get married?"

"Well, we have to wait till we graduate." His uncontrollable grin appeared instantly. "I can't be tied down while I'm around all these women."

Her eyes projected a playful scorn. "Bastard. I'll take you for every penny you have."

He chuckled, pleased her sense of humor overrode the extended seriousness of the engagement ordeal. "You'll get slightly less than two grand."

She continued, playfully indignant, "That little? I might as well stay married to you." Her smile widened. "So when do I officially lay claim to everything you own?"

"I don't know. What are you thinking?"

"I'd marry you tomorrow, but I think our mothers would be upset, don't you?"

"No doubt in my mind."

She casually brushed her hair back with spread fingers. "Besides, I'm washing my hair tomorrow, so tomorrow isn't ideal for me either."

"Ha ha." He motioned toward her finger. "Do you like the ring?"

"Jake. It's gorgeous."

"The diamond isn't very big."

She slowly twisted her hand and studied it. "It's the most beautiful ring I ever saw. It's from you."

"But do you think it's pretty?"

She circled the diamond with her fingertip. "Yes. I absolutely do." She stared into his eyes and whispered. "I love you."

He smiled softly. "I love you too, sweetheart." He knew damn well it could be the ugliest ring he found and she would have said the exact same words. *I'll never know if she really thinks it's pretty.* He caught himself smiling as he realized how much the idea tickled him.

She kissed him as he rose from his seat at the end of their period long break and pulled out her phone as they walked toward the cafeteria's double glass doors. She held it toward him. "…Gotta tell Vicky."

She watched Jake head in the opposite direction at the bottom of the expansive steps leading away from the building and dialed as she heard him say the goodbye he always offered. "I love you."

She held her phone next to her ear. "I love you too."

"I love you too. But don't you usually say that at the end of our calls?"

"Vicky!"

"Sister! How's my favorite sister of all time?"

She laughed. "Do you have any sisters I don't know about?"

"No." He paused a quick second. "Which is why I can unequivocally say you're my favorite sister of all time."

She shook her head. "You're a nut."

"Why yes I am. What's your point?"

"My point is…" She hesitated to increase affect, then raised her voice in excitement. "Jake proposed to me!"

He joked calmly. "Well what did you say?"

"What do you think I said?"

"Congratulations sister! I'm so happy for you!"

She felt herself blush. "Thank you. I'm so happy I can't believe it." She walked inside the stone building toward her next class.

"So …what you doing?"

"Walking into my next class. In fact, I have to go. I just couldn't wait to tell you."

"Thanks honey, but I need details when you can. …Lots and lots of details, hear me?"

"Yes Vicky. I promise."

"Good girl. Now go get smarter."

"I will. Love you."

"Love you and your hunk too."

~~~

Genna heard the side door open and rushed to the kitchen. When she saw Connor, she held out her arms and hurried toward him. "They're engaged."

Connor dropped his briefcase beside the door and hugged her. "Fantastic."

Genna bounced in his arms and laughed. "Finally."

"I agree." He kissed her. "…About time"

"Tell me about it. I feel like celebrating."

He gently rubbed her back. "You're too funny."

"Can you believe it?" She leaned away from him and made eye contact. "Can you believe they're engaged to be married?"

"Are they coming over? Are we celebrating?" He released her and lifted his briefcase.

"No. She has an evening class tonight. I just said that for us. She called me between classes today so the conversation was short."

"Did she say how he proposed? How clever did he get?"

She followed him toward their bedroom. "She told me he tried to think of something, but this wasn't planned. She said she *needed* it."

He dropped his briefcase against the wall in their closet. "Needed it? Did she know he had a ring for her?"

"I didn't ask what she meant. She was extremely excited and I was too excited for her." She sat on their bed. "I can't wait to hear details."

He kicked off his shoes and undid his tie. "Me either."

She watched patiently as he changed into more comfortable clothes. "Can you believe it though? Would you have ever guessed this is where we'd be, the day we moved here?" She extended her arms behind her and leaned back. "In a million tries, I would have never guessed this."

"Nope. Never." He turned into the bathroom and his voice increased from behind the door. "Did she say when she's coming over to show us the ring?"

She raised her voice. "No. It honestly was a short call."

"Did they tell Chris and Morgan?"

"I don't know."

He came out of the bathroom, walked to her and kissed her quickly. "You don't know anything." He reached for her hand and lifted her off the bed. "Can we call next door or do we have to wait for her to tell them?"

"You know we can't until we know."

He paused and frowned. "Well this sucks."

"I'll call her a little later"

His mind wandered as he followed her toward the kitchen. "I just pictured her in a wedding gown. I bet she looks gorgeous."

She glanced at him and smiled. "I pictured that earlier."

"Can you believe our adorable little boy became an even more adorable woman?"

She opened the refrigerator door and removed a few items. "Funny how when you love someone …you can completely see them as they need to be seen."

"And when they believe you see them properly, how they thrive?" He rubbed his stomach as he took her place in front of the open fridge. "What's for dinner?"

"I'm making a salad and heating leftovers."

He reached for a container. "Beautiful. You take care of the salad. I'll get the leftovers, as long as I don't have to put them in another container."

Her voice lowered. "Put them in another container."

"All that work?" He breathed audibly. "Alright …I'll do it."

She spun and smacked his bottom. "Thanks, ass."

# Chapter Two
## Revelation

"Your skin color is my favorite to work with." Vicky applied the finishing touches as the woman sat patiently, then cleaned the applicator in his hand before handing her the small mirror on his cart. "What do you think?"

"Wow. You're talented." The woman moved the mirror closer, examining the blended shades over her eyes.

"I'm glad you're pleased." He dabbed the applicator on a cleansing cloth. "And try that scrubbing machine. I think you'll like it."

He casually looked at the continually moving mass for anyone interested in his next make-up session, as his client examined his work. The aisle next to his make-up chair was crowded, even for a Saturday, but the eyes that caught his attention made him stop and watch a single individual for an extended moment.

"Thank you for your time today." He spoke to the lady as he continued watching this person move with the people surrounding him, then the person turned and made eye contact with him again.

His heart dropped as the young individual held his wide eyed gaze longer than normal, conveying a pain that seemed to beg for help. He remembered seeing the person before. He passed every so often during evenings or weekends. He was easy to remember; his long bleached hair offered a hint of peripheral lifestyle, though it wasn't an assumption Vicky made without care.

But this instance was different. Their eye contact continued longer than previous times. It also seemed more significant; still fleeting, but deeper and with more than a hint of desperation. The person appeared to want to stop. At least, their eye connection conveyed that message, but the crowd resigned him to continue on.

Then he watched the person cringe as someone bumped his shoulder, though the contact was far less than the reaction it produced. The person gave one fleeting look back as he moved past the corner of the opening between the store and the mall walkway.

"Have a wonderful day." Vicky glanced behind him for any sign of his boss, as he offered the parting thought, then rushed after him, maneuvering hurriedly through the slow moving crowd.

He quickly caught up and placed his hand on the person's shoulder and the young individual flinched, causing Vicky's heart to jump. He shifted the person away from the procession and stood in front of him, and the look on the person's face made his heart sink. Without a word, he took the person's other hand and quickly maneuvered against the continuing parade of shoppers until they reached his make-up chair.

"Sit."

The person stared without moving, then glanced around as if worried someone would spot them.

"Please sit?" Vicky discreetly searched the area, looking for anyone watching them. "Don't worry. I won't let anyone harm you. Are you in trouble?"

The individual made eye contact with wide desperate eyes, but offered no confirmation.

"Do you think someone's following you?" Vicky watched the person's breathing increase as his question registered, causing his own lungs to fill and his eyes to narrow.

"What's your name sweetie?"

Still looking in the direction behind him, he uttered, "Colin." and then dropped his head and whispered, "Colleen, but you can call me Colin if you want."

Vicky registered the defeat accompanying the compromise. "Hi Colleen. I'm Vicky."

Colleen's eyes narrowed and head twisted slightly.

"Yeah. If I may judge, I'm assuming we're more alike than you understand. I'm also not going to let anyone harm you in any way while you're with me, and I've faced many with that intention."

Vicky moved his make-up cart, then adjusted his stool to face the aisle. "Who are we looking for?"

Colleen's back straightened as if he'd suffer more by revealing the person responsible. "No one."

Vicky stood behind him, leaned close, and whispered. "I promise I'm on your side. Who are we looking for?"

"I can't tell you."

"Why not?"

"I'll get in trouble."

Vicky sighed and paused for a moment, then caressed Colleen's shoulder and he flinched. "Sorry."

Colleen glanced at him. "It's okay."

"No it's not. Come with me."

Vicky took his other hand and walked to a hidden door, marked; employees only. "This is a good hiding place. It'll allow you to not worry for the time being. I have to go let my boss know I'm taking a break. Will you wait a few minutes, so I can tell her and not get in trouble? I promise I'll help you. I want to help you. Will you wait here so we can at least talk?"

Colleen squinted curiously. "I guess."

Vicky sighed. "Do you have a phone?"

Colleen pulled out his phone, then eyed Vicky.

Vicky gently reached for it, then dialed his number and hit send. "There. Now we each have each other's number. Save mine and I'll save yours...Vicky." He handed Colleen's phone back. "Got it?" He watched her type. "Be right back ...okay?"

Colleen looked down. "I guess."

"If anyone comes by and asks what you're doing, tell them I told you to wait here for me." Vicky hesitated before hurrying out to the retail floor.

Vicky hurried back after gaining permission, then sighed and smiled as he saw Colleen waiting. "Thanks."

"For what?"

"For trusting me enough to wait for me."

Vicky's answer produced the opposite reaction he hoped, and his heart dropped a little further. He took Colleen's hand and walked to two dingy chairs in a corner of the staging area. "Are you hungry?"

"No."

He motioned for Colleen to sit. "Then can we discuss some things?"

"I guess."

"Are you done high school?"

"Yeah. I just turned nineteen."

"Do you have a place to live?"

Colleen's eyes lowered. "I guess. But I try not to be there if I can help it."

"Why?"

Colleen hesitated. "My father."

Vicky pointed to Colleen's shoulder. "Did your father do that to you?"

Colleen looked down and nodded.

Vicky's heart dropped and he could feel his eyes fill with moisture, for the pain he understood all too well and the resulting disheartenment it produced. "Why?"

Colleen stared into his eyes. "If you don't know, you won't understand."

His eyes narrowed. "You know I understand." Vicky inhaled slowly, realizing his immediate life had just changed. He knew he had to be the person he desperately sought when he sat in the chair facing him. "Where's your mother when this happens?"

"She's around, but she doesn't say anything."

"Do you work in the mall?"

"No. I try to stay here after people come home, but sometimes the security guards kick me out."

Vicky frowned. He knew every answer before he asked and not one answer was different than expected. "You realize our lives just changed."

Colleen's head shifted. "Why?"

"Because I love you more than your parents, and I don't even know you yet."

Colleen's eyes widened and filled with moisture, and for such a small reaction, displayed all the thank you Vicky needed. "Can you understand we're related?"

"Maybe alike, but I doubt we're related. I don't seem to be related to anybody."

Every sentence Colleen uttered gave Vicky more resolve. "Oh, you're going to be surprised how many people you're related to. You have another brother and sister you're going to meet in a short while." He pointed tentatively. "What's wrong with your shoulder?"

"Nothing. It's just a little sore."

"Is it hospital sore?"

Vicky's question produced a tear from Colleen's eye. "I don't know."

He noticed the dark circles under her eyes. "Did you sleep last night?"

"No."

"Come." Vicky led Colleen through a large gray metal door leading to an outside walkway, down hidden stairs and out to his car. "Would you sleep here until I'm done my shift and can figure out a plan?"

Colleen's soft sigh let him know the answer before he replied. "Can I?"

Vicky smiled. "Can you? You *have* to. I want you to lock yourself in and call me if anyone threatens you. Meanwhile I'm going to work on a few things. Do you trust me?"

She shrugged. "I guess."

Vicky inhaled. "I have to go back to work. I'm done in two hours. Please be here?"

Colleen's expression shared her lack of choices. "Sure."

Vicky dialed Steph as soon as he locked Colleen in his car and started walking back to the store's employee entrance. "Steph. We have a problem."

Stephie voiced instant concern. "I'm sorry. What'd I do?"

Vicky smiled, "No not me and you with each other, sweetie. Me and you *together*."

"Oh. Don't scare me like that."

"Will you relax girl. I ain't ever gonna be mad at you. I love you."

"Good, because I love you too." Stephie's voice softened. "What's going on?"

"Remember how I found you?"

"Of course. It's my most special memory of you."

"It's a great memory for me to." Vicky hesitated. "I found another like you, only this situation is a little different."

"How?"

"Remember the first questions I asked you?"

"Yeah…" Her voice turned solemn. "Was I being harmed in any way."

"This sister gave the opposite answer, and I think her shoulder or arm is broken…and we need a plan."

"Jake and I are in."

"I know. It's why I called you first."

"Where is she? What's her name?"

"Colin…Colleen. She's sleeping in my car till I'm done work, but I don't know how bad her shoulder is."

"Who hurt her shoulder?"

Vicky's voice lowered. "Her father."

"Why?"

"…for being like us." He stood on the walkway outside the outer door and marked the line of sight to where he parked.

"What do we do about it?"

He turned to the outer door. "The shoulder or the father?"

"The shoulder first?"

Vicky gave his car one last glance, then entered the inside staging area. "I'm not sure."

"I'll make a few calls."

"I'm done work at four. Can we meet at my house? Order pizza or something?"

"Jake and I will bring pizza. See you around four thirty."

"Thanks for helping."

"No problem, Vick."

After a pause, Vicky's voice rose. "Why do people like you find me?"

"Because you're obviously one of us." Stephie voice increased in confirmation. "You're a lifeline."

Vicky sighed into the phone and after another pause, spoke in a more somber tone. "Done my break. Gotta go. Love you."

"Love you too."

Two hours later, Vicky gently knocked on the window before unlocking his car. "Thanks for being here. Saves me the trouble of hunting you down tonight."

Colleen flinched as she sat up. "You would look for me if I wasn't here?"

"Me and eight other people. Thanks for saving us the trouble."

Colleen offered a sleepy smile.

"How's your shoulder?" Vicky motioned toward it.

"It hurts."

Vicky sat next to her, buckled in and started the car. "Well …we're having pizza with my sister, brother, and boyfriend, then we're taking a look at it. I hope that's alright but you don't have a choice."

He glanced at her as he headed toward the mall exit. "Do you ever not go home at night?"

She struggled to buckle her seatbelt. "I try not to."

"Do you want to stop at your house for some clothes or is that not a good idea?"

"Do you mind if we don't go right now?"

"Of course not." Vicky could feel his breathing deepen.

Vicky met her eyes and watched them well up. "It's alright if you need to cry. I cry sometimes but I no longer worry about a reason." He pointed to the glove compartment. "There's tissues in there."

Vicky pulled out his phone and dialed. "Steph. You have any clothes Colleen can borrow for a bit?"

"Boy or girl?"

"Both if you can. Loose, baggy stuff."

"I'll bring some."

Vicky ended the call as his experience fought his emotions. He wanted—needed to ask questions to learn more about Colleen's situation, but hesitated, trying to allow this new acquaintance time to pause and get comfortable with him. But he had to have a little more information. "Would you like to be Colleen full time or do you prefer being both Colin and Colleen?"

Colleen dropped her head. "I wish I could be Colleen, but I'm not allowed."

Vicky smiled. "Well you're allowed with me, so get used to the idea."

He opened his phone and hit a few keys, then held it out to Colleen. "Do me a favor? Text this message for me?" Vicky paused a moment. "Bring more girl clothes than boy clothes."

He waited for Colleen to finish. "Hit send for me?"

He finally entered his apartment complex and parked. "This is it. You need help or can you manage?"

"I'm alright." She walked next to him, to the closest apartment and stood as Vicky unlocked his front door and stepped aside. "Come on in."

Colleen entered and scanned the small apartment. "Wow, this is nice."

"Thanks. I'm glad you think so." He casually moved to the kitchen and removed two water bottles from the fridge, thinking about his one bedroom apartment and wondering where Colleen had slept in her journey to this point in her life.

Colleen accepted the bottle as she glanced down the short hall, then back at Vicky. "It's alright if I have to sleep with you."

Vicky's heart sunk. All the past situations he had endured were forcing their way back into his thought process, sapping more energy than he felt he had to give. His forearms suddenly felt weak. "You're very attractive, but you don't have to offer that to be safe here. You have a choice again, who you sleep with." He opened his bottle and drank half.

Colleen's brows lowered as she recapped her water. "Why are you being nice to me?"

Vicky softly inhaled and let the sigh out slowly. "Because I am you, and when I was where you are, I couldn't find the person I will be for you." He offered a slight frown and said the next words with hidden pain, "I desperately needed to find that person and I never did." then looked at Colleen and smiled. "And I won't let you go through the same thing. I wouldn't wish the same thing on a dog."

Vicky stared at her for a moment, then lightened the mood. "Go freshen up. Family will be here shortly and I'm sure they'll have dinner with them. Then we're going to take care of you for no reason." Vicky walked to his sofa and plopped down, then regained eye contact. "But not to worry. You'll pay this back. If people keep on the current course, you'll be offering this exact thing to another you in the years to come."

Stephie and Jake arrived soon after, with two pizzas and soda, along with two bulging carry-all bags. Vicky answered their knock. "Hi, sis. Come on in."

Both echoed, "Hi." as they kissed him hello.

Stephie entered, anxious to meet another girl like her. She knew they were around, but they weren't easy to find in real life, and she knew exactly why.

Colleen stood and extended her hand as Stephie walked toward her. "Hi."

Stephie met her eyes. "Hi. Can I hug you hi?"

Colleen's eyes widened and she offered a soft nod. "Sure."

Stephie gently wrapped her arms around Colleen. "It's great to finally meet someone like me."

Colleen let go and slowly backed up. "You're like me?"

Stephie smiled. "Yeah. I am."

"You're male?"

"Technically. But not my heart, mind or soul."

Colleen's eyes widened. "No way."

"Yep." Stephie nodded.

"And he's your boyfriend?" Colleen glanced at Jake.

Jake walked next to them after placing the pizzas on the dinette countertop.

Stephie glanced at him, then took his hand. "He's my fiancé."

Jake shook Colleen's hand. "Nice to meet you."

Vicky yelped, "Oh I forgot. Congratulations!"

Stephie held her hand out and displayed her new ring. "Look!"

"Oh my god." Vicky scurried to her and took her hand. "I'm so happy for you." He hugged her tight.

Stephie held her hand out to Colleen and she inhaled. "Wow. He knows and he loves you?"

Stephie smiled. "Yeah. There are guys out there not afraid to love us."

Colleen breathed deeper. "Wow. What's that like?"

Stephie raised her focus from her ring to Colleen's eyes. "Fantastic." She looked at Jake, then back at Colleen. "Hang around with the right people. You'll find out."

Colleen's eyes scanned Stephie's outfit. "You look so feminine."

Stephie pointed to Vicky. "So will you when he's done with you."

Jake placed his hand on his stomach. "Can we eat? I'm starving. I've been smelling that damn pizza for too long."

Steph glanced at him. "First things first. I need to see her arm." They turned to Colleen, and Stephie took her other hand, then motioned to Jake. "You eat. Vicky and I have this."

Stephie walked Colleen toward Vicky's room and Vicky shut the bedroom door behind them. "Okay. Let us see your arm."

Stephie watched Colleen gingerly lift her shirt off. "I called Jake's dad after you and I talked. He's in construction and trained in first aid. He told me what to do, and my grandmother told me what doctor to take you to if we need to."

After watching her struggle with the shirt, Stephie eyed Vicky and made a decision. "We're eating quickly then going to the doctor. I already made the appointment."

Colleen glanced from Stephie to Vicky. "But I can't go to the doctor. I can't pay."

Stephie offered a comforting smile. "It's already been taken care of."

"You're not telling anyone who did this to me, are you?"

Vicky offered in a soft determined tone. "Not yet."

# Chapter Three
## Prioritization

Stephie rose the next morning as quietly as possible, made a half pot of coffee, then sat patiently, inhaling the fragrant aroma of the slowly rising liquid. She had all intentions of seeing her parents and sharing their engagement later, but Colleen's sudden appearance made that news seem almost unimportant. She finished pouring a cup, then dialed her phone. "Hey mom."

"Hi sweetheart."

"Can Jake and I come over for dinner later?"

"Wait. Let me check my schedule."

"Mom!"

Genna laughed. "You're too easy to mess with. Of course you can come over. Just call and let me know you're on your way."

"Are you sure your schedule can fit us in?"

"Your come-back is way too late. I already got you. Of course I want to see you, even if I have to feed both of you."

Stephie's voice filled with playful sarcasm. "We can go out if you want."

"I'm sure we can." Genna offered playful exasperation in return. "But that'll cost me money."

"Dinner at home?" Stephie hesitated. "Want to just buy take-out?"

"Nah. I'll cook something simple."

"Whatever you decide. See you then. …Love you."

"I love you too sweetheart."

She hung up and immediately dialed her grandmother. "Nana."

"Hi cipolline. What's new?"

"Jake and I are engaged and he gave me a ring."

"That's fantastic. Are you happy?"

"Very, Nana. The happiest I've ever been."

"That's wonderful and I'm very pleased. I can't wait to see it."

"I can't wait to show you. Can I come over soon and show you …and talk about some things?"

"Whenever you want. You know I love when you visit."

"Let me figure out my schedule and I'll let you know."

"I'll be waiting."

"Thanks Nana. I'll talk to you soon. Love you."

"I love you too."

She ended the call with a feeling of unfinished purpose. She wanted to tell her about Colleen, but didn't quite know how at the moment. She appeased herself with the thought; she would share things with her mother first.

She dialed the phone one last time. "Hey Vick."

"Hey sister."

"How'd everything go last night?"

"Fine. She slept. We're gonna do some girly stuff together today."

"Like you used to do with me?"

"Yep."

She quickly reminisced about her first make-up session with him and a warm feeling came over her. "Good memories."

Vicky chuckled into the phone. "I'll never forget your face when I handed you the mirror that first time. I thought you were going to have some kind of anxiety attack or something."

"I *did* have an anxiety attack or something. I *dreamed* of looking like that since I was old enough to dream, and you're the one who answered that prayer."

Vicky joked, "And with my excellent tutelage, you can now do it any time you want."

"Yes, sensei."

She heard him snap his fingers through the connection. "I'm your damn *professor*, girl ...and don't you *ever* forget it."

Stephie laughed softly, "Yes professor." then her voice turned loving. "You're my brother, sister, and my only true life professor."

He replied proudly. "Correct."

She registered her sincere smile and shook her head. "Do you need anything else from me, to help with her?"

"Not at the moment, but it'd be great if you can spend some time with her soon."

"I will. Jake and I are going to my mom's for dinner tonight. I plan on talking to them about the situation too."

"Let me know if they have any ideas."

"I will. Talk to you soon. *Love you!*"

Vicky's voice deepened with affection. "Love you little sister."

~~~

Vicky walked quietly to his kitchen, and removed a can of soda from the fridge. He opened it as noiselessly as possible as he peeked through the nook opening at the new acquaintance sleeping on his sofa. Colleen stirred, then slowly sat up and slid her free hand through her hair.

31

Vicky sipped his soda. "Good morning. How's your arm?"

"Good morning. Sore."

"Did you sleep alright?" He raised his drink and pointed to it. "Want one?"

She nodded. "Yes please. The throbbing woke me a few times but at least I wasn't worried about getting woken for other reasons, so …better than usual." She adjusted the sling on her arm. "Do you have work today?"

Vicky's breathing increased for the implication Colleen's answer conjured. He walked her drink to her. "At five, but you and I are going to do something before I leave. Did anyone ever do your make-up?"

"Only me, but that's what started …everything."

Vicky could feel his anger build, and his tone turned serious. "Did he swear he was going to beat who you are, out of you?"

Colleen's mouth opened.

Vicky took another sip, "Told you …we're the same." then noticed Stephie's carry-all bags, and moved them closer as he sat next to her. "Let's see what Stephie brought you and then I'm doing your make-up if that's alright."

Vicky watched a smile appear and continued his soft reinforcement as he reached toward the bag closest to him. "I do make-up for a living, but I love making up girls like you and Stephie. It's my therapy, believe it or not." The statement wasn't completely true. His true enjoyment was watching girls like her and Stephie come to life after he made them up. "I also have a group of friends I want to share you with. We all enjoy helping girls like you. You're like a live dress-up doll to us, and we teach you every girl thing we can. We helped Stephie with her transition. She looks beautiful now, doesn't she?"

Colleen's brows rose. "She looks great."

"We'll teach you girl things too if you want."

Colleen lowered her head. "Yeah, but I'm not allowed to be a girl and I definitely can't be caught wearing make-up or having girl clothes on."

Vicky reached for her hand. "I know that's been your situation until yesterday, but things change." His breathing increased as he refrained from sharing his entire plan at the moment, for all the uncertainty surrounding it. He didn't want to be added to the list of people who've let her down in her life. Then he registered another aspect of her last sentence and his head tilted. "Do you have to be somewhere today?"

Colleen answered hesitantly. "No."

And Vicky's tone offered further comfort. "Then what are you worried about?"

"Where I'll go while you're at work."

Vicky scanned the room as if confused. "I don't know. The kitchen? …The bathroom?" He glanced at Colleen and smiled. "Promise to appreciate having friends who care about you, and a safe place to sleep?"

Colleen's back straightened. "More than you know."

Vicky tilted his head. "Promise not to hurt me or my house?"

Colleen's voice softened, "I promise."

Vicky's enthusiasm increased. "Okay then."

They each opened one of Stephie's bags. "Oh. She brought you more things than I thought she would." He pulled a delicate blouse from the bag. "Oh girl. How fantastic."

They unfolded each garment and Colleen lifted a few for further inspection, then carefully laid them in a pile. But one soft dress, she held against her and Vicky watched her subtle sigh. "Oh you should definitely wear that today. That's adorable."

33

Colleen met his eyes with a smile, then it disappeared instantly. "I don't have much money."

Vicky patted the back of her closest hand. "Relax, girl. We ain't there yet."

~~~

Jake exited their bedroom and stretched as he stepped into the kitchen, "Good morning sweetheart." then wrapped his arms around her as she spun toward him and kissed him.

"Good morning."

"Do we have any plans today?"

"Yeah. Dinner at my mom's." She held out her ring toward him. "I have to show our parents."

He smiled as he opened the fridge and stared inside. "I figured. Just making sure."

She paused in front of the stove. "You hungry? Want eggs?"

"Sure. Did you talk to Vicky this morning?"

She squeezed behind him at the fridge and reached for the eggs. "Yeah. They're doing fine." She placed a frying pan on the stove. "I want to talk about Colleen tonight too. I think we need to figure out some things for her."

"You have a good heart." He shook his head unnoticeably. "You're beautiful."

Stephie straightened. "Thanks but who wouldn't help someone going through what she's going through?"

His face turned serious. "You know the answer to that, just like I do."

He disappeared into the living room. "We have anything between now and your mom's?"

She raised her voice. "I have some studying to do."

"I do too."

Moments later, she heard the TV announcer rattle off a sports score. "…Sounds like it."

~~~

Vicky finished his soda and casually glanced at Colleen as he motioned toward the hall. "Take a nice relaxing shower and fix your hair if you feel like." He pointed to her arm, "Be careful." and smiled softly. "…Then put on the cute dress and whatever else you want, and we'll enjoy a little girl time together, and gab like only girls can."

His offer seemed simple enough and without purpose, but he had a motive. His life experiences taught him enough about where she was at the moment, to influence the therapy he planned to secretly administer. He wasn't anxious about getting answers. He had learned the answers would come, but his first priority was support. He would let her control the speed with which she shared her life, and any additional information she wished.

He waited for her to finish her soda and took the empty can. "Towels are in the sink cabinet and shampoo's in the shower. We're friends now, so help yourself to all the things in the bathroom without hesitation."

Colleen breathed deep, then stood and wandered down the hall as Vicky sat back and tried to relax. He had no idea where their situation would take them, and any attempt to see too far into the future overwhelmed him, but then he stared down the empty hall and realized she needed him. He decided he would focus on the present and be strong for her …then collapse later.

Colleen finally reappeared from down the hall and Vicky placed his hand over his heart and smiled. "You look adorable."

The statement made Colleen look down and blush. "I wish."

Every time Vicky heard a similar response, his determination strengthened. "Wait till you see what I can do. Even you'll be surprised."

Vicky had learned techniques, allowing him to use make-up for more than just enhancement. He had honed his skills to artist level and could now manipulate shades to feminize as well as enhance. He saw his skill as his personal gift to people like Stephanie and Colleen, and that purpose fed his being.

He had prepared the counter while Colleen showered, and motioned her to sit at the stool in front of the kitchen opening. "I can't wait to see how beautiful you are, all made up."

Colleen's eyes narrowed as she approached the chair, then her head lowered as his words registered. "I wish."

Vicky answered with confidence. "Oh, you'll see."

Vicky cleaned one of his brushes as Colleen made herself comfortable, then held a rectangular container filled with smaller squares of different colors next to her face. He spun the tray and held it close to her again. "You're one of the lucky girls. I think you could wear both earth and jewel tones. You're going to have a ball experimenting with different looks."

Colleen's breathing increased as she followed Vicky's movements. He reached for another rectangle container of colors and held it close to Colleen's face. "Now I'm not teaching today. I'm just playing with another pretty face. I'll teach you everything I know in due time though. …Not to worry."

Colleen relaxed as Vicky began the make-up process. "How long have you been making people up?"

"Since I was old enough to get someone to sit still and let me." Vicky laughed softly, then his voice calmed as he began working his magic. He whispered after a pause. "I love doing this."

Colleen whispered in return. "It feels nice."

He watched her reposition herself and get comfortable as she began placing her trust in him. "Good. I'm glad you're enjoying it." Vicky watched her relax further, and continued for a few moments before breaking the silence. "How are you feeling?"

Colleen softly inhaled. "Okay."

Vicky's heightened sensitivity registered the subtle non-verbal response accompanying the answer. "No. I mean …how are you really feeling?"

Colleen took a deeper breath and her shoulders drooped as she released it. "I don't share how I really feel. I don't mean that in a bad way. You're a very nice person, but nobody cares, so I don't share my real feelings with anyone."

Vicky felt her statement deeper than he let on, then softly offered, "You maybe haven't until now …but maybe I can be that person."

"You can't." She met his eyes. "I don't want you to be that person if we're friends, and if we're not friends, you aren't that person."

"You never had anyone you could tell inside secrets and feelings to?" Vicky closed his hand and patted his heart as he met her eyes.

Colleen's voice lowered. "No. People like me don't have anyone we can share with."

Vicky rummaged through his make-up box. "Well sometimes it takes a little longer to find those people, but the good news is; once you find them, they're far better friends than those who come and go. And I can be one of those friends."

"Then I don't want to tell you all the things that's happened to me." Vicky raised an eyebrow and tilted his head and Colleen squinted curiously. "You don't really want to know …do you?"

Vicky stopped his application, looked directly into Colleen's eyes, and softly nodded. "Yeah. Yeah I do."

"But why?"

Vicky reached for a different applicator without turning away from her. "Because I've been through the same things you're going through and if we share them, you're going to find out two things; first, I'm the same as you and you're going to be alright, and second; I have a few answers to what's happening to you that you maybe don't have or at the least, don't understand yet."

"How can you think there are reasons for the things either of us have gone through?"

Vicky gently caressed her uninjured shoulder. "Because there are, and once you learn them, you're going to be a lot less confused about things than you are now. The reasons won't help the problems go away or make them less hurtful, but they will give you strength you don't have now. *That*, I promise."

"How do you know these reasons? Where did you learn them?"

Vicky rummaged for a specific small container of color in his box. "You're gonna love this. My new family. Stephanie's grandmother is studying about girls like you and Stephie, and every once in a while she shares what she found with all of us. She's the cutest lovingest older lady you'll ever meet."

"Are you serious?"

"Dead serious. And you have no idea how much lgbt information she's shared. Jake too. He's ferocious." He dabbed a brush in another container, then the back of his hand as his voice lowered to a whisper. "…no idea. …wait till you see."

Vicky lightened the moment. "I love the way you did your hair. It's a beautiful color."

"Thanks." She held her arm carefully and readjusted herself in the seat, then met Vicky's eyes. "Does Jake really love Stephie?"

Vicky smiled. "Yeah." He dropped his hands and paused for a moment. "He's impressive."

Colleen's eyebrows rose as her voice softened. "Do you have a girlfriend or boyfriend?"

Vicky carefully blended colors with his thumb. "I do. His name's Jonathan."

"How did you find him?"

"By being in the right place at the right time."

Colleen kept eye contact. "Did you go somewhere purposely to meet him?"

Vicky snickered softly, remembering how they met. "No. He came up to me at work and gave me a note."

Colleen sighed and whispered. "I'll never meet anyone who'll love me."

Vicky registered her primary concerns and how her situation affected her hopes and dreams. He planned on rebuilding her confidence and outlook and if possible, would use her priorities to make that happen. He responded with soft adamancy. "Oh yes you will."

Vicky's next question wasn't as casual as he made it sound. "Does it matter what gender that person is?"

Colleen's brows rose and her eyes widened. "I dream about him but how can I refuse someone for gender when I'm hoping someone doesn't turn me away just for gender?"

Vicky met her eyes with slight astonishment. "That's a mature perspective. I'm impressed."

Colleen inhaled deeper. "Don't be. It's just a perspective from my place in life."

Vicky's head rose and he silently stared at her. Colleen's words showed a hint of wisdom which only comes from knowing the difference between opposite perspectives and he knew the only way to comprehend those differences were through the lessons the wrong side taught.

Vicky didn't announce he was done. He just held the hand mirror in front of her, stepped back, and watched her reaction. Colleen's eyes grew wide and she softy gasped, then eyed him. "Vicky. I never looked so much like a girl. You're an artist."

She stared into the mirror as she moved it in front of her, viewing every angle.

Vicky started closing jars and containers. "I'm glad you're pleased. It's just one of the things going to get better. I promise." He paused for a minute. "Let me clean this and we'll eat something before I get ready for work. I'm not the best cook but I make certain things."

Colleen happily volunteered, "I cook too. I like to cook. I'll make things if you want."

Vicky smiled at her while his brain registered Colleen's willingness to offer something for his kindness. He wasn't measuring the amount of the offer. He only measured the offer. "Not with one arm. I'll cook today. We'll see what tomorrow brings tomorrow."

Vicky finished packing his make-up away then fixed a simple breakfast, still curious about the details of his new friend's life, but showing as much patience as possible. They enjoyed casual conversation during the quick meal, discussing music and television. Colleen broke the silence of a short pause. "Do you have a vacuum cleaner? I can do a few things while you're gone."

"You'd do that for me? That'd be a big help."

Colleen's meek smile confirmed her need to do something for his hospitality, and the offers pleased Vicky. He pointed to the front door. "It's in the front coat closet, but I vacuumed yesterday, so take the day off."

Vicky glanced at his phone as he exited his apartment complex, heading toward the mall, then lifted it and entered Chris's name and his number appeared. He hit the send button and listened.

"Hey Vick."

"Hi. How are you?"

"Good. What can I do for you?"

Vicky inhaled. "I was wondering; can we have a beer together? I'd like to talk to you."

Chris answered immediately and calmly, "Of course we can. When works for you?"

"I'm off Monday."

"Good. Meet me at Logan's around four."

"Can you keep this between the two of us?"

"Absolutely. You have my word."

"Thanks."

"No problem. See you Monday afternoon."

# Chapter Four
## Comprehension

Stephie smiled and stared at her ring as Jake drove. "Should I have asked my mom to invite your parents over tonight?"

He shrugged but offered no response.

"I hate doing that though. It makes extra work for whatever mom we do that to. But our parents live way too close not to see them both, don't you think?"

Jake nodded. "Yeah. It's one of the crazy things about living next door to each other all our lives, but I'll take the good with the bad." He chuckled and glanced at her with a strange grin. "I loved living next door to each other and wouldn't change a thing."

Stephie stared at him as he drove. "You are such a romantic. I love it." Her eyes widened. "Am I your girl next door?"

He laughed. "You have no idea how many times I thought that."

"Aww." She extended her hand and they held hands as he drove.

She broke another short silence. "Colleen's cute, isn't she?"

He nodded. "Yeah, but I can see the pain and confusion. In fact, it's helping me make a little more sense of your confusion before you revealed what was going on inside you."

"I don't have her level of rejection though. I was afraid to share who I really was, but I knew my parents loved me." She stopped and thought for a moment. "I'm not sure I would've been able to survive that level of rejection. I was deathly afraid you would hate me too. I wanted to show you when we were young but always chickened out." She ran her fingers slowly through her hair. "I remember wanting to wear girl things when we played alone and how scared and confused that made me feel."

Jake glanced at her. "There are parts of this I can comprehend, but I'll never know the full depth, will I?"

Stephie's brows rose as she contemplated the complexity of her existence and the depth of his awareness. "Probably not, but I appreciate the love you show me and that makes up for not fully understanding."

He frowned and gently shook his head. "Every time you say something like that, you show me your courage, and it gives me courage. I understand your hesitation telling people …even people you love, because I hesitate and my differences are far less than yours. I get it."

"I know you do. But you still show more courage than me, every time the situation comes up. You always share who you are …we are, without hesitation and that's the most courageous thing I've ever seen."

"That's because I have more courage for you than I do for me." He paused as his eyes narrowed. "But I can't imagine how strange it must have been, knowing you were a girl when you were younger. I used to see the difference. I didn't understand back then, but when I look back, I remember seeing it." He glanced at her, then quickly refocused on the road. "You were smart but sometimes you seemed confused, and I never understood how you could be smart and confused."

"That's interesting, because when I look back on it, I think I was confused *because* I was smart enough to know something wasn't right, but I wasn't old enough to ask what was going on inside me. I didn't understand the feelings weren't common. I just tried to be what everyone told me I was. I even kept waiting for the feelings I had to go away."

"Don't beat yourself up over that. You were always smart but that doesn't mean you understood enough to know there were others like you, or that scholars wrote things that would help you. There's a big difference between a smart twelve year old and a smart fifty year old. The fifty year old doesn't question their ability to self-evaluate or have trouble finding existing information, and intelligent twelve year olds aren't sure about their evaluations and aren't aware they can research their conclusions."

Stephie jumped in her seat. "Shit. I was supposed to call my mom when we were on the way."

Jake smiled. "Why? Are we going to catch them doing something?"

She hit his arm. "Idiot."


Stephie exited the car as soon as Jake shut it off, ran to the side door, knocked quickly, then opened it. "Mom ...Dad!"

She heard their reply from the family room. "We're in here."

Stephie ran toward them and immediately held out her left hand. "Mom ...we're engaged!"

Genna examined the ring, then hugged her. "Oh sweetheart, I'm so happy for you."

Jake walked in behind and Genna embraced him. "I love you."

He hugged her tenderly. "I love you too Mom B."

"Can you just call me mom now, unless we're all together?"

He kissed her cheek. "Definitely."

Connor extended his hand toward him as he finished hugging Stephie. "I'd like to say welcome to the family, but you've been part of it forever already. But I think it's fantastic you're both making it official."

Jake joked, "You mean I'm invited to the Blair reunion this year?"

Connor laughed. "You could have come."

Jake raised an eyebrow and responded with mock sarcasm, "Yeah…"

Genna held Stephie's hand. "Are we heading next door?"

Without reply, Stephie and Genna headed toward the side door, with Connor and Jake following. Stephie knocked, then opened the Harrison side door. "Mom H!"

She heard Morgan reply from toward the family room. "We're in here dear."

Stephie and Genna hurried toward the family room. "Mom H, look what Jake gave me." She held out her hand.

Morgan smiled as she took Stephie's hand and admired the ring, then hugged her dearly. "Welcome to the family …since you were five."

"My mom said the same thing to Jake."

Chris glanced at the ring then hugged and kissed her. "We've always been family but this is great."

"I agree." She took a calming breath. "I always wanted our families to be related for real."

Chris slid his hand down the back of her hair. "Nothing could make me happier."

Morgan reached for Genna's hand and shared a thought. "Can we celebrate this together? …Here? Now?"

"Sure. I made a casserole we can finish in your oven if you want."

Morgan laughed. "And I just bought a box of wine in case we got together soon."

Chris grinned. "God, I love this family." He turned to Connor and mocked the two ladies. "And I keep beer stocked, just in case you visit, but it's better fresh, so I rotate it regularly. It's a tough job, but nothing's too good for my family."

Connor rested his hand on Jake's shoulder, "And you do a fine job keeping it nice and fresh." and everyone laughed.

The party quickly moved to the family room, after Jake and Stephie found snacks and everyone fixed a drink.

After they were situated, Chris motioned to Stephie. "Well what are you waiting for? Details woman. We want details." He eyed Jake after his request, and enjoyed his grin.

Stephie sat straight as her eyes widened. "The story's a little strange."

Connor interrupted, "Perfect."

She gazed at her father and paused for a moment before continuing. "I was kind of hurting and having a really bad day, and he asked me what was wrong and I started crying…"

Jake reached for her arm, breaking her train of thought. "Tell them *why* you were crying."

She smiled awkwardly. "I saw him with another girl." Her voice rose. "A gorgeous blonde girl."

"You're an idiot." He glanced from one parent to the next. "She spotted one of my classmates touching my arm as we left class." He shook his head.

She mock imitated him, swaying her head, "She spotted one of my classmates…" then hit his shoulder.

"Would you two tell the damn story already? Get to the happy ending, will you?" Everyone laughed at Genna as she looked around, playfully annoyed. "God."

Stephie's eyes widened as she softly raised her hands. "Mom, we're setting the scene."

Jake rubbed his shoulder. "She's telling you she's crying because I'm so handsome; women can't keep their hands off me."

Stephie's hand came down immediately on the back of his head, making him flinch. "Ow!"

"Kick his ass." Chris pointed at her with the top of his beer.

"Dad! Ain't you supposed to be on my side?"

"Hell no son. You know I love her more."

She playfully refocused and continued. "So, I was upset he was letting this girl paw him, and I could tell by his face he was enjoying it way too much."

He grinned. "She *was* cute." then flinched before the next slap. "Ow!"

"But by later that night, he realized I'm much prettier than her." She wrapped her hands around his neck and shook him. "Right?"

"Yes dear." He covered his head with his arm.

Morgan snickered. "You two are comical."

Jake continued, "So to stop her balling, I gave her her damn ring." He covered his head with both arms and ducked, and four parents laughed.

"…and now I have to marry him."

Genna stood with her empty glass, shaking her head. "That's so romantic. Someday, the two of you will have to tell us what actually happened."

Chris raised his beer as Genna walked toward the kitchen. "Can you get me another?"

"Sure."

Connor rose, "I need one too." prompting everyone to head toward the kitchen.

Chris placed his new beer on the kitchen table as others replenished drinks and searched for more snacks. "We're finally making our family official."

Stephie hopped excitedly. "Finally."

Chris caressed the back of her hair. "Took you two long enough."

He caressed her hair again, before reaching for his beer. "You were always family, but I'll love when it's official."

Stephie stared at him and sighed. "I not only get to marry the man I love but I get the in-laws I dreamed of having. You both not only accepting me, but me and Jake, means the world to me. I've never said it before, but I've been grateful for it always."

Morgan spoke softly as they headed back to the family room. "You being in my life is one of my greatest gifts. You helped me see the difference between things childishly believed and wisely evaluated. You were always a beautiful loving person but you helped me grow. I love you."

Stephie stood and they hugged, "I love you too." then Morgan held her face with both hands. "And I'm looking forward to helping you with your wedding ...and there'll be times when I cross from your mother-in-law to your second mother. Don't be mad at me."

Stephie kissed her. "I count on you crossing that line, forever." She glanced at everyone else. "I want an old fashioned traditional wedding."

Genna watched Jake smile softly, but kept her first thought to herself. She wondered how many social roadblocks stood between Stephie and her dream wedding. She knew all too well there were going to be more than any cis girl would ever have, and planning a wedding was already an enormous task. She sat quietly and inhaled unnoticeably, as she realized the work involved with this coming celebration.

Chris looked at Connor, then extended his right hand. "We're finally gonna be related."

Connor took his hand. "Maybe grandfathers to the same kid?"

Jake turned to Connor. "Definitely."

Connor smiled. "Nice thought."

Morgan and Genna coordinated dinner, after Jake and Stephie transferred everything across the drives, and they ate, drank and celebrated the official future joining of their families. Chris was the last to rejoin everyone in the family room after dinner and jokingly asked Stephie, "So what's new?" then watched her take a breath as her eyes narrowed.

"Remember the other night when I called you and asked what we should do for the friend who hurt her arm?"

Chris's voice turned solemn. "Yeah…"

She sat up and glanced at Genna, then back at Chris. "There's more to the story." She eyed her father, then Morgan. "A lot more."

Genna sat forward. "What's going on dear?"

"Vicky found another girl like me." She reached for Jake's hand. "Only she wasn't as lucky to have parents like us." The conversation turned serious as she and Jake shared the details concerning Colleen, and the six of them discussed past events, then present and future implications.

~~~

Logan's was comfortably quiet for a Monday afternoon, as Chris sipped his beer and glanced at the front door intermittently. Finally, Vicky appeared and Chris bellowed, "Vicky." loud enough

50

to get his attention. Vicky paused for a moment as his eyes adjusted, then walked to the stool he watched Chris pull out for him. He sat and Chris immediately placed his hand on his back and gave it a quick rub. "Hi. How are you?"

"Good Mister H."

"You're more than welcome to call me Chris." He waved to the barmaid, then glanced at Vicky. "How's my third kid?"

Vicky quickly inhaled. All of Chris's caring registered deeply inside him. He knew why. The thing he yearned for most, was a loving and accepting father. He had a biological father, but had come to learn how little the biology counted when measuring a father's worth. His father physically abused him, kicked him out of his house when the beatings didn't *fix* him, then disowned him, and left him on the street. His crime; being different. But being different wasn't anything he could control.

There were enough pictures showing his differences from before he was old enough to realize, and his expulsion from his family was something he always failed to understand. He wasn't overcompensating when someone showed love. He had a lot of love inside and was happy to share it. Not receiving any from the people he thought were supposed to love him was his greatest confusion, so when Chris ...when all four of Jake and Stephie's parents accepted him completely, with all his idiosyncrasies, he returned their love instantly and completely. He craved acceptance, and no one offered a more complete and down to earth acceptance than Jake's father Chris.

The barmaid walked over. "What can I get for you?" Chris momentarily interrupted, "Alicia, this is my other child, Vicky."

Alicia never flinched and welcomed him. "Nice to meet you. I'm Alicia."

Vicky responded, "Thanks. Can I have a lite beer please?"

Chris finished his glass, then placed it at the other side of the bar. "Another for me too, Alicia."

"Sure." Alicia moved immediately toward the taps.

Vicky's heart pounded as Chris's introduction registered in his heart. It seemed natural and without apology. He would have accepted being introduced as Vick. Many adults compromised when introducing him to others, but Chris continually never compromised him and never failed showing complete and unapologetic acceptance of him.

Chris turned on his bar stool. "I'm glad you took me up on my beer offer. I enjoy your company."

Vicky's breathing elevated. "Thanks, but there's a reason I did."

Chris smiled, "Which is a reason to have a beer together. Don't ever hesitate to ask me anything, including meeting for a drink." Chris sipped his beer then faced Vicky. "So what's on your mind?"

"Did Jake or Stephie tell you about Colleen?"

"Yeah. She called me about her arm, then we talked when Stephie and Jake came over to show us her ring."

Vicky brightened. "Their engagement is great, isn't it?"

Chris chuckled and nodded. "Yeah, it is." But Vicky was his concern at the moment and he brought the subject immediately back. "She's living with you?"

"Yeah." Vicky's eyes widened and his voice softened. "I don't mind the inconvenience, but there are other things about her stay that scare me a little. I'm not asking for help, but is it okay to talk to you about things?" He sipped his beer and eyed Chris. "I don't have anyone older to ask advice. Don't get me wrong. I don't mind figuring things out on my own, but sometimes it helps having someone to run things by, if that's alright."

Chris knew Vicky didn't have a father he could talk to. He knew he had been rejected by his family and that rejection led to confusions, other young adults don't experience. Chris gently placed his open hand on Vicky's shoulder and offered overcompensation without explanation. "You can talk to me about anything, always." He spoke lower, but with emphasis as he met his eyes. "Anything …always."

Vicky inhaled deeply as he met Chris's eyes, measuring his sincerity, then shared Colleen's situation and his concerns regarding taking care of her. Chris quickly caressed the back of Vicky's hair, then rested his hand on the back of Vicky's chair. "I love that you came to me."

Vicky sighed, "I don't know what else to do with her, and I won't leave her on the street. That's what happened to me and I desperately hoped for someone who would help me, and never found that person. There's no way I'll do that to her."

His words made Chris slowly shake his head. "I've watched you with Stephie and now you're doing this for Colleen. You're beautiful."

Vicky frowned, "I'm not beautiful. This scares me. The extra costs. Feeding her. How long she's going to need to stay with me. Then not having parents, it's hard to know what to do next sometimes." He glanced at Chris. "It's all a little scary."

Chris smiled softly as he spun his beer glass on its coaster. "Of course it is. And that's what your new parents are for; exactly what we're doing right now."

He waited for Alicia's attention and motioned for their check. "Your new family won't let you down." Chris opened his wallet, pulled out a credit card and searched for another. "Do you have room in your fridge for food?"

Vicky laughed. "More room than I want."

Chris rested his wallet on the bar. "Let's get out of here and go shopping. I'll help you with the groceries for now, at least. And we'll figure out the rest as we go."

Vicky's jaw opened and his eyes widened. "You don't have to do that."

Chris glanced at him as Alicia walked over. "Like you don't have to let Colleen live with you." He tilted his head to make his point. "Drink. We're going shopping with a buzz."

~~~

Stephie hopped excitedly as she spotted the brown cardboard shipping box leaning against their front door when they returned from school. She faced him and pulled his hand down, making him look at her as they approached the package. "I bought you a present online the other day and it's here!

He laughed. "For what?"

She smiled and skipped the last ten feet to the package, then looked up at him as she reached for it. "Because I love you."

He reached for her and gave her a playful kiss before unlocking the door. "Thank you. What is it?"

She frowned at him. "I didn't keep this secret for three days, so I could ruin it fifteen minutes before giving you the present."

He laughed. "Three days huh? I guess I can wait till I'm upstairs to open it."

She teased further. "Wrong again. You can't open it when we get upstairs either."

He peered at her with a playful smirk. "Okay, now you're driving me nuts. You bought me a present and told me about it and you have it in your hand but I can't open it?" The tickling she had initiated started showing on his face. "When do I get to open it?"

She removed a book and handed him her backpack, squeezed between him and the open door and hurried up the apartment stairs in front of him. "Oh you'll see in a bit. Set up our books to study in the living room."

He playfully exhaled and then spoke in mock resignation at his inability to get a straight answer from her. "Whatever you say."

"Don't come in our bedroom either."

He followed slowly up the stairs with both backpacks, shaking his head with a half grin. "You're a nut, know that?"

She walked out of sight at the top of the stairs. "Let's see if you think so in a few minutes."

He felt the weight of her backpack as he lifted it onto the coffee table. "Do you have every book you own in here?"

She didn't answer and he just smiled at his own statement. He loved how studious she was and her drive to succeed in school always amazed him. He opened her backpack and piled her books on the coffee table, then set his next to hers. He paused, then walked to the refrigerator. "You want a soda or anything to drink?"

Her muffled reply came from behind their closed bedroom door. "Water please."

He grabbed a can of soda and a bottle of water, then went back to the living room.

Minutes later, he glanced up from his text book as she finally turned the corner into the living room, and his heart jumped. She stood there, wearing a short red and black plaid schoolgirl skirt, semi-transparent white blouse tied at her waist, revealing a beautiful lace covered white bra, and below the hem of her skirt, equally beautiful white lace-top stockings, with little lace anklets covering the tops of her black patent leather high heels. His eyes scanned back up her outfit and noticed her hair pulled back on the sides, with two matching berets, and her lips covered in vibrant red lipstick. She cradled a textbook, holding a pen.

"I'm sorry I'm late for my tutoring session, professor."

He sat straight. "You're forgiven. I'm glad you made it. Come join me." He patted the sofa seat.

"On the office sofa, professor? Next to you?"

"Of course." His grin appeared. "Isn't that alright?"

She hesitated. "I guess."

She began walking toward him and accidentally dropped the pen. "Oops." She playfully eyed him, "I'm so clumsy sometimes." then turned her back and bent over straight legged to pick it up.

He whispered, "Oh my."

She stood, raising her hand to her mouth. "I hope I didn't show you too much!"

"Well…"

Her eyes widened. "I'm sorry. I'm so embarrassed. Sometimes I forget I'm wearing my uniform."

He broke character and laughed, "Yeah…" then ran his hand over his smile, trying to regain composure. "I actually like your uniform …very much." He fought his uncontrollable grin.

She held out her arms as she moved closer. "Well, I obviously added the stockings. My legs get cold. Plus, I think they're pretty." She stared submissively into his eyes as she stood close to him. "Don't you think they're pretty?" She pressed the front of her skirt and peered down her legs, then back into his eyes.

"Yes." He swallowed noticeably. "They're a very nice complement to the rest of the uniform."

She sat daintily next to him and he immediately grabbed her. "Jake!"

"I can't take it. Holi shit, Steph!"

He leaned over her and met her open mouth with his, as his hands began fondling the new gifts, covering his most precious gift.

~~~

Stephie daydreamed as she drove to her grandmother's house for their casual dinner date, and realized how much she had changed over the last few years. She reflected on the joyous reaction she knew Lorraine would offer when she saw her ring, but knew the meal wasn't just a celebratory get-together.

She had a purpose, though the purpose wasn't for her. She also knew Lorraine had certain connections, or at least connections to connections but lately, Stephanie had also come to count on her as a source for knowledge into people like her and she wanted to know how Lorraine sourced the information.

Her curiosities had always produced questions, but lately she realized; the right questions seemed to open doors to information not revealed without prompting, and the more specific the question, the more precise the answer if the right person was asked.

As soon as Lorraine opened the front door, Stephie excitedly held out her hand. Lorraine laughed and held it to better examine her new engagement ring. "Oh it's beautiful. I'm so happy for you."

Stephie kissed her as she walked in. "Thanks. It's the best thing ever. I love him so much."

Stephie told her the entire story as they drove to the restaurant, and Lorraine reached for Stephie's hand before exiting the car. "I appreciate your insecurities, cipolline. They're well earned." She patted her hand. "But I don't think you have to be insecure about his love."

The dinner started casually, so Stephie had no need to rush her remaining concerns. Lorraine always portrayed a comfortable graciousness and Stephie practiced her graciousness when she could, but especially when they were together. They ordered drinks, and Lorraine refocused as the waitress walked away, "How's school?"

Stephie sat straight and smiled. "Great. We both should finish this semester. I can't wait."

Lorraine held Stephie's hands across the table. "And I'm proud of you." You both held to your word and I couldn't be more pleased. In fact, I have a graduation present I have to share with you now. I renewed your lease for another year, to help you both get the next step in your lives organized without worrying where you'll live."

"Oh Nana, thank you." She stood and kissed her.

They sat casually enjoying the activity around them, and discussing everyone close to them, until Stephie paused and took a deep breath. "Nana, can we have another family meeting?"

"Sure dear. What would you like to discuss?"

Stephie leaned back as the waitress placed their plates on the table. "Well, there's a new *someone* in our group. Vicky found another girl like me. Her name's Colleen, but her situation is a little different. Her father physically abuses her, and Vicky's taken her in." She glanced at Lorraine. "She has issues I didn't have and my issues were traumatic. Vicky, Jake and I …and some of our friends are trying to figure out how to help her and I think you confirming how normal she is, like you did with me …is a great place to start."

Lorraine rested her hand on Stephie's. "Tell me more."

Stephie shared everything she knew about Colleen, including Vicky's role and the strain Colleen is causing him, then asked, "Can you share some of the basic information you shared with the rest of us, again for her, and can the whole family come so they can support her? She's needs to know she's normal and there are people who are on her side and care about her."

Lorraine smiled. She knew Stephie's definition of *the whole family* included people who weren't necessarily blood. "I'd like that. I can share some of the latest things I've learned with everyone and we can have a small family meal together and show her what a family's supposed to look like."

"Thank you, Nana."

"You're welcome, dear. Could Vicky use a little grocery money too?"

"I know he'd appreciate it."

After pausing for a few bites, Stephie glanced at Lorraine, "This is the first time we ever went to dinner alone together with me as an adult." then offered a big grin.

Lorraine smiled softly. "You're too cute."

Lorraine casually watched her grandchild as they ate, and Stephie's mannerisms and maturity confirmed her normality. She made no outer acknowledgment, but recognized the child's special differences had also made a softer and more accepting heart.

Lorraine sipped her drink. "When and where do you want to have the get-together?"

"That's up to you Nan. Do you want us all to come over your house or do you want me to pick you up and bring you to mom's?" Stephie straightened. "If it's at your house, Jake and I will clean everything, like we're hosting the party."

"Then let's have the party at my house. I feel like a dinner party."

~~~

Jake fiddled with the radio buttons on the steering wheel and caught himself smiling as he headed toward home. He appreciated how peaceful the ride seemed when the cars were sparse, especially compared to the daytime traffic. And with fewer cars, the winding highway arced like a piece of art as it skirted the city. The number of off-ramps increased as the buildings rose higher and he marveled at the majesty of the structure as the entire road elevated in preparation for the water crossing ahead.

He finally found a decent song and sat back, thinking about his new job, and how his adult life was starting to come together, but his network of thoughts quickly changed from his intended path. He wanted to concentrate on the positive aspects of his future but his thoughts drifted uncontrollably to his new work associates and a recent lunch-break discussion about spouses and families.

He didn't offer any personal information in return. There was no sign his personal life wouldn't be accepted but he knew the potential ramifications of his orientation. He also knew he had to be careful revealing it until he was sure the information wouldn't affect his job. The news shared stories of people like him getting fired. There were laws against discrimination, but companies always seemed to know what reasons couldn't be contested.

The thought turned his mood darker as he became aware of his inability to focus on the positive. He hated the idea others measured certain things not only personal, but also private. He had learned; his personal life harmed no one. He had learned; people with his orientation have existed since recorded history, and this new round of social backlash against those like him made no sense in his mind. There was no reason for the hate, but some people were more accepting of war and men holding guns, than they were of love and men holding hands.

He forced his thoughts to focus on Stephie, and felt his tension release. Thoughts of her never failed to lighten his frustrations. He pictured her waiting for him at home …greeting him with a projected love that touched his soul …making her undeniably worth the social risks. Her love was worth any risks, but he still couldn't rationalize negative consequences for loving someone.

He recalled a flashback of an African-American husband and his Caucasian wife wearing matching shirts and holding a sign at a marriage equality protest, explaining how their parameters of marriage didn't include same gender couples, and sighed knowing they weren't allowed to marry as recently as nineteen sixty four and the pre-civil rights act, then wondered if the world would ever embrace true equality and the acceptance that couple now enjoys.

He loved studying the history of certain paradigms which seemed questionable on merit alone. The idea others had fully developed opinions which obviously were not only under-studied, but selfish and self-serving, lowered his hopes for his future. Instead of a tendency toward tolerance, there was a growing rift between those wanting tolerance and acceptance of differences and those with a tendency toward exclusion and hate; especially religious hate and intolerance, which made absolutely no sense to him.

He loved his ability to weigh ideas and concepts, but often, that ability made him aware of that same inability in others. He also knew what would help his mood. He anticipated Stephie's eagerness as he fantasized seducing her, and made a mental note to seduce her as soon as he arrived home. Making love to her would help him in more than a few ways.

# Chapter Five

## Regeneration

Vicky spent the next few weeks working on Colleen's psyche, and finally decided it was time to take the rebuilt Colleen out for a test run. This wasn't a final test; just another level of healing. With the help of Stephanie, Jake and a few other friends, Vicky had secretly coordinated a special event for Colleen, within the safe surroundings of a night out together.

Vicky came home from work and found Colleen making dinner. He walked into the kitchen and kissed the back of her head. "Hi. How was your day?"

Colleen placed the lid back on the pot and smiled. "Good. I did a little cleaning and made us dinner."

"It smells fabulous, sister. What is it?"

"Rice and beans, but it's an old family recipe. I hope it's alright."

"Are you kidding? I love you cooking for me. I'm famished." Vicky lifted the lid, inhaled, leaned his head back and smiled in pleasure. "My stomach's grumbling."

Colleen brightened with Vicky's response. "Ten more minutes." She opened a cabinet, removed two bowls and placed them on the counter.

"I'm going to throw on some sweats." Vicky turned toward the hall. "…be right back."

Vicky walked back into the kitchen minutes later, and Colleen handed him his dinner. He lifted the bowl to his nose and inhaled, "Yummy." then headed into the living room and Colleen followed.

"This is nice, isn't it?" Vicky smiled at her as he tasted his dinner. "Oh, this is very nice."

Vicky noticed over the short period, how Colleen brightened whenever he offered her positive reinforcement, and savored her reaction to his latest compliment. "I have something planned for us tonight."

Colleen finished her mouthful. "Okay."

"This is a different something our group likes to do every once in a while."

Colleen responded more hesitantly, "Okay…"

"We're going dancing." Vicky sipped his drink. "Did you ever go dancing at a club?"

Colleen's eyes widened. "No. I'm not old enough. Don't you have to be twenty one?"

"Normally, but I have a special arrangement, so you don't have to worry." Vicky grinned playfully. "And I'd ask you if you wanted to go …if you had a choice. But you don't. Time to play, little sister."

He scraped the last few morsels of dinner from the bottom of his bowl, "Damn that's delicious." then faced Colleen. "Let's each take showers, then I'm doing your make-up and then we're finding a cute outfit for you, and going dancing."

An hour and a half later, Vicky stepped away from Colleen and his make-shift make-up chair to answer the knock at the front door. "Hi. We're almost ready."

Stephie stepped in the apartment and kissed Vicky. "Hi." She had a brown paper bag with her, and examined Colleen's outfit. "Hi. You look cute, but I brought you some other choices. When you're done, we'll take a look?" She and Jake had made a detour on the way and discreetly placed a few newly purchased choices Stephie hoped would be more her size, inside the hand-me-down bag.

Colleen and Stephie disappeared down the hallway after Vicky finished, and reappeared a short time later with Colleen in a cute short pleated skirt and feminine matching top.

Vicky brightened, "Oh girl, you look beautiful."

Colleen ran her hand over the front of her blouse and skirt. "I love this." She sighed. "I love being feminine."

Stephie met her eyes and sighed. "I remember the first time Vicky took Jake and me dancing. I was so nervous." She took Colleen's hand. "And we had the best time." She shook her head softly. "I'll never forget it."

"Aww, little sister." Vicky scooted to her and hugged her.

Stephie noticed Colleen holding her healing arm. "How's your arm."

Colleen's eyes widened. "Good enough to dance I think."

Jake spoke from the stool at the dinette opening. "Who we waiting for?"

Vicky turned toward him, "Nobody." then eyed Stephie and Colleen. "We ready?"

Stephie smiled at Colleen and took her hand. "Ready."

Stephie held Colleen's hand until they sat next to each other in the back of the car. She watched Jake glance at her as he leaned inside. "I'm gonna sit with her." She didn't explain, but the vivid memory of her mixed emotions during her first dancing excursion gave her the feeling; even a simple hand-holding could help Colleen through the initial tentativeness of the experience. She smiled

65

discreetly as she realized how much simple physical contact meant to her and then wondered if Colleen needed it like she did. But then she thought; *well ...just in case*, and gently reached for Colleen's hand.

Colleen held Stephie's hand the entire ride, and tightened her grip as the car slowed before turning between the tall pine trees lining the road. The large parking lot was as gloomy as Stephie warned, but she had now been dancing enough times to know the building facing it held an energy and enjoyment she excitedly anticipated.

Stephie watched Colleen's unsure reaction. "You're gonna love this, I promise."

Colleen's eyes widened. "I know I will, but I'm still nervous."

"Well you've never done this before. Believe me; you'll want to come back again and again if you're anything like me." She opened her side door, but leaned toward Colleen before exiting. "I feel so feminine here. It's almost like a dream, being with all these people and no one upset with who I am. I love this place."

Jake quietly watched Stephie walk in front of him, holding Colleen's hand like an older sister and caught himself smiling at how feminine Stephie's heart and soul was, and then thought what a loving mom she would be. No one in his mind had a more beautiful and natural nurturing instinct. No one.

They made their way to the corner of the expansive wood deck surrounding the double front doors and found a few friends. The ladies immediately began fussing over Colleen, hugging, complimenting, and surrounding her with attention. Introductions continued and every male in the group offered their complete acceptance.

Stephie whispered in her ear as everyone began heading toward the entrance line. "I know the crowd's a little scary. It scared me the first few times, but I promise you're safer here than most places." She pointed to one of the two large people guarding the open double doors. "See him?"

She watched Colleen study the man for an extended moment, then turn toward her. "He's one of Vicky's closest friends. They dated for a while."

Colleen's eyes widened as she glanced back toward the doors. "Him?"

Stephie chuckled and nodded. "Yeah him. His name's Desmond."

She motioned to the other large gentleman on the other side of the grey metal doors. "He and Mick rule this place. But the best part is; he's as gentle as a lamb and the sweetest guy you'll ever meet. We're all friends with him and every once in a while, he hangs with our crowd and dances with us when he's not working ...and the regulars know."

Their dancing group had grown since Stephie's first time, and the diversity of the group always made this event special. Everyone was represented, and the acceptance dynamic was the strongest reason to participate. More than a few college friends had become part of their inner circle, along with Dawn and Brittany who had joined the transition group that first helped Stephie, but had lately spent their time helping Colleen. The group allowed everyone the freedom to dance with whomever, further eliminating barriers between them, and the mindset seemed to strengthen as these gatherings became a regular occurrence.

Vicky stood quietly in line behind his two new sisters, daydreaming about the night's event. He told everyone in the group, well in advance; this excursion was for fun and camaraderie, but primarily, it was another step in Colleen's healing process. Vicky asked everyone to take care of her, dance with her, and make her feel like part of the group. He knew he was overly sensitive to her situation. He couldn't help it. Every time he came across someone like Colleen, his past ordeals flooded his memory and heightened his compassion.

He pictured her face when he first saw her and wondered how many could spot the trauma on his face when he had just been abandoned. He knew people could see it. Enough people avoided him after the quickest of casual glances. Others tried to take advantage of how lost and frightened he must have appeared.

After he realized he was going to survive, he grew strong enough to handle the small battles that continually followed, but the original trauma left a permanent void inside him.

But the demons who robbed him of a typical life left him something in its place; a sensitivity to others in distress. Since then, he developed the ability to spot others with the same unsettled aura, and the need to prevent them from experiencing the trauma he knew …and wouldn't wish on anyone.

On any given day, reminiscing about being forced to leave, for nothing more than being born different, could break him down to the point of collapse. On a good day though, he was glad he took one being's burden. He liked to think he at least saved someone else from experiencing his special existence.

He knew there were times when small confrontations still hurt him more than they should. He came to appreciate when they affected him more than he felt they should. They helped him realize he'd never fully heal, but those traumas honed his senses and connections to every part of the living universe. He came to realize the sensitivity and connections grew more acute as his level of emotional discomfort increased, so he decided as he grew older, he didn't want to fully heal.

He eyed Stephanie, then thought how they met. She had become a dear friend and trustworthy equal … intelligent and mature, yet as fragile as him for the lessons her existence demanded she learn. He loved her soft heart and unique awareness when it came to helping others. He joked that he had adopted her as a way to show what she meant to him, and his proclamation proved to be his greatest gift. Her extended family immediately declared him family.

He reminisced spotting her as the confused young male who sat staring at him for hours at the mall while he worked. The memory brought a contented smile and accompanying sigh, though he realized he had never asked her why she sat watching him before he introduced himself, then chuckled silently, realizing how obvious his orientation is and what a two-edged sword it was.

He smiled at how Stephie also had the personality and demeanor to help people. He couldn't find those people when he needed them, and he never told another soul, but he had decided in his heart to be the person he couldn't find when he was lost and hurting. He chortled at the thought, then shook his head in amazement at the strange place he occupied in this strange world.

Jake tapped Colleen's shoulder as she held Stephie's hand in front of him. "You can borrow that but you can't keep it. That hand's mine." He grinned lovingly as her mouth dropped. "I would never." Jake waved his hand dismissing her need to reply. "I'm just messing with you."

Stephie pulled on her arm as she motioned jokingly with her head. "He's an idiot."

Vicky took Colleen's hand as their turn in the entrance line approached, then revealed it in his as they stepped in front of Desmond. "This is Colleen. She's with me."

Desmond met Colleen's wide eyes and his deep voice resonated, "Hi Colleen." and warm smile amazed her. "It's great to meet you. Vicky told me about you and I hope we can be friends."

"Sure." Colleen's mouth unconsciously opened.

He extended his hand toward her and she placed her hand in his. Vicky watched her inhale and stare as Desmond's smile broadened. "Let me stamp your hand."

He gently rolled the stamp over the back. "See you inside."

He dipped the stamp in a small tin box and lifted his head toward Stephie. "Hi Steph …Jake."

Vicky pulled her through the door and into the expansive club, still watching Colleen try to keep her eyes on Desmond. She finally faced him. "He's a dream."

Vicky chuckled as he stepped to the side, waiting for the rest of the crowd. "There's nothing wrong with your eyes. He's impressive, isn't he?"

Colleen glanced back. "He's gorgeous."

Vicky laughed. "You're going straight for the home run, eh?"

She sighed. "He could never like a girl like me." She fluffed her hair and ran her hand over the front of her blouse.

Vicky laughed louder as Stephie walked next to him. "That's funny, because he does like girls like you. But be warned. He'll ruin you for everyone else."

Stephie glanced from Vicky to Colleen. "You already spotted someone you'd like to dance with?"

Colleen sighed. "Dance with? …fall in love with."

Stephie hopped. "Who?"

Vicky spoke for her as he pointed back at the door. "Desmond."

The group gathered near the door until most were inside, then walked to a large table on the other side of the expansive room. Three of the friends took drink orders and headed to the bar as others headed immediately to the dance floor. Stephie turned to Colleen at the end of the first song. "Are you ready or do you want to sit and take it all in for a bit?"

Colleen glanced toward the front doors, then at Stephie, and smiled. "I'm ready." She stood and reached for Stephie's hand and they walked to their friends already dancing. Stephie started dancing with her but everyone in the group switched partners constantly. Jake came out to the dance floor and Stephie motioned to Dawn and as Dawn started dancing with Colleen, Stephie slipped her arms around Jake's neck and slid against him.

The group continually moved from the table to the dance floor in every number and combination imaginable. In the middle of their little crowd, friends were giving dance lessons and everyone danced without judgment; taking breaks when exhaustion demanded.

During a short rest, Colleen met Cody's eyes from the other end of their long table and her heart sped as she watched him stand and look at her. Her mind flooded with thought as he began walking toward her.

They had greeted earlier but she didn't know him, though Stephie told her the group had one dominating premise; everyone accepted everyone with no exceptions, no matter who or what they were. But she heard he was one of Jake's college friends, and Jake held no qualms about sharing his place in life.

She heard he was also a member of Jake and Stephie college club. They had started a student group at the university, with one dominating decree; differences were not only welcomed, but celebrated, though all were welcomed not to share if they weren't comfortable.

She understood they celebrated different foods, cultures, religions, sexualities, genders, and any other differences anyone could think of, under one rule. No judging. No fixing. Only acceptance and possible friendship. And they shared one cause; to celebrate the amazing diversity.

She was told; those who joined all had one past thing in common though; they had all experienced being shunned; even ostracized at some point in their lives, for who they were, and wanted not only to be accepted, but make their world a more accepting place. But the tolerance wasn't an assumed mindset. Members of the group had set a precedent where these attitudes were purposefully addressed before anyone became part of the inner circle. They were also forgiving, if someone slipped up. Forgiving was their second most important paradigm.

She registered the slow song beginning to play and her heart beat faster as Cody extended his hand without a word. She slowly took it and stood, and he held her hand as he led her to the dance floor. They walked to a far dark corner where he softly turned to her and extended his arms, and she walked into him, sighed and wrapped her arms around him.

She held him in silence as they slowly spun, but she couldn't stop wondering if he knew her secret. Finally with a whisper, her curiosity broke the silence. "Are you okay with me being like I am?"

He whispered, "I'm very okay with you being who you are."

The potential of his response gave her excited hope. "Could you like a girl like me?"

He caressed her deeper in his arms. "Yeah I could like you. I could like you very much."

Her heart jumped and breathing increased. His words were the nicest thing anyone ever said to her.

She wrapped her arms softly around his neck and rested her head on his shoulder. "I could like you too if that's alright."

He whispered, "That's very alright."

Kyleigh and Giana walked next to them, holding hands and started slow dancing together. The second slow song ended and the music quickened. A few moments later, their group joined them and she stepped away from Cody and started dancing faster. Paige grabbed her hand and spun her further away from Cody and they began to separate physically, but he never left her thoughts. She intermittently glanced at him and every so often caught him looking at her.

The entire group filled the rest of the night with laughs and dancing, until the crowd began dispersing. Desmond came over and visited after he finished admitting people for the night and danced with everyone, including Colleen. A few friends left early, then the remaining friends finally decided to end the night and headed toward the front doors together.

Stephie took Colleen's hand and walked in front of Vicky and Jake through the front entrance and onto the wood deck, where everyone said their goodbyes and headed toward different corners of the parking lot. Stephie anxiously waited until they were away from all their other friends, then hopped as she faced Colleen. "So?"

Colleen smiled wider than Stephie had ever witnessed. "*That* was fantastic."

Stephie's excitement increased as she watched Jake and Vicky's pleasant reaction, then focused on Colleen. "I told you."

Vicky eyed her as he walked to the passenger side of the car, "Did you enjoy the group? Everybody treat you alright?"

She smiled at Vicky across the car top, "Everybody treated me great." She paused for a moment, "Cody asked me on a date after slow dancing with me."

"Ahhhh!" Vicky scurried around the back of the car as Stephie shrieked in joy. "Yes!"

Vicky hugged her. "Yay girl!"

Jake laughed softly. "He's nice, isn't he? He's a friend from college."

Stephie chuckled as she sat in the back and slid over so Colleen could sit beside her. "I saw him say goodbye to you. Nice."

Colleen's grin radiated on her face. "He made this so special." She breathed deep, then sighed and in a softer voice repeated, "So special."

Stephie broke the comfortable silence as they pulled in front of Vicky's apartment. "My grandmother wants to have another family dinner with all of us soon."

Vicky spoke as he opened his car door. "I love her family dinners. The woman always prepares a feast."

Stephie nod softly in Colleen's direction. "You're going to love it."

"I'm invited?"

Stephie didn't share the idea the dinner party was for her, and part of her healing process. She patted Colleen's hand. "Yeah. You're part of our family now." then watched her inhale as if her words were a sweet fragrance. They said their goodbyes in front of Vicky's apartment as usual, then returned to the car.

Stephie reached for Jake's hand as they drove away. "Thanks for letting me take care of her tonight; holding her hand and everything."

He glanced at her and softly chuckled, "I love how you took care of her. I love how caring you are." then inhaled and confirmed, "You're gonna be a great mom."

She shivered. "Oh my god, Jake. I love that you think so. I think you're gonna be an amazing dad."

She held his hand between hers and leaned her head back. A few minutes later she lifted her head. "Do you like the idea we've been dating long enough to know we love each other?"

He glanced at her and then at his hand in hers. "Yeah, I love that."

"So do I." Then she hesitated and eyed him curiously. "You really love me?"

He shook his head in amazement, as his heart filled. "You're too much."

~~~

The short texts between Genna and Morgan went back and forth a few days before, planning the dinner outing, and as the time approached, their outside landing lights went on and side kitchen doors opened, as they had been doing for nearly twenty years. Connor led Genna out their side door first, and Genna locked the door as Connor opened and started the car. Chris and Morgan joined moments later.

Morgan had spotted a new brew pub in a neighboring town and suggested they explore for a night. Chris opened the car's back door. "They better have regular beer."

Genna fielded his playful complaint. "Oh will you give the place a chance before you decide you don't like it. I hear the beer's really good."

They found a table for four and sat in their usual configuration; Connor and Chris next to each other and next to their wives. The bar was new and clean, and every seat faced multiple

TV's, but Chris decided the place wasn't as nice as Logan's. "I don't see light beer on tap."

Morgan responded without looking at him, "You're an idiot."

A server immediately came over. "Do you have regular beer on draught?"

The server faced Chris. "Yes we have lagers. We have a wide variety of different beers. If you've never tried most of them, I recommend our 5 variety sampler."

"Sure, do you have five regular beers on draught?"

The server asked a few qualifying questions, then made recommendations. After a few samples, they all found a beer they liked.

Chris offered a pleasantly surprised face as he sipped his first beer. "So what's new with the kids?"

Morgan lowered her glass, "When do we start planning their wedding?"

Genna eyed Morgan. "I don't know. She and Vicky have been concentrating on Colleen."

Chris scanned the room. "Did they set a date?"

Genna met his eyes. "Not that I'm aware."

Connor smiled. "I love how they're focused on more important things. They're good kids, aren't they?"

Chris lifted his glass. "Real good kids."

Morgan shook her head, then smiled. "They're grown-ups now." She inhaled and faced Genna. "I can't wait to go dress shopping with her. Can I come dress shopping with you?"

Genna's eyes widened and answered with playful confusion. "Morgan. Do you honestly think you have to ask?"

"I'm just making sure."

"Morgan." Genna tilted her head as if scolding her for thinking she was going to be left out of any part of their children's wedding preparations.

Morgan's eyes widened. "I didn't want to assume."

"Please assume. We've both been their mothers since we've known them and we're about to be related." Genna rested her hand on Morgan's. "Please assume from now on."

Connor sipped his beer, "She said she wants a traditional old fashioned wedding." then his voice turned serious for a moment. "I wonder what issues we're going to have."

Morgan tensed. "They better not have too much trouble."

"Are you going to kick some ass?"

Her eyes narrowed as she looked at Chris. "You bet your ass." She wiped the dew off her beer glass, then met his eyes. "Anyone hurts my babies, and I'll declare war."

Chris chuckled softly as he reached for her hand. "Weren't you defending the other side a short time ago?"

"Yeah, well everyone's allowed to learn, aren't they?"

Chris sat back and rested his hand on his stomach. "Are you kidding? I've never been more proud of how you went from unquestioning acceptance to evaluating things you were once afraid to evaluate, and then changing your opinion as a direct result. That's not only difficult but scary." He made a perplexing face. "When I went through the process, I questioned myself more than I questioned the bullshit. I remember being a little afraid to think what I was starting to realize."

Connor lowered his beer as his eyes glanced at Chris and Morgan. "Our kids have given us a perspective on certain things, we wouldn't have had otherwise, haven't they?"

Morgan shook her head. "How weird. I'm ready to defend something I had completely the opposite opinion of once."

Genna nodded in agreement. "Funny, the lessons we're taught in our lives." She softly hit the table top and energized. "But not to worry about the venue for the wedding. There are enough friendly chapels around to have a beautiful wedding. And we don't have to declare war on any group. Let's ignore the immature assholes instead. Hell, let's even hope they mature sometime before they die."

Morgan made eye contact with all three, then breathed deep. "Okay, but I'll go to war if we have to."

"Relax. I'm sure we won't have to." Connor turned from Morgan to Genna. "Don't they graduate this semester?"

Chris finished his pint, "Damn, this is pretty good." then answered Connor, "I've been meaning to ask Jake." He took out his phone and began texting. *Jake are you 2 graduating the end of this semester?*

He laid his phone on the table and waved at the server.

Genna motioned with her hand as a thought came back to her. "My mother wants to have a family dinner soon. She told me Stephie asked her to, for Colleen."

Connor looked at Chris. "I wonder how many more lost children there are floating around" His eyes narrowed. "...or huddled in an alley."

Chris inhaled and frowned as Morgan's eyes widened. "Are we invited like last time?"

Genna's smile grew. "Morgan. Of course. You know you are. Will you start assuming more please? We're family."

She sat back, relieved. "Good. I loved sharing information the last time. I'm amazed at how the more you learn, the more strength you get."

Chris smirked as he ignored Morgan, leaned forward and stared at Genna. "Then we're coming to the Blair family reunion this year, dammit."

Genna countered, "You could have come last year, ass."

"Ugh." Chris placed his hand on his heart as if she shot him. "If only I'd known."

Morgan lowered her glass and met Genna's eyes. "Can I cook anything for the dinner party?"

Genna sat straight, paused a moment, then snickered. "I'd be afraid to ask."

Morgan lowered her empty glass. "I'll call her and ask. She won't give me any problems."

"Yeah, but don't expect her to say yes either."

Chris's phone beeped on the table, and he read Jake's reply. *Yeah. We're done the end of May. No idea when graduation is.*

Chris raised his phone displaying the text. "They're graduating."

Morgan covered her mouth with her hand. "I'm so proud of them. I never thought Jake would do it. I don't know why." She met Genna's eyes. "Stephie had so much to do with this. She's awesome."

Connor sipped his beer. "They're a pair, aren't they?"

Chris sat back, enjoying the relaxed atmosphere. "They're a couple."

"Who would have thought?" Genna smiled at him, "We're gonna be related." then it transformed into a playful smirk. "Who would have thought?"

Chris pulled his new glass closer. "Have we known each other twenty years?"

Morgan waved at the server. "They need to sell pitchers. This is tasty, but a pain in the ass."

Genna held out her fingers as she counted. "Holy shit. I think it's twenty years this August. ...next August."

Chris patted Morgan's hand as he watched Genna count. "Logan's has pitchers. We'll go there next time, if you want."

Connor glanced at Chris and laughed.

~~~

Vicky walked out of his bedroom to the smell of bacon cooking, and the aroma increased the speed of his last five steps to the kitchen. "That smells fabulous."

Colleen turned away from the stove, and gave him a quick glance and a deep smile. "Good morning. I figured you'd be hungry after last night."

Vicky smiled. "Good morning. You're in a great mood."

"I am." She took a deep breath. "I had a great time."

"I'm glad." Vicky walked to the stove and eyed the frying bacon.

She stepped to the side and watched him. "Can I come to the mall with you today? I don't feel like staying home."

Vicky's eyes narrowed as he casually moved to the coffee pot, but he didn't ask why. He remembered all too well, needing human connection when it was lacking in his past. "Sure, but where do you plan on hanging for seven hours?" He discreetly inhaled and sighed as he casually watched her. He felt she was safer locked in his apartment, but her emotional needs took precedent over his better judgment.

Colleen flipped the bacon as she responded without looking toward him. "There's that back room you took me to."

Vicky frowned, not at the request, but the idea her need to continue the human connection was so strong, she was willing to stay in a dingy staging area for hours. "Want me to see if I can find anyone in the group not doing anything today?" He backtracked.

"It's not that I don't want your company. I actually do. But I won't be able to spend any time with you except lunch."

Colleen answered in a quieter voice. "I understand." She patted the last three pieces of bacon with a napkin, and placed them on the plate. "How do you want your eggs?"

"No, you need to get out and live life." He opened the fridge and removed the eggs, "Over hard." and placed them next to her on the counter. "Especially after last night."

"No. You're right. I should stay here." She met his eyes. "I need to look for a job soon though."

Vicky's heart sunk. "Damn girl. I guess I'm just being overprotective."

She glanced at him as she readied the egg pan. "No. I love how you look out for me. No one else ever did that …ever."

Vicky rotated a kitchen stool to face her and sat on its edge. "You have no idea how much I worry about you …how much I want to take care of you." He watched her at the stove and inhaled. "I know this may sound crazy, but do you officially want to be brother and sister? I mean, we already are in my mind, but do you want to make it official?"

Colleen spun from the stove and her entire demeanor brightened. "I would love to be your sister." Her eyes widened. "…officially? For the rest of our lives?"

Vicky's heart continued to respond to her every reach for connection. "For the rest of our lives. After we each get married. After we have kids. After we're old and I have to come live with you. It won't necessarily be pretty, but I can promise it'll be for the rest of my life."

Vicky read Colleen's reaction, and extended his arms. "Sister?"

Colleen hesitated leaving the eggs, then quickly wrapped her arms around him and hugged him without a word. He kissed the side of her head, and then she kissed him on his lips. He caressed the back of her head as their embrace broke and she immediately continued preparing his eggs. She glanced at him as she slid his eggs onto the small plate, gently added a few pieces of bacon, then handed it to him.

They sat next to each other at the counter between the kitchen and dinette as Vicky broke the momentary silence. "And if you ever want or need to talk about your past, I'm here for you, but I understand if you can't. It's still hard for me to share parts of my life, and my past is far more past than yours."

Colleen's eyes widened and Vicky immediately reached for her hand. "It's okay."

It had been a month since Vicky rescued her, and no one had confronted or questioned him at the mall regarding her, but he never did ask her the details of the events leading to their chance meeting.

"Do you think anyone's still looking for you?" He tilted his head as their eyes met, then watched Colleen's expression turn worrisome.

"I hope not."

"So do I, but do you think?"

She shrugged. "I don't think so."

His head tilted as a lighter smile grew. "Do you have a driver's license?"

"Yeah." Her eyebrows rose.

He wiped his mouth and pushed his plate away. "Why don't you drive me to work just to get out of the house. Then you can visit the mall and come home after a little while."

Her excitement increased. "Oh. I can do some food shopping or run any errands for you if you want."

"Sounds wonderful. Get in the shower while I do the dishes and I'll do your make-up before we leave."

She softly chided him. "You're not doing the dishes. I'll do them when I get home."

He raised his hands palm out. "Fair enough."

# Chapter Six
## Contemplation

Jake pulled Stephie closer and covered her back with his arm. Her heavy breathing matched his. "Oh Jake. I love when we make love." She inhaled trying to catch her breath, "There's nothing better." then snuggled under him further. "Do you think it's great?"

Jake smiled as he watched the Friday morning sun peak between the edge of the window shade and the corner of their bedroom curtain. "You aren't sure? My eyes almost popping out aren't enough indication I think it's the greatest thing ever?" He slid his spread fingers through the back of her hair as he caressed her head and snuggled with her.

She looked up at him as she exhaled contentedly, "I love you." …her words, more breath than voice.

He kissed her deeply as he ran his hand over her soft body, and she shivered, then burrowed herself further under him. "Jacob?"

He breathed contentedly, hearing his name.

"Do you think any of the things in the news about people like us is true? Do you think we're condemned to hell?"

Her question immediately took him out of his contentment. He could feel his heart quicken as he registered its depth, and his breathing followed, though he instantly tried to quell the sudden change. And after a moment's pause, offered, "Do you know the difference between humans and God?"

She gave no response.

"You understand we're normal. We're just another minority."

"Kind of. I want to."

"I've proven to you people like us have existed forever. You know we're mentioned favorably in more than a few ancient societies throughout history, and on every continent."

"Yeah, but I thought the Bible says we're not okay and I worry about going to hell." Her back stiffened. "I'm not a bad person. I don't harm anyone. Does God really hate me?"

He inhaled deeply. These questions were the exact reason he took his chosen college electives…exactly why he was grateful being who he is. "Sweetheart, God is perfect love, He loves you, and you're more alright than you can imagine."

He felt her relax. "Once your child is yours, whether born from you or legally adopted by you, what would your child have to do to remain your child?"

She thought for a moment. "I don't understand. Nothing."

"The answer is so simple it's hard to figure out where the catch is, isn't it? But you're right. Once your child is yours, there isn't another thing she or he has to do to remain your child." He paused for a moment. "Why, if that's the rule for beings twenty years old, does anyone think God, who is twenty universe lifetimes old, doesn't have enough love or wisdom to have the same rule for you?"

He inhaled slowly. "Who do you think wrote those religious books?"

She answered softly. "People."

He softly stroked her hair. "What people?"

"Special people?"

Her answer in the form of a question brought another soft inhale followed by a sigh. "Those special people; did they write about how the universe was created?"

She responded immediately. "Yeah. Six days, right?"

"What do you know about how long the universe has taken to get where it is right now?"

"It's fourteen billion years old, give or take a half billion."

He paused another moment so the conversation remained tranquil. "Does that sound like they knew God or how He created the universe?"

"No."

"A hell of a difference regarding the truth and the information in the book, don't you think?"

"Yeah..." The way she answered conveyed her desire for him to continue.

"They asked God His name and He refused them. When they insisted, He gave them four purposefully unpronounceable consonents." His right eyebrow rose as his head tilted. "And people think the authors know His purpose, His intentions, and His plan? Seriously, He wouldn't tell them His name." He inhaled audibly. "...Woman from a man's rib doesn't sound ridiculous, yet evolving over hundreds of thousands of years does? Seriously?"

"Religious books are more human, and more about the time they were written, than most people understand. People think those books are timeless. Existential psychology proves it's impossible for humans to not be influenced by their societies and their time of existence. And story discrepancies like the creation story prove there are inaccuracies in the book that signify the influence of the authors' time and place. Pretty significant inaccuracies."

She stared at him with heart-melting submission. "Yeah, but how do we know other parts aren't correct? I need to believe I'm not condemned to hell just for being who I am. Nothing scares me more." He felt her breathing quicken and she tensed as the sentence ended.

"Who told you God had a problem with who you are?"

"I think the Bible, but I'm too scared to read it and find out it's true."

"Sweetheart …I read the passages multiple times. I studied the passages. I've read their interpretations, and I've studied the history of the book."

"What does it say?"

He chuckled at the eagerness of her request and how her desire for knowledge overruled her fear of that knowledge. "The actual words, the interpretation, the legitimacy or ethnocentricity of the supposed writers, or the relationship and difference between the writer's thoughts and what God thinks?"

"Why do you study things like this?" She rolled on her side to face him, then snuggled tighter against him. "Why don't things like this scare you?"

He wrapped his arms around her and felt her loving warmth, kissed her softly, then whispered as their kiss broke. "Because some of the things I heard people say about God hating me …hating us …hating in general, scared the life out of me."

She inhaled deeply. "You too?"

"Come on. Who the hell wouldn't be devastated to find out God hates them? I used to be deathly afraid of what hell is supposed to be. That's some scary shit." His voice reflected a new level of emotion. "Who the hell would be alright with the belief that the ultimate being is uncaringly hateful, hates certain groups specifically and has full intentions of sending most of us to hell?" He inhaled. "The only thing a person could hope for at that point is God doesn't exist, and I definitely believe God exists."

He focused on her eyes. Her eyes were mesmerizing, and through her eyes, he could see a heart and soul; unequaled in his mind. "I was afraid to read about it at first. I think that's normal. Then after a couple of psych classes and philosophy classes, which taught me that knowledge is a strong defense against fear, I became brave enough to start, and once I did a little homework, I found out knowledge not only conquers the fear, but conquers the stupidity and inaccuracies too." He caressed the back of her head and brought her head tenderly into his neck. "The classes gave me the guts to look and the skill to learn how to study the issue. What I found after a little study gave me the power to recognize where the human influence redirects the perfect love message." He shook his head softly. "We're so alright it's ridiculous. I promise."

He chuckled ironically. "But if it makes you feel any better. Hell didn't appear in religion until the story passed through a Greek interpretation, with Greek mythology proudly and strongly embedded in a fully developed culture at the time, and which has Hades as their underworld, which was dreamed of as a way to explain their lava hot-spots throughout their country. And as far as taking a core evaluation and generalizing it, almost the entire story has a perspective that reflects specific tribal influences in both time and place, of the people who controlled the first drafts of the story.

Whatever humans were told about a higher plane of existence ...good or bad, was filtered through a mindset that operated within the parameters of the knowledge of the time. Everything we can verify about any reference to another plane of existence can be measured against what the writers thought was the explanation of this universe, and their explanation of creation is pathetic at best ...childish at worst. They thought the earth was the only planet in the universe and they didn't know where the sun went at night."

She snickered.

"No. I'm serious. They literally didn't know where the sun went at night."

She inhaled the scent of his skin. "But didn't Jesus mention hell?"

"How do we know? How do we know those words weren't adjusted for the benefit of the religion that controlled the writings for years and years, with complete impunity?"

His voice softened. "Hell's only referenced in one religion and it happens to be in one of the two major religions that fail every chance they get to preach love and acceptance, or move forward with current knowledge. ...Where women are still not equal to men. ...Where the reason priests don't marry, is one of their most hidden embarrassing secrets."

She interrupted him. "What do you mean?"

He responded with a single soft snort. "Did you know catholic priests were allowed to marry until A D eleven hundred?"

He felt her pull away to look at him, but she offered no response. "Before that, priests married, but they kept leaving their homes to their heirs and the church was losing too much money in real estate." He paused. "How's that for the difference between truth and what's believed?" He breathed deep. "All indication also suggests women were priests in the beginning of the religion. Somewhere along the line, some impressive thinking males decided they knew better and changed certain rules." He shook his head as he held her in his arms. "The history of religion is a history of blind unquestioning acceptance coupled with the threats of manipulative bullies. Take a look now. Current religious hate and exclusion still verifies the immaturity."

"But you keep telling me you absolutely believe in God."

He inhaled deeply and his voice turned sincere. "I definitely believe in God. God is perfect and beautiful."

"Then I don't understand why you attack religion."

She felt him take a second deep breath followed by a sigh. "I'm only attacking what attacks me. But it's amazing how many people think religion and God are connected." He paused and stroked her hair. "And the hate gave me the first clue the two weren't connected, and I should look into the separation. Do you think certain religions would be doing the shit they're doing if they knew God? I mean, is there anything easier to believe than certain religions have no clue who God is or what He stands for?"

"I try not to think about it."

"*Everyone* tries not to think about it, until some of us can't live with the bullying that comes from the disconnection. Every dominant western religion right now hates or excludes. Some are waging war as if the war will please or prompt God, as if God would ever be prompted by the childish antics of the inhabitants of this planet, when there are millions of planets in this universe, probably with millions of forms of intelligent life who have taken responsibility for their own actions and aren't counting on higher life forms to save them from their own immaturity."

She squeezed his neck and gave him a kiss. "Told you."

Her inflection made him smile. "Told me what?"

"That you're as smart as me."

He poked her hips and made her jump in his arms. "As smart as you?"

She moved suddenly in his arms, climbing on him and playfully straddling him. "Well almost as smart as me."

He tickled her waist and she twisted in response. "But not as cute as me. I'm definitely cuter than you."

Her playfulness lightened his disposition. "Okay, I'll give you that. You're definitely cuter than me. Especially this." He grabbed her bottom.

She leaned forward and softly kissed his lips, then whispered, "You're cute too." then opened her mouth softly on his.

Their kiss ended and she stared into his eyes. "You're positive God doesn't have a problem with people like us?"

"Sweetheart, I don't just believe in God; I studied Him. I begged for a connection, and sure enough, I came to feel and understand a love beyond description. She's perfect, and you're ...we're more alright than I can ever explain. We're His. We're just here to learn and She throws no one away."

"Why do you always use both pronouns when you talk about God?"

He held her to his chest, and silently registered their connection. "The perfect Being doesn't have a gender but it's hard to talk about God without using a pronoun, and I use both because She is both; perfect mother and perfect father ...just love."

Stephie rested her head on his chest. "I love our Fridays off together."

"Me too, but you know after we graduate, that ends, right?"

Stephie kissed his chest. "Yeah ...you suck."

"I can't help if we both like to eat."

They lay together in silent bliss as he ran his fingers over her back. "We have anything planned for today?"

"No, but we have nana's dinner party tomorrow."

He smiled at the thought. The information that would be shared, would feed each of them more than the accompanying feast.

~~~

Stephie knocked on Vicky's door as Jake sat waiting in the running car. She had called Vicky moments before, telling him they were minutes away, and after a moment, it opened. "Hi."

"Hi Colleen. How are you …how's your arm?"

"I'm fine and my arm is better." Stephie gave her a kiss on her cheek as she moved toward the car, waited patiently as Vicky shut and locked his front door, then hugged and kissed him.

"Hi little sister." His loving voice always touched her heart. She cherished the connection they had. They were related more than blood could ever represent.

She smiled as her eyes met his. "Hi big brother sister."

He playfully sashayed in front of her. "You know me well."

Jake pulled onto the street as Stephie spun excitedly toward Colleen sitting in the back. "These dinner parties are for teaching and learning. Anyone who wants shares anything they want about anything lgbt, so we all learn as Nana words it, *how normal we are.*" then she faced Jake. "What are you sharing tonight?"

He glanced at her, reaching for her hand as he focused back on the road. "What we talked about the other morning."

She smiled impishly. "In between making love?"

Vicky let out a playful yelp. "Yeah girl."

Stephie watched Colleen blush, then placed her arm over the back of her seat. "When's your date with Cody?"

Colleen's blush deepened. "We're going out tomorrow night. I'm so nervous. I never went on a regular date." Her eyes widened. "Please don't tell him."

Stephie waved her hand in Colleen's direction. "I wouldn't do that to you. Girls like us need to stick together."

Vicky reached across the back seat, for Colleen's hand. "He's as sweet as can be. Just relax and be yourself."

93

"But I don't want to be myself. I want to be a girl."

Vicky held her hand as Jake spoke without taking his eyes off the road. "You *are* a girl and I bet he'd tell you the same thing."

Stephie watched her sigh as his words registered. His words had always been powerful, but they had increased in strength over the last few years. He had become so sure of himself and the knowledge he now possessed. She discreetly watched him as he drove. He never demanded anyone's attention, but she was impressed with how easily he commanded it. She shook her head in amazement and her heart filled. Was he really hers? He was the wisest and most masculine man she knew and he loved her? Every time she focused on his character, she filled with emotion.

"I can't wait to see what she cooked tonight." His words lightened the mood. "Wait till you taste this woman's cooking. She makes feasts every time we visit. She used to own a restaurant."

"I got news for you; Colleen can cook. She's been cooking for me since moving in." Vicky's voice hinted playful concern as he reached for his belt. "My pants are getting snug." He eyed Colleen and raised his eyebrows.

Stephie glanced from Vicky to Colleen. "Really."

Colleen blushed, "I love to cook."

Stephie brightened, "So do I! We have to cook together. I learned from my mom and grandmother. Nana loves giving lessons. She says it's an honor when someone wants to learn her way of making something. I think it's an honor learning it."

Stephie watched Colleen relax, then faced forward and sat back, pleased to find another common interest.

Jake parked the car in front of the house next to Lorraine's. She knew why. She had asked once and his answer amazed her enough that every time he parked less than close, his answer came back to mind. No one would ever know and he wouldn't ever tell, but he did it out of respect for their parents, so they could have the spots in front of the house. Who else would ever do that? Who else would think of that? She sighed and discreetly shook her head.

Lorraine opened the door with her usual smile and Stephie hugged her immediately. "Nana."

Stephie's greeting produced a joyful reply. "Hi Cipolline."

Stephie stepped back as soon as their hug broke and motioned with her hand. "This is Colleen."

Lorraine extended both hands with a welcoming smile. "It's great to meet you dear. Come in and make yourself at home. You're family when you're here, okay?"

Colleen took her hands and her eyes noticeably widened. She blinked as she tried not to release a tear, but offered no response, as if any word would defeat the effort.

Vicky inhaled as he waited to greet her. "What is that delicious smell? Are you trying to fatten me up, Nana?"

Lorraine hugged him. "How are you dearest?"

Vicky hugged her deeply. "I'm wonderful. How are you?"

Stephie loved when Vicky called her grandmother *Nana*. She knew he did it for her. Vicky showed as much loving consideration as anyone she knew. And the longer they were family, the more confused she became when she envisioned his actual relatives discarding him.

Lorraine stepped back, making room for those already greeted. "I'm excited to enjoy your company tonight. I love when you all visit me. You feed my soul."

Jake held out his arms and joked. "And you feed my gut."

She laughed softly. "Then we both win." They kissed and hugged tenderly. "And you know I love win win."

Jake breathed deep. "Did you cook my favorite?"

She glanced at him and chuckled as she closed the door. "Jacob, is there anything that isn't your favorite?"

He grinned. "Not that you cook."

She shook her head lovingly as she cupped his face with her hand. "Come on in and make yourselves at home."

The door opened behind them. "Hello everyone."

All turned as Morgan and Chris entered, and the welcoming greetings continued. They moved to the family room and settled around the expansive fireplace, which provided a soft glow and soothing warmth, until Connor and Genna finally walked in. After light and loving greetings, Lorraine reached for Stephie's hand. "Will you help me in the kitchen?"

Vicky heard her and motioned to their new friend. "Colleen's an excellent cook." He patted his belly. "She's cooking me fat too."

Nana smiled at her. "Do you want to join us? I love cooks in my kitchen."

Stephie reached for her hand and answered for her, "Yes." and Colleen eagerly hopped up in response.

"Can I come too?" Vicky sat straight. "I wanna learn."

Lorraine laughed softly. "You know you're one of my children and my children don't have to ask. Please be home here."

Vicky moved two full serving trays and placed the last bowl on the table between them as he heard Colleen announce dinner. Jake held the head chair for Lorraine, and she cupped his cheek before sitting. Stephie insisted Colleen sit between her and Vicky, and the party continued during the feast.

Chris passed a serving dish then glanced at Colleen. "Did anyone share what we do after dinner?"

Colleen answered softly. "Kind of."

He passed another serving dish. "Not to worry. You'll see."

Genna added as everyone passed serving plates. "There's no rules or subject that's off limits. We're family and these dinner parties are for learning and sharing."

Morgan passed the bread. "Lorraine started this. She started studying lgbt and transgender topics when we realized who Stephie was, and the information was so beneficial, we realized the more information we knew, the stronger every one of us became." She gazed at Lorraine. "Thank you for being awesome."

Lorraine smiled gracefully. "I'm not awesome. I'm in love. I learned who my granddaughter was for that reason only. Nothing more."

Stephie raised her focus from her plate. "I love you."

Lorraine met her eyes. "You're my life." Lorraine spoke softly, but the table had become quiet as all eyes focused on her. "All of you are my life."

They all raised their drinks and saluted her and each other, and continued eating, joking and laughing.

They gathered in the family room after everyone helped clear the table. Morgan pointed to both Chris and Jake who were holding their stomachs, and laughed. "Suffering now? You two ate what the rest of us ate combined."

"I can't help it. I love this food." Chris glanced at Jake as he tried to get comfortable. "Me too. I'd weight four hundred pounds if I ate this all the time."

Morgan responded indignantly. "What are you saying? I'm not this good a cook?"

Everyone else began chuckling, anticipating his effort to try to escape his new predicament. "You know I love your cooking, but I love feasts like this and every meal you make just for the two of us can't be a feast."

Connor raised his beer. "Well done."

Everyone laughed louder.

"Thank you. Thank you very much." Chris bowed from his seat and Morgan smacked the back of his head.

"Ow!"

Genna motioned toward Colleen. "So, how much do you know about the history of transgendered and other lgbt people?"

Colleen raised her eyebrows and inhaled noticeably. "Besides how I feel and the hurt it's brought me, not much I guess."

"Did you know their history is as old as written history? Almost every culture around the world has recorded lgbt in its history."

Jake passed his open computer to Stephanie, sitting next to her. He had opened a map document verifying Genna's statement.

Morgan sat forward. "...Throughout recorded history. Did you know in certain cultures, you were considered elite and part of the ruling class?"

Stephie pointed to the written paragraph on the map. "Native Americans revered transgender people. We were called two-spirited, which meant we understood both genders deeper than just males or just females." She looked at Jake and then studied the screen. "How many documents do you have in here now?"

He smiled. "Roughly four hundred. And I found some new stuff I want to share today, I think you'll all enjoy."

Stephie handed him his computer.

"I found some interesting articles about the six bible passages which supposedly argue against lgbt lifestyle, and the information destroying their argument." He glanced around the room. "That's what I want to share."

Lorraine shook her head softly. "So much evidence verifying the validity of lgbt people." She eyed everyone in the room, though she shared the information mainly for Colleen. "From scientific documents explaining everything from genetic to hormonal proof, to historical documents ranging back to the beginning of recorded history, to psychology based Peer Review Journal Articles stating irrefutable evidence of the normalcy of everything lgbt."

Jake straightened in his seat. "Oh yeah, I learned something the other day I almost forgot. I was studying the Noah and the flood story, and I found out the story is a plagiarism of a much older story, and Noah's character was named Gilgamesh, the king of Uruk. It's a twelve tablet story predating Noah, and the ark story is the eleventh tablet, but I have a better twist. What if God told Gilgamesh about the flood, not because He was the perpetrator who needed to destroy people, but because the flood was an upcoming natural event He knew He shouldn't prevent, due to the Earth's natural development, and wanted His children to survive?"

Stephie shifted her head away from him. "Huh? Where'd you come up with that?"

"It's called re-framing; something psychologists suggest doing when explanations don't align with other more dominating paradigms. Perfect love doesn't hate, so I re-framed the story, only to find out the story is contrived anyway."

"But I'm not calling out a religion for plagiarizing a story. I'm calling them out for plagiarizing in a way that twists a perfect loving God into an ogre. My God isn't."

He quickly eyed everyone, then focused on his screen. "Okay, back to this other article I found, identifying all the bible passages against lgbt; the one Christians say is the most damning is in Corinthians."

Connor leaned forward. "I thought it was Saddam and Gomorrah."

Jake glanced at him then back to his computer. "It used to be, but scholars now believe that story is about corruption and greed. I'll share that study after I explain this if you want."

Connor shook his head in disbelief, "Amazing." then nodded. "Okay."

Jake refocused on the computer screen. "So, the two damning operative words in the original Corinthians passage are the Greek words, *malakoi* and *arsenkoitai*. *Malakoi* literally translates to gutless or *spineless*, but can loosely translate to *soft*, which has then been bastardized to mean effeminate, and or gay, but neither re-translation is accurate. The passage's initial meaning calls out those who are spineless or morally weak …and nothing more."

*"Arsenkoitai* is a little stranger. It's a very rare word and because it's so rare, scholars believe its actual meaning has been lost forever, but the word doesn't refer to homosexuality. There were, at the time of the original writing, many common words representing things homosexual during that time and place in history, and if that's what the writer intended, he would've used one or more of those well understood common words."

Morgan sighed noticeably. "Why?" Her eyes narrowed. "Why is it necessary to fabricate false meanings when the initial meaning is wiser and more important? Why make something up that's less important …even senseless?"

Jake looked at her and softly shook his head. "Because the misinterpretation serves specific agendas."

He glanced toward her. "But I saved the best for last. I just found something by accident that's beyond this world. I found a gospel passage where God talks about lgbt being His, for His purpose." He looked around as everyone stared. "Matthew nineteen, eleven and twelve." He typed, read the passage, then repeated the first and last sentence. "Not everyone can receive this saying? Let the one who is able, receive it? ...Is that mind-boggling? ...*Eunuch* is a mistranslation for lgbt. The definition back then was; men not comfortable sleeping with women. Think about it. In their own book and they're told they're not allowed to understand."

His eyes narrowed and breathing quickened. "I think He's using lgbt to separate sheep from wolves. Who can love ...who can accept ...who can avoid judging and just love, as ordered."

Genna broke the momentary silence and stood. "Can we take a quick break?" She pointed to the bathroom.

Connor stood. "Beer break."

Morgan waited until everyone rose, then motioned to Jake and led him into the foyer. When they were alone, her voice softened. "Jake, I'm sorry I believed things without questioning them, and still don't do as much homework as I should."

"Oh mom, it's alright." He reached for her arm. "That's what love is for; to automatically forgive things. I love you and I knew you'd be alright. I told you when we had our long discussion."

"It's not alright. I love you and I hurt you."

He hugged her. "It's so alright. I love you and my situation hurt you."

"Only because I believed shit I shouldn't have." She held his hand.

"But mom, how were you supposed to know you shouldn't believe those things? We trust our teachers and preachers to be wise. How are we supposed to know when they aren't?"

Her right brow rose as her chin lowered. "Then why did you start questioning these things? You studied this. Why don't more people study this and let the world know the problem with the interpretations?"

He sighed. "People are too busy with their own concerns. People care. They're just too busy. I study these things because they directly affect me; otherwise I doubt I would."

After the short break, Jake shared the other five modern interpretations of the supposedly condemning passages as everyone enjoyed the fireplace and additional drinks.

He closed his lap-top and glimpsed at everyone. "Anyone have any questions?"

Vicky turned toward Colleen. "What do you think?"

Her eyes widened. "I'm blown away. I wish my family knew even a little of this." She pointed to Jake's computer. "I don't know where or how I could even share proof we're normal, with them."

Vicky reached for her hand. "But isn't the information overwhelming?"

She gently shook her head. "I had no idea."

Vicky frowned. "Not many do."

Lorraine spoke softly. "You're so intense, Jacob. Thank you. Now let's spend the rest of the evening on a lighter note."

Chris reached for the wine bottle on the coffee table. "I'm head of the beverage refill committee."

Genna laughed. "You do know your expertise."

Chris topped Stephie's glass. "Be nice to me or *no wine for you*."

~~~

The goodbyes and laughing extended to their cars, as Lorraine stood at her front porch waving. Morgan watched as Chris followed Connor's car down the street. "I can't believe how strongly I feel now about the kids being completely normal. I can't believe I went from thinking this was some abnormal form of existence to thinking beyond a doubt, they're unbelievably normal and our religious structure is immature, and maybe mean. Why would anyone…how could anyone think these people are anything but normal?"

Chris glanced at her quickly. "You know, it took me two years to be completely comfortable with my new perspectives about this stuff way back when. I pretend I figured it out and was immediately fine with the new structure I was adopting, but your adjustment has been smoother and faster."

She shivered but wasn't sure its cause was the cold car seat. "Yeah, but look at the help I have. You study these things privately and in silence. I have you, Jake, and the Blairs helping me."

He tilted his head in confirmation as he glanced at her. "It was disquieting, coming to these realizations secretly." He turned onto the highway. "Each bit of information; each new discovery was upsetting. Are the books no one questions, not the perfect wisdom those who praise them insist they are? Each new revelation led to more exploration, until I finally fit it all together; until I finally realized what all the information had in common."

She turned the car radio off. "But you talk more favorably about God than you ever did."

He held out his hand for hers. "Because at first, I thought the hate and condemnation were God's edict. At first, I thought religions were carrying out God's rules; then I realized there are more rules telling us to love each other, then there are any other rules, and that's when I realized God and religion aren't the same thing. Humans rule religions, not God. Humans manipulate religions. And since realizing that, I've been able to see God differently. Remember when I told you I read that alternative Dead Sea scroll? It stated how God wants us to learn from our mistakes, which takes precedent over Him stepping in and fixing our problems. I've also read other things that offer better understanding of ancient beliefs."

"Do you and Jake talk about this?" She twisted in her seat.

"Yeah. We talk. He's matured so much, and shares new perspectives with me as he comes up with them."

He paused and smiled, "He makes me think." then inhaled fully. "And he has an understanding of things, like no one I've ever met."

# Chapter Seven
## Incarnation

Colleen sat on Vicky's bed, as nervous as could be. She had decided on a casual and modest purple skirt, and matching silk blouse more for its femininity than any other reason. She liked the way she looked, but actually wanted to wear something a little sexier; something she hoped Cody would really like. She knew what cis girls would wear and how they would act, but she knew she didn't fit either paradigm.

Her mind played tricks on her as she sat. She wanted to be excited. She had dreamed about this. Well, at least dreamed about dating someone when her mind let her. Most times she was afraid to have this fantasy, for fear the reality was beyond her. But now that it was here, she felt apprehensions not part of her first date daydreams. Apprehensions blocking her ability to feel the excitement she felt when she dreamed of this moment.

Her thoughts wandered to Vicky sitting in the living room, and how different it was having a family member who cared for her and willing to guide her. She wondered what he would think of her outfit and felt her heart jump. The last thing she wanted was to disappoint him.

She reminisced about dancing with Cody. She hadn't stopped thinking about him since he asked her to dance, and couldn't get the way he held her, out of her mind. She had never been held like that ...ever. At least not by anyone she wanted to hold her. He wasn't the best looking guy she ever saw, but he was cute and he liked her? He could like a girl like her? *And* he was a regular guy; in college even. Every time she imagined having a real boyfriend; someone to care for and who cared about her, the thought overwhelmed her.

She took a deep breath and stood, hesitated and took another, then exited the room toward Vicky. She felt her face blush as she walked past the hall corner and into Vicky's eyesight. He turned toward her and clasped his hands in front of his chest. "Oh honey, you look adorable."

She blushed deeper, and smiled bashfully. In the short time she had known him, Vicky's approval had come to mean the world to her. After all, he was the only person who ever volunteered to be her family. Family for no reason. She knew she had little to offer, and the thought made her sigh. If she won the lottery, she would happily give him half ...but she knew the odds of that fantasy occurring. She knew the odds of all pleasant fantasies occurring.

Vicky stood and pointed to the dinette stool. "Ready for make-up?"

She hesitated, inhaled deeply, and watched Vicky's eyes widen. "Are you nervous, honey?"

She could feel her eyes well up in response to his caring tone. "I can't believe how different the reality is, compared to the fantasy. I feel overwhelmed." She sighed.

Vicky placed a few applicators on the dinette counter. "Why?"

"I feel like this is my one chance to have a boyfriend, and I'm not ready. I don't know how to be his girlfriend." Colleen sat on the stool.

Vicky's voice turned soothingly confident. "I used to think like that. When I finally found someone who accepted me, I was deathly afraid of losing him, and absolutely sure I'd never find someone else if it didn't work. The odds of there being one person who liked me were ridiculous, right?"

He glimpsed toward Colleen, then rummaged through the make-up box. "The odds of a second guy would be astronomical."

He found the specific applicator and blotted it on a folded paper towel. "Then I met a second guy and was *positive* I had to hold onto him for the rest of my life."

His concentration divided as he started applying her make-up. "Yep. You're so normal it's a crime, and I'm going to give you some older sister advice."

He held a palette of colors close as he transferred color to her face. "There will always be another special someone you never expected. You can hold onto any single one that comes along, but there will always be another. I promise."

Colleen squirmed as if the words didn't apply to her …couldn't apply to her. Vicky shook his head and secretly sighed, motioned her to stand, then hugged her softly. He didn't say anything, but his breathing and warmth felt so comforting.

"Sit."

She sat as directed.

"Where's he taking you?"

"I have no idea." She squirmed in her seat.

"Stop fidgeting."

"I can't."

He paused and stepped back as his head tilted. "Is this your first date ever?"

Her eyes scrunched. "Can you tell?"

He hopped with excitement. "I did your sister's make-up, her first time too." He waved his hand at her. "You're gonna be fine."

After a short silence, he stepped in front of her and raised her chin. "Beautiful, if I do say so myself." He handed her the mirror. "What do you think?"

She inhaled as she stared at her reflection. "Wow Vicky." She examined closer. "My eyes. Thank you."

"You have beautiful eyes." He placed his hands under his chin then made a funny voice and batted his eyelashes, "Tell me more about my eyes." making her laugh.

"Okay honey. Go relax while I clean up."

She stood. "Yeah …like that's possible."

The doorbell rang and Colleen jumped, covered her mouth, then whispered, "I don't know if I can go through with this."

Vicky glanced toward her as he stood to answer the door. "Sweetie, I bet it ends up being one of the best nights of your life."

He opened the door and greeted Cody. "Hi, hon."

"Hi Vick." Colleen caught his eye and he did a double-take in her direction. "Hi Colleen."

Vicky discretely smiled at the positive reaction he displayed as he eyed his date. "Come on in."

He walked immediately past him and toward Colleen. "You look beautiful."

"Thank you." She blushed.

Vicky jokingly cleared his throat with a mock cough. "Excuse me. Where you taking her tonight?"

Cody turned to Vicky, "Just a movie." then nervously faced her. "Is that alright?"

Vicky secretly enjoyed his unease, then lightened the mood; jokingly waiving his finger. "I'll be asking her details about the movie, mister …so you had better just be watching. Hear me?"

Cody smiled as his shoulders straightened. "Yes sir."

Vicky continued pointing at him. "And have her home at a decent time. …Understand?"

"Yes sir."

Colleen hit Vicky on his shoulder as she took Cody's hand, "Thanks Vicky. Good night Vicky." and led him to the door.

His voice softened. "You two kids have a good time. I love you both."

Colleen answered as the door shut. "We will."


Colleen was too nervous to notice Cody's nervousness, and he startled her as he suddenly ran to open her door as they approached his car. At first, she was confused by the gesture, wondering why he was hurrying. Then it struck her. *Oh my god. He just opened my door for me!*

Then she became aware of how he perceived her and her nervousness increased. *Why does he see me as female? How can he see me as female when he knows I'm not. Wait. I am. …but I'm not. How can he not care? How can he like me?* The thoughts were starting to overwhelm her. She became aware of her breathing and peered at him, realizing she didn't remember him getting in the car next to her. She breathed deep and the words that followed felt like they came from someone else's mouth. "Why …how do you see me as a girl?"

Her words seemed to startle him and he paused, making her heart beat faster. "You are, aren't you?"

She lowered her eyes, "Yes." then whispered, "But my parents can't."

He glanced at her and took a deep breath. "But I can."

She narrowed her eyes in confusion. "And everything's all alright with you?" She waved her hand at the front of her outfit.

He glanced at her, then turned back to the road. "Yeah, it's alright. I see a girl. A cute girl." He smiled and his voice gave a hint of relief. "A really cute girl." He glanced at her again, then back to the road. "Is that okay?"

She inhaled deeply. "Yeah." She paused, then offered quietly. "Very okay."

He extended his hand across the arm-rest between them and her heart jumped. She placed her hand in his, leaned her head back, and tried to calm down.

Cody pulled into an almost empty movie theater parking lot and she sighed with relief. She opened her door as he shut the car off and he paused before getting out. Was he this caring? *I think he would have opened my door.* Her heart beat in response. She had never imagined a man treating her this nice.

She met him at the back of the car and took his extended hand. His inhale was noticeable and his attentiveness, wonderful. The large glass vestibule listed the six choices in the ten theaters, and she watched Cody glance at her between staring at the board. "Do you want to see anything?"

Her eyes widened. "It doesn't matter to me. I'll see whatever you want."

He smiled at her. "I don't go to many movies." He pointed. "Did you see that?"

"I didn't see any of these."

She stepped a half step closer to him and held his hand quietly, then followed him to the ticket window. The theater was almost empty and they sat quietly sharing a soda and popcorn. She reached for his hand as the movie started and they held hands the entire movie. She sighed as she realized he was also reaching for the soda between them with his far hand and wondered if he didn't want to let her hand go either. She glanced at him and sighed.

The movie ended before she was aware and her first thought was Vicky! She didn't remember a thing about the movie. Her heart beat faster as the lights brightened and she stood as Cody stood.

His eyes widened as he focused on hers. "Did you like it?"

She didn't know how to tell him it was the best thing she ever did, and sitting for two hours holding his hand was all she remembered. "Yeah. Did you?"

His smile and his voice softened as he met her eyes. "Yeah."

He found an open spot and parked the car on the busy street in front of Vicky's apartment complex, shut it off and faced her. "I really had a good time tonight."

She smiled at him. "I did too."

She could feel her heart race. The kiss was next. She was losing her calm. He wasn't moving.

His voice rose. "Do you have to go in yet? Want to talk for a bit?"

"No. Sure. I mean, no, I don't have to go in. Sure, we can talk if you want." She forcefully controlled her breathing.

He exhaled and smiled, then she watched his eyes narrow. "Mind if I do something I wanted to do since we danced?"

She inhaled as her heart jumped in reaction to his words, then shrugged her shoulders. "Sure."

He reached behind her head and pulled her slowly toward him as he moved closer to her, and softly kissed her lips, then just as tenderly, opened his mouth on hers. Her heart immediately jumped as if a spark had hit it. The spark was soft but deepened through the entire kiss. She felt her reaction grow, then slowly wrapped her arms around his neck and opened her mouth wider. Then felt his arms wrap further around her and her heart began yearning for more as the embrace deepened. The kiss ended naturally and her sigh matched his.

He smiled. "I wanted to do that since we danced."

"You could have." She smiled as he leaned toward her and fulfilled his desire a second time.

She took a breath as their second kiss ended, and looked at him curiously. "Are you gay?"

He gave a half shrug as he tilted his head toward his right shoulder. "I don't consider myself gay. I don't know. I don't like guys. I'm not attracted to masculine guys, anyway." Then he thought for a second. "But I think I had a crush on a guy friend once." He shrugged. "What does it matter anyway? I like whoever I like for all different reasons, I guess."

"Why do you like me?" Her eyes widened and her brows rose as she asked. She knew it was a strange question and definitely a premature one, but qualified it in her mind; her existence was also strange by all current social ideals.

He met her eyes. "You're feminine. There's something about how feminine and..." He paused for a moment and his eyes narrowed. "I don't know how to explain it. Stephie has it too. You both don't think you're special ...and there's something really feminine about how you act ...that I like." He breathed deep. "It's hard to explain." He faced her. "It's like, you don't think you're anything special and that makes you special to me."

He watched her confused reaction and his face formed a frown. "Is that too weird for you?"

Her eyes widened, and her breathing quickened. "Yeah. Like you could out-weird me."

They both laughed at her candor, then he sat straighter. "I think the rest of the world out-weirds you. I learned you're normal."

She sighed. "But there are parts of me... I mean... Are you okay with ...everything?"

He offered a knowing smile. "You know Kaden?"

"Yeah."

"Do you think you could touch Kaden?"

She grinned at the awareness he just shared with her. "Yes."

He continued even though he could tell she understood. "Why."

"Touching him would be touching a guy."

His eyes widened as he nodded softly. "And you're attracted to guys?"

Her grin broadened. "Yeah."

He reached for her hand. "It's the same thing. You're a girl and touching you is touching a girl." He studied her eyes. "And I like the idea of kissing and touching girls, so I like the idea of kissing and touching you."

Her mouth slowly, eagerly opened as he leaned toward her for another kiss, and for the first time in her life, she realized she could revive the hopes and dreams she had abandoned, since she gave in to her need to be who she knew she was.

~~~

Jake hugged Kyleigh hello, then turned toward the rest of the group. "Alright everybody. Let's do some official business and then we'll get back to the social."

He moved to the front of the classroom, shaking Anthony's hand as he passed. "Hey everyone."

Return acknowledgments filled the room. "It's always great to see everybody." He scanned the room and enjoyed the smiles and nods of agreement, then met Stephie's eyes last and her smile triggered a deeper reaction he silently registered. He dropped his backpack on the desk and unzipped it, "Okay." then removed a paper.

"The agenda."

The room quieted.

"I wanted to discuss something my father says every once in a while, that gives me strength every time he says it. This is him. He's a construction worker and doesn't mince words, but the bluntness adds to its strength."

He paused... "What's it to you if I'm fucking chickens?"

He tilted his head as the sentence had its normal effect on him. "Everyone lgbt seems to feel pressure to *come out* or *share their sexuality*. Every non-lgbt person feels absolutely free to ask lgbt people intimate details they wouldn't think of asking a cis or hetero person, and I'm a little confused by it. No one ever expects a hetero or cis person to declare their sexual preference or gender. And why do lgbt people feel obligated to comply? Why do hetero people feel empowered to ask?"

Giana called out. "Society. We're not equal."

Jake faced her. "Exactly."

Stephie spun in her desk toward the group. "Try being transgender. People ask you what genitals you have. ...Like *that's* anyone's business."

Kaden responded with his continually deepening masculine voice. "I get people demanding to see mine once they find out I'm transgender. *No* answers leave some people confused and have led to more than one fist fight."

"Saying no doesn't work?"

Kaden firmly responded to Anthony's question. "*Fuck you* is a form of *no*."

Everyone in the room snickered.

"Like my father says…" Jake sat on the top of a desk, facing the group and glancing at all gathered. "Do any of you feel like we're actually trying to change the world for the next generation? Ever notice how much more accepting people our age are?"

Kyleigh confirmed his observation. "More people our age, than our parents' age know we're normal and it's reassuring, but I wish our parents and grandparents thought lgbt people were normal." Her voice turned solemn. "I wish we didn't have to keep arguing we're equal to everyone."

Giana added, "Maybe the next generation won't have to have meetings to tell each other they're normal and equal."

James moved his desk to face the group. "The world's changing, but if people like us have existed for as long as that website says…" He motioned to Jake's computer. "…then why aren't we just another group of normal equal people yet?"

Jake's brows rose and he inhaled. "That chart on the history of lgbt is eye-opening, isn't it? Isn't it strange finding out we were more accepted throughout history, by societies we consider more primitive than ours?"

Giana offered in a lower voice, "But equally frustrating we aren't considered normal or equal now, when we're so much more modern and aware of our universe."

"The world's almost splitting." Anthony ran both hands through his hair. "Half the population wanting to go back to a more primitive time for mindlessly confusing reasons and half wanting to use our new knowledge to go forward, and I'm scared of who's winning."

Jake glanced from James and Anthony to Giana. "That's why I share the things I share; so all of us can understand how normal we are, and the more we share with whoever will listen, the more we'll be treated equally."

He eyed Anthony then pointed to his computer. "I see the same split, and it's scary thinking there's no clear-cut winner of the argument yet."

Everyone watched Michaela as she offered a thought. "When I try to share the information we've all shared, some tell me I'm trying to shove my agenda on them. It's hard when people won't hear we just want to be considered equal. I don't want to be better than anyone. I know I'm not better than anyone." She peered down and her voice softened. "But I know I'm no less than anyone either." She raised her stare. "It's frustrating. I get tired trying to convince people."

"Don't you wish someone in the past had spoken for us?" Jake stood and started pacing. "Don't you wish this had been settled by now?"

Kyleigh shared her frustration. "Yes!"

Kaden took a noticeable breath; the air passing through his nose, audible to the rest of the group. "I'm going to spend the rest of my life defending everyone like us."

Kyleigh reached for his hand. "You're more of a man than any cis man I know."

Jayjay interrupted, "So different from me, stuck between genders."

Jake nodded in agreement and his resolve reflected in his voice. "All these reasons are why it's necessary for us to keep educating everyone who'll listen …for us to be strong and give each other strength. For those who will follow us. We need to do what our parents and grandparents failed to do. We need to keep educating until every different human is accepted as equal."

A voice shouted from the hallway… *faggot* …but no one appeared.

They stared at each other for a moment, then Jake immediately ran to the classroom door and shouted. "Come on in and join us. Everyone's welcome."

A male in the distance, turned and yelled. "I'm no faggot."

Jake raised his voice. "Neither am I. But hate isn't the opposite of love; indifference is. You yell hate in order to fight being included, and now I want to become your friend. Your outburst is just your way of forcefully staying away from us because your feelings run against everything you've been taught. I understand more about your need to find our room and share your remark than you realize, and it's okay ...I promise." He waved his arm. "Joining us doesn't mean you're gay...come find out who we are. I promise I won't tell a soul you came. This is a no judgment zone. I won't hurt you like you just tried to hurt us. I promise."

The male shouted back, "No way. I'm not gay."

"We don't categorize. Everyone's just human. If you're human, you meet all our requirements. Every first and third Tuesday four PM right here. You don't have to be gay. We accept friends."

"I'm not your friend." The man disappeared from Jake's sight.

Jake yelled a little louder, "Not yet."

He walked back in the room with a wry grin, and Paige stared at him with wide eyes until he made eye contact with her. "That was unbelievable. You took his hate and offered acceptance. That was brilliant."

His grin widened. "Psychology is a bitch." He paused intently, enjoying her reaction. "We're taught most active haters are fighting their own inner conflict between having lgbt feelings and the prejudice they've learned from the people they love. Some people don't have the guts to admit their confusion so they fight the feelings actively. People who have no feelings are indifferent, not actively hostile." He narrowed his eyes as his grin changed. "That psychological perspective sure does add a new twist on preachers who constantly, unsolicitedly rail against lgbt, doesn't it?"

He looked around, displaying his uncontrollable grin. "Anyone have anything to add before we close the agenda?"

"Yeah. I have something I found online, I thought was interesting." Linda opened a piece of paper, and started reading. "I don't have to like lgbt. I have to coexist with them. I don't have to agree or disagree with lgbt. I have to not judge them. I can or if I don't feel like, don't have to learn more about lgbt, but if I choose to not learn about lgbt, I have to not have an opinion about them." Linda turned the paper over. "A Muslim, Jew, Christian, Sikh, Buddhist, African, European, Latino, and Asian all came together and you know what happened? They became friends because they weren't assholes." Linda lowered the paper, prompting everyone to look at all the other smiling faces.

The walk home from the meeting was quiet and pleasant. Jake had taken her hand as soon as they left the classroom, and hadn't let go. She knew it was silly, but she loved holding his hand. She loved the different ways they held hands. The car was different than walking. And nothing was as nice as going to sleep holding hands. She looked down at her hand in his and then raised her eyes until they met his beautiful face and her heart filled. "Can we pick a date?"

She saw her question break his trance and he moved her arm, spinning her toward him, then took her in his arms and kissed her tenderly in the middle of the walkway, and she sighed as he released her. "Oh Jacob." She looked into his eyes, then placed her head on his chest under his chin. "I want to be your wife so badly. ...I love you so much."

He stroked her hair. "That's funny, because I already think you're my wife. Not that I don't want to marry you." He took her hand as they resumed walking home. "We're definitely having a ceremony and party, but that's nothing more than the confirmation. We're already married in my heart."

"God, Jacob. You always say the most perfect loving things."

"And you always show me complete love. What date do you want?"

"Saturday."

He glanced at her and smiled. "Didn't we already have that discussion? Our mothers would shoot us."

He slid his arm around her and gave her another kiss. "Do you have a serious date in mind?"

She focused on his eyes. "I was thinking January. January is always a big letdown after the holidays and there's no celebrations the entire month. This would give us a celebration in January."

He inhaled and grinned. "January it is. When in January?"

"Right between New Year and Valentine's day."

He let go of her hand to unlock their apartment door, and glanced at her as he dug for the key. "How long have you had this figured out?"

She hopped as he swung the door open for her. "Not long."

~~~

Colleen turned away from the stove, placed Vicky's dinner plate on the breakfast counter and met his eyes. "Need anything?"

"Nope." Vicky leaned forward and inhaled. "This smells delicious. You're spoiling me."

She smiled deeply. "I love cooking and I *love* when people think it's good."

119

"But you're ruining my girlish figure." He leaned back and patted his stomach.

She slid her plate next to his, then opened the refrigerator door. "You can't get fat eating this food. Want a soda?"

"Sure." He glanced at her as he took the first bite and moaned in pleasure. "Damn, girl."

Colleen placed the two sodas next to their plates and walked around to the dinette side of the breakfast bar. As she sat next to Vicky, her phone rang on the small counter, and she reached for it. He watched her face turn solemn as she read the name, then hit *end*, and sat still for a moment.

He waited another moment for her to volunteer a reason for the reaction, and then broke the silence. "Who was that?"

"Nobody."

Vicky reached for her folded hands, resting on her lap. "If you were my girlfriend and gave me that answer after I witnessed that, we'd be having a fight right about now."

Colleen's impish smile confirmed her lie.

Vicky reached for his soda. "So?"

She inhaled slowly. "My father."

"Is this the first time he's called you since you've been here?"

Colleen finally lifted her fork. "No, but he's calling more."

"Have you answered any of them?"

"No."

Vicky could feel his breathing quicken. "Please don't."

"Believe me, I'm not gonna." Colleen offered a deeper smile, but he could tell it wasn't genuine.

"How's your dinner?"

He decided to accept her polite request to change the subject. "It's fantastic," He patted his stomach. "but you really are starting to make me fat ...and we ain't even married."

~~~

They had been sitting next to each other, studying in relaxed silence for hours when Stephie closed her books. "Can we take a break?"

Jake looked up from his notes. "Sure. You want to watch TV?"

"No." She bounced in her seat and faced him. "I feel like playing a game."

"Okay. ....What game?"

"Let's call it *Lap Dance*."

Jake's heart jumped and his voice lowered, "Oh ...that sounds like a nice game."

Her smile brightened. "I think you'll like it."

He closed his books and pushed them away. "I already do."

"Then let's play." She stood.

"Okay." He sat straight. "What do I do?"

She thought for a second. "You go to the door to enter the club, and I'll greet you there and share the rest as we go. Okay?"

"Okay."

"But first, give me a few minute to get ready, okay?"

"Okay." He started chuckling at all the *okay*s, and how she made each one sound more feminine than the last. He smiled at her like a child promised candy and thought; *God, she's frigging adorable.*

"I'll be right back." She spun and headed toward their room.

He reached for the remote, stared at the television, then returned it to the end table, stood, straightened the pillows on the sofa and plopped back down ...then popped up and walked into the kitchen. He made a face. There wasn't a thing he wanted or needed in there. He glanced at the hallway leading to their room and considered barging in, then straightened as the next thought entered his head; *And ruin the game? What the hell's wrong with me?*

He walked back to the sofa and sat …waiting impatiently. The momentary forever finally ended as she yelled from the hall out of eyesight, "Go out the door and shut it behind you. When I open it, you'll understand."

He chuckled and replied in a loud voice, "Sweetheart, if you told me to drive to Canada right now and wait for you, I would."

She heard their front door shut, quickly turned on music, and raised the volume enough to make the mood in the house match her skimpy outfit and dancer's amount of perfume. Then went to the door, inhaled deeply and slowly opened it. "Hi! Welcome to the Fantasy Club. Please come in!"

"Thanks. Hi." She eyed his uncontrollable grin as he quickly studied her short silk skirt and delicate blouse, then watched him breathe deep. "You smell nice."

She curtsied. "Thanks. You like my perfume?" She lifted her neck, offering him unspoken permission to enjoy it more, and he eagerly obliged.

"Have you ever been here before, or is this your first time?"

"This is my first time."

"Well it's great you came, especially since you're so cute." She started up the stairs. "Please follow me to the lounge."

She turned to him at the top of the stairs and stood extremely close without so much as an accidental touch. She was playing the part and off limits to him unless he paid for a dance. That was one of the house rules she'd soon explain. But flirting seemed just as natural a rule, and she was playing her part to its highest degree.

She kept complete eye contact and the look on his face told her he was pleased with her choice of music, outfit and perfume. "Since it's an afternoon in the middle of the week, there aren't many girls here, but since you're so cute, I'd love to be your host and make you feel comfortable." She walked a few steps into the room and faced him again. "Can I get you a drink?" She was trying to make him pleasantly uncomfortable, and his breathing gave every indication she was succeeding.

"No thanks."

She pointed toward the kitchen. "We have free water in the other room. Help yourself if you want one."

"Thank you."

"What's your name?"

"Jacob, but my friends call me Jake."

"Oh, I love that name." Her voice rose playfully. "Do you have a girlfriend, Jake?"

"No. I don't …and I'm starting to get on my guy friends' nerves, so they told me about this place."

"But you're really cute. How is it you don't have a girlfriend?"

He ignored the question. His girlfriend was the one asking. "My friends said there's a girl in here they think I would really like."

"Oh? What's her name?"

"Stephanie."

"I'm Stephanie." She daintily extended her hand.

He took it softly, "Oh wow …I was hoping."

"Really?" Her smile turned genuine.

His smile widened. "Definitely."

"So …if I treat you right, you might be back?"

"I'm already pretty sure I'd like to visit weekly."

123

"You're quite a flirt!" She placed her hand lightly on his chest, and with glistening eyes, gazed into his, "So, Jake ...what can I do for you?"

His eyes widened. "My friends told me you'll dance with me?"

"They did, did they? Would you like me to dance with you?"

"....Very much."

"Do you know what kind of dances we do with boys?"

"No. I mean, I've heard, but I'm not really...." He let the sentence fade off.

"Well cutie, we take boys like you and we sit them on one of our couches, and we make them all comfortable, and then we dance against them, on their laps. ...Which is called a lap dance." Her eyebrows rose. "...Would you like a lap dance Jake?"

His grin widened. "Sure. Very much."

"Would you like one from me?"

"Oh yes definitely absolutely."

"Wow. That's a lot of different yesses all at once. Are you a little horny, sweetie?"

He blushed for real. She was so convincing, he was starting to wonder if she was secretly moonlighting and the momentary jealousy tickled him.

"Oh, you're such a cutie." She turned away, then tilted her head as she reached back, took his hand and walked him to the middle of the sofa. "Sit and get comfortable." She stood in front of him and spread his legs, then moved to the edge of the sofa and watched him grin as he stared at the lace top stockings her short skirt failed to conceal.

"The rules:" she raised a finger like a second grade teacher making her point. "...or the bouncers will throw you out." She smiled teasingly. "You can caress my legs but don't get caught caressing my butt. You can have your hands on my stomach and back, but you're not allowed to touch my breasts," She playfully slid her hands over her chest. "or the bouncers will throw you out and there's no refund." Then she winked and whispered, "Or at least don't let anyone catch you."

She paused as she noticed him having a hard time concentrating as he stared at her slinky outfit, and his distress fed her enjoyment; further fueling her desire to play the role to its ultimate degree. "The regular dance lasts two whole songs, and the special dance lasts three songs each. And if you want a double dance, I'll throw in an extra song at the end too. My treat."

He stared at her, absorbing every minute of the fantasy; his forceful breathing continually raising his chest. She casually ran her fingers through her hair, discreetly hiding her awareness as the rules continued. "We're supposed to get off a guy immediately, if he looks like he's about to ...you know, but I think I'll ignore that rule too for you." She gave him another big smile, "You sure are cute."

He grew more excited as she continued sharing the rules, and the result became obvious as it strained against the front of his sweatpants. She peered down, and without taking her eyes off his lap, toyed, "Oh my. I see you think I'm cute too." She continued staring. "...Wow. ...You must think I'm really cute!"

The music set the atmosphere, and her perfume filled the room as she continued standing in front of him ...teasing him with her casual contact and mesmerizing eyes. "Are you ready, Jacob?"

He inhaled. "If you don't hurry, I'm going to be done before you start."

"Aww sweetie!"

They both heard the next song begin, and she took her cue and started her slow teasing dance. She placed her hands on each of his thighs, lowered her head close to his hips, stared suggestively into his eyes, and slithered up his body as if she was slinking under a limbo stick. He felt her silk covered chest brush softly against his manhood and she continued her slow slither up his body until her face passed his. Her almost kiss …like sweet torture.

Her silk covered breasts were next to approach his face. They came from the bottom of his vision, moving slowly closer …then tantalizingly close as they deliberately passed his mouth, which opened in amazement. He inhaled her intoxicating perfume and filled his senses as her chest magnificently came into fractional distance of his eyes. Her precision was breathtaking. He sat there with his hands by his sides, mesmerized by the teasingly playful show being performed for his pleasure.

Once she had reached the height her legs would allow, she arched to full extension over him, then curled both arms around his head and gently pulled down on him until her upper belly pressed against his lips. Then she slid down until his nose was between each sweet soft bra covered breast, making it impossible for him to breathe anything but her intoxicating scent.

She whispered, "Aren't you going to touch me at all?"

He offered no verbal response. Instead, he reached with both hands and gently caressed her waist, guiding her as her slinky travels torturously teased.

She then lay on him and without breaking eye contact, provocatively spun until her back faced him. With an arched back, she lowered her head onto his shoulder, pressed her derrière into his lower stomach, then took hold of his wrists, and guided his hands over her belly; teasing his fingertips with the bottom edge of her delicate bra, while her arched round bottom playfully provoked his bulging lap.

Then she started her slow descent, wiggling over him, taking every opportunity to rub his pounding excitement, pausing where she desired so she could feel its pulsing warmth on her silk covered bottom. She moved ever so slightly up and down… side to side… as she breathed loud enough he could hear, giving special attention to the height where, without purposefully touching him, she could feel his arousal almost between her silk covered bottom. She let out a soft gasp as she felt it throb against her, engorged with anticipation.

Her overwhelming enjoyment of his reaction to her control, made her realize she wanted to extend this fantasy, and decided to playfully delay his release as long as she could. She slid down until she slid off him, then paused after facing him; casually calming him from the edge of ecstasy.

She ran her fingers sensually through her damp hair, before pressing his legs together and climbing knee first to straddle him, then teasingly restarted her slow sensual grind over his warm hard bulge. She extended her arms and slipped her hands behind his neck as she playfully arched back, swaying her head, and slowly manipulated his throbbing bulge with the sensuality of an accomplished dancer.

His heart raced, and his chest heaved to accommodate it, and in unison, they fed every sense he had. He was so excited, there was no way he could do anything but open his hands wide, boldly grab her hips and move with her. She began grinding against him as deep as she could, staring intensely into his eyes, but when the second song ended, quickly rose from his lap; placing her chest in his face as she moved off him. He breathed deep as her perfume continually flooded his senses.

She paused as if done, and gave him a look of pure sexual control. With a stranger, her gaze would have silently told him this was just business, but between them, the look was just another playful tease telling him she was in charge of the game they were playing. But she was only delaying so he would enjoy himself for as long as he could tolerate. She had tantalizingly denied him his release again, but he wasn't complaining. He knew it would come and he knew it would probably blow the top of his head off.

She loved being this much of a tease, and it was coming so naturally. She took a moment to gather herself. "Don't get up. I'm going to pretend you wanted two dances in a row. I'm not done talking to you."

She paused before the next song started, and he noticed her intense breathing, then realized he was breathing harder. Perspiration had started forming on her neck, and he was dying to taste it, but knew that would interrupt the game, and this fantasy was too intense to break.

The next song started… and she slowly continued with perfect timing. Facing away with her back arched, she started softly grinding into his pulsing manhood as she took his hands and slid them over her silk covered belly. She maneuvered his hands slowly upward until his fingertips touched the bottom edge of her delicately covered chest, before gently stopping their progress, then paused and whispered with more breath than voice, "So, can I ask you a personal question?"

He huffed, "Sure."

She tilted her head slightly, letting her hair fall innocently into his face. "Would you like a girlfriend?"

His heart jumped. He wasn't sure why, but hearing her pursue him at that moment, was incredibly hot.

She leaned close and whispered. "I mean, if you like me and you wanted one …you wouldn't have to pay for lap dances anymore." She looked around, then whispered. "…I'll even let you have a secret feel right now, if you say yes." Her breathing deepened.

He offered with more breath than voice, "You would be my girlfriend, for real? You're so beautiful and sexy."

"Is that a yes? Are we going out now?" Her voice sensually delighted.

"Oh yes, definitely ...absolutely."

"There's all those different yesses again." She smiled, "You're so cute!" then twisted her head and glanced playfully into his eyes. "And I guess since you're my official boyfriend ...you can place your hands wherever you want."

She slid his hands slowly over her silk covered chest and felt his chest expand.

He cupped her soft chest, then realized he had sat quietly through the entire event and wanted to encourage her. "You're a really good dancer."

"Think so?"

"Oh yes. You're unbelievably good. ...and unbelievably gorgeous ...and unbelievably sexy."

"I absolutely love being told that." She lowered her voice and seductively whispered. "But did you know there's a way a girl knows when the boy thinks she's cute, even before he says so?" And as she said it she gyrated into his lap as she glanced back over her shoulder with the slyest smile.

Her hands gently rose to her hair and as she slid her fingers slowly underneath and casually lifted it, she began rubbing his concealed erection with the softest and slowest sensual gyrations. She noticed he had remained rock hard during their short conversation, raising her excitement to its limit. She was facing away from him, but her smile was as wide as possible. She was having the time of her life.

She twitched as she suddenly felt his hands on her hips and as he took control of their embrace, she let go completely; her heart pounding as she let her boyfriend control her …fondle her …desire her …every bit of her at peak excitement. Her faint gasps of pleasure now all she could offer, as he started their climb together to the fantasy's end.

He motioned her to face him and as soon as she sat straddling him, their mouths instantly opened and sealed together; his tenderly forceful hand holding her head perfectly to his. He was now taking her where she had led them. Pulling her down tighter onto his lap, he ground into her adorably cute bottom like only a young lover could, and as they both lost awareness of everything in the universe, his movements went from rhythmic to erratic. Her heart pounded, her eyes popped open, and she gasped into his mouth.

Though the rubbing had her as excited as possible, the sight of him reaching his pleasure sent her over her edge, and with her open mouth sealed against his, she crossed her threshold; her muted whimpers of pleasure, forced into his mouth by the grip he had on her head. And as she shared her pleasure, he let out a deep sensual vocal cue signaling he had passed his release.

They gripped each other tighter as they came together, both releasing the evidence of their love and lust, beneath their clothing. Finally, he relaxed his grip as their passionate kiss turned tender, then broke slowly, and he immediately laughed out loud.

"Wow Steph! Oh my god, wow!"

She arched her back delightedly. "Did you like the game?"

"Where the fuck did you learn how to do all that?"

She kept smiling, and sung playfully. "I dunno …Did you like it?"

"Did I like it? Holi shit!" He leaned his head back onto the sofa. "I can't believe what just happened!"

Her voice raised. "You liked it?"

He laughed and raised his head enough to look into her eyes. "That ...was amazing."

"Really?" She smiled softly as she caught her breath.

Her need for more reviews touched his soul. "Oh sweetheart. I think it'll take me a week to digest what just happened, and I may have mental residuals for a month. I feel like I need to do something for you. Can I buy you a car or something?"

She smiled as she absorbed his accolades and they gave her an instant energy, "Want to go do something or go somewhere?"

He smirked, keeping in character. "But aren't you working?"

She brushed off his statement with a quick hand wave. "Oh no. I don't work here. I only came here today to give my friend a ride home. She's getting her car worked on." She smiled playfully. "You were just too cute to let someone else play with. ...So if I leave with you, I can just give her my keys and she can drive my car. But funny enough, my name is Stephanie." She raised her chin. "By the way, the Stephanie that works here isn't right for you at all."

He laughed out loud. "You're frigging adorable."

They tenderly held each other as she watched him close his eyes, registered his soft smile, rested her head on his shoulder and closed hers.

# Chapter Eight
## Consternation

Vicky walked into the kitchen. "Good morning."

"Good morning. How are you?"

"I'm doing great. How about you?"

Colleen smiled at him. "I'm fine."

He stretched his arms wide then tried to crack his neck. "Excellent."

"Coffee is ready."

Vicky inhaled deeply. "I smell. That and the spicy sausage smell like heaven."

She glanced at him. "These are the last of the eggs." She tilted the pan and slid his eggs onto his plate, then placed the plate on the dinette counter. "Can I go food shopping for us today? I'll make you something special for dinner."

Vicky moaned in satisfaction as he took his first bite. "Everything you cook is something special." He glanced at her. "Of course you can use the car. Get me gas?"

"Sure."

Colleen dropped Vicky off at work and immediately pictured the store she intended to visit, and a pleasant feeling came over her. There were definitely parts of her old life she missed, and the specialty grocery store her and her mother frequented, was one of them. She could feel an excited smile appear as she remembered the two gentlemen who own the store. They always treated Colin like family. She reviewed the informal shopping list in her head as she parked, and the special meal she had planned that evening, then hesitated a moment before exiting the car, realizing she was in full feminine attire and make-up, and her heart reacted with an anxious thump.

She inhaled deeply, trying to calm down as she reached for the door and walked in the small store. One of the owners stood behind the register on the far side of the front glass wall, ringing up a customer as she walked to the high middle shelves filled with items not available in the larger grocery stores. She placed a few cans in the small carry basket and headed further toward the back, for a few potatoes.

Her breathing increased. She knew the second owner would be behind the back counter, and he stood, weighing something and talking to a customer just as she pictured. She sighed knowing there was no way to avoid him. He had to weigh the potatoes she was purchasing, before she brought them to the front register.

"Hi Mister Marin."

The man behind the counter squinted curiously, then lowered his brows. "Colin?"

She smiled demurely. "Hi."

"Where have you been? Your mother and father have been worried sick about you. We've all been worried about you." His eyes narrowed as he leaned forward on the counter between them.

Colleen stepped back as she felt her breathing increase. "I'm fine."

His head tilted, as he quickly glanced over her outfit. "Are you sure?"

Her eyes widened. "Yeah."

She held the potatoes toward him, but had to step closer to reach his open hands as he offered further thought. "Then you should let your mother know you're fine."

He took the potatoes from her, placed them in a bag after weighing them, then marked some numbers on it before holding it out toward her. "Promise me you'll call your mother and stop her worrying?"

She took the bag, "I promise." and continued toward the front counter.

She picked up a few items on the other side of the tall dividing wall before reaching the front register, as the store phone rang. The man behind the counter raised his hand as he faced away from her for a moment, listened, laughed, then lightheartedly spoke into the phone. "Sure. I'll see what I can do." He listened for another minute. "Okay I will."

He hung up the phone and turned toward Colleen, "Hi." then glanced down at the purchases she had placed on the small glass counter.

"Hi Mister Cantor. How are you?"

He glanced up, and did a double-take. "Colin? Our Colin? Is that you?"

"Well, Colleen now."

He quickly glanced down at her outfit. "How've you been?"

Her voice softened as her breathing quickened. "Okay."

"We miss you. We miss seeing you with your mother."

"I miss you too." She saw sincerity in his eyes and an idea came to her. "Do you and Mister Marin need any help? I'm kind of looking for a job."

Mister Cantor immediately straightened. "Good idea. Very good idea. Why don't we go in the back and you can fill out an application. I'll hold your purchases here for you." He finished bagging her items and lowered them to the floor behind the counter.

"Come with me. I'll get you an application."

She followed him to the back of the store, then through the private door behind the back counter. He closed the door behind them, searched for an application and pen, then placed them on the rectangle table in the middle of the small room. "Sit and fill this out and I'll be back to talk to you in a bit."

She met his eyes and inhaled deeply, "Sure Mister Cantor" and sat in the metal folding chair facing the application. He seemed to be accepting her for who she is and the feeling was heartwarming.

She filled out the application, intermittently daydreaming about working here …as a female. …and the underlying feeling of acceptance made her feel optimistic. *Wow, I always liked Mister Cantor and Mister Marin.* She sat patiently, straightening the papers strewn on the table, thinking how she could help them more than any other hire. They were her friends, and she would benefit them in ways they didn't realize, cleaning shelves and the dust on the tops of the cans better, and the corners of the floor, which had been passed over longer than she dare ask. So many things …little things that would make them happy they hired her. The store was her favorite food store, but it wasn't the cleanest. She smiled at how the dust and dirt didn't bother her though. Her mother had been taking her here for as long as she could remember, and this is how it had always appeared in her mind.

Then the door burst open. "There you are!"

Her shock muffled her vocal response and all she could express was a soft cry. Her immediate reaction was a level of disheartenment she knew all too often. Her father stood there for a moment, and she quickly felt torn between wanting …hoping for a loving greeting from him, and the shock of seeing him burst in the room unexpectedly. He rushed her before she could stand, covering her mouth and lifting her off the metal chair. Tears of shock and dejection began flowing and her eyes grew wide as she saw Mister Marin right behind him. He grabbed her legs as her father lifted her, and they carried her backward to the back metal door, only feet away.

She didn't fight or kick Mister Marin. Despite his actions, she cared for and respected him, though she also knew any resistance would lead to a discipline beating compounding the upcoming beating she was sure would accompany this already irrational act.

Thoughts began speeding through her mind. *He doesn't have to kidnap me.* He could have asked to meet with her at any time or place and she would have relented. She loved him. She was afraid of him but she loved him.

Her heart jumped with fright as her father stepped down the first of four steps outside the back door and yelped into his hand as they spun her sideways and laid her in the open trunk of their family car. She shut her eyes in utter defeat as her heart sunk, and all she could do was cry as the light quickly disappeared with the thud of the closing lid.

The ride was bumpier, and with more uncomfortable turns than she realized. She was sure he was taking her home, though the ride was frighteningly different than any previous ride she had taken between these two familiar locations.

~~~

Vicky pushed his make-up cart through the swinging service doors and into the wood and metal grate lock-up area, then locked the cage behind him and proceeded to the punch clock at the entrance of the small employee break room.

He leaned in the room, "Bye Dawn." and heard her reply as he walked toward the outside service door. "Have a good night Vick."

He pressed the silver bar on the gray metal service door. "Thanks." then walked along the outside service walk toward the parking lot, looking for his car as he dialed his new friend and roommate. He shivered, then zipped his jacket wondering what she made for dinner, and his stomach grumbled. He scanned the closest parking spaces as his call connected to her voicemail so he hung up, waited a minute then redialed and as the phone went to voicemail a second time, he stared at it. Why wasn't she answering? He sighed as he continued to scan the lot, quickly identifying every moving car then dialed and waited until the call went to voicemail. "Colleen, honey. Are you at the mall?" He paused. "Are you here?"

He could feel his heartbeat increase as he stood for a few more moments, then hit the send button twice, and the call immediately went to voicemail. He walked to the center of the service road circling the building, for a better view of the lane leading to his location, then dialed a different phone number.

"Hi."

"Steph, I'm stuck at work."

"Car trouble?"

"Yeah. It's missing, and so is Colleen. I lent her the car to go food shopping today and she was supposed to pick me up. She's not here, and she's not answering her phone."

"You don't think she forgot, do you?"

"I don't know what to think, but right now I need a ride home." Every moving car distracted him. "Will you come get me and then we'll panic together?"

"Sure"

He faced the building. "Pick me up at the back service entrance."

"I'll be there as soon as I can."

Stephie lowered her phone and looked at Jake. "Vicky's stuck at work and needs me to get him, and he's not sure what happened to Colleen."

He rested his hand on his open text book and looked up. "Can you explain in more detail?"

She walked to the coat hooks where the living room met the entrance stairs. "Vicky lent Colleen his car to go food shopping while he was at work and she never showed to pick him up, and she's not answering her phone."

"That's not good." He dropped his book on the coffee table and quickly stood. "Grab my coat too. I'll drive."

Vicky spotted Jake and Stephie's car as they drove toward the back service door. Jake barely stopped when Vicky opened the back door and hopped inside.

Stephie twisted to face him. "Hi Vick."

He lovingly covered the hand she had placed on the back of her seat, "Hi honey." then his voice turned solemn. "I'm worried."

Jake drove the car toward the main road. "What's going on?"

Vicky grabbed the back of Jake's seat. "I honestly don't know. A thousand things are going through my mind, and none of them good."

"Is there anything else you didn't tell me on the phone?"

Vicky met Stephie's eyes. "Nothing I can think of. I know we don't know her long, but I guarantee she didn't steal the car …or forget me. Something's wrong."

Stephie's breathing increased. "Do you think she was in an accident?"

Vicky inhaled deeply. "I don't know what to think right now."

"Do you think she's hurt? ...in a hospital or something?"

Vicky frowned and shrugged, but didn't reply.

Jake spoke as he drove. "Do you know what grocery store she went to?"

Stephie held her phone and dialed Colleen's number and they heard the call go directly to voicemail.

Jake finished his thought. "Maybe we can spot your car."

Vicky leaned forward. "I have no idea where she went." He leaned back and ran his hand through his hair. "How are we going to do this? Where do we even begin?"

Stephie twisted in her seat. "We need to call and see if there were any bad accidents, then I think we should call all our friends and search for her."

Jake looked into the middle rear view mirror at Vicky. "Do you need to stop home for anything first?"

Vicky met his eyes in the mirror. "No. I need to find her."

~~~

The sudden light and accompanying shock from the trunk lid opening made her flinch and cover her eyes, and then Colleen felt forceful arms awkwardly lifting her. "Ow!" She whimpered as she banged her knee, then an abducting arm pulled her hair as it reached further under her.

As her eyes adjusted, she recognized her surroundings. Her abductor and the car were in the alley driveway behind their house. She contemplated screaming, but hesitated. She didn't want to get her father in trouble. She loved him. She was deathly afraid of him, but she loved him. A silent sigh exited her nose. She seemed to love him more than he loved her. Maybe he loved his child in his own way, but he didn't love her. Instead, he loved this alternate reality of who he wished his child was. Her heart sunk further as she realized; she and that child were not the same person.

He twisted her arm behind her as he stood her upright behind the trunk. "Don't fight or I swear I'll break it."

Tears flowed down her face; not for the pain in her arm or knee. That pain was nothing compared to the pain her heart felt, as she resigned herself to his anger and control.

"Dad, you don't have to hurt me. Please don't hurt me. I love you. I promise I won't fight. I don't want to fight you."

He was silent until they were inside the house, then his voice projected the gruffness of a contrived anger. "Fight me? You raise your hand to me and I'll break it off." He held her still as he shut the back door behind them and locked it. "But you're a fucking sissy anyway. Do you think a sissy like you could ever stand up to me?"

He pushed her toward the basement steps and she stumbled away from him. "Look at you. You disgust me."

He reached for her and ripped the dress down and it tore off her. She immediately covered herself with her arms. "In fucking panties and bra? Jesus Christ, son!"

She fell to her knees, crying harder. "Dad …please."

"Please? Please what? …You fucking girl." He shook his head as he stood over her. "Get up the stairs before I kick you up them." The rest of her immediate world went blank as her mind registered overwhelming unexpected pain from the back of her right thigh. The blow nearly buckled her leg and the accompanying pain temporarily erased her vision and momentarily stopped her leg from responding to her desire to move quickly away from him.

She stumbled up the stairs, holding the back of her bare and bruised leg, expecting the continued physical abuse which always accompanied his anger. She waited for the next blow that would express his irritation at her momentary hesitation as her injured leg failed to respond, and pressed on her other leg, trying desperately to continue moving to avoid his further displeasure.

~~~

Stephie wrapped her arm around the headrest and faced Vicky. "I think we should call our friends."

Jake interrupted, "Do we know her last name or where she lives?"

Vicky sat with narrowed eyes, breathing intensely. "Damn. I almost took her home once." He inhaled. "I can't believe I can't remember her last name. She only said it once. Damn."

Jake made eye contact again through the inside mirror. "I think we should call the police to see if your car was in an accident."

Stephie turned to Vicky as Jake finished. "If it wasn't, then we should search some local food store parking lots." Stephie's increased breathing matched Vicky's.

She dialed the police and talked to a desk Sergeant and he searched for them. "None? Thank you sir." She sighed as she ended the call. "No accidents with your make and model, thank god …I think."

Jake pulled into a convenience store parking lot. "Time to call friends. I'll call Cody, Lauren, Kaden, and Paige."

Vicky offered, "I got Desmond, Mick, Kyleigh, and Giana."

Jake opened his door. "I'll step out so we're not yelling over each other. Where should we all meet?

Stephie held her palm out. "Stop a second. I know we're rushing because every minute matters, but we need to organize so we're not wasting time."

They set a plan and made their calls. Friends made plans to drive through food store parking lots closest to Vicky's apartment, looking for his make, model, color, then the few unique identifying marks he shared. Vicky suggested searching small ethnic food stores also, since Colleen loved cooking with certain unusual brands. He remembered joking he never heard of the names on some of the cans and boxes sitting on his counter as she cooked.

They quickly moved back to the car after finishing their calls. "Cody's in a panic. I never heard him like this. Her last name is Raphael and he knows the general neighborhood she's from. They talked about school on their date. She went to Saint Ignatius grade school and Middle Township High. He's heading to the area he thinks she lives."

"How can we find out if there are any small food stores around there?"

Stephie typed away on her phone. "On it."

Jake ran his hands through his hair. "I just decided we need to head there too. The more I think about it, the less comfortable I am with Cody finding something and doing something alone. I hope this whole situation is nothing, but I doubt it."

Vicky gasped. "Oh my god I just remembered; her father's been calling her. She received one of his calls in front of me and her face turned pale." He dialed his phone. "Desmond, are you with anyone?" He explained their new situation, then paused and listened. "Will you meet me so I can partner with you? We have a few ideas. Meet us in front of Saint Ignatius grade school. We may get lucky and we'd be luckier if you're with us." He shared the location, then ended the call and Stephie dialed. "Cody. Four of us are heading to Colleen's neighborhood." She listened for a few seconds. "Yeah. Jake told me. We think you're on to something. We're meeting Desmond in front of Saint Ignatius grade school." She switched her phone to the opposite ear and glanced at Vicky. "See you in a bit."

Cody was the last to arrive. He parked behind Desmond, and ran to the group breathing heavily. "I just remembered she told me she used to walk to grade school. We had the whole *uphill both ways* laugh."

Vicky scanned the street. "That makes the search a little easier, but I'm still not sure it's possible."

"This may take all night, but I'm not letting her down." Desmond's voice produced a momentary silence and Jake's nervous grin. Stephie glanced at him and shook her head, then nodded once toward Desmond. "None of us are leaving this area unsuccessful."

Cody pointed. "I'm heading that way."

Stephie scanned both directions. "Okay, there are four directions and three cars. Should we call another car?"

"No sweetheart. By the time someone else gets here, I think we can cover the walking area with three." Jake studied the potential directions. "Mind if I suggest a plan?"

He met everyone's eyes as they paused and waited for him. "Who has GPS? We need to pair up by that."

Vicky raised his hand and glanced at everyone quickly. Stephie and Cody both confirmed. "Okay. Every car has one. Let's all pull up this grade school so we can search methodically."

Jake waited as the three worked their phones, then offered, "Steph and I are headed that way and making a left at the first street. Cody. You make the first right."

Vicky studied the opposite direction, then pointed. "We're making the first left that way."

He eyed Vicky. "We'll work the school side of the streets we drive down. Cody, stay to the right of that street since we're working within walking distance of the school."

Stephie raised her phone. "And try to keep an eye on your GPS to know what you've covered."

"If you see anyone walking, especially anyone about her age; ask them if they know a Colin. Maybe we get lucky."

Vicky offered a final thought, "Good luck." then headed to Desmond's passenger door. "Now let's go rescue our sister!"

~~~

Collen crawled into bed and held her covers over her head as she cowered in a ball. No matter what thought went through her mind, it caused tears to flow. She strained to hear his footsteps on the stairs, between bouts of tears and inner panic. She imagined the beating she was in for, then recalled the shock of seeing him barge into the back room of the food store. Her heart sunk as she realized how Mister Marin and Cantor betrayed her. *Why would they do that to me? I never did anything to them.*

The bed dropped below her and she fell uncontrollably, waking her in an instant panic. Even her dreams offered no escape. Her heart dropped as she remembered the inevitable beating coming. Momentary optimism followed since it hadn't occurred yet, then her torment deepened as she recognized the anxiety of the wait. How demoralizing, the morbid hope he would be so disgusted with her, he couldn't bear her presence even to beat her?

The waiting and wondering were distressing, but the thought he was disgusted with who she knew she was, hurt deeper. She shivered in fear, but her heart sunk with disappointment. She knew her existence repulsed him. She revolted him …her own father. The more she focused on that devastating realization, the further her heart fell and her tears continued flowing. She felt the wet sheet under her hair but was afraid to move even an inch.

Her heart tensed as she instantly felt his presence, immediately expecting her beating, then realized the panic was her mind playing games …just her mind betraying and torturing her too. But she wasn't mad at herself for the torment her mind also offered. She was sure she deserved it.

A blow came down on the blanket covering her and she startled, instantly aware she hadn't been awake, then realized he was in the room! The strike didn't hurt but it frightened her, and that emotion instantly turned to shock as the covers suddenly disappeared from her grip.

She yelped in fright. "Dad! No!" His fist came down on the side of her right thigh and the pain seared white through her eyes. "Dad! Please!"

His low angry scowl filled her ears. "Put fucking boy clothes on …NOW!"

She scrambled off the bed in the opposite direction, knelt at her dresser and searched for clothes.

Each new sentence produced a new shock and accompanying fright. "You make me so angry, I want to kill you."

She fell backward away from him as she tried desperately to pull jeans on.

"Do you know how embarrassing you are to me? Do you know what it's like to admit you're my son? I'm embarrassed to go to places where people know me!"

She lowered her head, speaking barely above a whisper. "But dad, you made me. Why can't you just accept me? Why can't you love me instead like I love you?"

"I can't love you. You disgust me. You embarrass me. People look at me as if my family is something to be laughed at because of you." Her father moved closer; his presence even more ominous as he stood over her. "And I'm going to make you a fucking man if I have to break every bone in your body."

She looked up at him through streaming tears. "Then I'll be a broken girl." She stared down at the floor, realizing she was already a broken girl. Her voice trembled. "Do you really think I wouldn't love being a man and ending your hatred of me? Do you think I would invite the abuse if this wasn't who I am? I'm not playing, dad." She slowly shook her head. "I'm really not."

She paused, "I'm sorry." then covered her head as she faced the floor.

He stood over her but she didn't look up. "This conversation isn't over."

She startled as he banged the wall exiting her room and she followed his sounds as he walked down the stairs, then gently lowered herself completely to the floor, and finished crying.

They had been driving longer than they hoped and the streets were starting to blend together. Keeping track of each turn was more daunting than originally thought. Stephie's screen suddenly displayed Cody's picture as her phone rang. She pressed the button and immediately turned the speaker on. "Hi."

"Get here! Get here!" She looked up as Jake glanced at her, then her phone; his eyes narrow with intensity.

She held it in front of her. "Cody! Where are you?" His anguishing cry pierced her.

"Cody! Where are you?"

"In a drive through alley between the backs of two rows of houses!"

She glanced at Jake, then at the phone. "Where though?"

"Wait! Let me go to the corner."

She raised her voice. "Drive slow! Don't raise any suspicion!"

"Fuck that! Fuck that!"

"Cody. We're going to rescue her! Don't worry! Where are you?"

Jake had already turned their car around, knowing where they sent him.

Cody yelled through the phone. "Eden! Eden and Cheyenne. The alley behind Eden. There's a car with the trunk open! I can feel it! This is where she lives! I *know* it is!"

Her breathing intensified. "Call Vicky! Tell him. We'll be right there!"

The wheels screeched as Jake turned and she swayed against the middle console. "Go slow enough for me to pull up a map."

Jake whispered gruffly, "Hurry."

She typed then spread her fingers on the screen. "Go past the street the school's on, then go straight for three intersections."

A car honked as Jake sped across the intersection and Jake responded. "Sorry buddy."

"Give me your phone." She held out her hand.

"What's the next turn?" He placed his phone in her open hand as she studied her screen. "Next left, one block, then a right into the first alley."

She dialed his phone as he pulled next to Cody and rolled his window down. He watched Cody stare at the top windows of the three story house, raised a finger and paused as he let Stephie share their situation. "Vicky. We may have something."

She gave him the simple directions, then Jake directed Cody, pointing to the end of the alley behind him. "Drive to that end." He motioned forward. "We'll sit at that end and I'll call you to explain."

They drove to opposite ends of the alley and Jake dialed Cody. "Hey. When Vicky and Desmond get here, I'm thinking you and I go around the front of the house in one car. One of us gets out and the other honks until a neighbor pops their head out a window or door. Then ask if they know where Colin lives."

"I'm getting out."

Jake heard his friend speak through clenched teeth. He knew he would be less confrontational, but he also understood how he would need to be hands on for any rescuing Stephie needed, so he wasn't about to deny Cody the same consideration for Colleen's rescue. Desmond's car turned into the alley and pulled next to Cody's. Jake watched them talk for a moment, then dialed him, and Cody spoke immediately. "I'm sharing our plan. Desmond wants to leave Vicky in his car and come around front with us."

"Then let him drive and the two of us will be outside. No one is going to open a window or door if they see him." He paused. "Ready?"

"We'll count the houses, then pick you up."

"Okay." He ended the call, leaned toward Stephie and quickly kissed her. "You drive and have your phone ready in case anyone comes out the back and takes off in that car."

He watched them drive slowly toward him, then stop. Jake stepped out and opened Cody's car door as Stephie replaced Jake in their car. They drove around, counting the houses, then double parked in front of the sixth. The front doors stood on a landing, five concrete steps above the fifteen foot walkway connecting the sidewalk. All but the end units had two adjacent doors per landing; each aware the front door was technically on the second level.

Cody and Jake exited the car and walked half way between two separate front landings when Desmond started pressing the horn as if summoning someone for a ride. When the action didn't receive any curious onlookers, he laid on the horn and a woman in the house they perceived as next door, opened her front door.

"Does Colin live here?" Cody pointed to the door to her immediate right.

He spoke as she paused curiously. "We're his friends and we need to tell his parents he may be hurt."

Jake's heart jumped as he deciphered Cody's twisted truth.

Cody shared a second request. "Please help. Does he live here?"

The lady answered in disgust, "If you're friends, how come you don't know he lives there? Now go away or be quiet." and slammed her door.

Cody ran up the steps and pounded on the front door. The flickering of the TV through the curtain covered front window stopped, then the room went dark. Cody pounded harder, without an accompanying word.

He whispered loudly to Jake. "I'm ready to go through this fucking door." He looked around in frustration. "Can I yell her name?"

Jake stood at the bottom of the five outside steps and held the iron railing. "Let's do this the right way instead."

Cody pounded with the side of his fist as he stared at Jake. "How?"

Jake raised his hand as he brought his phone to his ear. "Vicky. Call Stephie. Surround that car front and back and lock your doors!"

He refocused on Cody as he held his phone. "Time to call the cops." Jake no sooner said the words when the red and blue flashing lights began reflecting off all surrounding buildings and the siren whelped through the closest intersection.

Jake flinched as the bang behind him rung in his ear and a man charged out the outer screen door and tried to shove Cody backward. "Get off my porch motherfucker."

Jake ran up the stairs as Cody recovered and wound his arm back to retaliate. Jake locked his arm around Cody's. "Only one of us is going to jail tonight, my friend."

The siren whelped again as the police car stopped behind Cody's car. Desmond stepped out as Cody yelled at the top of his lungs, "COLLEEN!" waited a second and yelled louder, "COLLEEN!!" He coughed then tried to break Jake's grip. "Let me search!" He fought Jake's grip. "Please! I need to find her!"

Jake whispered, "Cody, the cops are here. Let them do their job. We'll find her, I promise."

Colleen's father stood against the wrought iron railing on his neighbor's side of the landing, then bent over at the waist with his hands on his thighs as the first officer walked to the three of them. "What's going on gentlemen?"

Jake rested his hand on Cody's shoulder and whispered. "Cody. Let me." Jake inhaled. "Officer, we have a friend who we think was taken by her family and this is where they live. She ran away from an abusive father and didn't show up tonight where she now lives, and we're all worried she's here against her will."

The officer faced the man standing away from Jake and Cody. "Sir, are you the father of the person they're referring to?"

"Yeah, but he's my kid and I can discipline him any way I want."

The officer didn't acknowledge the statement. "Is that person inside?"

The father squatted where he stood. "Yeah."

Cody interrupted. "Can I go get her? I'm her boyfriend."

The father mumbled loud enough to be heard. "Fucking faggots."

Cody spun quickly toward him. "Fuck you."

The father stood and pointed. "Fuck you! You're the one gonna rot in hell!"

Cody yelled back, "On your judgment or did God anoint you judge?"

Jake spoke calmly as Vicky and Stephie approached the concrete steps. "Officer, can someone go in and get her please? She now lives with this friend." He pointed to Vicky.

The officer pressed the side of the inch wide speaker attached to his uniform collar and talked into it. All Jake understood was *domestic disturbance* and *backup*.

The officer turned to his partner, "We may have an abuse victim inside." then turned to Colin's father. "Are there any other people or animals inside?"

He lowered his head. "My wife. She's sitting in the kitchen in the back."

"Where's your child?"

"Upstairs in a back bedroom."

"What's the child's name, sir?"

"Colin."

Cody instantly spoke over him. "Colleen! Her name is Colleen! That's the problem! This asshole won't let her be who she is!"

Colleen's father leaned against the neighbor's railing, without replying.

The second officer stood one step down from the top landing as the first called inside the house. "This is police officer Devlin. Colleen? It's safe now."

A second patrol car pulled behind the first and three officers met quietly, then the first two officers announced their presence a second time at the open front door and with hands on their holsters, disappeared inside.

The friends gathered on the walkway in front of the house as they waited. Jake discreetly watched Cody wring his hands and clench his fists as he paced beside the others.

They all turned in response to new movement at the front door, and Cody ran toward Colleen as she appeared on the top landing, wrapped in a blanket. "Cody! Cody!" She hunched forward crying as Cody hurried to her, surrounded her in his arms and held her. The group silently watched from the walkway.

Colleen's father eyed Vicky as an officer led him toward a patrol car. "Hey." He pointed at him. "You're that make-up faggot from the mall. He lives with you?" He stared and nodded.

"Hi." Desmond smiled at him, and he stared with an open mouth, at the previously quiet giant standing to Vicky's right. Desmond winked, then mimicked a kiss to him as he was led away.

Stephie's stare moved from Colleen's father to Vicky, then watched until the officer helped him into the cruiser.

The group walked to Colleen, each waiting their turn to hug her, but no one interrupted Cody as he held her. The officers stood with patience. All could hear Colleen crying in Cody's arms. Finally she looked up and offered the group the best smile she could, as she wiped her eyes. "You all rescued me? You all came to rescue me?" She broke down again as Vicky held out his arms and she spoke through a teary voice before walking into her dear friend's embrace. "I can't believe you all care this much!"

Vicky stroked her hair. "I told you, you'd find friends worth waiting for." She shivered in his arms.

Stephie held her phone out. "I just sent a text to everyone and told them we found her and where we're headed."

When each finished hugging Colleen, the officer stepped next to the group. "We have to take your friend and her father to the station, to get statements. You're all welcome to meet us there and take care of her after we've done our job." Five quick thank you responses followed in reply.

Desmond spoke over the group, toward Colleen. "Did he hurt you?"

Colleen met his eyes but offered no response as the officer gently led her to the first patrol car.

Friends began trickling into the police station lobby and they gathered as if waiting at a hospital for someone in surgery. Stephie explained their situation to the front desk sergeant and apologized for the crowd she expected. The officer smiled at her. "I'm glad your friend has support. With support, we're all stronger." He pointed to the small table off to the side of his desk. "I'll make coffee for everyone. Help yourselves."

"My car!" Vicky raised his hands. "I forgot to ask her where my car is." His eyebrows rose as his voice softened. "My precious booboo. I hope my booboo's alright."

Desmond leaned toward him. "Your fucking car's name is booboo?" His deep laugh echoed through the hall.

When Colleen appeared further down the hallway accompanied by the two officers, Vicky jumped up and spoke just loud enough to get Colleen's attention. "Where's my car?" He held out his arms.

"In front of the little food store in the Plaza Shopping Center on Sherwood."

"Do you have the keys?"

Colleen raised her hand to her mouth as her voice rose in response. "My purse! My purse is in the back room of the food mart."

Desmond watched Vicky sigh, then discreetly whispered, "I'll drive you home and pick you up tomorrow and we'll visit the food store together."

Vicky smiled at him. "Thanks."

The group mingled together for longer than expected, until Vicky gathered those who had found Colleen. "You're all welcome to come back to our apartment with us if any of you need to be with others to decompress."

Cody straightened as he motioned to Vicky. "I was going to offer her to come home with me, so she can sleep in my bed instead of your couch." He contritely held out his hand. "She doesn't have to, but I want to offer her the option. I'll sleep on the floor beside her."

Jake patted Cody on the back as he overheard his suggestion, but didn't say a word. The idea impressed him. His friend had proven his loyalty and worth.

"That's a wonderful thing to offer, Cody. She can decide where she'd feel best tonight," Vicky reached for his hand. "but we all need to get together as soon as she can. She needs to fill us in on details."

His smile widened as he registered Vicky's conditional approval.

Everyone spotted Colleen's father and mother as they appeared down the hallway with an officer. They were escorted out a side door facing the parking lot as the group stared in silence. Vicky quietly exited the front double glass doors and quickly walked around the corner of the building. "Excuse me. Excuse me!"

Colleen's mother turned to him apologetically as her father continued walking toward the car Vicky recognized from the alley. He offered in a soft but stern voice. "You can always visit your child, as soon as you indicate you love her like we love her …unconditionally." He wanted to offer her a smile, but produced a smirk. "I won't ever deny her the love of her parents …when they offer their love."

The mother wiped her eye with the tissue in her hand, but offered no response. Vicky paused patiently, shook his head, and hurried back inside.

Colleen finally appeared down the hallway, accompanied by an officer who walked her toward the group. Everyone stood as she approached and took turns hugging her. When all had greeted her, Vicky motioned discreetly to Cody. He hugged her and whispered in her ear as she stood resting in his arms. "I want to offer you my bed tonight. I'll sleep on the floor next to you. I don't want you to sleep alone, if you don't want."

She leaned away and stared at him, as tears softly rolled down her cheeks. She leaned against him and whispered, "I'd love that."

Jake parked the car in front of the apartment after a fairly quiet ride, and Stephie didn't speak until they were behind their locked front door. "Why is it, most parents don't care if they have a baby boy or girl, but have a problem when that same baby tells them they need to be the other gender?"

Jake followed her up their stairs. "To be honest with you, I know it's all just social influence. Certain corners of our society have this unexplainably negative and vocal preoccupation with people like us."

She continued to their room. "I can't imagine telling my baby I can't love them, for any reason."

He thought; *neither can God*, then ran his fingers through the back of her soft shiny hair as she walked in front of him. "That's because you know how normal you are, even though you know how different you are. But some people can't imagine the two concepts coexisting."

"I'm glad you can. I'm happy you understand." She spun toward him as she entered their bedroom and wrapped her arms around his neck. "All our parents …Nana …they all understand."

He kissed her softly and held her close. "Believe it or not, some who look like they understand still actually don't. They accept because their love is greater than their confusion, but since they have no experience feeling what it's like to be someone like you, they really don't know."

She hugged him tight and stood with her head resting on his chest. "But you understand."

His breath indicated a different level of thought. "Sweetheart, I love you. I love you beyond an explanation or understanding, which allows me to work hard, caring and learning who you are, but I can't imagine how it feels to be you, with your unique place in this world." He kissed her tenderly. "I think you're special and amazing. I agree with how native Americans regarded people like you; a gift to their people …two spirited; able to understand both genders, like only God understands. I get to know you and love you, but psychology says I don't get to experience what it's like to be you, so I'll never truly understand, just like a cis guy never truly understands what it's like to be a cis girl." He kissed her face and neck. "That doesn't mean I can't love you more than anything, though."

She watched him slip under the covers as she finished undressing, then snuggled next to him as he continued. "…Just like some straight people can completely accept lgbt people. They can't know what we feel, but they can love and accept enough to understand we're just another definition of normal. And many can consider us completely equal, but other people can't accept *different* and for some reason feel threatened by it."

She snuggled close. "But we aren't different."

He rolled toward her, softly pinning her under him. "You and I know that, but they'll never believe it; especially since they're told not to."

"But why are they told not to?"

He kissed her softly and settled comfortably. "I haven't figured that out yet. He pressed his head next to hers. "...but I'm working on it."

# Chapter Nine
## Recognition

Vicky heard Desmond's horn the next morning and immediately opened his front door. He knew Desmond better than any of their other friends. Not only had they gone out for an extended period, but he had since confided a few secrets in Vicky and their relationship had grown accordingly.

Vicky could be boisterous, but he hid a seriousness behind his overt idiosyncrasies, and he and Desmond had made a pact quite a while ago; certain things they shared would always remain locked behind a deep caring friendship that would serve both in distinct and necessary ways. This special friendship had matured past the necessity for either to question the secrecy with which they went about certain activities, and today's ride and visit was just another of those private occasions.

Desmond dropped Vicky off, well away from the front of the small food mart and then drove around the back of the building. Minutes later, he called. "Back door's locked and I'm back in the car."

"Okay. You're on speaker. I'm going in."

The door chimed as Vicky entered. He casually glanced at the gentleman behind the register by the other side of the front window and proceeded down the aisle in line with the front door, heading toward the back. He casually pretended to inspect the items on the high dividing shelves, then noticed the second gentleman behind the back glass display counter working with his back toward him, cutting chicken with a long thin butcher knife. He continued around the back of the store-length center divide and toward the front counter, then stood on the opposite side of the flat glass top counter in front of the first gentleman. "Hi."

The man looked up from the magazine resting on the glass counter. "Hi. Can I help you?"

Vicky smiled. "I believe you can. I'm interested in a small light brown purse I understand is in your back room."

"Get out." The man's face paled as he pointed to the door.

Vicky smiled but didn't move. "If you insist, but the cops will be here in five minutes to make the same request. Would you rather explain the purse to them?" He moved so he could see the aisle leading to the back counter, then heard the door chime as Desmond walked in and Vicky's voice lowered. "I'd just as soon feed you to a monster." He moved his hand, indicting they were together. "But Colleen seems to have a soft spot for you, so pick your poison."

He eyed Desmond as he answered Vicky. "I don't know where her purse is."

Vicky waved him toward the back room. "She told us it's in your back room on the floor next to where she was sitting." Vicky decided to keep the gentleman on edge as he motioned him to lead them to the back of the store. "Kidnapping? How many years is kidnapping?" The gentleman glared at Vicky; his face still pale.

The man behind the back counter turned from his work table when he heard the voices behind him and raised his butcher knife as he saw them approach. "We being robbed?"

His friend raised both hands. "No. Everything's alright."

He eyed Vicky. "We good?"

Vicky motioned to the door. "Purse."

The man opened the door and held it from the other side.

"There it is." Vicky walked to the purse peeking from under the table, as soon as he entered the room, and picked it up with a smile. His smile brightened as he pulled out his car keys. "Thank you for your wonderful cooperation." Vicky headed back toward the retail area, and Desmond stated in an overpoweringly deep voice. "Wait out there for a second. I want to talk to these two."

Vicky watched the man from the front counter pale. "Sure. See you in a minute." He laughed. "I'll watch the store."

Desmond appeared a few minutes later and greeted his friend with a wry grin. They left the store and walked to Vicky's car in silence before he turned to Desmond, and Desmond took the cue. "Colleen starts work there whenever she wants. I got her a nice raise too."

~~~

Stephie walked through the cafeteria doors after her first class and instantly spotted Jake at their regular table, head buried in his textbook. She walked wide enough around him to sneak behind him and plant a kiss on the back of his neck. He lowered his head to accommodate her. "Hi sweetheart."

She playfully countered, "But which sweetheart am I?"

He grabbed her ass as she walked in front of him, and she jumped. "The only sweetheart I have." He met her eyes. "Why? How many do you have?"

She plopped in her seat as she swung her backpack onto their table. "I'm not telling."

He felt his grin appear, knowing this teasing was one-directional, and it tickled him to his soul knowing if the conversation was reversed, she wouldn't find it at all amusing.

"Vicky texted me, inviting us to come over tomorrow. He wants us all to hear Colleen's story, straight from her. We're all chipping in for pizza and bringing our own drinks."

"Sound's good." He lowered his eyes toward his text book.

They worked silently, until Stephie raised her head from her notes. "When do you start your internship?"

Jake rested his hand on his open book. "Monday."

She grinned. "I thought so." Her back straightened and voice rose. "I need to make you lunches. What do you want?" He started replying, but she interrupted. "We need to buy you a to-go coffee mug and a lunch bag with an ice pack."

He shook his head and smiled. "I love how you take care of me. I never thought of any of those things."

"We'll go shopping this weekend. Do you have enough shirts and ties?"

His eyebrows rose. "I have enough to start the job. I don't know if I need ties. I don't know how they dress in the office or when they go out to clients."

"Are you nervous?"

His eyes widened. "Of course I'm nervous. This is what I've been working toward for the last five years."

She waved at him. "You'll be fine."

She looked back down at her notes, then startled him as she quickly looked up. "Don't forget to ask about getting off for our wedding."

He chuckled. "It'll be the first thing I tell them when I walk in."

She eyed him and grinned. "Are you making fun of me?"

"No dear."

She flipped her pen at him then immediately held out her hand. "Give me that."

~~~

Stephie rang Vicky's doorbell cradling a two liter bottle of soda as Jake stood patiently behind her, holding two boxes of pizza. She felt the instant smile on her face as the door swung open and Vicky appeared behind it. "Hi little sister. Thanks for coming early."

"No problem. Have you heard from Colleen or Cody?" They hugged and kissed.

"We texted this morning. He's letting her sleep as late as she wants, but he'll text us an arrival time when she's ready."
Vicky waited for Jake to place the pizzas on the counter, then hugged and kissed him.

Friends trickled in over the next hour and the gathering morphed into a casual party, until Cody and Colleen showed. Everyone greeted her with muted love and concern, following Vicky's suggestion, and once greetings were finished, fixed plates buffet style before gathering in his living room to discuss Colleen's ordeal.

Jake smiled as he watched Stephie, Vicky and Cody show her a love beyond the depths of friendship. The conversation remained casual until Vicky finally focused on her and asked, "Are you ready to share?"

Colleen sighed, made eye contact with Cody sitting next to her, then proceeded to share details. After she shared as much as she could, Shelbie asked about the outcome. "Did you press charges?"

"No." Her eyes glanced at friends sitting around the room. "He's my father and I love him. I don't want him to get in trouble. I don't want my mom to suffer."

Gianna questioned softly, "But she doesn't stop you from suffering."

Colleen face contorted. "She can't stand up to him." Her wide eyed expression begged them not to judge her mother. "And it's alright." Then she lowered her eyes.

Vicky discreetly acknowledged his connection with Desmond, before turning to her. "What about the store owners?"

She met Vicky's eyes then looked down. "I couldn't …I didn't mention their involvement. I've known them since I was little."

She straightened in her chair and offered consolation. "The police were very understanding but told me if there was a second incident, there would be no prosecution leniency." Her shoulders dropped. "I'm scared he won't let this end here. I know him. He doesn't like to lose …at anything."

Dawn broke her silence. "I'm worried he'll misinterpret your kindness."

Colleen face appeared apologetic. "But he isn't horrible. He just doesn't understand. Mom told me he thinks if he makes my life miserable; I'll choose to be a straight boy …as if the way I feel is a choice." She looked down as if the weight of her statement affected her ability to hold up her head.

James broke the momentary silence. "Has anyone shared any information with your parents, explaining how no one would choose this lifestyle if it was just a choice?"

"My parents aren't very open to the information. They're old school and think any information supporting our lifestyle is evil and wrong."

Jake's eyes narrowed. "Evil."

Colleen's eyes widened. "Honest."

"No, I'm not disagreeing with you. I read the same viewpoint whenever I read about certain groups' opinions of our corner of society. I just can't figure out why people would be so unwilling to at least hear what higher learning has discovered over the last twenty five years." He inhaled in frustration. "All I want is to share information ...read something ...learn something ...then judge. That's all I ask."

The room fell silent for a moment, then Stephie made a face at Vicky, changing the focus of the conversation, and offering her own insight into bullying. "I don't like the way he identified you as they led him away."

Colleen raised her hand to her mouth as the color left her face, then glanced from Stephie, to Vicky.

"I can handle myself." He grinned wide, offering a reassurance neither had seen before.

Colleen inhaled in desperation. "But I don't want you to have to."

Stephie motioned toward Jake. "I'm talking to our family, to see what they think."

Vicky met Colleen's eyes. "I'm just worried you're in danger."

Desmond finally spoke. "We have more strength and resources than we're giving ourselves credit. Let's let this play out before we start planning for the worst." He offered the slightest head nod as he made eye contact with Vicky.

Vicky discreetly registered Desmond's insinuation. "Desmond's right. Let's consider the ordeal over until we're given reason not to."

Everyone seemed to relax per Vicky's instruction and the rest of the gathering became a celebration of their successful liberation of one of their dear friends. The party slowly disbursed over the next few hours, until only Jake and Stephie remained. Stephie patted Jake on his thigh, then rose. "Are you ready?"

He stood as she walked toward Vicky with her arms extended. "I'm going to tell our parents and nana. You'd be surprised how they always find ways to help."

Vicky tenderly slid his hand down the side of her hair, then embraced her. "I'm counting on it. The more people on our side, the more clout we have if anything strange happens."

Stephie kissed him, "I agree." then moved toward the door as Vicky hugged and kissed Jake.

Stephie removed her phone from her purse after Jake turned onto the highway. "When do you want to share this with our families?"

He shrugged. "Text both moms and let's see when we can have a small dinner party."

She started typing, then held her phone in her right hand as she held her left toward him. Her phone beeped twice in succession and she read the replies, then quickly typed another without explanation.

Jake glanced at her. "What's going on?"

"Both moms miss us and we're discussing where we're meeting for dinner." She continued typing, then faced him. "Any preference?"

He projected the satisfaction only love produced. "It doesn't matter to me. Whatever everyone decides."

She hopped in her seat, twisting toward him. "Want to have a dinner at our house?"

"Sure, but six around our little table won't work."

She eyed him and he glanced at her before refocusing on the road. "Mom and dad have a folding table in the basement. It'll fit in the trunk. They've done it before."

"We'll need folding chairs too. I'll get everything. It'll definitely fit in this thing."

She continued texting until she read the last, then lowered her phone to her lap as she bounced in her seat. "We're having our first dinner party next Saturday. I'm inviting Nana."

He glanced at her. "Definitely."

"We may have to give her a ride."

He patted the steering wheel and glanced at her. "With the car she gave us?"

He reached for her hand, and discreetly shook his head as he realized he'd been smiling the entire conversation.

~~~

Jake's phone vibrated in his pocket, interrupting his concentration. He removed it and discreetly read the incoming text, *How do you like your new job?* then smiled as he lowered the phone to the space between his keyboard and lap, and quickly replied. *Considering I been here 4 days -I'm liking everything …but I keep getting txts fr a certain PITA …*He hit send.

His phone beeped within seconds. *Hey!*

He caught himself grinning and glanced around the room as he buried his phone in his pocket. It vibrated almost immediately.

*Whatcha want for r dinner party dinner?*

He breathed deep and quickly typed. *cant u ask me that tonight?*

His phone vibrated in his hand. *I was goin 2 go shopping*

He typed. *Sweetheart …I cant rite now. Call u @ break*

His phone vibrated a moment later. *U suck …love u!*

He grinned as he buried his phone back in his pocket.

"Jacob?"

Jake glanced over the wall of his cubicle and his heart jumped as he heard the lady four cubicles down the aisle. "Jacob. It's Jacob, isn't it?"

"Jake."

She rose and walked toward him. "Well, Jake…" She pointed at her chest. "I'm Beck, by the way."

"Hi Beck." He extended his hand.

She quickly shook it, then rested on the partition panel at the edge of his cubicle and addressed him loud enough for the entire area to hear. "Since you've showed up every day this week without running screaming for the door…"

Two people out of sight clapped lightly. "Hooray!"

She paused and frowned at the interruption. "…there must be something wrong with you, which means you fit perfectly with the rest of us loonies, and we like to go out and get some beer …and food we shouldn't eat at all, complain about the bosses, and share and spread immature rumors …about once every six or eight weeks or so, and due to the terrible timing of your hire, that's tonight. So call you wife or girlfriend and tell her you're coming home late tonight. Her voice rose. "…Unless you don't have a wife or girlfriend." Her face contorted and her head tilted teasingly as snickers could be heard in multiple directions, then she turned and walked away before waiting for a reply.

She wandered out of site and a moment later Aaron popped his head around the corner of their connected cubicles. "She ain't so bad. A little intimidating and definitely scary, but not so bad."

Jake smiled at the gesture his cubicle neighbor made. "How long have you been here?"

"About six months." He slid his chair closer. "Where you from?"

"I live by the university. You?"

"I have an apartment down the street, near the bar they all go to. It's a decent sports bar." Aaron stood and glanced over their shared wall. "You into sports or anything?"

Jake smiled. "Yeah."

"It's close. You can follow me." He disappeared behind his side of their partition.

"Thanks."

Jake studied the orientation book open on his cubicle desk, waiting for an opportunity to text Stephie and let her know he had to go out after work, then decided he couldn't wait and headed to the bathroom. *Steph I hav 2 go out after work w/theoffice. I'll call u @ 4 love u*

The workday ended and Jake followed everyone to the parking lot as four different conversations filled the hallway, then the stairway. He noticed Aaron's effort to stay next to him, and the kindness registered solidly in his mind.

Aaron adjusted his backpack on his shoulder. "Sorry."

Jake smiled. "No worries."

"So, what teams do you root for?"

Jake glanced at him as they reached the outer building door. "All the local teams. Only the local teams."

Aaron's enthusiasm increased. "Me too! I'm tired of people cheering for cities on the other side of the country."

"Tell me about it."

"Do you like talking about sports?"

Jake nodded, "Sure." and sighed with relief as he recognized Aaron's potential in the acclimation process of this new job. Jake followed him to the bar and they parked next to each other, continuing the conversation without interruption. Once inside, Janet grabbed Jake's arm and introduced him to everyone, whether they had already met or not, and as introductions ended and everyone began mingling, Gina stood in front of him. "So, what's your story? You married?"

"Engaged."

"And I guess, in love?" Lauren laughed and hit her on the arm. "Stop picking on him." She turned to Jake. "Don't mind her. She just likes to joke around. It's her way of breaking you newbies in, that's all." She motioned to Gina, "Don't' scare him away or I'll get you in trouble." then pointed to Jake without looking at him. "Now buy the man a beer and let's order some pizza and wings."

Lauren whispered to him before walking to the bar. "Don't worry about her and feel free to give it back to her whenever you want."

Aaron waved him over to a bar table and pulled out the stool next to him. Jake could hear his breathing. "Don't let any of them get to you. This is what they did to me a few months ago and by the end of the night, they were taking care of me like you wouldn't believe."

Jake smiled. "I can handle it. I've been through worse."

"Good. Don't quit."

The row of TVs on a high wall caught his eye and he strained to see the score of the local game. "I won't."

"You a baseball fan?" Aaron hit his forehead. "I already asked you that."

"It's alright. Yeah."

"Ever play?"

Jake glanced at him as he lifted his beer. "Yeah. Through high school."

Aaron straightened in his seat. "Me too. Catcher."

"Third base."

"What'd you hit?"

"Fifth."

Aaron raised his glass at the connection. "Me too."

They both focused their attention on the TV. "You're engaged?" Aaron sipped his beer. "Too great. I have a longtime girlfriend, Kristen.

Mine's Stephanie, but I call her Stephie or Steph.

"College sweetheart?"

"Best friend since I was five, but we didn't start dating till we were in college."

"You were best friends with your girl since you were five?"

Jake's heart jumped as he realized how fast circumstances prompted him to expose his distinctive social situation. He felt himself flush and his breathing quicken. "Kind of. It's a little complicated."

Jake poured them both another beer from the pitcher on the table. "Where'd you meet your girl?"

Aaron chuckled. "At a dive bar. I was with my brother and I asked her to slow dance. We've been together since."

"Nice." His breathing eased as he realized he didn't have to reveal anything personal. He had no problem telling anyone who he was or who he loved; just a problem with that information potentially costing him and Stephie, things it didn't cost others.

The rest of happy hour went smoothly and Jake could see the acceptance level change as they joked and talked. He was reserved friendly, and as soon as the crowd started to thin, he said his goodbyes and excused himself.

~~~

Stephie rested the knife next to the half sliced onion. "Jacob! Are you going to vacuum?"

He popped his head in the kitchen opening. "I told you I was."

"Well we're running out of time!"

"Will you relax? Everything's going to be fine." She heard him open the hallway closet and remove the vacuum, then listened as its squeaky wheels allowed her to follow its location.

"No it isn't and this is important."

The vacuum cleaner wheels stopped squeaking. "*This* …is *not* important. They're our parents." The squeaking resumed. "The night could be a complete disaster and they'll consider it a raging success." Jake darted in the kitchen and attacked her from behind, tickling her as he kissed her neck. "Jake!" She elbowed him and he stepped back, then she reached for the knife and spun toward him. "Don't make me have to cut you!"

"Goddamn woman!" He backed up with arms raised as she playfully pointed with the knife. "Now go vacuum or I'm gonna make you clean up the blood with the one arm I leave you." She pointed the knife at him again. "Now!"

He began walking away, then looked back as he exited the kitchen. "You know you're going to pay for that tonight."

She smiled playfully. "How many times do I have to tell you, you don't scare me?"

He wondered into the living room. "I have to run to the car for the last two chairs."

She raised her eyes toward the kitchen ceiling. "Vacuum first!" A moment later she heard the vacuum and sighed. The vacuum went off and after a pause of silence she heard, "Did you hear me?"

She shut the faucet off. "No."

He walked into the kitchen and kissed her. "I'm going to go get the last two chairs from the trunk. Be right back."

She faced the mound of mushrooms. "I'll probably be in the shower when you get back."

"Okay."

She heard their front door shut, and shook her head. Their parents were coming to dinner. She squinted in disbelief. Their parents were coming to dinner at their house; her and Jake's. Her eyes slowly scanned her surroundings, as she tried to memorize the moment. Where she was at that moment, was exactly where she pictured herself in her happiest fairytale, but she couldn't begin to identify the details leading to that instance.

The scared girl in the boy body, with the best friend who she desperately wanted to tell, but couldn't for what seemed like forever, complicated by a crush on him that seemed longer than forever. And now, allowed to not only be female, but allowed to love that best friend and love of a thousand lifetimes, preparing a meal for him, and both sets of parents. The joy frightened her for a moment. She quickly thought of Colleen; so much like her, yet with so much in turmoil, and her bliss ended instantly.

The sounds of metal banging at the front door ended her introspection, and she listened as Jake brought the last chairs up the apartment stairs. She finished wiping the counter as he appeared at the kitchen opening. "Oh good."

"What?" She turned to him as she dried her hands.

"You didn't shower yet?" His smile grew. "Now we have to take one together since we're running out of time." He lightheartedly stared at her.

She fought her smile. "You're an idiot."

He walked to her and lifted her without warning. "Jake!"

He playfully met her volume. "What?"

She offered no reply.

After spending twenty five more minutes than Jake getting ready, she walked back into the living room and shook her head at him calmly sprawled on the sofa. He casually looked up. "…'Bout time."

Her heart offered a single strong beat as she watched him relax, thinking about their shower and the unplanned lust they just shared, then smiled at her inability to think of a clever retort. Making love to him always wiped her sarcasm repertoire clean.

He casually watched her. "We ready?"

She knew she was about to hear it if she answered the truth, but she secretly loved this game they played. "Yes."

He grinned conceitedly without offering a word, so she jumped him and he feigned injury. "Ugh!" The doorbell immediately rang and she quickly jumped off. "Company!"

She ran down the stairs and swung the door open. "Hi Dad!" She kissed him quickly. "Hi Mom!"

Both parents chimed, "Hi sweetheart."

Connor handed Stephie a bottle of wine as her demeanor caught his attention. He hesitated. "Are you alright? You seem a little wound too tight."

"I am! I'm trying to get everything ready all day and Jake isn't running around panicking like I need him to."

Jake pointed at her as he stood at the top of the steps waiting to greet them. "She pulled a knife on me!"

Connor extended his hand at the top of the stairs. "Did she cut you?" He quickly examined his torso and before Jake could answer, Genna kissed him. "Well you're bigger than her and probably deserved it sweetheart." She patted his cheek as she passed him into the room.

Stephie hopped with delight. "He did mom!"

And Jake stood there playfully dumbfounded until Connor patted his back. "Let's have a beer, son."

They returned to the family room after fixing drinks, when Chris and Morgan rang the doorbell. Stephie raced Jake to the front door. "Mom, Dad!"

"Oh, I like that a lot." Morgan handed Jake desert, then followed Stephanie up the stairs.

Greetings followed, and they gathered in the living room, enjoying conversation and waiting for dinner. Genna and Morgan helped when requested, but Stephie had been cooking for years and had everything nicely under control. Finally, Stephie announced dinner and the conversation moved to the makeshift dining area.

They ate and joked until Morgan raised her glass, half way through dinner. "To the cook." then faced Stephie. "This is excellent."

Chris confirmed with a full mouth. "It definitely is."

Connor saluted with his glass, in agreement.

Genna sipped her wine and met Jake's eyes as she lowered her glass. "Are you finally coming to the family reunion this year, sweetheart?"

Jake's eyes widened in playful disbelief. "You say that like I declined the invite for the last ten years."

Chris reached for his napkin and laughed as he covered his mouth. "If you only knew how miserable he was each year ...especially a few years ago. It was like someone shot him. Please take him this year."

Jake's heart jumped at the memory and his face flushed as he met Stephie's growing eyes. Stephie froze with her fork half way to her mouth. "Really?"

His breathing quickened noticeably as they locked eyes. "What do you think?"

"Oh my god, Jake." She lowered her fork, hurried around the table, and hugged and kissed him.

Connor watched with confusion. "What the hell just happened?"

Chris reached for his beer and leaned back. "If I didn't know better, I'd say Jake just told her he loved her years ago."

Morgan smacked his arm. "You're such an ass."

The night was like any other the two families spent together. Chris did his best to lovingly torture everyone. Morgan spent her night trying to rein Chris in. Connor quietly observed and laughed constantly, throwing in a sarcastic remark whenever he could, and Genna mothered everyone, but as soon as the door closed after the extended goodbyes, Stephie wrapped her arms around Jake's neck and swallowed his tongue. When the kiss finally broke, his eyes widened. "What was that for?"

She stared into his eyes with her arms still around his neck. "You loved me when I was Steven?"

"I told you I had a crush on you for a long time."

She held his hand as they walked up the stairs and toward their bedroom. "Did you ever want to kiss Steven before you met Stephanie?"

"Yes, I wanted to kiss Steven." His mouth curled upward against his control. "I wanted to do a few things to Steven." He kissed her softly. "In fact, I've done a few things to Steven."

"You cheated on me?"

He reached for her as she started undressing and tickled her. "You're an idiot."

She pointed at him after he let her go, swishing her hips and taunting him, "Yeah, but you loved me."

He feigned exasperation. "Yeah yeah …I loved you and I still do. What's your point?"

"When do you feel the difference between Stephanie and Steven?" She tried hard to continue flirting, though her words now showed signs of loving curiosity.

He laughed at the sexy motions still accompanying her words. "You're both to me, and sometimes when we make love, I feel a connection to Steven, my feminine guy best friend since I was five. But it happens most when we kiss. I love kissing Stephanie and Steven."

They both climbed under the covers and he extended his arms to her. She moved voluntarily to him, and as she lay close, he immediately felt her arousal. His heart jumped. "Do you like the idea I find both Stephanie and Steven sexy?"

She knew he felt the answer without her verbal confirmation. "Very much. I think it's sexy in a different way, but it's something else too." She eyed him curiously. "I just got the feeling I don't have to pretend at all..." Her eyes narrowed as she stared into his. "You really love me? ...The real me?"

He buried his mouth in the crook of her neck. "Yeah. Yeah I do. And I have for longer than you know."

She gasped as his mouth and tongue teased her neck and offered with more air than voice, "You can call me Steven right now, if you want."

He didn't hesitate. "I love you Steven." He stopped making love to her neck and placed his forehead under her chin. "I love you, Steven. You have no idea."

She pulled at the sides of his face, trying to look into his eyes. "Are you alright?"

He inhaled. "I never said that to you."

She lay silently under him as her breathing deepened.

His breathing matched hers. "I wanted to say that to you for a long time, and didn't because I was worried I'd upset you; you'd get confused or not understand what I meant." He kissed her passionately.

A tear slid from the corner of her eye as her head lay in his hand. "You needed to tell Steven you love him?"

He wiped the tear from the corner of her eye. "I never told him …and I needed to. He kissed her softly. "I never realized how bad I needed to." He kissed her again. "I love you Steven …and I love you Stephanie."

~~~

The next few days were uneventful, and both were in a productive routine. They were spending less and less time at the school complex, unless resources couldn't be accessed from their apartment. Jake closed his textbook on the coffee table as he sat studying next to her. "Aren't you going out with Vicky tonight?"

Stephie smiled immediately. She seemed to smile whenever she heard Vicky's name. "Yeah. I told him I wanted to go out just him and me; a little alone time with my brother."

"And he bought it?"

His statement produced a smirk. "Why wouldn't he?"

He leaned over and smothered her under his larger frame and she slid down the sofa as he kissed her passionately. "Don't meet anyone."

"You're an idiot."

He buried his mouth in the crook of her neck. "Are you asking him?"

"Yeah. That's why we're going out."

He tasted her earlobe. "You know; he's going to cry, then you're going to cry, so bring tissues."

"Good idea." She started pulling tissues from the box next to the sofa. "There's lunchmeat and rolls in there."

He stared into her eyes and smiled, then paused and placed his hand over his heart. "I swear I'll survive a night without you."

Her eyes widened. "Yeah, but *I* don't know if you can."

"Ha ha." He smirked. "Thanks. I love you too."

She slid her hand on the side of his hair. "I'm so in love with you, I feel like I'm going to explode sometimes."

He smirked. "You don't mean your weight, right?"

She playfully smacked the top of his head, then pulled him to the living room floor and straddled him. "You're such an ass sometimes." She repeatedly poked his sides.

His soft laughter turned to a frown as he attempted to control her hands. "Hey. Idiot to you, and don't ever forget it." He tickled her waist as he rolled on top of her. "Do you have time to make love to your idiot?"

She inhaled deeply and opened her eyes seductively as she stared into his. "I always have time to make love to you." Then exhaled with pleasure and draped her arms lovingly around his neck as he lifted her and carried her to their room.

Jake wandered back into the living room and sat facing his text books. He opened the top one realizing he was still smiling, then also noticed his breathing and how relaxed he felt. He stared at the open text book and inhaled deeply, then forced himself to focus on the words. He felt his smile widen as he quickly recalled what they had just done, then reached for the remote and contentedly sat back.

Stephie came out of their room some time later, gathered her purse and jacket, then kissed him. "Don't wait up."

He grabbed her bottom as she turned toward the door. "Have a great time, sweetheart. Be careful. And call me if you need me."

She disappeared down the steps toward the front door. "I will. Love you."

She daydreamed the entire twenty minute drive to Vicky's, anticipating the joy of Vicky's reaction to the undisclosed purpose of their night out. She stopped the car in front of Vicky's apartment and quickly texted her adopted older sibling. *In front waiting 4 U*

She sent the text and honked lightly. Her phone beeped seconds later. *B rite there*

She watched Vicky lock his front door, hurry to her car, and open the passenger door. "Hi honey!"

She hopped in her seat, "Hi!" then leaned toward him after he sat, and kissed him.

"Little sister …how are you?"

She grabbed his hand excitedly, "I'm great. We haven't done this, just the two of us, in an age. I'm so excited!"

He chuckled, "Ha! You energize me." then paused. "Where we headed?"

"I'm in the mood for finger food." She met his eyes and smiled deviously. "Like some fattening fries."

"Of course."

They picked a restaurant, asked for a quaint booth away from the noisy bar, sat cozy and comfortable, and began gabbing as Vicky loved to say, 'like only girls can'.

They ordered junk food and experimented with more than a few drink choices, and after a while, were giggling and making their corner of the restaurant, as noisy as the bar area. Stephie was never much for gossip, but listening to Vicky tell stories in his unique animated way, had her laughing out loud more than not, and all Vicky ever needed for even the most impromptu performance was an audience, and Stephie fit that bill all too well.

Stephie finally reached for his hand across the table. "Okay." She tried her best to be serious, only to have Vicky make a face and the giggling resumed.

She mock-hollered at him. "Will you stop a second?"

"Girl, I'm just getting started." He snapped his fingers and swayed his head. "Girls night!" He leaned forward. "We have to do this more often."

Stephie shook her head softly but her giggle came from the bottom of her heart. "You are one of the most beautiful people I have ever met." She stared at Vicky intensely. "How are you so beautiful?"

Vicky paused for a moment. "Don't do me with those eyes girl. I'll lose all focus on anything else." He sighed and rubbed Stephie's hands across the table. "I love you. I need you." He sniffed, rubbed his nose with the back of his hand, then breathed in, staring into Stephie's eyes. "You're gonna make me all emotional." He glanced down at her hands in his. "I love having people to love. I need having people to love." He smiled. "And you offer to be one of those people and never looked back. You don't judge. Instead, you love me back. And for all my weirdness, for all the times I act different; you do nothing but think I'm special, and love me."

He sipped his drink. "And it's the one single thing I need most in the whole world. You know what's in my heart, you see my other side, even though I don't wear it on the outside like you do." He tilted his head. "It's who you are too; born boys but we have the ability to love with a female intensity. And I know you know that's deeper than men can." He tried to breathe deep. "And that's what my family denied me. I was denied the people I wanted to love deeper than they realize." He stared at their interlocked hands. "But you offer love without judging. It never comes with any expectation, but it's always unmistakably there." The smile on his face displayed a relaxed pleasure, then his entire countenance brightened. "Do you know who's told me they love me, the most in my life?"

She moved her head back, and thought for a quick second. "Who?"

"You." He breathed deep as he sat up. "You tell me almost every time we talk on the phone, and when we're together and we say goodbye. And especially when we're being strange or doing something that brings us closer. Do you know how you feed my soul? Do you know how I live for our connection and what it means when you constantly make sure I know?"

He shook his head. "I'm sorry I took our party down, but I've been thinking for a while how you're one of the best things ever to happen to me and your wedding and happiness make me feel joy." He squeezed her hand. "I love you, little sister."

She sat straight. "And that's why I invited you out tonight." Her smile widened. "To show you what you mean to me." She placed her hands on his. "Will you please be my person of honor?"

He gasped as he raised both hands to his mouth, "Me?" then quickly stood as he began crying, pulled Stephie from the booth and squeezed her; kissing the side of her head repeatedly as he rocked her in his arms. "I'm so very grateful for you and I love you."

She moved so she could look into his eyes. "I know. You show me by everything you do for me."

She softly exhaled as he continued the embrace. "You really are my sister, aren't you?"

"Completely."

He wiped his eyes, then hugged her tighter and whispered, "We're so girly, aren't we?"

She laughed in his ear.

Her ride home after dropping Vicky off was sheer bliss. She locked the apartment door behind her, quietly climbed the stairs, and stared at Jake sprawled on the sofa. "Why aren't you in bed?"

He mumbled, half asleep. "I wanted to make sure you didn't meet someone."

His droll response raised the right side of her mouth. "Very funny."

He slowly rose. "How'd it go? Was he excited like only he can be?"

She smiled. "Of course."

He walked to her as she hung her coat. "Did you enjoy tonight?"

"Of course. He's zany and makes me giggle." She sighed. "I love him." Her smile never lessened as she continued to relive the event in her mind.

He matched her smile and nodded softly. "So do I."

She reached for his hand. "Then it wouldn't hurt saying you love him every once in a while, to let him know."

She watched his brows dip and tilted her head. "I know you love deeply, but some of us need to hear the words a lot, even though we know it. Some of us have had rough adjustments into this world. You know that." She leaned toward him and kissed him. "Not that we aren't loved, but people who've been beat up by the world have a need to be told more often, whether they say it or not, but it means even more to them when they don't have to ask." Her eyes widened, causing him to shake his head. He wrapped his arms around her, lifting her off the carpet, and squeezed her. "I love you I love you I love you!"

She quickly fought against his playfully torturous grip. "Jake!"

# Chapter Ten
## Delineation

Days turned into weeks, and the group collectively assumed Colleen's father had decided to let her move on with her life. The living arrangements weren't perfect, but Vicky knew the closeness they developed far outweighed the less than adequate sleeping arrangements, though he wished he could think of an option which would allow her the dignity of her own room.

He parked his car in front of his apartment and instantly wondered what she made for dinner. She was cooking and cleaning to offer something for the inconvenient arrangement and open ended intrusion on his life and privacy, but lately, he wasn't sure he wasn't getting the better end of the bargain.

He was about to shut his apartment door when something caught his eye and made his heart jump. The car sped away, but there was no mistaking it. He had sat facing it in the back alley, long enough to memorize it and though it was dusk, the face behind the wheel confirmed it. Colleen's father had tracked Vicky down.

Vicky's heart sunk. The peaceful last few weeks had just come to an unannounced end.

He watched the car make the left out of their complex and disappear into traffic, and he froze with the handle of the open door in his hand. He sighed as he realized how inevitable the end of the calm was. He had paid attention for longer than a few weeks, making sure their specific car wasn't somewhere behind him as he drove home from work, but had stopped paying attention without realizing, and now it was too late.

A second thought occurred; at least he knew her father wasn't done bullying. He breathed deep and stood straight, exhaled and breathed deeper. This new situation was not going to show on his face as he greeted Colleen, nor was he going to let it ruin their night. He was too far in the door to make a phone call or leave without raising questions, no matter how innocent. The pause at the open door was already too long.

He forced a smile and the appropriate accompanying mood, locked his front door behind him, then entered and greeted Colleen in the kitchen. "Hi, honey ...I'm home!"

Colleen turned from the stove. "Hi Vick! How was your day?"

"Uneventful. Yours?"

She looked back, attending to the pan in front of her. "I took the bus to the mall and filled out applications. If I get a job there, I'm thinking maybe we could drive together to work when our schedules match."

Vicky buried his concern and greeted the news with the casual joy it deserved. "That's wonderful." He paused. "I appreciate how hard you're trying to pull your weight, and I want you to know your success doesn't have to match your effort. Your effort counts for everything and others control your success." He walked next to her and slid his hand down the back of her hair. "But I know everything will work out."

He motioned toward the short hall leading to his room. "I'm going to change into sweats. Be right back."

He shut his bedroom door behind him and started typing into his phone. *Desmond we have a problem. I just spotted Colleen's father in his car @ our complex*

Moments later, his phone beeped in response. *We don't have a problem. We have an inconvenience.*

Vicky quickly typed. *Nothing stupid*

His phone beeped and he read the reply. *...maybe a little stupid*

~~~

Genna ended her call with the last client she had on her agenda, marked her itinerary on the open computer program, then sat back and dialed her cell. "Mom."

"Hi cara." Her mother's soft reply brought a warm smile to her face.

"I had a light day today and managed to finish everything early ...so you want to go to lunch?"

"You know I always want to go to lunch with you."

"Then it's a date. See you in an hour?"

"I'll be waiting."

Genna's smile continued as she straightened her desk and prepared to leave. She took her time; her mother's house was only thirty five minutes from her office. She forwarded her work phone to her cell, locked the office and left.

She watched her mother lock her front door as she pulled up, and smiled as Lorraine opened the passenger door. "Hi mom. How are you?"

"Not bad for this make and model."

She laughed. "Oh god mom; that's one of dad's old lines."

Lorraine laughed. "Yeah, and it felt good saying. I like keeping him alive in my heart and mind."

Genna glanced at her. "Don't get too deep or I'll start crying."

She heard her mother breathe deep. "I agree. He always said he wanted us to laugh when we remembered him after he left, so let's adhere to his wish."

Genna shook her head. "I still miss him."

Lorraine nodding softly, "I miss him too. I loved him while we were together and under those terms, have no regrets." She patted the armrest between them, then faced forward. "Where we going? ...I feel like a burger and a beer."

Genna tapped the steering wheel and giggled. "I've never heard you ever say you feel like going to a bar for a beer."

"It has been a while." Lorraine laughed. "Your father and I used to go to this dive bar and get pitchers all the time when we were young. We used to play a drinking game called *buzz* when we had beer left we couldn't finish." Lorraine's voice softened. "I'll never forget the place. The paneling was so old, you could see the outline of a person at the inside seat of the booths against the wall."

Genna glanced at her. "Ew?"

"Oh yeah. What a dive. Great memories."

Genna pulled up to a local casual restaurant. "Is this alright?"

Lorraine lovingly chided, "You know it is."

A young woman greeted them inside the second set of glass doors. "Welcome. Any preference?"

Lorraine moved her focus from the young lady, to Genna. "Can we sit at the bar?"

Genna laughed. "Mother. Yes. I believe we both qualify age-wise, though I don't think we've ever sat at a bar together. You're too funny."

She glanced back as she walked toward the long stone bar top and line of matching black leather stools. "Sometimes I feel young."

Genna quipped. "You just want to see if any guys will hit on you."

Lorraine chuckled, then cupped her hand at the side of her mouth, "Maybe we can get a free beer or two."

Genna scanned the empty bar area. "Not with this crowd."

"Can I help you?" The young barmaid stood attentively on the other side of the counter.

Genna watched Lorraine motion to the taps. "Do you have the beer that comes with an orange slice?"

"We do"

"One of those please?"

The server focused on Genna, as she read the tap handles. "Light beer please."

"Would you like menus?"

"Please."

They watched the young lady remove two glasses from a metal chest and head toward the taps. Then Lorraine smiled at Genna. "What's new?"

"Not much. How about you?"

Lorraine watched the young lady place their beers on the bar, then reached for her glass and held it. "Cheers."

Genna responded, "Salute." and sipped.

Lorraine lowered her glass. "I've been thinking about something since our last extended family gathering, I want to discuss with you."

Genna straightened in her chair. "Okay. What do you need?" She lifted her beer and took a gulp as Lorraine's statement raised her concern.

Lorraine squeezed the orange into her drink. "Colleen."

"What about her?"

"Do you want to order something?"

Genna turned to the server. "Yes, but not right now. We're going to relax for a while."

The young lady stepped back softly. "Oh no problem. Let me know when you're ready."

"Thanks. We will." Genna rested her arm on the back of the stool and faced Lorraine. "Colleen?" She watched her mother inhale.

"I want to help her."

"Okay. What are you thinking?"

Lorraine's brows rose. "I don't know why, but I've taken an instant liking to her. She's sweet, and scared, and lost, and the older I get, the less comfortable I am when one of our children fits all those categories."

Genna knew her mother and would have bet she was going to propose something beyond anyone else. She did it often, and could feel the knowing smile it produced on her face. "What are you thinking?"

Her mother smiled back. "I'm getting older, but I don't want to leave my house yet. But the house is too big for me, and the older I get, the more alone I feel inside." She lifted her beer and sipped it. "And I want someone to worry about …to guide …to care for." Her voice rose. "And she needs a place to stay …a bed of her own." Her breathing steadily increased. "And Vicky has already done too much …and she's sleeping on his couch …not to mention the financial burden."

"Are you thinking of asking her to live with you?"

Lorraine scrunched her nose. "Would that upset you?"

Genna raised her glass and softly saluted her. "It wouldn't upset me at all. My only concern is your safety."

Lorraine lifted her beer in response. "You're okay with the idea?"

"Of you helping someone in need? Mom. I love when you take action. Of everything I admire about you; that's number one."

Lorraine tilted her head. "What do you think of the idea? Do you think her situation and the offer for another start would be appreciated enough she'll respect the opportunity?"

Genna inhaled deeply. "That's the only hesitation, but you can feel her out." Genna placed her beer on the coaster. "I know you'll open a dialog with her that'll allow discussions on necessary levels."

Lorraine nodded in agreement. "I'll offer with a level of communication that'll help her respect the opportunity, without making her feel like a stranger in the house." Her mother placed her hand on Genna's closest hand. "I'm doing it."

Genna shook her head softly. "Your actions always blow me away."

"Another?" Both turned to the young server. "Yes." "Please."

Genna finished her beer. "Vicky's birthday's coming. We have to have a birthday bash. He's our child now."

Lorraine slid her empty glass to the inside edge of the bar, "I agree." then faced Genna. "And we can show him his actions have been well recorded. Find out from Stephie what he needs, and let's do something special for him."

"Want to order? I'm getting hungry." Genna opened her menu.

Lorraine patted hers. "I know what I want."

They ordered, and sat back, enjoying the quiet atmosphere, then enjoyed the casual meal and another drink.

"Can I get you anything else?" The server lifted Lorraine's empty plate, then motioned to Genna. "Finished?"

Genna wiped her mouth. "Yes, thank you."

"Anything else for you, ma'am?"

Lorraine leaned back. "Just our check please."

The server lifted the second plate. "Be right back."

Genna watched Lorraine move her purse to her lap. "Oh, the kids are graduating at the end of this semester and I was thinking of a graduation party. What do you think?"

Lorraine smiled softly. "At my age, I'm always anxious for the next family gathering on happy terms." Her smile turned into a laugh. "I don't want the next one to center around me." She motioned as if slicing her neck with her fingers.

"Mom!"

~~~

The next day was bright and sunny but as soon as the taproom door shut behind them, the room reflected the appearance of night. The two large men casually paused for a moment as their eyes adjusted to the change, then proceeded toward the outdated and almost empty bar. Desmond scanned the room and counted four patrons and a bartender, then noticed the single miniature window high on a far wall, covered with a dingy cigarette-smoke stained cloth curtain. He inhaled and smiled. The dank odor of stale beer accompanying the aged grime oddly comforted him.

Desmond and Mick had already discussed the plan and as Desmond sat next to a man sitting alone at the far end of the bar, Mick moved a stool and sat so the man was snugly between them. The man looked up, and his back immediately straightened. Desmond smiled as their eyes met. "Hi."

The gentleman immediately tried to stand but Mick placed his hand on the man's shoulder and spoke softly. "Have a beer with us."

The bartender walked over and waited without saying a word. Mick met his eyes. "Light beer for me and I'd like to buy my friend here another of what he's having."

The bartender focused on Desmond and he responded. "Light beer for me too."

The elder gentleman placed the last drink on the bar top without a word, and Desmond waited for him to walk away. "Remember me?"

The man's wide eyes let him know the answer without a response.

He mouthed a soft kiss, then smiled. "I'm one of your daughter's best friends."

"I don't have a daughter."

Desmond offered no reaction and continued to casually look around. "And I'm going to need you to honor that thought until you grow the fuck up." Desmond's smile projected an intimidatingly uncomfortable calm. "Understand?" He twisted his head slowly toward the man.

The man's breathing noticeably intensified. "And why should I?"

"Oh you don't have to. In fact, I hope you don't." Desmond sipped his beer. "If you don't, we're gonna become friends." Desmond's voice continued to project calm. "Good friends." He methodically adjusted his mug on its coaster, then met the gentleman's eyes. "Would you like that?"

The bartender stopped wiping the bar top close by and without lifting the rag, interrupted the quiet conversation. "Hey. I don't want no trouble in here."

Desmond met his eyes and smiled, then pointed to the furthest corner of the room. "If you go clean that bar top over there, until we're done having a few beers with our friend, you'll see a lot less of us than you will if we discuss this further."

The gentleman raised his hands. "I'm not starting anything."

Desmond grinned and nodded once, "Good." then turned toward the man next to him and his knee intruded the man's space. He leaned slowly toward him, resting his arm on the bar top almost in front of him. "You were spotted in a place you need to stay as far away from as humanly possible."

The man's demeanor betrayed his words, as he attempted to hold his ground. "I can go any damn place I want."

"Then you'll find, we can take you anywhere *we* want." Mick's voice noticeably startled him.

Desmond finished Mick's thought. "And if we spot you where we don't want you again, we're gonna take you someplace you don't want to go."

"And we promise you'll be amazed where that is." Mick's voice at the back of his head made the man twitch.

The man's head spun as Desmond confirmed. "…amazed."

Mick moved the man's beer closer with mock hospitality. "Drink."

The man did a double-take in Mick's direction, then obediently lifted his beer. Desmond lifted his and they both drank. Desmond lowered his slowly, projecting an eerie calmness. "I decided I won't be visiting you more than one more time."

The sentence caused a relaxed smile on the man's face, and Desmond let it fade before continuing. "I don't believe in threats." He met the man's eyes and held his stare. "We're grown men." He took a deliberate breath, making his sentences almost painfully slow. "We know there's no such thing as intimidation." His eyes narrowed as he tilted his head. "This isn't a reprieve though. …This is how I work." He leaned closer and whispered. "I disappear before I act."

Desmond leaned away and reached for his beer, sipped it, then smiled. "Others have misinterpreted my disappearance as a lapse in vigilance." He slowly placed his beer on the coaster, and meticulously adjusted it, then turned his head toward the man. "I hope you make the same mistake."

Mick whispered to the back of the man's head. "See, you already struck first, so you already set the rules of engagement."

Desmond raised his empty beer glass toward the gentleman standing as far away behind the bar, as possible. "Another round please."

Mick whispered to the man. "Drink." Then lifted his beer and finished it before sliding the mug toward the approaching bartender.

After the third beer was placed in front of them, Mick smiled at the bartender, "Thank you." then stared at him until he was sure the message was received. The gentleman moved immediately to the far side of the bar.

Mick moved the man's chair toward him, with little effort. "But we're not unreasonable. We like teaching too." He wrapped his hand around his beer mug without lifting it, then met the man's eyes. "Your daughter…" He moved his seat closer. "…is a beautiful kind loving person."

Mick paused as Desmond continued. "Not only didn't she press charges against you, she didn't press charges against the two store owners either."

The man straightened as the sentence registered.

Mick finished the thought. "Kidnapping?"

Desmond slowly scanned the leak stained tin ceiling, "We asked her why."

Mick placed his arm on the back of the man's chair. "Do you know what she said?"

The man turned his head from one to the other without offering a response.

Desmond's eyes narrowed as he inhaled, "Because I love them." then exhaled slowly. "Because she loves you three assholes."

Mick finished the point as he nodded in agreement, "She loves you," then shook his head in the opposite direction. "…but the rest of us haven't developed that deep a relationship with you yet." Mick slid his hand tenderly over the back of the man's hair. "So we're hoping to forget you exist instead …but you're not helping."

Desmond watched Mick's hand produce a shiver and bit his lip. "We're hoping our beers together helps. Do you think our beers together helps?"

Colleen's father froze and his mouth opened. Desmond leaned close. "I'm going to take that as a yes."

The bartender walked over, but stayed beyond reach. "Are you gentlemen almost done?"

Desmond eyed him, then glanced at Mick. "I think we're good." He faced the gentleman next to him, "We good?" and watched his eyes widen but received no reply.

He finished his beer, watched Mick finish his as he reached in his pocket, then threw a twenty on the bar top as he stood. "Thanks for your hospitality."

Mick stood and after a purposeful pause, patted the man's back slightly harder than friendly. "Great meeting you." then turned and followed his friend out the front door.

# Chapter Eleven
## Supplication

Vicky's phone vibrated on the table as he sat in the employee break room eating the lunch Colleen prepared. He sipped his ice tea to clear his mouth, then quickly grabbed his dancing phone. "Hello?"

"Vicky?"

He immediately straightened in his chair. "Nana?"

"Yes dear. Is now a good time to call?"

His voice exuded permission. "Of course." He took a small breath. "Is everything alright? Are you okay?"

"You're such a dear for asking. Yes, I'm fine. But I've called to share a thought, if that's alright."

He laid his fork in the plastic container. "Of course it's alright."

He concentrated on her soft voice. "I've thought of a way we can help Colleen, and I'd like to ask your permission before sharing with her." She paused for a moment. "I'd like to offer her to come live with me."

Vicky gasped. "Wow. That's generous."

She countered, "Not as generous as you think."

He paused and she continued. "I'm getting old and this house is big. I could offer her a home but she could help me with many things. I also wouldn't be alone, though I have no intention of intruding in her life."

His breathing increased. "Wow."

"There's something else I'd like to offer her, but you mustn't share."

He replied immediately. "I promise."

Lorraine's soft voice continued. "I want to help her with her future; get her back in school, and intend to pay for her Associate's degree at community college. I'm sure she's had a rough life, with little support, and I'm sure opportunities haven't been abundant. I think this would be a way for her to regain missed opportunities. What do you think?"

He energized at the thought. "What a fantastic offer. What a generous gift."

Her voice stayed soft, but turned serious. "I would do it for any of my children." Then he heard her soft laugh. "But I want you to understand how selfish the offer is."

He breathed deep and listened. "She would be someone to focus on …talk to, someone to cook for, someone to care for …share stories and experiences with …to love if she's interested in being loved. All I'm giving her in return is an unoccupied room."

He felt his eyes widen. "You're amazing."

"I'm not amazing at all. I'm old, though I'm not asking her to be my nurse. Old age teaches lessons, being young doesn't. Nothing more." Her voice softened. "May I have your permission to ask her?"

"Of course, but why would you think you need my permission?"

"Because you've volunteered to be her guardian, and with that responsibility comes a certain authority."

He took another deep breath. "Oh no. I'm just a friend."

"You may downplay the inconvenience and financial burden your support is causing you, but that doesn't mean some of us aren't fully aware of the actual gift. But I believe it's time for a more extended plan regarding her living arrangements."

He stared ahead. "I don't know what to say."

"You can think about the idea and let me know."

"Oh no. I think it's a fabulous offer" He joked. "…Will you adopt me?"

She giggled delicately. "Oh dear …I already have."

~~~

Morgan removed the upper half of the cake from the baking pan, gently placed it on the bottom half, then carefully aligned them as Chris glanced at her with his hand on the fridge door. He watched for a moment longer and her demeanor caught his attention. He tilted his head, then released the refrigerator door. "What's wrong?"

She broke her concentration, but didn't meet his eyes. "Nothing." She refocused on the plastic icing container.

He opened the refrigerator door without turning away from her. "I don't know what it is, but I'm betting it isn't *nothing*." He reached for a water bottle. "Do you want me to ask again?"

She lowered the container and the icing knife. "I'm mad at myself."

"For what?" He sat across from her at the kitchen table and inhaled the sweet cake aroma.

She sighed. "Oh it's silly."

He snorted with empathy. "It's usually silly when we're mad at ourselves, but what do you think you did that's making you mad at you?"

She sneered as she glanced at him. "I'm mad I ever thought people like Jake, Stephanie, Vicky, Colleen … were anything but how they were made, and every time Jake or Lorraine share information about how normal they are, I get mad at myself for not being able to figure everything out on my own." She held the knife

199

lower and met his eyes. "What am I stupid, or ignorant or something?" She sighed noticeably. "I'm trying to figure out what's wrong with me."

His right eyebrow rose as he cracked the water bottle lid. "Nothing's wrong with you."

She rested the knife on the container. "I always loved our children, but I never let Jake know he could come to me with something as personal as his inner feelings. I never asked him who he was. I told him who he was, instead. Why?" Her eyes narrowed. "I should have been alright with whoever he was, but it wasn't the case."

She frowned. "He had to have a talk with me, Chris. *He* had to teach *me*." She rose from the table, walked to the counter and pulled napkins from the holder. "My son; the love of my life, had to teach me how normal he is …and I hate me right now."

He stood and hugged her. "But look where you are."

"That's not good enough." She gently freed one arm from his embrace and wiped her eyes. "My god!" She looked up in exasperation. "And my original opinion of them. Was I kidding?"

"Stop already." He laughed as she wiped tears on his shirt sleeve. "Stop. Who do you think you should be? Super Morgan?"

She stared at him curiously.

"Everything you were told to believe, before you were old enough to evaluate, gave you your opinion of people like them. You can't beat yourself up for being an obedient daughter and listening to your parents, or for being a faithful religious person because you listened to your pastor. God, Morgan …that ain't how you're supposed to judge yourself."

Her voice turned self-deprecating. "How am I supposed to see myself?" She reached behind him and grabbed the napkin holder.

He inhaled deeply. "By being thrilled you now know things about this subject, others will never understand. By being excited you've come far past some of the mindless bullshit you were taught. By applying this lesson to all other potential lessons; don't have an opinion on anything you haven't studied and measured yourself."

She placed her arms around him and kissed his cheek. "You know, you're pretty smart for a construction worker."

He smirked sarcastically. "Thanks."

"It makes me mad though." She blew her nose. "It makes me mad as hell that certain sons of bitches teach people shit, and you have to damn near ruin a child to learn how wrong the bastards are. And you can see it." She moved to the sink and washed her hands. "You can watch certain children almost twist inside out trying to deal with being told they're not okay being who they are." She turned as she dried her hands and met his eyes. "And now I'm mad I don't have any..." She searched for the right word. "...power; influence to tell the whole world what I learned."

She sat facing the cake and continued icing it. "Is it that hard to learn common sense lessons?" She peered intently into his eyes.

His face contorted as the answer appeared. "I'm afraid it is." His eyes narrowed. "You have to want to learn before you can, and life's too damn busy to pay attention to everything."

She made one last pass over the top of the cake with the knife, then gently pushed it away and motioned toward it. "And I feel really good giving Vicky a party and making him a cake. He's impressive ...so loving." Her eyes narrowed as they met his. "I mean, how many of us would've taken Colleen in?"

Chris grinned. Isn't it interesting how a person's heart has nothing to do with who they're attracted to or where they fall on a gender spectrum?"

She tilted her head. "They have *nothing* to do with each other."

"They have less to do with each other than the world realizes …unless society convinces those children they're cosmic trash; then society says, *told you,* when they react negatively to the condemnation."

He softly hit the kitchen table, instantly changing the depth of their conversation and its accompanying mood. "Anything else you need me to do for the party?"

She leaned toward him and jokingly sniffed. "Take a shower and shave?"

He grinned, "Wise ass." then walked around the table and kissed her, before walking out of the kitchen.

She raised her voice as he disappeared. "Genna texted. All the pizza was delivered over there. Would you bring it here after your shower?"

He yelled out of sight. "I'm on it."

Vicky heard Jonathan honk and blinked his porch light, letting him know he'd be right out. He opened his door and raised his hand in shock as Jonathan greeted him in the doorway, "Happy birthday!" then kissed and hugged him. "Your gift's in the car."

"Oh you didn't have to buy me anything."

Jon laughed. "Yeah, right."

Vicky chuckled. "…maybe you did." He shared a quirky smirk before sitting in the car. "But I'm allowed to say that too."

Jonathan shook his head and smiled but didn't offer a reply.

Vicky eyed him after buckling in. "How've you been?" He sung the question.

"Good. You?"

"Okay. I miss you." He paused, then added, "You know I hate your job."

Jon glanced at him. "Not as much as I do."

He watched Jon turn toward the highway. "Where we headed?"

Jonathan lied as instructed. "Chris texted me asking if we wanted to go to Logan's with them so they could celebrate your birthday with you. I said sure." He glanced at him as he entered the highway. "Is that okay?"

Vicky's tried to sound upbeat, "Sure." then his voice faded to dejection. "The rest of our friends are all busy."

Jon offered solace for Vicky's disappointment. "You love Chris and Morgan. And I bet we have a great time."

He sat back and sighed. "You're right. It'll be fun."

Vicky pointed as Jon drove past the exit for the little tavern. "That's the turn." He faced Jon. "I think we can get there from the next exit."

Jon casually lied again. "Chris asked if we can drive together." He quickly moved his focus from the road to Vicky's eyes. "...drinking. He's pretty sure some of us are going to drink too much."

Vicky's voice turned resolute. "Smart man."

Jon pointed toward the phone on Vicky's lap. "Text him and let them know we're close."

Vicky raised his phone and stared at it, amazed at how little text activity he had received on his special day, then opened a new text. *We're almost there. C U in a few* He shut his phone and glanced at Jon. "Mind if I get drunk tonight?"

He nodded as he concentrated on the road. "Not at all."

Except for the birds singing, the neighborhood was noticeably quiet for a spring evening, but the air had the soft fragrance of newly awakened vegetation. Vicky led Jon up the drive to the side kitchen door. He hadn't been here often, but family seemed to only use the side door. He knocked, then faced Jon as the door opened.

"SURPRISE!"

Vicky jumped, then covered his open mouth with his hands and immediately started crying. Morgan, Genna and Stephie stood in front of a crowd of friends jammed into the kitchen, all still discordantly yelling *surprise* and *happy birthday!* He stepped back gasping, as tears fell.

Stephie opened the door and extended her arms, "Happy birthday! Surprise!" then stepped aside as Vicky made his way into the crowd, kissing and greeting everyone. He pointed and yelled as the celebration slowly moved to the family room. "Five minutes ago I was mad at all of you!" He wiped his eyes. "I thought you all forgot my birthday."

Jake yelled over the crowd. "Yeah, like that would happen. You're the glue of this group. You're the one thing everyone here has in common."

"Oh my god." Vicky's smile brightened as he scanned the room. "This is remarkable. I never had a surprise party."

Connor patted his back, then hugged him. "Sorry we missed so many before this one."

"Hey!" They hugged. "It wasn't *that* many!"

He hugged Genna, keeping his eyes on Connor. "And this makes up for all of them."

Morgan kissed and hugged him tight. "You're going to find out, we tried." She caressed his face. "What are you drinking?"

"White wine please?"

Morgan stepped away, revealing his newest dear friend, waiting patiently to greet him. "Happy happy birthday, big brother."

Colleen wrapped her arms slowly around his neck and held him dearly, then whispered close to his ear. "Thank you for taking care of me."

"Stop. You're going to make me cry." He leaned his head away from her and peered into her eyes. "I'm exhausted from all the crying already." He hugged her tight. "It's my absolute pleasure, honey. I have another sister because of it." He breathed deep, then squeezed her tighter.

He made the rounds, hugging and kissing everyone else. Morgan handed him his glass of white wine, and the party amped up until a quiet hush came over the room and someone switched the lights off. Lorraine, Morgan, and Genna came down the hall from the kitchen, all carrying homemade cakes with enough candles to light the room, and Connor prompted everyone. "Happy birthday to you…".

Colleen led Vicky to the middle of the sofa and the three cakes were placed on the coffee table in front of him.

He gazed curiously at Morgan. "Three?"

She beamed proudly. "For past missed birthdays." Genna chimed. "Besides, we didn't know what kind of cake you like."

Morgan pointed to the white iced. "This one is chocolate."

Genna opened her hand over hers. "This one is vanilla with chocolate icing, obviously."

Lorraine continued the love. "And this one is spice cake with cream cheese icing." She raised her brow. "It's my favorite."

"Blow out the candles already!"

Someone else yelled. "Keep it dry."

He took the prompt and blew the candles out to everyone's cheer. "Speech! Speech!"

He smiled passively, pretending he didn't want the attention and someone yelled, "You know you want to."

He stood, instantly energized. "If you all insist."

Someone yelled. "Excellent speech! Short and sweet."

He glared. "Smart ass." Then looked around. "First, I want you to all know I was devastated earlier. You all got me good, and I love all of you, but damn," He motioned to everyone. "...you got me."

"Second," He scanned the room. "where are my mothers?"

Connor called out with his arm raised, pointing down. "Right here."

Vicky placed his hand on his heart. "To my adopted moms." He wiped his eyes. "I prayed for you. I prayed for any one of you. And one would have been my greatest prayer answered. Three? Three moms? It's unbelievable! I love you. Thank you for adopting me."

Tears flowed down his cheeks as he made his way to them and they to him. Someone yelled, "Tissues. Tissues up front!"

The three cakes disappeared with the moms. Minutes later, plates of cake and ice cream made their way around the room.

Connor held the outer side door as Genna entered their house with a quarter of a birthday cake on her platter. He shut and locked the door behind him as she slid the plate onto the counter. "That was a blast."

He stood there as she covered the cake, obviously wanting to reminisce about the evening. "It was, wasn't it?"

"Those kids are so..." His eyes narrowed as he searched for the word. "...loving. They're so loving toward each other."

He paused in thought, "Even Stephie." then held his hand out. "Wait. That came out wrong." He stood there as she walked toward their bedroom, then followed her. "I mean, even Stephie's more comfortable and loving than she's ever been." The pitch of his voice rose. "Have you noticed how loving she is now? She's come alive since she decided who she is."

Genna sat on the edge of their bed and grimaced as she gingerly removed her shoes. "I've noticed, and it's wonderful. She's happier than I ever remember seeing her."

He laughed softly. "She was bopping around the entire night, having a blast."

Genna continued rubbing her foot. "And I love the way her and Vicky treat each other. She loves him."

"I love him. He's an impressive young man." He headed into the bathroom. "And Jake's right. I think he is the glue holding that group together."

Genna leaned back. "I think he assembled them …and he finds additional strays."

He stepped back into the room. "Stephie was a stray he adopted."

She gasped. "She was never a stray."

"Not physically, but there's a chance she was emotionally and mentally. But he didn't know when he found her."

Her eyes widened. "Oh my god, you're right. He knew Steven was a girl before we did, so in a way, I guess she was. Oh how cute."

He pulled the covers down. "Have you ever seen her happier though?"

She chuckled. "No, and I'm thrilled she's finally happy. Who knew she'd have a completely different demeanor than Steven." She shook her head as she pulled the covers up, "I can only imagine the confusion she lived with for all those years." then leaned toward him and kissed him goodnight. "I need to remember to thank Vicky for taking care of her through her transition. He's adorable."

"Jake's funny too, isn't he? He's like an old man."

She rolled toward him and wrapped her arm around him. "He is. He thinks too deep sometimes. I think he carries certain problems of the world on his shoulders."

He ran his fingers through her hair. "He's trying to make the world right. I never knock a man who's willing to act, and not stay silent when things need fixing." He kissed her. "I'm proud of his mindset along those terms ...as long as he tempers the seriousness."

She cuddled closer. "I think he's fine. He has an old soul though."

"I don't think Stephie does." His voice rose. "Do you?"

She chuckled. "Who can tell? She's technically a brand new person; living ...discovering herself and the world from her new perspective."

"I never considered that." He kissed her. "Night sweetheart."

"I forgot to tell you. I have an appointment down the street from them Tuesday and I know Jake's working in the evening." She paused. "I'm going to see if I can spend the evening with my daughter."

"Sounds good to me. There's a basketball game on. I won't have to fight you for the remote. ...I may even have a beer."

"Perfect. Especially since I won't have to watch."

She stroked his hair. "...Do you remember discussing this possibility before we were introduced to Stephie? Do you remember me asking you if you'd be part of his ...her world, even if it was different than yours?"

She felt his short quick breath and affirming nod. "Yeah. I remember."

"I love how you honored your promise." She kissed him.

"I told you I have true love for our child, and her reaction proves it's the only thing a child counts on."

~~~

Genna walked out of her appointment and scanned the street as she usually did when she left this particular building. The street was quaint, with its brick townhouse businesses and residences, matching trees and decorative street lights for as far as the eye could see. She inhaled the clean crisp air. *What a beautiful college town.*

She descended the five steps to the sidewalk and hesitated. She knew how close she was to one of the most important people in her life, and she wanted to see her, but for Stephie's age, didn't want to inconvenience her or interfere with her normal day. She walked toward her parked car, then stopped, removed her phone from her purse and dialed. "Hi sweetheart."

"Hey mom."

"I'm in the neighborhood, mind if I stop by?"

"Not at all. Jake's working." Stephie's voice rose with eagerness. "Where are you?"

"At the account where I first saw you and Jake. I just finished my sales appointment."

"Come on over. I'm only sitting here watching TV."

"Are you sure?"

"Mom. You have to visit me now or I'll be upset."

Genna laughed lightly into the phone. "Well, since you put it that way. I wouldn't want to upset you. See you in a few minutes."

"Okay. Love you."

Stephie hung up, scanned the apartment, measuring its readiness for a guest and immediately began straightening the living room. They both kept the apartment clean, but their daily activity showed. She then made sure the bathroom was clean, replaced the hand towel, then moved across the hall and quickly washed the two dishes and single empty pan sitting in the sink.

The doorbell rang followed by a faint knock, and she quickly straightened the coats on the hooks at the top of their entrance stairs before heading down to the front door. "Coming."

She opened the door, "Hi mom." and kissed her. "This is too great."

She let Genna pass before locking the door behind them and following her up the stairs.

Genna hesitated half way up. "Are you sure I'm not bothering you?"

"Mom." Her response filled with playful exasperation.

Genna handed her a brown paper bag covered bottle and Stephie knew immediately what it was. "When did you stop and buy this?" She pulled the bottle of white wine from its wrapping.

"I had it in the trunk. I was hoping…"

Stephie smiled and hugged her. "You can visit anytime."

Genna hung her coat as Stephie headed toward the kitchen. "I'm respecting your privacy."

"Well don't. You're my mom." She popped the cork and filled two glasses, then rejoined Genna in the living room.

She sat at the other end of the sofa and raised her glass. Genna clinked her glass and they each took a sip. "This is nice." She watched Genna scan the living room. "This place really is quaint and cute."

"We think so." Stephie shook her head. "I still can't believe Nana did this for us." She glanced around the room, then inhaled deeply. "It's one of the greatest gifts…"

She lowered her glass onto the coffee table in front of her. "I'm actually glad you stopped by." Stephie sat back, turning toward her mother.

"Why is that sweetheart?"

"I've been thinking about Colleen. I'm trying to understand her situation better." Her back straightened and her enthusiasm increased. "Want to stay for dinner? Would dad mind?"

Genna chuckled. "Mind I'm spending an evening with my daughter?" Her smile twisted. "I'm not sure he'll be alright, but I'm sure he won't mind."

Stephie laughed. "I promise I won't tell him you said that."

"He'd say the same thing." Genna reached for her closest hand. "Hey, want to go to the Cajun restaurant we went to, for dinner? My treat."

"No." Her eyes met her mother's. "I want you all to myself. I'll fix something or we'll order a pizza or something."

Genna smiled and raised her drink. "To our first girls' night alone."

Stephie clinked her glass again. "I'll drink to that."

Genna lowered her wine to the coffee table and reached for Stephie's hand. "So what's on your mind?"

Stephie's eyes narrowed. "Colleen."

"What about her?"

"I'm curious why her father can't accept her; why parents abandon their own children." Her eyes widened. "Oh my god. Vicky's parents too. How could I have forgotten that?" She breathed deep. "Mom, how hard was it to see me like this? Did it upset you a lot? Was it devastating?" She offered a contorted half-smirk. "Please be honest …brutally honest. I need to understand."

Genna's eyes widened and she rubbed the back of her hands as if they were cold. "My main emotion was my disappointment in myself." Her eyes narrowed in concentration. "I failed you."

"Oh god mom, just the opposite!"

Genna inhaled slowly and deeply. "No sweetheart. I failed you to that point." She faced Stephie, frowning slightly. "Now I know how little it matters whether you're a boy or a girl. Hell, half of the paradigm is nothing more than a social construct. Infants in the hospital receive blue or pink blankets. Two years later, trucks or dolls." She softly shook her head. "It's pathetic, and for the most part it's harmless, but not completely. ...Completely mindless but not completely harmless."

Stephie tilted her head. "But why do you think you failed?"

Genna stared into her eyes. "Because I never told you how little it mattered what you are. I skipped that message and it turns out that message was most important in your life." Her eyes widened as she offered an apologetic smile. "I failed."

Stephie leaned across the sofa and hugged her. "You didn't fail at all. You were sensational."

Genna wiped her eye. "After the fact, and that's arguable ...semantics; we'll go there later. What I know I didn't do, was offer you support without you asking for it. ...Sitting you down and letting you know how little what you are matters and how, who you are, is everything. I waited too long to share that." Stephie watched Genna reach for her hand. "I waited way too long ...and I'm sorry."

Stephie inhaled deeply. "Oh god no, mom. I could always see and feel your love for me."

Genna pointed to the center of Stephie's chest. "You have a good heart ...quick to forgive."

"Mom, there's nothing to forgive."

"I'll prove it to you." Genna tilted her head. "Did you wish through your transition, you could tell us but hesitated for fear of our reaction?"

"Of course, but that's natural." The tone of her voice defending Genna.

Genna breathed deep. "See; we didn't convince you early enough of our unconditional relationship." Genna lovingly slid her hand down Stephie's cheek. "You just confirmed."

"If you failed, then what do you call what Colleen's and Vicky's parents did?" She tilted her head, making her point.

Genna snickered softly. "I love you."

She smiled and stared deeply into her mother's eyes; her voice echoing the years of tenderness her mother conveyed from as far back as she could remember. "…that's all that counts. You don't have to be perfect." Her voice lightened. "Look at me." She ran the back of her hand down her chest. "I'm the definition of imperfect, and you love me. Do you really think you have to be perfect for me to think you are?"

Genna slid closer to her and they hugged as Genna whispered in her ear. "I didn't know I needed that but damn, I needed that."

Genna sipped her wine, then placed her hands on her thighs. "Okay, let's get down to business." She inhaled. "Colleen. But before we discuss her situation, I have one more question. Why did you have such a hard time telling me who you were – when you know I …your father …your grandmother love you with all our hearts?"

"I'm glad you asked." Stephie's smile grew by the moment. "I thought about that more than any other part of the revealing, and I finally came up with the answer, and ever since I did I've wanted to tell you." She hopped with excitement. "The reason is; because I love you and wanted to be everything you wanted me to be, including some things I only guessed you wanted me to be. I was afraid I would disappoint you and I wanted to delay disappointing you for as long as I could. I didn't want to be anything but perfect in your eyes because you love me." Her brows rose as her head tilted.

"Tell me you didn't feel the same way to Nana and Pop ...I dare you."

Genna slapped her thigh lightly and her entire countenance brightened. "You think that much of your father and me?"

She held out her hand "Mom, what do you think?" then lifted Genna's glass as she stood. She glanced back as she walked toward the kitchen. "This is fun!"

Genna's melodic reply followed her. "It is, isn't it?"

Stephie placed the two filled glasses on the coffee table. "Can I order a pizza?"

"Absolutely."

She finished ordering, laid her phone on the table and then looked seriously into Genna's eyes. "Okay. Colleen."

Genna inhaled noticeably. "What about her?"

"First, why do you think Colleen's father or Vicky's parents can't accept them? Why do you think they aren't interested in hearing proof that people like us are natural and have been around forever ...everywhere?" Stephie tilted her head curiously. "How could you dad and nana accept me and Jake, and they won't even consider it?"

Genna shook her head softly. "Oh sweetheart. The answer is complicated."

"What's complicated about loving your child?" Her eyes narrowed and she could feel her breathing quicken and become shallow. "What could possibly make a parent throw away their own child?" She could feel her frustration building. "...for *any* reason?"

She sighed as she stared deeper into Genna's eyes. "People don't throw away their child if they have a disease. They don't if they're born with a birth defect or handicap." Her eyes narrowed. "Yet they do if the child is lgbt." She inhaled. "Is lgbt worse than all those things?"

Genna looked down as her eyes welled. "The closer you are to situations and experiences like this, the harder it is to rationalize some of the insensitive human reactions." Genna's brows raised in confusion. "It's hard to rationalize irrational actions. All the attempt seems to do is frustrate and exhaust."

"I mean, Colleen is absolutely sweet and kind. She isn't pressing charges against her father, who's been beating her ever since discovering who she is. He kidnapped her, mom." She pleaded with her eyes. "Who does that? What normal person does that?"

Genna's eyes widened. "I don't know what to tell you. It makes no more sense to me than it does you."

"Oh, and she's not pressing charges against the two guys in the little food store, because she's known them her whole life and she thinks of them as part of her family." She lowered her chin and shook her head.

Genna softly stroked Stephanie's hair. "Oh child."

Stephie inhaled. "I'm sorry. I didn't mean to upset you."

Genna did her best to offer a smile. "I understand your confusion. Believe me, I understand." She met her eyes. "Well, we don't need a reason to drink, but it's nice to know we have one."

Stephie laughed, making Genna chuckle lightly.

A heavy knock on the entrance door interrupted them.

Stephie stood quickly. "Pizza delivery man!"

Genna met her eyes. "Ever have a delivery man fantasy?"

"Mom!"

Genna rose and headed toward the steps in front of her. "...pay him some other way, instead of money?"

"Mom!"

Stephie followed her mother to the bottom of the steps and watched her open the door. An old sweaty guy held out a box. "Fifteen seventy five."

Genna glanced at her as she held out a twenty. "We'll pay for this one with cash."

"Mom!"

Genna handed him a twenty, "Keep the change." then laughed as she shut the door.

"Mom!"

"Oh relax. I'm completely screwing with you." She motioned Stephie to lead back up the stairs. "I've decided dad and I are finished raising you and I want to be best friends for the rest of our lives. Share secrets. Be bad together." Genna raised her tone. "Is that alright?"

Stephie turned to her at the top of the stairs. "Oh mom, I would love that."

Her mother smiled deeply. "So would I."

# Chapter Twelve
## Reflection

The morning was lazy; routine in a comfortable way as the semester's workload came under control. Stephie excused herself after sharing their normal weekday morning ritual of casual conversation and multiple mugs of coffee, with books open in front of them.

She re-entered the living room, sat in front of her pile of books, and pretended to refocus on the information, though she had a completely different activity in mind. She impatiently delayed her plan, trying to increase the surprise but was afraid the intensity of her own breathing would raise Jake's suspicion, and decided to act before she gave her intentions away. She closed the textbook on her lap, and placed it gently on the coffee table, before leaning toward Jake and shutting his.

"Hey. What'd you do that for?" Jake squinted in confusion.

She took the book from Jake's hand without answering, dropped it to the floor, and straddled him. "You know what we haven't done in a long time?"

Jake slid his hand over her soft blouse covered chest. "I can think of a few things we've done recently."

She interlocked her fingers with his, and attempted to pin them to the wall behind the sofa, producing a smile matching the one she wore.

He leaned forward, trying to kiss her and she leaned back, twisting her head away from him; producing a quick giggle at the play hostility. He lightheartedly forced his arms around her waist. "I thought you quit trying to wrestle me, since I always kick your ass."

She pulled at him, trying to force him to the floor. "You never won and you know it."

He twisted as he carefully rolled off the sofa, and landed on his back with her safely in his arms; but the move still frightened her. "Jake!"

She watched him pause for a moment, as she struggled to gain control of his hands. "You're getting weaker." He let her pin them to the floor next to his head, as she sat on his chest.

He smiled at her declaration. "Think so?" He reached an arm behind her shoulder and gently forced her mouth to his. After sighing with complete submission, she broke the kiss. "I know so." She swung her hair away from her eyes. "I've been winning our wrestling matches lately and you know it."

He laughed. "You couldn't be more wrong, because I've been extremely happy with the results for years now, every time we *wrestle*."

She struggled against him as he brought her mouth to his. "Hey! No kissing. You're not supposed to kiss your wrestling opponent."

"But I love kissing my wrestling opponent."

She paused. "And how long have you wanted to kiss your wrestling opponent?"

"Ever since eleventh grade."

She gasped as her eyes widened. "What?"

He laughed softly. "I wouldn't have minded if we accidentally kissed back then. I look back and wish it had happened." He let out a soft snort. "I wanted to go to the prom with you."

Her breathing widened his eyes. "Are you alright?"

"Jake!" She sung his name in disbelief.

"What?"

"Do you have *any* idea how bad I wanted to be your date prom night? ...What I would have given?" Her chin lowered and eyes glazed as her face twisted in defeat.

He tilted his head to meet her eyes. "No. Really?" He moved her down his stomach far enough to sit up, with her now in his embrace, and the consolation in his heart echoed in his voice. "I had no idea. I didn't even think we were close back then."

She inhaled deeply. "Why do you think I stopped doing things with you?"

"I thought you were getting tired of me or we had different interests."

She smiled innocently and stroked his hair. "No. What we had was the start of me realizing I was in love with you and every time I saw you with another girl, I got depressed."

She watched his pleasant reaction and began play choking him. "Enjoying that fact, are we?"

He leaned over and tickled her neck with his mouth, then sung, "You loved me."

She fought futilely against him and sighed as his words brought back memories of hopelessness. "You're an ass." She pushed his shoulders and he let her have the upper position.

"I have a secret too." His uncontrollable grin broadened. "I wanted to go somewhere with you prom night but I didn't know how to word it so I quit trying to figure it out."

Her eyes widened. "What?"

"Not like a date, but I thought about going to the movies or doing something together." His face contorted into a smirk. "Then Gabrielle asked me and I didn't know what else to say." He shrugged, then the smirk turned into a smile. "I imagined making out with you while I was kissing her. I used to fantasize about you …if you know what I mean."

Her mouth dropped open as her breathing increased. "You used to think about doing things with me, in high school?" He laughed. "Hell yeah. Why do you think I always wanted to wrestle you?"

She sat proudly on his chest. "Ha! I loved you but you *lusted* for me?" She wiggled her bottom on his chest. "I win!"

He laughed and grabbed her ass with one hand as he placed the other on her back and brought her mouth down to his. "As long as I get to have this …you can declare yourself the winner of everything between us." He rolled her over and smiled as his voice turned playfully confident. "But we both know I'm still the wrestling champion between us."

She squirmed under him. "Wanna bet?"

His eyes widened. "Hell yeah."

She forced him to let her up without saying a word, then ran toward their room. "Don't come in here."

He rolled on his side. "I won't."

Moments later, she reappeared wearing the white babydoll nightie and matching lace thigh highs she wore their first night together and he immediately stood, then reached for her but she pushed his hands away. "Oh no."

He laughed. "I take it our wrestling match isn't over?"

She teasingly taunted him, "Correct." then fluffed her hair and pranced in front of him. "And I'm raising my game a notch."

He sighed as he examined her, from her lace covered toes to her soft brown eyes. "I notice."

She slowly slid the back of her hand down her outfit. "And I'm going to make you declare me the winner of all time."

He raised his hands laughing and blurted out, "I quit. You win. You're the champion of all time!"

She held up a finger and waved it at him. "Oh no mister. You're not getting off that easy." She spun and hurried back into their room. "Forgot something."

She pulled the comforter off their bed and drug it to the living room. He immediately helped her lay it out on the floor, then stood facing her. His eyes met hers but he pointed to her hips. "I see you don't have panties on." He lowered his eyes. "…and you're all ready to wrestle."

She tried to stifle her giggle and pointed back. "I see you are too."

He swung his arm like a gentleman. "Shall we begin?"

They stepped onto the comforter and she attacked him; wrapping her arms around his neck and shoulders. "Yes!" But he didn't budge.

She struggled for another moment. "You suck."

He giggled. "That's exactly what I'm thinking." He inhaled, then lifted her and gently laid her on the comforter, "goddamn Steph." his breathing increasing with every passing moment. "You're fucking sexy."

She slid her arms tenderly around his neck and whispered, "What were your high school fantasies about me?"

His open mouth met hers and she melted at the feel of his soft delicious tongue. Their kiss broke and he immediately smiled. "One was, I wanted to kiss you, which you already know." He inhaled, then softly exhaled shaking his head. "I wanted to kiss you more than I ever wanted to kiss any girl."

They rolled side by side and she stared deeply into his eyes as their faces almost touched. "What else?"

He slid his hand softly over the side of her face, spreading his fingers and letting her hair slide between them. "I used to fantasize about your eyes. Your eyes are unbelievably sexy."

She felt his breathing increase. "And?"

His brows lowered. "Ever notice me staring into your eyes as we make love?" He slid his hand around to her exposed bottom. "And when you stare at me...how I explode?" He inhaled deeply.

"And?" She cuddled against him.

"No. You tell me a secret."

She inhaled. "When we were younger, I wanted to wear girl's clothes for you and play boyfriend and girlfriend. When we wrestled sometimes, I used to pretend we were doing more."

He let out a single snort. "I did too." He moved his other hand to her bottom and softly gripped her with both hands. "And I always wanted to play with this."

Her voice rose. "Always?"

His voice lowered. "...always."

"Even when I was a boy?"

"You were always feminine, and this was always nice."

Her eyes momentarily narrowed. "You always liked me being feminine?"

"I've liked you for a long time, so I'm not sure I used that more as an excuse to combat the confusion I had about my sexuality or not, but I don't question it anymore." His eyebrows rose as he tilted his head. "Especially since I've proven to myself how natural and normal we are." He paused a moment in thought. "But I know

I'm more attracted to feminine than I am to masculine, yet I'm more attracted to you than I am to cis girls."

"I don't know who I'm attracted to" She energized. "...but I love every masculine part of you." She straightened in his arms. "I always wanted to explore you."

He tickled her waist, then rolled her on top of him. "Damn. We could have gone out since we were twelve."

She looked at him curiously, "We kind of did." then hit him on the shoulder. "Except for the times you cheated on me in high school."

"Well I was handsome and popular. It was only natural." He flinched at the incoming reaction.

She pushed him back, "You're an idiot." and he moved her until she was straddling his shoulders and close to his mouth. He pulled her forward a bit more, opened his mouth, and began adoring her. She arched back as her breathing went immediately into overdrive. "Oh Jake!"

~~~

Colleen parked the car in front of Lorraine's house and took a deep breath. She had no idea why Vicky, Stephie, and Jake all insisted she meet with her. She was friendly and obviously smart, but still a stranger. She sighed. This visit was strictly in honor of the respect and trust she had for her new friends. They had rescued her more than once and she owed them, but she couldn't help feeling intimidated. Reminiscing about the dinner party she enjoyed here a few weeks earlier had produced an instant fondness for Lorraine though, but for all the turmoil her situation had always caused, she expected only disappointing news from even those who wished her well.

She shut off the car and focused on the gently curving street and the houses lining it. Everything was so different than where her family lived. Each house seemed like half the size of the entire row of houses in her neighborhood, and the trees surrounding each house made the entire picture, elegant.

She took a breath and exited the car. Lights lined the winding walkway to the front entrance and the light above the door gave the entryway a majestic glow. She knocked and moments later, Lorraine opened the door with a soft welcoming smile and softer voice. "Hi Colleen. I'm glad you came. Thank you."

The thank you raised her curiosity, though she tried to project the grace she was being shown. "Thank you for inviting me." She hugged the elder woman with respect.

Lorraine took her hand "Come in, come in." and walked her to the family room and the already lit fireplace. She paused then smiled at her. "Let's get a small glass of wine before we sit. Thank you for visiting. I've prepared a simple dinner."

Lorraine continued to the kitchen. A bottle of red and white wine sat on a side counter, with two glasses placed stylishly, though she was sure it was more her perception than by design.

"Red or white, dear?"

"A little white, please?"

Lorraine met her eyes and smiled softly, then poured a different wine in each glass. Colleen accepted the glass Lorraine presented. "Thank you."

Lorraine gently squeezed Colleen's other hand. "You're very welcome."

Colleen followed her into the family room and sat in the loveseat as Lorraine placed her glass on the end table and sat on the sofa, with her arm gracefully resting on a corner pillow.

Colleen studied the room. "Your house is beautiful."

"Thank you. I think so too." She reached for her glass. "Every room holds so many memories, I hesitate to leave, but I'm afraid it's now too big for me to maintain." Lorraine scanned the room. "But I'm not ready to move out yet." She set her glass down. "It reminds me of the gifted life I've lived and the wonderful marriage I had."

Her statement struck Colleen deeper than expected and she stammered with her response. "How long have you lived here?"

Lorraine smiled softly and met her eyes. "Not yet long enough, which is why I've invited you here tonight." She leaned forward and folded her hands on her lap. "I don't want you to respond to my next thought. I have a habit of thinking out loud, and to be honest with you, those thoughts are equally divided between clever and crazy, and I'm not always able to put them in their correct category until after they're shared." Her eyes widened. "May I share my latest thought with you?"

Colleen swallowed hard. Her immediate thought; *I'm scared but how could I refuse?* She hesitated, "Sure." then watched Lorraine breathe deep.

Lorraine's voice softened. "It's always difficult sharing things prematurely with someone you hope will be a close friend, but there are times in our lives, when timing doesn't cooperate as fully as we would hope, don't you agree?"

Colleen nodded softly, then looked down. "I couldn't agree more."

Lorraine straightened in her seat. "I'm happy you agree."

Colleen watched Lorraine move closer to the arm of her sofa and place her hand on Colleen's folded hands resting on her lap. "I want to make you a selfish offer, and I don't want you to answer right away. Many things would have to be discussed before I would accept an answer, anyway." Lorraine moved her focus from Colleen's hands to her eyes. "Understand?"

Colleen responded immediately. "Yes ma'am."

Lorraine instantly smiled and shook her head. "You make me very pleased." She met Colleen's eyes with raised brows. "I want to offer you an extended invite into my house." Lorraine breathed deep, her hand still resting on Colleen's folded hands. "You would have the privileges of the entire house, the privacy someone your age deserves and needs, and the love and hopeful relationship of an adopted grandmother who can share life's experiences in ways I hope will benefit you."

She felt her eyes widen and her breathing deepen, and swallowed hard as Lorraine continued. "But it's by no means a gift. It's instead, what my late husband and I used to call; a win win opportunity, though the timing is less than perfect."

Lorraine reached for her wine. "You in turn would allow me to have someone to care for on a daily basis, someone to talk to …to get to know and someone I can share things. You can help me with cooking and silly things like changing a lightbulb. I'm now wobbly, two steps up a step stool." Lorraine sipped her wine and continued. "And we'll work out all the complicated things we need to work out as we progress, openly, as equals. We'd also have to agree we would need to be able to share expectations out loud without assumptions."

Lorraine placed her glass on the coffee table and met her eyes. "But there is something I'd like to strongly insist on." She watched Lorraine breathe deep and her face turn serious. "Your continued education."

Colleen watched Lorraine register her reaction and nod affirmatively. "Oh, I'll be paying for your associate's degree from the local community college. We won't discuss your bachelor's degree until then, but this is non-negotiable. No child of mine is starting adulthood without at least some level of college degree."

She stared at Lorraine through glassy eyes. "Why would you offer me so much. I have nothing to offer back."

She watched Lorraine's expression soften. "You may not understand for years, but you'll offer me more than you realize. Oh, there's another thing I'd like to demand." A soft smile appeared. "I demand we become friends who care for each other. I'm not your disciplinarian. You're a grown young woman now. You know right from wrong. I'd rather be your friend; an older friend who has passed potholes you haven't come to yet, but a friend like your other friends who don't judge you and only accept you."

Colleen breathed deep. "I know you want me to think about this, but how can I say no? I don't have anywhere else to go and I can't continue being in Vicky's way."

Lorraine raised her glass. "Then may we assume this is an idea worth considering seriously?" She sipped her wine. "I told you it has the potential to be a win win situation, but considering our friendship, the offer is premature."

Colleen lifted her glass. "But how would I ever pay you back?"

Lorraine placed her glass down and tilted her head. "There is no payback. You'll pay this forward, if the opportunity presents itself. Oh, I'm also not expecting you to be my nurse. I'll live with my daughter when that need comes to pass."

Lorraine extended her glass, prompting her to reach for hers. They clinked softly and Lorraine offered. "To deeper friendships."

She sighed. "To deeper friendships."

Lorraine swirled the last drops of wine in her glass then eyed Colleen with a more devious smile. "Join me in the kitchen for another small glass, while I make sure dinner is alright?"

Colleen stood, "Sure." then raised her nose and inhaled. "It smells like heaven."

"Thank you dear." Lorraine led them to the kitchen. "I hear positive things about your cooking skills too. We're going to have to exchange recipes."

Colleen hopped with excitement at the thought. "Oh, I would love that."

She motioned her to the stove and lifted the lid off the simmering pot. "This is my grandmother's scallopine recipe. If you like peppers, this is heaven."

She leaned closer and inhaled the complex aroma. "I make stuffed poblano peppers... oh I have to make them for you."

They ate and shared the evening, enjoying light and casual conversation, until Colleen's eyes narrowed and her smile momentarily disappeared. "Are you sure you want to do what you're saying ...with me?"

Lorraine took Colleen's hands in hers and met her eyes. "I've never been more certain of anything. I'm guessing your opportunities have been limited. All I'm trying to do is redirect your path, so opportunities can present themselves as they do for others."

Silent tears dropped from her eyes and she wiped her face quickly with her palms. "I'm sorry."

Lorraine's eyes welled and she pulled tissues from the box under the end table between them. "For what?" She handed her a tissue.

"For crying."

Lorraine shook her head. "Don't ever be sorry for showing your emotions. Emotions take guts. They show your heart."

Colleen wiped her eyes, then glanced at her phone. "It's getting late. I should go."

Lorraine stood and took her hand. "Take your time and let me know your decision."

Colleen glanced at her as they walked to the front door. "Oh, I thought you already knew my decision. Yes. My decision is yes. This is a fantastic choice," She lowered her head. "even if I have no other choices."

She felt her brows rise as she hesitated asking the next question. "…When?"

"That's up to you. …It can be as soon as this weekend, but if that's too soon, we can make it your convenience."

Colleen studied the two story foyer. "I get to live here?"

"If you want."

She hugged Lorraine softly. "Thank you."

Lorraine softly stroked the back of her hair. "It's my pleasure."

They ended their hug and Lorraine opened the door. "Be careful driving home."

"I will."

~~~

Stephie walked to a quaint table covered in muted sunlight, sat with her back to the massive wall of floor to ceiling library windows, and sighed as she scanned the almost empty expanse, waiting for Jake. The last two years had been intense and busy, but the accomplishment made every anxiety before every exam …every anguish handing in every paper …well worth it. She smiled. This was going to be her alma mater for the rest of her life, and she couldn't be more pleased.

*I wonder if mom ever sat here working?* Her brow lowered. *Why haven't I ever asked her?* She shook her head, then straightened in the hard cloth chair and smiled. They had something new in common now. They were both graduates of the same college. *Oh, I hope we play dad's college in something. We'd have to watch together …and gang up on him!*

She caught herself tapping her foot and getting more impatient as the minutes lingered, then searched her bag for something to occupy her increasingly impatient mind. She reached for her phone and dialed. "Hi Nana."

"Hi Cipolline. How are you?"

"I'm good. How are you?"

"Content. You're graduating college and planning your wedding and it's making the entire family atmosphere festive. It's fun isn't it?"

"It really is." She paused a second. "Nana, can I ask you for something?"

"Oh dearest child, you can always ask me for something …and rarely do." Lorraine paused. "What can I do for you?"

"I want to ask Colleen to be in my wedding, but I know she can't afford a dress."

"That's a wonderful idea, cipolline, but I already had plans to buy her dress. It'll just be a bridesmaid's dress now."

"Wow. I didn't know. Thank you."

Lorraine chuckled into the phone. "You're welcome dear."

Stephie's voice rose with excitement. "You're coming dress shopping for me with mom and mom H, aren't you?"

"Of course I am."

"Great. Oh. Vicky's coming too, so it's all of us and Colleen."

"Perfect. Let me know when."

"I will Nana. I love you."

"I love you too, dear."

She hung up and sighed, then continued tapping her foot impatiently as she stared at the door she knew Jake would enter. She popped up and beamed at the sight of him, and let out a greeting way too loud for the location. "Jake!"

He walked to her slowly as she rushed to him, then dropped his shoulders. "Am I done?"

She hugged his neck and hopped excitedly. "Yes, you're done. We're both done. Isn't it fantastic?"

"I feel more relieved than happy." He quickly kissed her hello, then took her hand and led her toward the door.

"So how are we celebrating this time?"

He glanced at her and grinned. "We're sleeping late, then spending the day in bed together."

She jumped excitedly in front of him "Are we gonna make love and sleep all day?"

He grabbed her around the waist with one arm and playfully squeezed her. "Absolutely. ...Until we pass out. ...What do you think?"

She wrapped her arms around his neck and kissed him. "Perfect!"

They headed down the path toward their apartment, with Stephie bouncing instead of walking. She softly sung his name. "Jake."

He sung his response. "What?"

"What are we doing tonight?" She hopped in front of him and walked backward.

"Be careful." He reached for her as he adjusted his backpack on his shoulder. "I don't know. What do you want to do?"

She skipped backward and sung her reply, "I dunno." and grabbed his arm as she spun forward. She hopped again, as she lightheartedly looked up at him. "How come we're so bad at this?"

His brows lowered as he met her eyes. "So bad at what?"

"Celebrating." Her brows lowered and eyes narrowed as she continually peeked at him. "We really suck at it, you know."

He slid his hand over her skirt covered bottom and caressed a handful. "I kinda like how we don't need to."

Her head tilted as she glanced at him. "I never thought of it like that."

She walked a few more steps, then swung his arm. "Can we call our moms and dads and see if anyone wants to meet us for sushi?"

He grinned. "Sure. Sounds like fun."

She ended the second call as he hung his jacket on the hook at the top of the stairs. "Yay! We're all getting sushi." Her eyes widened and she made another call. "Nana?"

She smiled at Jake as she heard her reply. "We're officially done school." She followed Jake into their bedroom. "All six of us are going for sushi to celebrate. Will you come with us? We'll come get you."

She waved for Jake's attention and jumped slightly. "Yes."

She smiled at Jake. "See you around six." then paused for a moment. "Love you too."

She raised her arm in triumph, "Yes." then grinned at him. "We're all celebrating."

Her phone beeped and she read the text, then quickly typed a reply and hit send. "They're bringing the sake and beer."

Jake followed Stephie and Lorraine into the restaurant, and then to the table Connor and Genna occupied. "Hi."

"Hi everyone." Morgan walked up behind them and wrapped her arm around Jake's waist. "You're done? You have a bachelor's degree?"

His grin widened as he turned toward her. "Yeah mom. Can you believe it?"

She stepped in front of him and pulled his face down to hers. "I've never been more proud."

"Thanks mom. It hasn't totally sunk in. I mean, it seemed like a big deal when we finished high school, but not as big a deal now. I can't explain it. We kept plodding along and then we were done."

She caressed his face. "Well I think your degree is a big deal. ...A very big deal. And I'm very proud of both of you."

"Thanks Mom H." Stephie's voice caught her attention. She let Jake go and embraced her. "I hugged you years ago and declared you the most wonderful person in the whole world for your offer to help him with college, and I still think you are. Part of his degree is because of you. Thank you."

"He did all the work himself. I just supplied some company."

Jake reached for her hand. "I wouldn't have done this without you, and the fact you went to community college so we could go together is something you absolutely get credit for."

She grinned as they finished their greetings and sat down. "Then I have a confession." She faced Jake and reached for his hand after he sat, but shared with everyone. "Jake, I suggested community college together because I was in love with you and the idea we may be separating scared me to death."

Connor laughed. "That's funny! You mean, you were a manipulating woman before any of us knew?"

"Dad!"

"Oh no, sweetheart. You don't understand how I mean it. You staked out your man and claimed him, then educated him? You're my hero ...and more like your mother than I'll share."

Everyone laughed as Genna smacked him on his arm and Stephie blushed crimson. Connor rose, maneuvered around the table and gave her a deep kiss, then caressed her face tenderly. "I love you more than you'll ever understand."

They ordered appetizers, and Stephie lifted the plastic bag she carried in, onto her lap after they clinked glasses and had a drink. "I have something I want to share before we start eating and drinking." She reached into the bag and took out the first shirt; school colors with a picture of the mascot over the word *alumni*. She studied the tag. "This one's Morgan's but don't worry. You all get one."

Chris stood as he received his and pulled it over his shirt. He ran his hands over the front, "I love it." then met Stephie's eyes. "So what are your plans from here?"

"Jake has an internship and doesn't want to do any more school, though he may have to for whatever company he works for, but I want my master's degree." She looked at Lorraine with raised eyebrows.

Lorraine softly smiled. "Our deal is our deal…" She chuckled, "…and I like how you're using the opportunity to your full advantage. Well done." She held her sake toward Stephie, then sipped. "I personally think you need an advanced degree to get where you want nowadays."

Jake reached for a soybean. "We don't have a problem taking care of as much of the cost as you want though. We think we can handle it and we're not looking to bankrupt you."

Lorraine chuckled. "Oh dear …not to worry."

Genna motioned for Stephie's attention. "Where are you going?"

"Right there." She pointed to Chris's chest. "Close to my family. Besides, I like the commute. And we have a wedding to finish planning."

Connor lowered his beer and smiled at Jake. "Looks like she's planned out the immediate future for the two of you."

Jake smiled back with a mouthful. "That's completely fine with me."

# Chapter Thirteen
## Trepidation

Colleen gazed into the mirror on Vicky's bedroom closet door and straightened her dress for the hundredth time, then realized all she's been doing is wiping her hands down the front and sides. She purposefully held her arms next to her and stepped closer to the mirror, examining the make-up Vicky applied. For the few times Vicky made her up, she felt different than when she tried, then realized the difference was as much the caring conversation as it was Vicky's ability.

Vicky' talented results didn't help her nervousness though. A second date? She often daydreamed about a first date, but never considered a boy might want a second one. She raised her head toward the ceiling, sighed and wondered if cis girls felt like this before a date. She smiled in the mirror. Of course they did. She heard them talk in school, remembering listening secretly to conversations she yearned to join. There were things as different as possible, but there were things about being a girl, she imagined were exactly the same as every other female.

Her thoughts quickly moved to Cody, and she remembered how comfortable she was as they sat in the car during their first date. Her thoughts then wandered to him letting her sleep in his bed after rescuing her and wondered if he'd join her the next time. She frowned, then felt embarrassed by what he'd think of her naked and the pleasant thought ended. She sighed, turning so she could see her skirt covered rear in the mirror, hoping it was as feminine as she'd like to think, then remembered his scent on his pillow and the secret joy, smelling it all night had been.

*Not bad.* Her hand on her hip helped accentuate the view. Cody seemed to like what he saw. The thought he liked her enough to ask her out again produced another smile and allowed her to daydream about being intimate with him. *I wonder if I'll ever sleep on his pillow again.* The trauma leading to that first time experience suddenly connected to the thought and she quickly and purposefully ended the stream of thoughts.

She glanced at the mirror one last time in passing, and nervously exited the room. She heard Cody's voice as she approached the living room and it brought an instant smile, and suddenly her delay getting ready made no sense in her mind. She reached for her hair as she appeared, "Hi." and felt her eyes widen as she met Cody's. He was definitely getting cuter each time she saw him.

"Hi." He stood straight as he faced her. She loved the nervousness he projected. It was exciting having a boy think she was special enough to cause him discomfort, and then felt a feminine certainty she could ease his nervousness any time she wanted. A quick fantasy how, entered her mind and produced a smile that seemed to ease his tension.

"Where you two headed?"

Cody's nerves reappeared instantly as he faced Vicky. "There's this really nice park down by the river I wanted to show her. There's a long walking path next to the water and a view of the bridge." He turned to her. "Is that okay? We don't have to."

She blushed as she realized how intimate that setting would be. "That sounds nice."

Vicky sat back, "Bring a jacket." then pointed to her shoes. "And more comfortable shoes."

Cody's focus intensified on her. "Are you sure?"

"It sounds perfect." She pictured them walking alone along the river, holding hands. She softened her stare and her smile. "Be right back."

She hurried back to the two bags holding her borrowed clothes and scrounged through. She knew there was a pair of flats and as she searched for them, remembered they were a little tight. She grabbed them anyway since it was easier to bring them than explain to Vicky she didn't have any that actually fit. She didn't bother looking for a jacket. She knew there wasn't one. *I have to look for a job.* She found a second blouse and folded it in a way that hid the fact it wasn't something she could wear over her outfit, then lifted the flats and headed back to Cody, extending her hand out to his as soon as he was back in sight. "Love you Vick. See you later."

"Be careful you two." He stood and followed them to the door. "And have fun."

Cody opened the car door for her again and gave her a warm feeling. The idea he was this polite made her feel like she could trust him. His every thought and action indicated true caring.

He glanced at her as he backed the car out. "How've you been?" The tone of his voice, just high enough to project his continued tenseness.

The sound of his voice broke her daze as the tone of his question secretly tickled her deep inside. "Good. You?"

"Good."

She became conscious of her own silence as they continued driving. Her thoughts were preoccupied with the chill the water would create, and she finally shared the concern. "This sounds like a nice way to spend time together, but I only have the clothes Stephie lent me and I don't have a jacket." She scrunched her face. "Do you have an extra shirt or jacket in the car maybe?"

He glanced at her and reached for her hand. "Yeah. I have something."

She immediately leaned back and relaxed. Moments later, she broke another brief pause. "This is nice."

"What?"

"Just driving …the two of us." She leaned against the headrest and turned her head toward him, watching him tense as her words registered.

"It is." He glanced at her. "I like being alone together." His words didn't quite match his demeanor, and the sudden awareness of the gap between the two began to feel confusing.

She watched his breathing increase. "I like your company too. Where is this place?"

"South a bit. Not too far from here." He offered her a hurried smile. "But let's make a quick stop first." He pulled into a local shopping center. "Is that okay?"

"Sure." Though the change in plan caused a slight concern.

He tensed as he parked, creating a transient dark thought and a sudden feeling of overwhelming insecurity, and without warning, the feeling produced a sentence she had no ability to stop. "You seem nervous around me. Is anything wrong?"

He hesitated shutting the car off. "I don't know why I'm nervous around you." His eyes widened. "I never had a girlfriend …and I like you."

She matched his apprehension. "Cody, I never had a boyfriend. But you don't have to be nervous when you're with me. I like you too."

He spun toward her too quickly. "Really? I mean …you're not just saying that, are you?"

"Cody. You're great." She leaned toward him, and then hesitated but he took her lead and softly kissed her. She opened her mouth and returned his kiss, and as the kiss extended, felt her heart melt.

Though the kiss offered him yet another confirmation, he tensed as it ended. "Can we be going out?"

She snickered softly, and secretly coveted his insecurities as fuel to quell hers. "I thought we already were." She stared softly into his eyes.

"You thought I was already your boyfriend?"

"Well yeah."

"Oh wow." The energy he projected, at hearing this bit of information, fed her soul. Someone wanted to be her boyfriend? …really *wanted* to be her boyfriend? How could that possibly be? Why? And then she thought; *stop questioning it.* The idea was a fantasy she wasn't sure would ever come true, let alone happen so naturally.

He smiled at her and pointed to the store. "Can we go in real quick?"

She decided to continue feeding his confidence. "Cody, I'll go wherever you want. I'm your girlfriend." The words sent goosebumps through her, she didn't expect. She meant them for his uncertainty, but they had an unexpectedly agreeable effect on her. *I'm his girlfriend.*

He reached for her as soon as she joined him behind the car, and held her hand until they were in the women's clothing section. She tried to follow him quietly, but her curiosity took over. "What are we doing?"

He breathed deep. "I'm buying my girl a jacket."

"Oh Cody, you don't have to."

His eyes widened. "What if I want to?"

"That's so sweet." She smiled softly and kissed him quickly, as an accompanying thought entered her mind. *I can't wait to give him something in return.*

He brightened, then started examining the jackets on the nearest rack. "What do you like?"

They shopped for a bit as he held jackets up for her inspection, and she examined each jacket's tag, trying to find the least expensive, using size as the excuse. She finally found a reasonable one and decided it was perfect, modeling two different sizes for him. "What do you think?"

He smiled. "I think you look beautiful." He took her hand and headed toward the cashiers. "I can't wait to show you this park."

They hurried back to the car. "I love my new jacket. Thank you!"

"I'm glad you like it."

She slid her hand down the front, then faced him from her seat. "You're the first person to ever buy me something like this." Her voice softened. "Something feminine."

He didn't offer a response, but his smile definitely grew. She held his hand until they could see the park from the road. "There it is." He pointed to the right as he drove past, then turned down a small side road.

"I never knew this was down here."

He filled with enthusiasm. "Wait till you see. I love it here."

"Is this where you bring all your girlfriends?" She teasingly raised her eyebrows.

He answered too seriously. "I never brought anyone here."

She teased more. "I love the idea I'm your first. I can't wait to do other firsts with you." She met his eyes and watched him turn a beautiful crimson. And as his face reddened, her heart beat with a pleasure so powerful, it shocked her. Did she really have the power she just witnessed? Could she really just tease him and see its reaction so obviously on his entire being? She exited the car quietly euphoric. At that moment, being a girl was everything she imagined.

They reached for each other's hand and she swung his arm teasingly. "There is one thing we already did that I hope I do again."

"Okay." He looked at her and she offered a playful smile, but no words.

His eyebrows rose. "What?"

"Sleeping in your bed." She studied him carefully as the right side of her mouth gave her playful enjoyment away.

He finished blushing but his breathing remained fast. "You know you're torturing me, don't you?"

She glanced at him. "A little …but maybe it's not just torture." She spun in front of him and placed her arms on his shoulders. "Maybe all I'm doing is sharing a nice thought." She pulled him closer, until their mouths met, and slowly opened her mouth, and as he followed her lead, her heart registered how exhilarating, being desired felt. When the kiss ended, she turned and they resumed their playful stroll along the river.

"This is so pretty. I love it." She swung their arms as they held hands.

"I like looking at the bridge. I like how the cars and trucks look small from here." His excitement grew. "I hope a ship comes. It's neat watching it go under."

She heard him breath in the cool air, as the water gently lapped against the gigantic black stones a few feet below. He pointed to the gulls sitting on the thick round timbers which were once a pier extending into the river. "I wish we could sit out there."

She shivered. "No thank you. I like the view from right here."

"Is your jacket warm?"

"It's perfect." She held her arms forward, inspecting it. "It's the most wonderful gift anyone ever bought me." She met his eyes, not expecting to see such a satisfied reaction on his face and her heart melted a little more.

"Let's sit." He pointed to one of the swinging benches facing the water, and she followed him hand in hand. She waited for him to sit, then moved close. "This place is beautiful."

He grinned and slid his arm around her shoulder, and she snuggled closer as he pushed with his feet, making the wood bench swing softly. They walked the path twice after sitting on the swing seat and as they approached his car, he glanced at her. "Wanna get a burger and fries?"

She smiled softly. "I'd love to."

They drove a short distance in the opposite direction. "Want to use the drive-through and go back to the park?"

"Yeah." Her heart jumped as she realized they would be in the car, alone after dinner. There were no other cars when they left and she anxiously waited until they were back in the secluded park. They ate and teased and she quietly hoped he had additional plans after dinner. The longer she spent with him, the more she wanted to explore other aspects of being a girl.

They each finished dinner, then sat back and stared at the river as the sun dropped in the sky, until she couldn't take the anticipation. "I wish we could cuddle." The front seats were separated just enough, they could kiss, but not lay together.

He sat straight and suggested the solution she hoped he would. "We can move the seats up and sit in the back."

She immediately reached for the seat latch on her side and he followed her prompt. They moved to the back bench seat where she immediately snuggled next to him. "This is nice."

He held her softly. "Very nice."

244

He didn't take long to meet her lips with his, and they slowly found the most comfortable position to continue exploring each other. She felt her heart and breathing steadily increase as she concentrated on his soft tongue eagerly exploring her mouth.

She unzipped her new jacket as they broke their kiss. "I love my new coat."

She lied. "It's nice and warm." She took his hand. "Feel how warm my chest is." She slowly and softly moved his hand until it covered her blouse and bra, and he quickly covered her mouth with his in response.

He softly caressed her blouse and bra and her heart melted in his grasp. The desire he projected was like nothing she had ever experienced. He leaned over her and kissed her neck, as he continued to caress her chest and she suddenly felt how much he was enjoying their new level of intimacy.

She didn't know why she didn't expect to feel the proof of his desire, but her breathing increased exponentially and she had to somehow acknowledge this new thrill. "I'm sorry I don't have more up top."

He lifted his mouth off her neck. "I love exactly what you have."

"You do?"

He pressed softly against her skirt covered thigh. "Yeah. You're unbelievably sexy."

Her breathing quickened. "I love *feeling* how much you think so."

He quickly moved his hips away from her, never moving his hand off her silk covered chest. "Sorry."

"For what?" She wrapped her arms around his neck. "I think you feel wonderful." Then as they kissed, she slid her hand from his neck, down over the proof she had felt against her thigh and his kiss paused as he registered her caress. She sighed in his mouth, pulling away just enough to whisper his name.

He inhaled forcefully as she caressed him, then held his breath as she undid the top button if his pants. "Can I show you how much I like my jacket …and you?"

He didn't respond with words, but his breathing told her explicitly. He tensed as she lowered his zipper, then breathed deep as she slipped her hand inside and caressed his warm hard flesh. And he pulled her mouth tight against his as she lovingly explored him.

She shut her eyes and momentarily focused on the prize in her hand, memorizing the warmth and girth of her new boyfriend. She squeezed and felt its exciting resistance; secretly marveling in its message, then noticed his breathing intensify to an almost startling level. "Is this alright?"

He made another sound but still failed to produce any words, so she met his eyes and watched his reactions to her exploration. "I like the way you show me you like me."

He slid his hand down to her lap and his eyes widened as he felt her enjoyment through her soft skirt. She smiled softly. "Are you okay with that?" He kissed her longer and more passionately than any previous kiss, as his hand slid under her skirt.

Lights from an approaching car crossed their side windows as it wound along the path cutting through the park, then slowed and lit their location as they hurriedly zipped things, and sat straight. The car pulled close and the front passenger window rolled down as they both read *Police* in dark green lettering against the white background on its side doors. The single driver positioned a lit flashlight on them as Cody rolled the back window down, "Park closes at sunset. Please exit." and they hurried into the front seats, quickly obeying.

They held hands and drove in silence from the park, until Cody finally spoke as they pulled into Vicky's apartment complex. "That was the best date…"

She smiled at his inability to end the sentence. "It really was."

He placed the car in park and eagerly kissed her goodbye, then watched her exit and hurry to Vicky's front door; turning and waiving before disappearing inside.

~~~

Colleen delayed telling Vicky about Lorraine's offer, for days. She just wasn't sure she could explain the proposal without sounding ungrateful or hurting him. She knew she was infringing on his life, but he seemed to truly enjoy their time together, and continuously made sure she knew how much he loved her cooking and cleaning. But she couldn't sleep on the sofa any longer, and waking up with him passing through was something she also needed to end. Was he her new brother? Absolutely in her mind. Was he the opposite gender? Though closer to her gender than most brothers and sisters could be, the answer was equally absolute.

She woke early. She knew his schedule. The beautiful work calendar she made, now hung on the kitchen wall next to the breakfast bar. He had a day shift today. Not too early, unless normal days started later than the average worker, as his did. She quietly dressed, made coffee and started breakfast; deciding a quick fried potato would be an appreciated addition this morning.

Something came over her as she sliced the potato; a feeling of melancholy, and it produced a long sigh. What a strange feeling. For as awkward as the living arrangements were, he never offered any emotional perception other than loving happiness she was in his life. She never had that before, and felt her heart sink, realizing how much she was afraid to lose their connection by moving out. A feeling she overstayed her welcome, directly countered the sense of closeness which existed for too short a time.

She bargained with her anxiety. *It isn't like I won't see him. He said we were brother and sister.* She tried to shake the emotion, and concentrate on his breakfast. Focusing on him definitely helped take her mind off her. She learned that trick recently, and it seemed to work most of the time.

"Hi sweetheart."

She smiled and immediately felt love for him. *My god ...he is my brother.* "Good morning Vick."

She snorted once discreetly, as she watched him sleepily pour his coffee. *Who else would have taken me in when my only other choice was the street?* "How'd you sleep?"

"I was out until I had a dream I smelled breakfast." He lowered his chin but kept his eyes on hers as he patted his stomach. "I *never* ate breakfasts like this until we found each other."

Her heart lifted. *See? Who else would word it that way?* She blurted out, "I love you. You really are my brother."

He stood next to her at the stove, gently pulled her head toward him, and kissed the side of her hair, "Your *older* brother." then his voice softened. "...and don't you forget it."

He leaned over her shoulder, watching her cook. "How was your date last night?"

His question immediately signaled the warm memory last night now held, and she glanced at him. "I had a great time." She turned with the utensil in her hand. "He treats me like I'm special ...like he's excited to be with me. He gets anxious... nervous..." She smiled as she refocused on his eggs. "He makes me feel like I dreamed of feeling when I dreamed of having a boyfriend."

He kissed the back of her hair before moving to the breakfast bar. "I love that he's in your life now. It's about time you caught a break."

She glanced at him as she cooked. "He bought me a jacket before we went to the park. I'll show you after breakfast."

"You go girl!" He snapped his fingers.

She slid his eggs onto a plate, then placed their plates on the breakfast bar. "Things are starting to change, but he's only one of the things that's happened to me lately." She watched him begin eating and couldn't wait any longer. "There's something I have to tell you."

He casually glanced at her like an older brother not concerned with the next sentence's depth. "You're not pregnant, are you?"

She giggled. "No!"

He fanned himself. "Thank goodness." He drug out the next sentence. "Then what?"

She breathed deep and his eyebrows rose as he watched. "Is everything alright?"

"Lorraine."

Vicky brightened. "Isn't it incredible?"

She felt her eyes widen. "You know about it?"

He sipped his coffee as he glanced at her. "She asked me permission."

He offered her an older brother smile for the confused look she exhibited, "I know..." then shoved a piece of bacon in his mouth. "...our adopted family is strange." His voice muffled as he chewed. "They think everyone's equal." He offered her a playful grin then held his arms out and shrugged. "Ever hear anything so bizarre?"

"Is it alright?" She tried to project the love and submissiveness she felt a loving older brother deserved.

He laughed softly. "Oh honey, how could it be anything but alright? You'll have your own room in a beautiful mansion. Besides …I know where she lives."

She shook her head more purposefully. "No. Not that part." She felt her emotions build. "Will you still love me the same way?" She blinked, holding back the tears.

He immediately stood, gently grabbed her off her stool before she was ready, and hugged her tight. He started to speak, but she interrupted his words. "I don't think I can live without your love now."

"Holy shit, Colleen." He pulled back to stare into her glassy eyes. "I've been told someone loves me, for the first times over the last few years, but *no one* ...*no one* has ever told me they need my love." His eyes widened. "You love me that much already?"

She hugged him and rested her head on his shoulder. "I can't tell you how much I don't want to lose what we have right now. …what you did for me." She wrapped her arms around his waist. "Do you know how much, what you did for me means to me?"

He continued holding her. "Wow, little sister. Wow."

He patted his eyes with his napkin as he sat back down. "So when's my little sister moving out?"

She sat and lifted her fork. "Is next Saturday okay since the barbeque is this weekend?" She feared his assumption; a date too close would mean she didn't appreciate his hospitality, but she hadn't had a decent night's sleep since moving in.

He smiled as he lovingly toyed with her hair. "You know it is. …I have to work though, since I'm taking off for the barbeque, so I won't be able to help you move."

"Vicky." She looked around. "I don't have anything to move."

He raised his eyebrows, then slowly motioned with his hand to the entire room. "You mean you're leaving me everything?"

She couldn't help but laugh and pointed to the sofa. "Even my bed."

He pulled her close, and kissed the side of her head.

~~~

Vicky opened the fridge and reached for a bottle of water. Their welcomed Saturday morning started lazier than the previous weekdays. "Are you coming with me today? I was thinking of leaving around eleven to go over and help." He uncapped the bottle and drank it down, then reached for one of the bananas on the counter. "Steph said her and Jake would probably be there around then."

Colleen sat up and met his eyes as he walked into the living room. "Oh I forgot to tell you. Cody's picking me up. I think he wants it to be a date. Do you mind?"

"I don't mind at all. How are you two getting along?"

Colleen sat back, met his eyes and grinned. "Good." Her mind wandered to the back seat of his car. "He's so cute."

"That's great and I'm so happy for you. When is he done college?"

"I think he has at least another year, but I'm not sure."

"Okay, I'm getting in the shower. You alright doing your make-up today?"

She eyed him as he stood. "I think so."

He skipped the first step and sung. "Gotta go get beautiful."

She raised her voice as he disappeared. "Will Jon be there today?"

"Yeah. Finally. His job hours suck."

A while later, Vicky came down the hall, interrupting Colleen's focus on the TV, and sung again. "Beautiful." He held the back of his hands under his chin. "Don't you think?"

She snapped out of her daze and brightened at the sound of his voice. "You're definitely beautiful."

"Oh girl, that's my favorite lie."

He walked to her, leaned over, and gave her a kiss. "I'll see you there." Glass bottles clinked as he grabbed the small carry bag off one of the kitchenette chairs. "I have your desert and drinks. Love you."

Her heart jumped as he shut the door behind him. Cody was coming and she hadn't seen him since their date. She registered a strange feeling in her chest, accompanying the thought lingering in her head. When would she have a chance to finish what she started in the back seat of his car? She jumped up and hurried to the bathroom. Time to get ready.

Stephie juggled the covered food container and grocery bag, before reaching for the outer kitchen door. "Hi."

Genna rushed to the door. "Let me get that."

"Thanks mom." Stephie handed her the plastic container with her desert offering, then placed the bag near the steps at the opening of the laundry room.

"Jake's here, right?"

"Yeah. He has chairs and things he's taking around back."

They hugged and kissed. "How are you sweetheart?"

"Good, mom."

"Hey, let me in." Stephie turned toward the voice, then hurried to the door. "Hi, dad." It was one of the first times she ever left off the first letter of Chris's last name. She knew there was precedent. Her mom always referred to her father's parents as mom and dad without additional delineation, but there was the slightest feeling of betrayal to her father deep inside her, which she couldn't explain. She made peace with the thought, knowing it would come easier as time passed, though no one deserved the title alongside her father, as much as Chris.

"Hi Steph. This is heavy." He moved quickly and dropped the large pot on the stove. "Hi Gen."

"Where's Mom?"

"Cooking next door." He motioned with his thumb as he kissed her.

The two families crossed their shared drives more times than they could count, as both houses rushed to prepare for the Memorial Day party and parade, and as the morning continued, others joined bearing gifts of food and drink. Connor lit the barbeque a while later and the party moved to the joined back yards. An hour later, someone called out. "We have fifteen minutes."

This holiday had been a dual family ritual for as long as they lived next to each other, mainly because the parade passed right in front of both houses. Everyone who witnessed the event thought it was well outdated, but something about its heritage was addicting. Guests made fun and joked during the entire procession, but everyone looked forward to the next one, come the end of May.

The small old fashioned parade passed between one and two thirty in the afternoon with fire engines, old cars, little league and cheerleading teams, local high school marching bands and color guards participating; all throwing penny candy at the people watching along the sidewalks. Little ones darted into the street for the candy that didn't reach the curb, and young and old sat, laughed and cheered each passing group.

Vicky danced with the festive lady clown pushing her shopping cart full of balloons, and everyone voiced disappointment as the last few township trucks followed behind, signaling the end of the parade. They gathered chairs and drinks as the street emptied and Jake offered a thought to anyone listening. "Steph and I were in this parade."

Vicky pointed to the street. "So was I."

"No. I'm serious." He glanced at Steph for confirmation. "Three or four years?"

Colleen stopped with two drinks in her hands as she followed Cody carrying their chairs. "For what?"

Jake laughed. "We were on the same little league team. But we didn't have a flatbed truck to ride in, like they did today. We walked …and it was long. I was tired when it was over." He smiled as he studied the neighborhood. "Great memories."

Stephie's eyes followed his down the empty street. "And one year I rode my bike …you didn't want to."

"Oh yeah. I forgot." Jake laughed. "I got way too old and cool to be riding a bike in a hokey parade."

Michaela folded the last remaining chair. "I'd ride my bike in next year's if they'd let me."

"That would be fantastic. We can put matching streamers on our handlebars and clothes-pin baseball cards to the spokes." Vicky extended his arms looking for agreement, "Oh, we have to see if we can." then thought for a moment. "I'd have to buy a bike."

Kaden stopped collecting the unclaimed candy in the street, and energized. "Why don't we? We could represent our lgbt club."

"I wonder how well that would go over?" Jake eyed Stephie but spoke loud enough for everyone remaining to hear.

Vicky held his arms out. "We sure would get an idea what our little town thought about our existence."

Michaela waved at Vicky. "Nah. I'm sure everyone would see it as just wholesome fun."

"We could only hope." Colleen's statement made everyone pause.

Dawn waited for the rest of the group to follow her to the back yard. "I feel like we went back in time about thirty years."

Jake nodded. "It's old fashioned americana and definitely worth seeing, isn't it? We do this every year."

The rest of Vicky, Jake, and Stephie's family and friends arrived over the next few hours and the party continued late into the night as glimmers of other back yard parties could be seen and heard throughout the neighborhood.

~~~

Connor sat at his desk, in the expansive and almost empty work area, concentrating between an open file and his computer screen, until the sudden movement and accompanying voice startled him. "Connor, I didn't know you were here. What're you doing here on a Sunday?"

"Hey Dan. My wife, mother-in-law and daughter are going out wedding dress shopping. I figured I'd come in and clean up some stuff." He glanced at his work friend leaning on the partition. "My daughter is engaged."

Dan straightened. "I didn't know you had a girl too. I thought you only had a son."

"So did we. Then we found out we were wrong all along. We only had a daughter."

Dan rested his arms on the cubicle partition. "How the hell did you get that wrong?" He teased. "Weren't there certain *signs*?"

Connor smiled. "Just the opposite. The physical signs indicated boy, but the rest of the signs ...the more subtle signs ...the more abundant signs, showed us she wasn't. But neither Genna nor I knew what we were really seeing so we just assumed he was different" He pushed away from his desk and spun the chair to face his co-worker. "…but we had no idea she wasn't okay with her gender. Then a couple of years ago, she told us …showed us who she was."

Dan scratched his head. "That's wild. I read about this stuff but I didn't know anyone who actually knew anyone. Was it hard?"

Connor straightened the papers in his open file folder, then looked up. "Reading the subtle signs? We saw things. We even discussed what we saw, but we had no real idea until she told us."

Dan disappeared below the partition, then wheeled a chair around to Connor. "No. I mean accepting him as a girl."

"Her. She's a female. And no, it wasn't hard accepting her. I love my child. If she tells me she's a female …then that's exactly who she is, and that's exactly who we see."

Dan leaned his chair back and folded his arms. "I don't know if I could accept my child changing sexes as calmly as you seem to."

Connor corrected softly. "Genders."

"Crazy."

"I think you would, but I guess it would be a blow to some people's ego. I decided to love my child instead." He felt the intellectual fine line he was walking, and knew it was always better to try to educate than admonish, but sometimes the closest acquaintances said inconsiderate things …accidentally. He concentrated on understanding some things said naively aren't personal, but instead, only a lack of forethought or knowledge.

Dan stood, then pushed the chair toward the cubicle it came from. "Wow. Well said." Dan extended his hand. "And I admire how you're handling it."

Connor shook his hand.

"I'm glad I don't have to deal with that though. It sounds complicated."

Connor inhaled and calmed, hearing the sudden change in Dan's viewpoint. "I appreciate your honesty, but I'm glad I did. My son wasn't comfortable or happy. My daughter is both. And the love we gave her seemed to alleviate the anxiety, simplify the complication, and enforce our love and acceptance."

"And she's getting married?"

"Yeah. January."

Dan tapped the top of the partition before heading away. "That's fantastic. Tell her I said congratulations."

"Thanks. I will."

~~~

"Mom?"

Genna rose as she heard Stephie knock on the open kitchen door. "C'mon in."

They met in the hallway entrance to the family room and kissed. "I'm glad you could come early."

"Are you kidding? I'm so excited I can't stand it. I was bouncing off the walls at home. Mom, I'm going wedding dress shopping!"

Lorraine stood as they entered the family room. "Nana!" She hurried into her grandmother's arms. "I didn't know you were here."

Lorraine kissed her, then caressed her face. "Hi cipolline."

Stephie hopped lightly as her grandmother released her. "I'm so excited!"

The more enthusiastic Stephanie appeared, the more Genna hesitated sharing what she hoped to share. She wanted the idea to be the best idea her daughter ever heard, but she didn't want to influence any decision or temper Stephie's enthusiasm, shopping for her own wedding gown.

"Are we meeting everyone here?"

"We're supposed to." Genna glanced at her watch. "But not for a while yet."

She patted the seat on the sofa next to her then took Stephie's hand as she approached. "Your grandmother and I want to offer you something, and I didn't know how or when to tell you." She shared a quirky grin. "Because I don't want to influence anything you have planned in your mind."

"What? Is everything alright?"

She patted Stephie's hand. "Everything's great. It's just..."

The unfinished sentence made Stephie's eyes narrow. "I don't understand."

Genna rose and held a finger toward her. "You will in a minute."

She motioned, letting her know she'd be right back, then quickly left the room. Moments later, she reappeared holding a large thick zippered plastic garment bag and watched Stephie's eyes widen. "This was your grandmother's and then mine. I wore your grandmother's wedding dress and if you want…" She paused as her emotions built. "…it could be one of your options."

Stephie stood and raised her hand to her mouth as her eyes moved from the garment bag to Genna's eyes. "Mom!"

Stephie covered her mouth with both hands as Genna reached for the top of the bag and slowly …carefully unzipped it, and Stephie helped her as they laid it on the coffee table and continued revealing the dress.

"This is the dress you were married in Nana?"

"Lorraine answered lovingly. "It sure is, dear."

Stephie caressed the garment delicately, as Genna finished opening the bag completely. "Oh, it's exquisite." She moved her arms, making the material flow off her hands, then met Genna's eyes. "Mom. This is your and Nana's dress?"

Genna walked to the curio cabinet and removed a wedding picture from each side of the top glass shelf, then walked back to her and held them out. "Yep."

Stephie stared at the pictures. "Oh Nana …it's gorgeous." She moved her focus to her mother. "I can wear it?"

Genna's eyebrows rose. "Can you wear it?" She inhaled noticeably. "Can it please be one of your choices? Would you consider it?"

"Oh my god, mom. Can it please?" She stared at the pictures and her voice lost some enthusiasm. "Will it fit me?" She pressed her hand to her chest. "Parts of me aren't quite in either of your league."

Lorraine chuckled. "You'd be surprised the secrets that help with those concerns." Her grin widened. "We can alter this. We can alter those." She waved her hand. "Not to worry."

Genna watched her stare at the pictures then narrow her eyes with concern. "What am I supposed to tell everyone today?"

"Oh no, sweetheart. Let's go out and gown shop. You never know what you'll find. Besides, it'll be nice spending the day together …just us girls."

Stephanie delicately slid her hand across the lace bodice. "I love how old fashioned it is." She traced the embroidery. "I love all the lace and beads."

Lorraine laughed, "Old fashioned?" then shrugged. "It is over fifty years old now, so I guess it is old fashioned."

Stephie straightened apologetically. "No. I mean it as a preferred thing." She met her grandmother's eyes. "I love old fashioned." She lifted the bottom half and felt the weight of the slippery silk. "And then it'll be the wedding gown for all the women in our family? I need to wear it."

"Well you don't need to if you find something you'd rather have."

"Yeah, right. Like anything could compare." She followed the playful sarcasm with an enthusiastic hug. "And you want me to wear it?" She turned to Lorraine before giving her mother a chance to answer. "You want me to too?"

Genna stroked the back of her hair. "I love the idea. It'll bring back wonderful memories, and stories."

Lorraine smiled. "Yeah." She reached for Stephie's hand. "Nothing would please me more than knowing the three of us wore the same gown on our special day."

She stood there shaking her head, staring at her mothers. "You really do see me as a girl, don't you?" She glanced quickly at her grandmother after asking.

"You are."

Her voice lowered. "There's no doubt in my mind."

"Nor ours, sweetheart."

Lorraine rose as a knock from the kitchen door echoed into the room. She smiled at her daughter and granddaughter, before heading to the kitchen. "Coming."

They all heard Morgan's voice. "It's only me."

Genna quickly gathered the gown, glanced at Stephie, and hurried toward her room as Stephie registered the unspoken message and walked toward the kitchen to offer her mother a few extra minutes to hide their new secret. She heard Morgan greet Lorraine, "Great to see you." and watched them embrace as she entered the kitchen.

"And you too," Morgan extended her arms toward Stephie, and they hugged and kissed, "I've been looking forward to today since we made the plans." She held her hand as they walked to the family room. "I love that I've known my future daughter-in-law since she was five. Oh! A true girl next door romance."

Stephie quipped, "Yeah, but not a typical one."

Morgan laughed as she reached for both her hands. "I've learned love is love, dear. Oh how I've learned, love is love."

# Chapter Fourteen
## Rejuvenation

Colleen jumped as she woke, and immediately realized what the rest of her day entailed. Her first thought; she would sleep in a normal bed tonight, and maybe not be as tired during the day. Her next was the idea everything else would also be new and different. Lorraine seemed as sweet and understanding as possible, but new and different was always unsettling.

She thought about the new house, and her room. Both were gorgeous. Then her thoughts wandered to her bedroom in her parents' house. It wasn't half as nice, but she wished she was sleeping there tonight, then realized *that* fantasy also had a loving father …and wasn't reality.

She stood and folded the comforter, as she had every morning, then placed it on the floor on the other side of the sofa. She then laid her pillow carefully on top, as she had for weeks, realizing it isn't where they went anymore, and the thought made her heart heavy. She hadn't had a full night's sleep her entire stay, but there was love here; love she would miss more than anything, and meant more than everything. She removed some tissues from the box on the floor next to the sofa and quickly dabbed her eyes, but realized she was alone. No one would see these tears.

Would it be wrong to ask Lorraine if she could visit Vicky tonight …maybe make them dinner? Would the request insult Lorraine on their first day together? Why did her life have so many short and strange endings to every real relationship she ever had? Always strange …always abrupt. She wondered how she and Cody would end …her and Lorraine.

She sat on the sofa, holding the tissues to her eyes, missing her mother, and even her father …wishing she could be what they had wanted her to be. She would trade who she was for their love. She tried to force that trade-off all her life; fighting and hiding who she is for exactly that reason.

She never meant him to discover her secret. She hoped to keep it from him, his entire life. *Damn. I should've done better.* She shook her head slowly, blaming herself for her situation; the uncertainty of everything, no real home, no real family, no real future.

She had delayed the inevitable as long as she could, and dialed Lorraine. "Hi."

"Hi Colleen."

"I'm ready."

"See you in a bit, dear."

She sat and caressed the sofa pillow. Vicky's sofa now meant more to her than it ever should. She slept and healed here. She slowly scanned the room, studying every nook, and sighed. Her final transformation occurred inside this apartment; Colin finally ending and Colleen finally born. But why did so many demand she remain the former? Did anyone ever share a reason? There had to be a reason, though she couldn't remember ever hearing one.

She lay back and stared at the ceiling before shutting her eyes, then quickly rose to gather the few things coming with her. She emptied the clothes in the two nylon bags Stephie lent her then meticulously refolded and restacked them inside.

The bathroom …the kitchen! She hurried to the kitchen, only to find everything cleaned and put away, then quickly rushed to the bathroom, but there was nothing to clean. She straightened the hand towel, when she heard the doorbell. "Coming."

She walked the two bags to the door, breathed deep and purposefully changed her demeanor before opening it. "Hi Lorraine." Her voice failed to greet her as pleasantly as she thought she deserved, and consciously lightened her mood. "It's great to see you."

Lorraine lovingly slid her cupped hand along the side of Colleen's face. "I know how you feel. Turmoil is never comfortable, is it dear?"

"No, it's just that..." She looked back at the living room and stopped talking, knowing the next few words would produce tears.

"It's alright dear. It's alright to show feelings." Lorraine's voice brightened. "It's another proof your heart is where it should be."

Colleen turned to her, studying her eyes, and Lorraine's face softened. "We can wait till you're ready."

Colleen's eyes widened and after a quick glance back and single deep breath, lifted the two clothes bags. "I'm ready."

Colleen checked the locked front door twice before continuing toward Lorraine's open car trunk. She loaded the clothes then as she shut the trunk, noticed the car keys in Lorraine's extended hand. "Do you mind dear?"

Her eyes widened. "I never drove anything like this."

"It's one of your new perks." Lorraine smiled wryly before moving toward the passenger door.

"I'm not driving this."

Lorraine laughed before ducking inside. "Well I'm not buying another car just for you."

Colleen sat beside her. "Lorraine!"

Lorraine raised her fingers. "Let's go have some wine together before our company arrives."

Colleen refocused. "Company?"

"I invited Vicky, Stephie and Jake tonight. We're having a small pasta party." She smiled softly as she pointed forward.

Colleen took her cue and headed toward the road. She hesitated before exiting the complex. "Left?"

"Yes dear." Lorraine's voice softened. "I want to play a game with you."

Colleen's voice rose. "What kind of game?"

Lorraine pointed. "Left at the third light. Did you ever hear of one called *twenty questions*?"

"I'm not sure. I think so."

Activity on the side of the road caught Lorraine's attention. "I love being a passenger in a car. You can enjoy watching life while sitting back and relaxing. Robert and I used to always take drives." She turned her head toward Colleen. "Did I ever mention my late husband's name to you?"

"No ma'am."

Lorraine reached over the middle console. "No formalities, young lady. You wouldn't call someone your age ma'am." She laughed, "…ma'am." then shook her head. "I must be old."

Colleen's voice rose. "But you have a lot of energy."

"People your age give me energy. I've been envisioning all the things I want to do and share with you." Lorraine raised a finger. "Back to twenty questions… Let's call this game *two thousand questions*. Hell, let's call it *two million questions*." She smiled wide. "I like it. Two million questions." She nodded as the words faded.

Colleen didn't respond and Lorraine pointed to the restaurant on the right. "They have delicious burgers and beer there. We have to go."

She didn't know if that meant right now, but she continued past without further mention, so she figured Lorraine meant in the future. "Okay, but I'm not old enough to drink."

"You're not allowed to be served at your age. You're allowed to drink. I drank controlled quantities of wine since I was twelve. Everyone above twelve drank wine during dinner on special occasions. Only a little, but we did."

Lorraine straightened. "The game." She faced Colleen. "You can ask me any question and I'll answer honestly, and if you want …when you're comfortable, I'll ask some too but you never have to answer at all or right away. No question forbidden. Ask in the detail and depth you need to ask. And neither of us is allowed to be offended by the question or the answer." She glanced at Lorraine who glanced back. "I want to get to know you …the real you. And I want you to know me." She felt Lorraine's soft hand grasp her forearm as it rested on the console. "Does that sound like an acceptable game?"

Colleen sighed. "It sounds amazing, but kind of scary if we have to be honest."

Lorraine laughed softly. "Just the opposite. The true honesty solicits proof we can love each other after we start to discover and share our faults and imperfections." Lorraine paused, then opened the sun roof. "I love looking at the sky when I'm riding along."

Lorraine changed her focus from the sky to Colleen as her voice turned playful. "Ask something …I dare you."

"I don't know what to ask." She glanced out the side driver window at the passenger in the next car, admiring theirs. "This is a fun car to drive."

"I'm glad you like it. We're sharing but I don't drive much anymore."

Lorraine casually inspected her nails. "We need to get our nails done, don't you think? Oh, we need to stop at the wine store." She laughed. "You're going to come in handier than I originally thought."

They drove quietly until Lorraine broke another momentary pause. "Okay …so far, you're really lousy at my new game." She snickered. "I was married forty six years, to the only man I ever thought was more impressive than any other man I ever met. He was an inch shorter than me. Hell, he was pretty short, but his aura made him six foot seven."

Soft silence followed but the open sunroof offered its noisy share of the life outside. "Genna's my only daughter. Stephie was my only grandchild until we adopted Vicky."

Colleen glanced at her and Lorraine placed her hand on Colleen's forearm. "He's the cutest thing, isn't he?"

"I love him." Colleen exhaled noticeably.

"You should."

"We adopted each other too." Colleen's voice confirmed the significance of her declaration.

Lorraine eyed her. "Seriously?"

"Very seriously. He's more of a brother and father than any of my blood relatives. He promised me we would be family for the rest of our lives."

Lorraine's voice turned serious. "Do you understand what you just did?"

"What did I do?" Colleen looked around, startled.

"You declared your place in our family. We adopted him. If you two adopted each other, you're my newest granddaughter. I'll kiss you hello when we get home."

"What do you mean?" She tensed as the wonderfully confusing words registered.

"When he adopted Stephie, he became part of our family. If you two also made a sincere pact, then you have more new family than you realize. Now I'm very glad I invited your brothers and sister over for a feast tonight. We're celebrating your adoption."

Tears filled Colleen's eyes. "How can you do that?"

"I'll explain in significant detail some night when we're bored and nothing's on TV, but for now understand; I have the power to love and accept, like I have the power to hate and exclude. I choose love and accept. It's easy. You'll see."

"Then I have a question for our game."

Lorraine smiled and met her eyes. "Go ahead."

Colleen breathed deep, glancing at her. "Why can't my own family love and accept me? Why does my father hate me?"

"Oh dearest, I'm sorry to inform you; some people choose law over love …over loved ones …even after another part of the law explicitly explains not to. We won't go into the law's legitimacy or who destroyed the law. Let's just say, everyone has different levels of wisdom and maturity, and some people can't comprehend the cosmic place we occupy. Some think this earth and this life are the beginning and the end, though their own God whispered otherwise." Lorraine patted her forearm. "But it's okay. See, the rest of us not only understand more, but understand we need to have patience with those who don't. They need our love and patience too."

Colleen shook her head and narrowed her eyes. "How do you think like that?"

Lorraine reached up and pressed a small button between the visors. "Age." She pointed. "Do you think you're alright pulling into the garage?"

"I think so."

"Just be careful and if you're not comfortable; stop."

269

Colleen creeped forward until the car stopped at the floor gauges. "Well done, dear. Welcome home."

Lorraine exited the car, then walked to the inside garage door and held it open. "So don't hate your father; feel sorry for him. Pray for him if you're inclined. …He chose poorly, but maybe because he's not yet mature enough to accept that lesson." Colleen followed Lorraine into the kitchen, listening intently to her soft but deep explanation. "Often, lessons are presented, but we're not forced to learn them. My belief is; it only means we have to live the lesson over, until we learn it."

"They're not having any more kids."

Lorraine whispered. "I know."

She dropped her head, "And I don't hate him. I love him." then she straightened. "I forgot my clothes …Stephie's clothes." She pointed toward the garage. "Can I?"

Lorraine's eyes widened as she lowered her chin, "Will you stop asking permission? You *live* here." then pointed to the bowl on a side counter. "I have another set of car keys. Those keys are yours. The other two keys on the ring are for the front door."

Colleen smiled to herself as she heard Lorraine continue the conversation from the kitchen as she re-entered the inside garage door. "Take your things upstairs and get your new room situated to your liking. Dinner will simmer until everyone gets here." She reached the kitchen opening and Lorraine turned with a wooden spoon in her hand and a pleasant smile on her face." When you come down, we'll open a bottle of wine and continue our game."

"Okay." She headed toward the foyer stairs and Lorraine's voice followed her one last time. "A phone. I'm adding a phone to my plan for you. We'll work out the details."

The feelings Colleen experienced as she climbed the stairs confused her. The love being shown was overwhelming, yet her reaction to it ...unexplainable. This lady offered her wisdom, knowledge, love, acceptance, family and home without cost, but this wasn't where she wanted to be. She wanted a less impressive family, with far less wisdom and knowledge, love and home.

She opened the door to the room Lorraine had designated during her last visit and the division continued. The room was stunning. The curtains on the two large windows matched the pastel colors on the bed, which perfectly complimented the walls, carpet and four matching pieces of furniture. She opened the closest drawer and it slid smoothly in her hand. She ran her fingers inside the empty box. How different than the single wobbly dresser in her tiny room at home.

The smell caught her attention. She scanned each outlet for an air freshener, but there weren't any. She shut her eyes, recalling the permeating old smell that couldn't be masked by the fresheners in her parents' house. Then she looked down and moved her shoe over the carpet. She removed her shoe, then quickly removed the other, worried she wasn't allowed to wear shoes on such a pristine carpet. Her toes wiggled and the carpet surrounded her bare foot.

She sat carefully on the bed. It would never fit in her old room. Then noticed the length and realized she could probably sleep without bending her legs. She slowly scanned the room, pausing a moment to examine the desk and pictured herself happily working there. Oh, maybe with music playing. *I could sit there for hours. I could stay in here for days!*

A faint knock interrupted her peaceful inspection.

"Colleen?"

She quickly rose and opened the door.

Lorraine stood without entering. "I figured I would share some *do's* and *don'ts* about your room. Is that okay?" She paused. "May I come in?"

Colleen backed up and responded quickly as if permission was understood. "Of course."

Lorraine entered, keeping her eyes on her. "Not of course. This is your room. Yes, I gave it to you, but because I gave it to you, you own it. And with ownership, at any age, but especially since you're older, there'll be times when entering is an infringement on your space and privacy." Lorraine tilted her head. "You're absolutely allowed to tell me I can't enter. Do you understand?"

Colleen inhaled as she placed her hand on her chest. "Sorry. I didn't have that choice at home."

"You have it now." The smile on Lorraine's face widened. "And I won't ever take the refusal personally. It doesn't mean you don't love me."

Lorraine watched Colleen's eyes widen. "I see every indication your past rules were governed by a strict and unquestionable hierarchy, and you're going to need time to understand I work on mutual love and caring; better words than respect ...the foundational words to respect." Lorraine took her hand and sat her on the bed, and Colleen watched her eyes turn serious. Lorraine pointed around the room. "I want you to put holes in every wall for the things you hang, have too many gadgets plugged into too many outlets, and flat surfaces cluttered so badly, the actual surface can't be seen. I know all the scuffmarks on each piece of furniture, and if you don't increase the number regularly, I'll come in here with a heavy object and we'll do it together ...and I better hear some music, decent or terrible, coming from the walls of this room and invading every other room in this house. Do you understand, young lady?"

Tears fell from Colleen's eyes and Lorraine opened her arms immediately. As they hugged tenderly, Lorraine whispered, "I'll explain the difference between punishment and discipline in due time. It'll help you understand better. For now, believe I love you for no reason whatsoever." Lorraine leaned away, making eye contact, then raised her hand and caressed her face. "Convince yourself immediately there's nothing you can do to change that fact. You can break my heart but you can't lose my love." She smiled softly. "I'll demand less and less as our relationship develops, but right now I demand you understand you're loved for no reason whatsoever. Not something you do or fail to do, but because I have the ability."

Lorraine rose, but didn't move away. "Now, how awful is it to have so much of something wonderful; you want nothing to do with?"

Colleen looked up quickly. "How do you know that?"

"Love, dear. Love lets one see many things, hate and indifference block." Lorraine walked to the door. "Love also revealed you weren't comfortable sharing the idea this wasn't all just positive. Love hopes you'll share those things in the future, but also understands you would be worried I would be hurt, which hopefully is your way of saying you're starting to love me back."

Colleen inhaled and sighed as Lorraine softly shut the door behind her.

She lifted the covers and crawled under. *This is crazy.* She sighed and shut her eyes.

After an unmeasured time, she awoke to Vicky's voice following the knock on her door. "You in there little sister?"

Colleen jumped out of bed and ran to her new brother, opening the door fast. "Vicky!" She wrapped her arms around his neck, squeezing him tight.

"Yo girl, let me breathe!" He squeezed her and kissed her neck.

"I needed you tonight."

"I'm here little girl. I'll always be here for you." He lifted her off the ground. "Let me see my baby sister's fancy new room."

She took his hand and drug him inside. "Damn! Look at this shit."

Colleen's voice lowered. "It's beautiful, isn't it?"

Colleen straightened the comforter and noticed Stephie as she knocked on the open door. "Hi."

"Hi. Come on in."

"Hi, other little sister!" He snapped his fingers. "You look spectacular."

Vicky tapped his foot waiting for his two sisters to finish hugging, then hugged and kissed Stephie. He separated without letting her go. "Will you look at those eyes. Damn girl, your eyes could melt steel." He eyed Colleen as he held Stephie. "I'm not done teaching you how to do this." He waved his arm at her. "You're getting better, but you're not done learning."

Stephie immediately defended her. "She hasn't been a full time girl as long as me."

He stepped back. "Dang! Are my two sisters already teaming up on me?"

Stephie smiled at Colleen and nodded toward him. "Great idea!" then attacked him, making him fall back onto the bed. She glanced at Colleen. "Come on, help me!"

They each playfully tried to pin down one of his arms, but he wrapped one arm around each and squeezed them.

Stephie yelled, "Vicky!" as Colleen laughed.

He released them and they sat on the bed.

Stephie quickly glanced around. "I loved sleeping over in this room."

"You used to sleep here?"

274

"Yeah. This was my mom's room growing up."

"Wow."

Jake yelled from the bottom of the steps. "Hey! Can we move the party down here?"

Vicky yelled, "We're having a girls' night." then covered his mouth with one hand as he pointed to his two sisters with the other. "Ah! How funny is that? The three of us ...*girls' night!*"

They giggled at him, more out of love than any other reason

He took their hands and walked them to the stairs, followed them down, then held their hands at the bottom of the stairs and made a playfully flamboyant entrance into the family room. "Me and my two new sisters in my grandmother's house." He smiled wide. "I'm in heaven!"

Lorraine laughed and stretched her arms out. "Me and my grandchildren in my house. You spending time with me is *my* definition of heaven."

Vicky raised his arms, still holding their hands, "Yeah." then went to her and hugged her. "This is fabulous."

They laughed and gabbed through the feast, then moved the party into the family room without interruption. Jake lit the fire he built as the others prepared dinner, and casual conversation filled the remainder of the evening. Finally everyone said their goodbyes while Colleen stood with Lorraine at the front door and waited for her to finish waving. Lorraine shut and locked the door before turning to her new housemate, raising her eyebrows.

Colleen shook her head softly. "I can't believe you invited them for me." She smiled wide and extended her arms.

Lorraine embraced her. "I promise it'll only get better."

"Good night." She lifted the three bags of clothes, lying in the foyer.

Lorraine eyed the bags, then met her eyes. "What are they?"

"Stephie's helping me with clothes, till I get a job. Most of them are too small, but there's a few I can wear." She straightened. "I'm looking for a job, immediately."

Lorraine shut all but the stairway and upper hall lights off. "I'm sorry. I forgot to tell you; you have a three week vacation to get used to living here, during which you get an allowance. You can start looking after that ...but not until. There are more important things to take care of." Lorraine motioned her upstairs. "You can also charge four hundred dollars on my credit card for clothes, not counting your phone. We'll make a date to get your phone too, but we have to go there together." She walked toward a different bedroom.

"That's all so much."

Lorraine paused at her bedroom door. "I don't go into a plan without working it through in my mind. I knew what I was offering, even if you didn't." Lorraine smiled softly. "Good night dear."

"Good night."

~~~

Lorraine opened her bedroom door the next morning to the smells and sounds of kitchen activity and immediately smiled. Her decision was a tough and complicated one, but everything she had observed about Colleen, let her believe the invitation not only was a necessary decision, but the right one. She threw her robe on and wandered down to the kitchen and before she could offer a morning greeting, Colleen turned from the stove. "I found your bacon and eggs." She hesitatingly pointed to the bacon frying. "I hope.."

Lorraine raised her fingers and tilted her head with a loving scorn. "Don't you dare." She walked to the coffee machine "Good morning dear." and removed a cup from the cabinet above.

"Good morning."

"How'd you sleep?"

"I don't think I moved all night." Colleen glanced at the bacon.

Lorraine watched Colleen discreetly as she fixed her coffee. "I love the smell of breakfast." She sipped, "Delicious." then sat at the table. "Vicky said you were cooking him fat."

Colleen raised her head. "I love him."

"I know, and I see how he loves you. And it happened fast."

Colleen turned as her eyes narrowed. "Loving someone is a choice, isn't it?"

Lorraine casually sipped her coffee, but hid the sigh Colleen's words produced. The more she saw inside Colleen, the more that question hurt. *How could anyone not see how beautiful this child is?*

Colleen checked the cooking bacon, then faced Lorraine. "I texted Stephie about all you offered last night. She wants to take me clothes shopping today. Is that okay?"

Lorraine wrapped both hands around her coffee mug as it rested on the table. "Oh that's wonderful."

"A little overwhelming, actually. I never bought clothes…"

Lorraine listened to the sentence end before completion and decided it best to let the comment fade without response. "Tell her I said she can have a hundred too. But there's a cost. I want pictures of both of you with shopping bags in your hands. Deal?"

"Deal." Colleen laid the last piece of cooked bacon on the paper towel then lifted an egg. "How do you like your eggs?"

"Two over easy, please."

Lorraine sipped her coffee after she finished, then gently pushed her plate away. "That was delicious."

Colleen projected the pleasure of a true cook. "Thanks."

"Don't worry about the dishes. I'll do them."

"Oh no. Not today. And I call that job as mine." Colleen grinned playfully.

Lorraine looked up, smiling at her tone. "Thanks. But I can do them too if I feel like."

The doorbell rang roughly an hour later and Lorraine instantly realized there was a benefit to Colleen's accepted invitation, she hadn't considered. She was not only going to see her grandchildren more, but also be more in touch with their everyday lives.

She rose with an unexpected cheerfulness, and called up the stairs as she entered the foyer. "I'll get it."

"Thanks."

She opened the door. "Hi cipolline."

"Hi nana! How are you?"

"Oh, very happy. Colleen made me a beautiful breakfast and pot of coffee this morning, then did all the dishes for me."

They hugged. "Last night was special too."

"It was." Lorraine took Stephie's hand and walked her to the family room. "Can I get you something?"

Stephie grinned. "I'm not a guest here. I'll get myself a water." She headed toward the kitchen. "Want anything?"

Lorraine laughed. "No you're not. And no, I don't want anything."

Colleen walked in as Stephie reappeared. "Hi."

"Hi." Stephie hugged and kissed her. "This is going to be fun! I never had a girlfriend to shop with."

Lorraine softly corrected. "Or sister."

Stephie amended. "Or sister." She held Colleen's hand and paused. "Need anything from the store?"

Lorraine smiled at the sight of her two children standing hand in hand. "No. Just go out and enjoy yourselves."

"Thanks nana. We will."

"Oh, I told Colleen she has four hundred dollars to spend. And you can spend a hundred too. But don't worry about a few dollars."

"Thanks."

"You're welcome."

"Thank you."

"You're welcome too, dear." She kissed both, then followed them to the front door.

Stephie hit the key fob as they walked away from the house, and the car chirped.

"Nice car."

Stephie opened her door as she watched Colleen walk to the other side. "Thanks. It was my grandfather Robert's. Nana gave it to me and Jake on our twenty first birthdays."

"Wow."

"Wait till you get to know her. She's amazing." Steph smiled as she started the car.

"I already think she's amazing ...overwhelming even." Colleen spun after buckling in. "I don't mean in a bad way."

"Relax." Stephie waved the concern away. "I know exactly what you mean. She's caring and loving, but she's absolutely overwhelming."

Stephie glanced at her after a brief pause. "Do you know anything about her?"

"Not really, but she said I can ask her anything I want, no matter how bizarre or personal."

"Then I'll let her tell her story, but you're gonna be amazed." Stephie glanced at her, "Ask her about her restaurant, or where she's traveled to. They're great stories." then reached for her closest hand over the center console. "I love doing this with you. I finally have a girl like me to talk to. I mean …a girl *just* like me."

Colleen's eyes widened as she turned in her seat. "I know what you mean. I never met anyone like me and I was sure I never would. Especially when I was younger. I was different from everyone I met. Then I started getting beaten and I didn't know what to do."

"I can't imagine. That sounds scary. But I wasn't scared as much as I was confused. I had bullies all my life but I wasn't beaten by someone who's supposed to love me, so I can only imagine how horrible that was. Feeling like I did was confusing enough."

Colleen sighed. "It was devastating and I had no idea what to do or when it would end." Her voice relaxed. "But maybe it's over. We're right here, together." Colleen glanced at her. "And here's a pretty nice place to start the rest of my life."

"Wow. You can do that?" Stephie's head tilted. "You can look at everything that's happened and see how all those things led to here and now?"

"Not as much as the words say, but don't we have to? Besides, it helps me start to accept what's happened."

"Yeah, but do you understand what you said? Jake's totally into psychology and you just said something he's been saying out loud for years."

Colleen's eyes widened. "Vicky told me those words, and told me to repeat them out loud when I need to, but it's easier said than done."

"I have to ask Vicky where he heard them. I wonder if it was Jake."

Stephie pulled into a small shopping center and headed toward the discount store on the end. "Let's take a look in here first. We can get more for our money, and right now, more is better than nicer." She offered a twisted smile and shoulder shrug. "Though I'm not sure that was english."

"I agree, english or not." Colleen matched her playful shrug.

They walked together through the double glass door entryway and the lady behind the large return counter facing the entrance did a double take, then stared. They walked toward the female clothing and out of her hearing distance and for the first time in her life, Stephanie felt like an older sister, disheartened for her sibling, by the fleeting ...demeaning event. "Are you okay with that?" She gave Colleen the slightest head gesture toward the counter behind them. Sharing yet another uninvited experience in an existence where the lessons are either overabundant, or nonexistent.

Colleen glanced briefly, then stared straight ahead. "What choice do we have?"

They wondered to the middle of the clothing section, where they could be inconspicuous as well as shop and both forcefully buried another demeaning encounter deeply in their psyches.

"This might be cute on." Stephie held a casual denim dress. "Oh, I heard you and Cody went on another date."

"How'd you know that?" Colleen reached for the dress and examined it.

"Vicky and I text ...often." She glanced at Colleen. "Do you like him?"

"Steph, he so cute it's unbelievable." She excitedly faced her new sister. "He bought me this jacket."

"Wow." Stephanie touched the sleeve, admiring it. "...Rescued you. Let you sleep in his bed. Buying you clothes. Wow."

"Tell me about it." She pushed the dresses apart for a better view.

The sudden silence and lack of movement caught Stephie's attention. She looked up with heightened concern and noticed Colleen staring down with narrowed eyes. "You alright?"

"Yeah." She met Stephie's stare. "Why...?" A deep breath and exhale followed. "Why does he keep doing things for me?"

"He obviously likes you ...a lot."

"I know." A momentary pause passed before Colleen finished the thought. "How? Does he really understand? Do you think he'll be upset when he really sees the difference?"

Stephie pulled another dress from the rack and quickly returned it. "I used to wonder the same things about Jake and I'd get sick thinking there's no way our deeper relationship could happen, and if it did ...could last. I'd get so sick I couldn't do anything, and then I'd see him and realize all the worries were worth every moment together, so eventually I stopped trying to figure out why." Stephie continued the thought as they moved to another large round rack of blouses and skirts. "But I know what you mean. But why does anybody like anybody? Maybe he's wondering the same thing about you."

They shopped until they each had enough things to try on, then headed toward the fitting rooms. Colleen offered the thought suddenly going through Stephie's mind.

"I wonder if we're allowed."

With curious confusion, the lady guarding the fitting room handed them plastic number signs and let them pass, and they took stalls next to each other. After rustling silence and soft commentary, they reappeared at the fitting room entrance and hung their discards on the appropriate rack. "Let me see what you have?" Colleen held the items for Stephie's scrutiny.

"Nice. I like this." She lifted the arm of one of the blouses, then raised her focus. "Want to take a look at their shoes?"

Colleen nodded, "Sure. We're here." and headed toward the back of the store. As they entered the shoe isle, she spotted a pair of flats and held them for further inspection before slipping them on, then looked down as she raised her foot for further inspection. "I needed these that night."

"They're cute. Where'd he take you?"

"To a beautiful park with a walking path and swinging benches along the river, and a view of the bridge. The date was very romantic. We got a burger, fries and sodas and parked for a while." She shared a soft smile. "I had a great time."

She repacked the shoes, placed her clothes on the box and faced Stephie, "I think I'm ready." then followed her new sister to the registers.

After paying, Stephie followed Colleen out of the store. "Did anyone ever tell you Vicky found me too? I never told you, did I?" Stephie's excitement rose. "We have so much to talk about."

Colleen stopped half way to the car. "Lorraine needs pictures." Stephie removed her phone from her purse and they stood together with their purchases and sent her a few pictures before placing things in the trunk and heading to the next store.

"Where to?"

"We might as well go to the mall and use Vicky's discount, don't you think? Oh, you need more shoes." She pointed to the solitary shoe store at the street side of the parking lot. "They're not the best quality, but they're reasonable."

"Okay."

A short time later, they walked from the second store with another bag and headed to the mall.

"Can we just go in his store? I know what door leads into the women's department and I'm not comfortable walking in the mall today. Sometimes I'm scared of running into certain kinds of people." Colleen's breathing quickened. "I'm sorry, but there's days when being gawked at like I'm a freak, takes its toll."

Stephie breathed deep. "No need to apologize to me. I understand …probably more than anybody." She shook her head softly. "No need to ever apologize to me."

Colleen offered a compromise. "If the mall isn't too crowded though, we can say hi to him."

They shopped inconspicuously while talking privately about common subjects and friends, and Stephie began noticing Colleen relax and worry less about those around them; making her more concerned. She knew her most devastating disheartenments came when she wasn't prepared for them. In fact, they were the rejections she remembered longest and cut deepest.

Colleen casually examined a cute blouse. "Do you know what I don't understand?"

Stephie's back straightened as she reached for a top, then paused for a second, hoping to project calmness. "What?"

"Cody and Jake." Colleen lowered the blouse in her hand as her eyes narrowed in Stephie's direction. "Are they gay, straight, or bi? I mean, do they like girls or guys? …I'm confused."

Stephie hung the top in her hand, back on the rack. "We have so much to teach you, it's unreal. We've been studying about ourselves for a while, and found a lot of answers, believe it or not."

Colleen met her eyes, waiting. "Jake started by taking a psychology class. Wait. Nana started sharing. Oh my god." Stephie's words slowed as she concentrated on the thought. "It was Nana."

Her demeanor brightened as she paused in thought. "Somewhere a few years ago, I think because of me; Nana started researching about girls like us. Then Jake seemed to come alive with each new bit of information she shared about me ...him ...all lgbt people, and he seemed to get stronger because of the information. Then he took over the learning and sharing after taking a few psychology courses. She still shares stuff, but he loves psychology. Remember the first time we all met at Lorraine's?"

"Sure."

"I don't expect you to remember the details, but those get-togethers are what we do now every once in a while to share new information." Stephie readjusted the clothes in her arms. "You're going to learn so much, you're going to be amazed." She started walking toward the fitting room as she glanced back. "But whatever you do, be careful asking Jake any questions. He doesn't shut up when it comes to this subject. He'll corner you and share so much information, you won't remember a thing."

The conversation paused as they stood in front of the attendant behind the beige counter inside the dressing room entrance, and the woman showed grace if not apathy, but few would understand how discomforting even these instances of casual classification were. They each took a tag from her and headed to adjoining stalls.

Colleen asked as she disappeared behind the stall door. "So, what are they?"

Stephie raised her voice to a loud whisper. "Well, like anything else, it's complicated. But because of Jake, I know more about the true answer than the average person. He did a psychology paper on it. Ready?"

"Sure. ...Can I show you this top?"

"Sure." Steph opened her stall door. "Oh I like that."

"Thanks. I can't believe I'm shopping for girl things and taking them home to an adult who doesn't have a problem." Her voice rose as she shut the stall door. "You have no idea how weird that feels right now."

"Tell me about it." Stephie remembered a quick flashback; trembling and crying at the deep need to wear things she thought were forbidden, then quickly refocused on Jake. He had become more of a leveling mechanism than he was at the beginning of her transition.

"Jake was always confused why everyone thought guys who liked transgender girls were gay. He believes he isn't gay in the way everyone perceives, and according to the definition, he's not. He isn't attracted to masculine and he's positive about that." She fixed her dress and gathered the clothes she brought in. "I'm done. Need my opinion on anything else?"

"Yeah. Hold on."

"Sure."

"Then what are they?"

"I know we're just talking between us and I know how much information you don't have yet, but I'll start by saying; if a guy is attracted to girls or people who are feminine, then they're more straight than gay and if a guy is attracted to guys or more masculine people, than he's less straight, by definition. Jake calls it *points on a continuum* …but what's the difference?" She paused for a second. "How he words it is; I'm a person who loves a person. He flat out doesn't care who likes it or who doesn't. …And he hates labels and categories. He thinks they show the mindset of seven year olds. Seriously, that's what he told me he learned in psychology. Seven year olds sort crayons by color, and get confused when a color fits two possibilities. Most grow past it by the time they're twelve, but not everyone."

Colleen opened the door and modeled her outfit.

"I love that on you."

Colleen smiled and shut the door. "Cody's straight?"

"I have no idea, but I probably wouldn't go that far, but not because I'm thinking like you. More because I never asked him if he's attracted to guys too, but people aren't either or. People are all different measures in between either or, but those attracted to us are closer to straight than gay. Think about it."

Stephie heard Colleen open her stall door, then heard her in front of Stephie's stall. "I think I understand ...I think."

"But there's more. Jake learned, less people are one hundred percent gay or straight, than anyone will admit, and certain people in psychology believe the actual percentage of people with some level of attraction to different people is far greater than anyone realizes. But our society prevents people from being honest about it."

Colleen led them from the dressing room and waited until they were away from the attendant. "But I hear stories of guys who've been caught with girls like us, denying they like girls like us."

"That's another peculiar bit of information. Jake says in past societies, people like us didn't have a stigma. They were even revered, and it was considered an honor to be their mate. But in our society, we have a stigma, so men who like us feel the need to be secretive about it."

"What society didn't we have a stigma in?"

"Older cultures; ones that have been around way longer than ours. Native Americans right here in this country was one. They called us two-spirited and we were often spiritual leaders. They understood we could relate to both genders, like a genderless spirit God. Neither cis men or cis women understand both." Stephie led them toward the store exit. "But now guys don't want to admit being attracted to us because they fear being labeled lgbt and worry about the accompanying circumstances, but a woman like us once told Jake; more married guys make passes at her, when they find out she's transgender, than any other group."

"We need more pictures for Lorraine." Colleen pulled out her phone. "Jake and Cody don't seem to have a problem letting anyone know they like us."

Stephie stopped behind their car and they posed before placing the bags in the trunk and Colleen took another picture of the open trunk before shutting it.

"They don't just admit liking us. They adamantly defend us." She shut her car door and started the car as she waited for Colleen to get situated. "I heard Cody yell at your father; She's a girl!" Steph buckled her seatbelt and tilted her head. "I mean, he was ready to fight your father over the point."

"Well he doesn't know how much of a girl I'm going to be with him when the time comes."

Stephie laughed. "Vicky really helped me with that too."

Colleen watched curiously for further explanation but Stephie didn't offer any. She just patted her new younger sister on her arm before wrapping her arm around the passenger seat and backing the car out of the parking spot. "So much to share."

Stephie turned onto the road toward home. "Want to go to lunch?"

"Yeah, but I'm not comfortable being in public today."

"I understand." Stephie reached for her closest hand. "You'll get there, I promise. You'll get there like I did …physically and emotionally. …I promise."

Stephie glanced at her as she drove her home. "Oh, we have a school lgbt meeting next Friday night at six thirty, at our apartment. It's not so much a meeting as it is a small party. You have to come with Cody from now on, or without him if he can't come."

"Will everybody be alright with me there?"

"Colleen, in our apartment? You're more invited in my apartment than friends. Besides, Vicky comes too."

"But is it a school thing? I won't be in the way?"

"It's an lgbt thing, and you're never in the way. We just happen to know most of them from school, except Vicky, Desmond, and a few others." Stephie eyed her like an older sister and commanded in the form of a question. "You're coming, right?"

Colleen smiled. "Okay."

Stephie softly sold the invite. "You have to. They're necessary for a bunch of reasons. They help us deal with the social beatings we each take regularly. They help us be in contact with those who understand, accept, and even care for us, and you know we need that." She pulled into Lorraine's driveway, placed the car in park, then leaned over the console and they hugged and kissed. "That was fun. We have to go shopping more."

Colleen sighed as the thought of another shopping trip produced two opposite emotions; enjoyment and friendship carrying the risk of humiliation and even physical harm if they ran into unfriendly or misunderstanding people. She played off any sign of the thought, so she wouldn't upset her new sister. "Yeah, but I think I need a nap. Everything is kind of overwhelming and I'm beat." She glanced at Stephie and hesitated.

"I understand." Stephie reached for her arm as Colleen reached for the door handle. "Oh, next time we'll discuss our sexual preferences and how they have nothing to do with our gender identification. That'll probably help you understand people like us, better too." She popped the trunk open from the driver seat. "Need any help with your things?"

"No. I can carry everything."

"Alright. Talk to you soon."

Colleen hesitated shutting the car door. "Do you want me to cook anything for the meeting?"

Stephie scrunched her nose. "Nah. We order pizza. Everybody brings their own drink though."

"Okay. ...Bye."

"Bye."

~~~

The mall was almost vacant, as it was most weekday mornings, which met Lorraine's shopping preference, and for her new persona, suited Colleen's self-consciousness perfectly. Colleen drove, as Lorraine requested when they travelled together, and she parked at the entrance closest to the phone store. She knew what stores were closest to what entrances, from her countless hours hiding in and around the gigantic building.

They still had to walk together inside the mall for a longer distance than comfortable, and all three people they passed, watched her uncomfortably. She pretended not to notice, though she glanced at Lorraine to see if she registered the looks.

Lorraine didn't acknowledge as they walked together. "Do you know much about the new smart phones?"

"Yeah, but I don't need anything fancy."

Lorraine softly clasped her hand as they entered the store. "Yes you do."

"Can I help you?" A gentleman in a tailored suit jacket appeared behind them as they browsed the displays and Lorraine answered immediately. "Yes. I'd like to add my granddaughter to my phone plan and buy her a new smart phone please."

The gentleman did a soft double-take and Colleen's heart jumped at the reaction she caused. The man quickly recovered from his initial reaction, then as quickly, offered an explanation of the displays around the store.

They listened to his opinion and Colleen tried a few, as Lorraine watched silently, until Lorraine decided she had enough information. "I think we'll take this one."

Colleen's head quickly rose. "Oh no. This one's great."

Lorraine smiled then looked at the salesperson. "Is this the newest one?"

"Yes ma'am."

"Then this is the one we want."

Colleen's eyes widened as the man quickly responded. "I'll be right back."

They watched the gentleman hurry to the back of the store and disappear through a metal door. And as she scanned the store's front entrance, Colleen watched Lorraine offer no acknowledgment or explanation to any of the reactions anyone had given her. They concluded their business and as Lorraine paid for everything, Colleen lost herself in the new gadget; quickly escaping the uncomfortable present reality.

Colleen roamed out to the mall walkway only to realize more potential confrontations were on that side of the store, and quickly stepped back inside as Lorraine finished the transaction. She stood inconspicuously in a display nook, examining the new device until Lorraine approached. "Ready dear?"

Colleen answered quickly, "Yes." then caught her haste and paused for a moment. She held the phone out. "Thank you."

"Thank me outside where there are less people." The message Lorraine's accompanying smile offered, sent relief through her. She *did* notice. It wasn't just her being overly sensitive.

Lorraine walked gracefully through the exit and toward their car as Colleen cradled her new device. "Do you like your new phone?"

She glanced up. "Very much. Thank you."

Lorraine smiled as she reached for the passenger door handle. "But you don't have to thank me at all."

"You might not think I have to, but I want to more than I can explain."

"Well you just offered the perfect response and the more I get to know you, the happier I am with my decision. You're a beautiful young lady." Lorraine discreetly watched her as they drove home. "Remember our game?"

"Yes."

Lorraine opened the sun roof. "May I start?"

Colleen inhaled deeply. "Sure."

"You're not enjoying your purchase in the way I expected. Did those people cause you that much discomfort?"

Colleen's mouth unconsciously dropped, followed by a defeated sigh. "It hurts when people look at me like there's something wrong with me."

Lorraine paused to gaze at the sky, then softly touched Colleen's upper arm. "Did you know any of them?"

"Who?"

"The people whose paths we crossed today."

"No."

Lorraine gazed at Colleen and smiled. "Me either." She paused. "When do you think you'll see any of them again?"

Colleen glanced at her, then back to the road. "Those exact people?"

"Yes. Those exact people."

"Probably never?"

Lorraine continued without confirming the answer. "They were complete strangers who don't know your name, let alone your heart?"

She glanced at Lorraine watching her, "No," then paused for a moment. "they don't even know my name..." She straightened in her seat. "but it didn't stop them from having a complete opinion of me."

Lorraine's voice softened. "And that's where you're completely wrong, and as soon as I explain, you may start to see things differently."

Colleen eyed her curiously, but didn't respond.

"...Wrong about the complete opinion, dear. You don't have a complete opinion of you and you've been spending every moment with you from the day you were born."

She felt her breathing increase but still offered no response.

"They have no clue who you are. They have no clue what you've been through. They have no clue how beautiful, loving and forgiving you are, but I appreciate how they hurt you and I understand how their stares hurt. You've been mistreated for longer than a while now, and after a while, the smallest additional rejection weighs more on you than others could understand."

Lorraine inhaled deeply. "But they don't know you at all, let alone completely. You're beautiful. And every time someone looks at you in a peculiar way, remind yourself, they don't know you. They *don't* know you."

Lorraine raised her hand through the roof, just enough to feel the wind. "Do you know anyone who knows you and truly likes you?"

"I guess."

"Who?"

"Cody. Stephie. Jake ...Vicky. You?"

Lorraine raised her brows and lowered her chin. "Of course me, but go on."

"Chris, Connor, Morgan, and Genna seem to."

"And do all those who know you past your picture..." She waved her hand at Colleen as if displaying her. "...like or love you?"

"Not my father."

"I don't think that's an accurate assumption. Does he know you?"

Colleen frowned. "No."

"He can't see past your picture either, so my premise is; he gets lumped with the other group." Lorraine rested her hand on Colleen's forearm as it rested on the middle console. "When people ...strangers look at me, I know beyond a doubt, they have no idea who I am ...but I've had many more years practice. But it's time to start practicing. Certain beneficial activities take practice to perfect."

Lorraine folded her hands on her lap, "I want you to practice. Will you ...for me?"

"Yes, ma'am."

"You can call me whatever you want, but I hope you'll adopt a less formal nickname for me."

"Like what?"

"I love how Vicky always calls me Nana, in honor of Stephanie, but my husband used to call me *Rain*. Definitely more appropriate for our living arrangement, but don't hesitate to use Nana if you feel like."

"*Rain* is so pretty." Colleen glanced at her and smiled.

"I loved when he called me Rain." She leaned her head back on the headrest and showed peaceful enjoyment the remainder of their ride home.

# Chapter Fifteen
## Deliberation

"Can I have your attention?" Jake raised both arms. "Let's do something serious before this meeting turns into a party."

"Boo!" Assorted giggles came from multiple directions as Stephie openly and playfully provoked him.

He glared at her and held his arms out. "What ever happened to the cute shy girl who lived next door to me growing up?"

She hopped so she could glance over the shoulders blocking her direct view of him. "You brought the woman out in him and let her spread her wings, and now she can fly."

Cheers resonated around the room as she walked toward him. "Would you rather I remain lost and scared?" She stood tight against him in playful intimidation, with her head raised and her back straight.

"Kiss her, fool!"

He futilely fought his imminent grin and whispered, "Soar like a phoenix, sweetheart." He swept her off her feet with the embrace that followed and obliged the anonymous request with a passionate kiss, and as he kissed her, she noticeably melted in his arms.

He slowly released her, then acted as if nothing romantic happened; teasingly ignoring her and immediately scanned the room. "Does anybody have anything they want to discuss?"

She smacked his arm as Cody raised his voice without hesitation. "I told my mom about me and Colleen the other day, and…"

"Yeah!" Anthony and Kaden both yelled and pumped their arms upward.

Cody faced them but continued speaking to everyone. "Not so *yeah*. She wasn't happy." He took a noticeable breath. "She told me I made a terrible choice she couldn't accept."

Dawn stared at her phone. "Oh my god." She eyed Giana and Michaela as tears filled her eyes. "We just lost Britt." Tears covered her cheeks and she sobbed. "We just lost Britt!"

A hush came over the room as tears flowed and friends consoled friends. And muted frustrations released from every corner of the gathering. The quiet mourning extended for some time, until Dawn raised her beer, and with a quaking voice cried, "Oh Britt! My sister. I miss you, but I understand." She broke down as tears flowed from her eyes. "I understand …but I miss you." Kyleigh hugged her tight and she collapsed in her friend's embrace.

Anthony watched patiently through tears as the initial shock and consolations ran their course, then raised his beer. "Britt, we knew you were in pain but we never guessed how much." His red eyes darted around the room. "We knew she hoped for something that probably wouldn't come and she told us her timeline. Yet we never imagined." He raised his eyes to the ceiling. "I'm sorry we failed you. I'm sorry this life failed you. Please forgive us." He raised his bottle more. "To Britt."

Soft acknowledgments followed. "To Britt."

Someone softly exclaimed, "God damn. …To Britt."

Giana whispered to Dawn, "She hoped for something by a certain date?"

Dawn sighed. "Yeah."

"What?"

"Someone to love her."

Everyone mingled until the consolations faded, and Jake once again tried to refocus the group. With slouched shoulders, he raised his arm. "Let's continue."

Someone in the group called out. "How?"

He straightened. "We have to, and this is why we have to." He slowly examined the eyes looking back at him. "We don't honor her by fighting less. We honor her by fighting more. We just apologized for failing her. Let's continue so we don't lose another, as timelines of friends or strangers, secret or revealed, approach." Jake stared a beam of fire in his friend's direction. "Cody, What were you saying?"

"My mom. I really thought she'd understand, but she didn't …at all. How do we get our parents to understand who we are and that it's alright to love anyone?"

"I've been working on that question for years, honey." Vicky waved his hand in disgust. "…so long, I've given up."

Heads followed the conversation coming from different people, and anyone with a thought, shared as the process continued.

"Yeah, but we never attack the problem together."

"Maybe that's the problem. We're all trying to share the answers separately, but none of us know enough to be as persistent as when we're together. Ever notice how when we talk, someone always adds something that strengthens each idea?"

"Definitely."

"Maybe we should discuss it with our relatives the same way."

"Yeah, as a group. It doesn't have to be all of us, but we lose the argument when we don't have anyone backing us."

"Absolutely. Some older people are definitely harder to talk to, individually. How about we recognize the strength of our target and address them with the same strength; with the force in numbers, their beliefs hold against us?"

"You're brilliant."

Shelbie joked. "I know. I was only the fourth person to say the same thing. …Pure genius." Everyone laughed.

Kyleigh stood and raised a blank paper. "How about we start a list and people can sign next to what they want to research and become expert on?"

"Let's name the subjects or the perspectives. Anyone call them out."

"Remember, this isn't a test. This is when we take the methods we've learned and use them for something we want. More than one can research the same topic. No one's grading us."

"Then in a meeting or three, we'll cross-train then feed off each other, presenting it."

"Cross-train? What's your mother a corporate executive or something?" Soft laughter crossed the room.

"Kyleigh, you the note-taker today?"

"Yeah."

"Thanks."

"Topics and Sections…call them out."

"I know. Five parts being. Ready? Physical, Emotional, Mental, Spiritual, Social."

"Break social down into Religious, Historical, and Medical."

"And break history into history and geography. People think we're a western civilization phenomena, but we need to let them know lgbt is a natural occurrence around the world, and as old as humans."

"Religion. We need to break that down into history and geography too."

"Agreed. People think lgbt lifestyles offend God since the beginning of humans, but the word *homosexual* didn't appear in the bible until nineteen forty six."

"How the fuck do you know shit like that?"

"You wouldn't understand if I explained."

"Medical, which fits into physical."

"Psychological fits into emotional and intellectual"

"Intellectual also fits into history of education / social influence in our education system – how rules are skewed according to beliefs. How beliefs are skewed by people and organizations with agendas."

"Wait." Cody raised his hand and eyed Colleen. "Choice versus real nature. Who we are in the core of our being, and the idea this is as natural to some as heterosexuality is to others."

"Excellent."

"Guys, remember it's fine when things cross over. Don't stay away from evidence in your specific section because you think the information infringes on another. ...Just the opposite because it may be a different perspective on the same exact information and then the info looks even more legit."

Zelma stood and held her beer out. "Anybody else need another beer? All this work's making me thirsty."

~~~

Lorraine stood in a haze leaning back, holding her stomach ...laughing. "Can you come? ...You're driving!"

Jake woke as the echo of the sentence transitioned him from dream state to sentient thought and with an instant energy, leaned over, kissed Stephie in the pitch dark and shook her too enthusiastically. "Come on."

She squinted and rustled under the covers. "What the hell's wrong with you?"

He shook her again. "Come on!"

"What are you in such a rush for? The place isn't going anywhere."

His eyes widened. "Rush? I've been waiting for this for the last dozen years. ...More. Fifteen!"

She pulled her pillow over her head. "And I've told you every year ...it's nothing special."

He straddled her, pinning her under the blanket, leaned forward and covered her so she couldn't free her arms. "Bullshit. I know it's great. You just never wanted to make me feel bad." He tickled her neck with his mouth and she squirmed under him. "Jake!"

He lifted his head waiting for more, as she struggled against him in the dark. "You're an idiot."

"Yeah, well now I'm a Blair family idiot and I finally get to go to the Blair family reunion."

She shook her head as his words tickled her. "You could've gone to any of the other ones too. All you had to do was ask."

He tickled her, still not freeing her arms. "All I had to do was ask? You shit. All you had to do was invite." He leaned down and continued tickling her neck.

"Jake! If I ever get my arms free..." She struggled against him. "...you're dog meat."

He paused for a second. "Is that a threat?"

"No ...it's a promise." She squirmed. "And you have to let me up so I can get in the shower. So when you do ...run."

He grinned at her, "Be nice. I've been waiting for today, my whole life." then kissed her as he freed her arms. "What time do we have to pick up Nana?"

She reached for her phone on the end table and lit the screen. "A little less than two hours." Her voice rose. "I could've slept another half an hour!"

"No you couldn't. We have to get there early. I got years to make up for."

"Man…" She kissed him as he let her up. "I hope you're not too disappointed by Sunday night."

He hurried past her and quickly disappeared into the bathroom. "They have a balloon guy, don't they?" She heard the shower spit its first thrusts of water.

"I'm getting a matching blue balloon sword and hat."

"You're an idiot."

"And a cotton candy machine." He turned as she entered the bathroom. "With blue and pink cotton candy." He hugged and squeezed her.

"Jake!"

"I'm gonna eat cotton candy and wipe my fingers on my shirt."

"There's no cotton candy machine."

"Yes there is …don't lie."

He held the shower curtain back and she stepped in. "So you plan on being ten this weekend?"

He wrapped his arms around her as the steamy water cascaded over them. "I told you; I have to make up for lost time."

"Maybe you should stay home. We'll call it the special Harrison tradition part of the Blair reunion weekend."

"Too late. I'm a future Blair family member." He playfully tortured her by dancing as he held her and sung in her ear. "…I'm invited and you can't stop me!"

Her voice rose in playful exasperation. "Yes I can …because I'm going to kill you before we get there."

They walked out of the apartment, and into a magnificent August pre-dawn, and Jake inhaled the clean morning air as he locked their front door. "Get breakfast on the way?"

She reached for his hand. "Definitely."

They pulled into Lorraine's driveway fifteen minutes early and saw the front door open before they exited the car. Jake heard Stephie greet Lorraine as he made room for her luggage in the trunk, then kissed her dearly as she appeared at the back of the car. "Good morning."

"Good morning, dear."

Stephie eyed Lorraine's travel coffee mug as she helped her into the car. "We bought you a breakfast sandwich."

"That's sweet, but I'll just have my coffee."

Stephie turned toward the back seat. "How's Colleen doing?"

"Much better."

Jake interrupted. "Why didn't she come?"

"She's not comfortable yet in certain large gatherings, so I told her to enjoy the weekend in her own house. Invite Cody over for a nice meal. I'm glad she can have some private time with him, so it works out nicely."

"Oh that's great." Stephie's face brightened as Jake's voice rose. "Well she can't have my balloon sword when we get home."

Stephie answered Lorraine's confused look. "He's being an idiot."

They drove in intermittent peaceful silence as the sun rose in the morning sky, and pulled into the resort before noon. Genna and Connor arrived earlier, rented their three rooms, and met them at their hotel-room door. Connor greeted him with a beer. "Welcome to the Craven, Blair division of the Santi family reunion." He handed Jake a beer then clinked the bottle. "C'mon, I'll introduce you to everyone. The women will meet up with us later." He smiled. "You're my bocce partner this weekend."

Jake couldn't stop grinning. "Okay …What's bocce?"

Connor patted his back as they walked to his room. "You throw the pallino, a little ball …down the court, then you throw the other bigger bocce balls and try to get closest to it. The games are cut-throat friendly and all the men drink wine and get stoned. It's a blast."

He leaned inside his room. "Sweetheart, Jake and I are going to put our names in the bocce tournament." He motioned to Jake. "Go tell your other half I'm stealing you and we'll see them outside."

Jake ran back into his room and jumped giddily in front of Stephie as she unpacked. "I'm gonna go drink red wine and play bocce with your dad. *Bocce!* …I never even *heard* of bocce and now I'm in the family tournament."

She kissed him. "You really are an idiot."

He headed out the door. "I know!"

They didn't return to their room until well after two in the morning and Stephie had to guide him to bed. She plopped him down and reached for his sneakers as he draped his arm over his eyes, shielding the light. "Wow."

"Unbutton your pants." She pulled on the legs of his jeans as he lifted his rear.

"If I had cotton candy today, the day would've been an eleven."

"You had wine instead."

He raised a finger as he lay on his back. "…Turns out, it's a very acceptable substitute."

She smirked and shook her head. "I'm noticing."

"And we kicked ass in bocce."

"Help me, will ya?" She pulled his shirt over his head. "We have to get up in five hours. Nobody misses the family breakfast." She pulled the covers over him, then climbed next to him, kissed him and shut out the light. "Good night."

He answered with a snore.

~~~

The doorbell rang and Colleen shut the TV off before hopping up and heading to the foyer. She paused and pulled at the hips of her dress, took a deep breath and opened the door. "Hi."

He held out flowers. "Hi."

"Oh Cody." She brought them to her nose and inhaled. "Thank you." She kissed him and their mouths stayed locked as he shut the door behind them.

She softly broke the kiss and led him by the hand to the family room, then let go of his hand, intermittently looking at the flowers. "Let me find a vase for these?"

His breathing was already intense. "Can you just lay them in the kitchen and find something later?"

She hurried to the kitchen and laid them on the table, then hurried back as he sat in the corner of the sofa. Both knew this was the first time they had been alone in private and both considered it a gift from Lorraine. "She actually said you could invite me over?"

"She told me if I didn't, she'd be disappointed in me."

He wrapped his arm around her as she sat snuggled against him. "She isn't like any person I ever met."

"She sure isn't. I don't understand why all adults aren't like her, but she's amazing." She moved her lips to his and their mouths instantly opened and softly sealed together.

"I made a nice dinner for you."

"It smells excellent. Can we eat it for breakfast?"

She blushed, "Cody." and her breathing increased noticeably. She touched his cheek as she kissed him, "Maybe the leftovers." then met his eyes. "Did you bring an overnight bag?"

"Yeah, but it's in the car."

She wrapped her arm around him and lay her head on his chest. "Why didn't you bring it in?"

He held her and inhaled the soft feminine fragrance of her hair. "I don't want to pressure you."

She shut her eyes and felt the tenderness of his embrace. "Oh Cody, you're so sweet."

He twisted her in his arms, until he had her face to face and kissed her passionately. And when the kiss broke, his voice echoed his desire. "I can't believe I'm alone with you."

"Me either." She had decided beforehand to let him lead their pursuit of intimacy. Her strongest secret desire was to be seduced passionately, but his caring tenderness was making it more and more difficult for her not to abandon the fantasy. She decided to at least try to prolong the anticipation. "Can I play some music?"

"Sure."

She reached over him for the remote on the end table and felt his deep inhale and tender embrace, then twisted away enough to turn on a music channel; secretly registering his continuing effort to hold her. She playfully pressed against him as she placed the remote back in its decorative box and his breathing responded noticeably, making her more excited than she wished. She tried separating without sacrificing any of the sexual tension between them. "This is nice, isn't it?"

He exhaled. "Real nice."

"Are you hungry?" She tried to glance at his lap before meeting his eyes.

He kissed her. "Not really."

"Let me go check on dinner." She discreetly tucked herself so she could stand. "Be right back."

She walked into the kitchen and out of sight, then tucked herself better and breathed deep. This was the most fantastic torture she had ever experienced as a girl. She made sure he was still on the sofa, with a quick glance around the kitchen wall. "Want something to drink?"

She caught him adjusting his jeans, knowing it was only a matter of time before she would relieve his discomfort, and the thought exhilarated her. She had fantasized about being intimate with him; caressing him, tasting him …since their date in the park. She remembered her excuse to leave the room and opened and shut the oven door, then removed two bottles of water from the fridge, tucked herself and rejoined him.

He sat up and smiled as she reentered the room. "You look pretty. I really like when you wear a skirt or dress. You have nice legs."

She softly sat next to him, trying hard to hide her quickened breathing, and without answering, placed her mouth on his. And as they kissed she took his hand and gently placed it over her blouse and bra, and felt him squeeze softly. She knew she didn't have anything there, but the feeling of being felt up raised her arousal and her breathing further.

He moaned softly, then kissed her neck as his hand gently caressed her chest. "God, Colleen."

His open mouth and warm hand sent chills through her and she moved her hand over his lap. And the proof confirming his pleasure made her heart jump. "Oh Cody." She sighed as she held his mouth to her neck. "This feels nice."

He whispered as he kissed her. "Is everything off in the kitchen?"

"No." Every word he uttered made her heart jump.

He grabbed her hand and stood her up, "I can't take it anymore." his chest expanding and contracting as he stood there. "Can we shut off everything in the kitchen? I'm not hungry."

Her breathing increased as she watched his chest. "Me either." She rushed in front of him and made sure the oven was off, then reached for his hand as she reentered the family room, and they hurried upstairs without another word.

~~~

"C'mon bocce champ." Stephie rubbed Jake's arm. "Wake up. It's almost breakfast time." She leaned over and kissed his forehead.

"Ow. Do you have to kiss me so loud?" He massaged his temples.

"Sit up. I have something for your pain." She handed him two pills and a bottle of water, then imitated the witch from Bell Book and Candle, "DRRINKK!"

He covered his ears. "Very funny. What did you beat me with?"

"Homemade red wine, trampled tenderly by Aunt Rose's tiny purple feet and aged for weeks in Uncle Chick's smelly cellar."

He rubbed his eyes, "Oh yeah." then made dry swallowing sounds. "Now that you mention it, I think I taste her feet. Does she have corns?"

"You're disgusting."

She pulled the covers off him. "C'mon. Time to get in the shower. Day two's about to begin." She led him to the bathroom and turned on the water, then lifted the blow-dryer and laughed as he held his ears.

Breakfast lasted for hours and the goodbyes lasted longer. Genna and Stephie packed their suitcases and Jake and Connor loaded the cars for the ride home.

After walking to the loaded cars together, the five kissed, then decided to follow each other home. Jake helped Lorraine into the back seat, then sat in the driver seat with a gigantic satisfied smile. He waited patiently as Stephie buckled her seatbelt, then broke the silence. "You lied and been lying to me for years. That was fantastic."

Lorraine chuckled then playfully interrupted. "But you didn't get your balloon sword or cotton candy."

He peered through the inside rear view mirror at her. "So it wasn't perfect, but that was really fun." He glanced at Stephie. "I think we should build a bocce court in our back yard when we get a house."

She glanced at him with raised eyebrows. "Think so, eh? And I suppose the house has to have a basement so we can make our own wine?"

He grinned. "Now you're talking."

She twisted toward her grandmother. "Nana… help."

Lorraine raised both hands palms out and chuckled. "I refuse to take sides. I love you both equally."

Jake giggled as Stephie pleaded. "Nana!"

Jake broke the next temporary lull in conversation as he glanced at Lorraine in the rearview mirror. "How are you and Colleen getting along?"

"Fantastic. She's a beautiful young lady and the more I get to know her, the happier I am with my decision to invite her to live with me. She does things for me that show she appreciates the hospitality, though I'm still working on making her comfortable asking me things. But I think that's her way of treating me with reverence." She smiled and her voice brightened. "I may have to ply her with alcohol to loosen her up."

Lorraine paused for a moment. "I gave her orders to invite Cody over while we were away. I hope she did." She reached for the back of Stephie's seat. "Can you text her for me dear, and tell her we'll be home by nine …just in case she did? I don't want to embarrass her or Cody."

"Sure." Stephie worked her phone, then hit send. "Done."

A few minutes later, her phone beeped and she read the incoming reply. "Message received."

~~~

The sun was noticeably slower to rise and the night resumed its natural chill as another summer came to an end. Stephie asked Colleen and Dawn to be her bridesmaids and the group decided to invite everyone dress shopping on a crisp September Saturday.

Colleen and Dawn had both tried on a handful of dresses, though this was only the first of what they all assumed would be countless trips searching for bridesmaid dresses they would all be happy with. This first stop was more for elimination than anything, but they agreed on one thing; none of them wanted to wear traditional dresses which were useless after the actual wedding, as was common in Genna's day.

Vicky placed his hand on his hips as Colleen and Dawn disappeared into the dressing room to change out of their most recent sample. "What am I going to wear?" He turned half teasing, half disconcerted to his new mothers." I don't want to be different. I want to wear what the other bridesmaids wear." His eyes met theirs, then waved his hand and shook his head. "No. I shouldn't."

Stephie giggled as she stared at him. "Why not?"

"Nope. This is your day and I don't want to do anything to make it less than perfect, and people would be confused."

Stephie lowered her chin and lovingly chided, "But you don't understands what matters to me." She placed her hand over her heart. "You're my person of honor. And as my person of honor, what you want is most important to me. I want this celebration to be about us and no one in your new immediate family would be fazed at all. And everyone else will be too busy being confused by the boy in my wedding gown." Stephie moved in front of Vicky and took her hands. "I don't care what you wear. If you want one, I want you to have one."

"Stop." He began fanning himself as he tried to hold back tears. "Oh my god." His eyes widened as he faced her. "Should I?"

Stephie grinned at the perplexing reaction. "What does your heart say?"

Lorraine interrupted. "I'll pay for it."

"Oh I don't know what I should do." He shared a devious grin as he glanced at everyone. "I never wore a dress outside a locked bedroom." He play scowled at Colleen and Stephie. "I'm not as physically girly as some of my sisters."

They all laughed.

He rubbed his temples and scanned each person. "What do all you think I should do?"

Stephie answered first. "What your heart wants, no matter what consensus is."

Morgan broke her silence. "But this wouldn't be an issue if you didn't want to. I vote dress."

Genna met Morgan's eyes. "I vote dress."

He paused for a moment and waved a raised finger. "No. It's just the excitement of where we are. I'll be more comfortable in a matching color tux." He squinted as he stared at Stephie. "Is that alright?"

She shook her head at him. "Don't you understand you can show up wearing grocery bags and I'm going to be thrilled you're beside me on our special day, and that's all I'll remember."

He held his raised finger still. "But I'm getting ready with the girls that morning."

Stephie looked around, extending her arms. "What girls?"

Everyone giggled.

~~~

Colleen spent weeks searching for a job, with no luck. She first used the internet, but every time an opportunity went past the initial stages, and she shared her transgender orientation, the opening disappeared. Most people politely ended the preliminary proposals with vague excuses, but some were very direct regarding their reason they couldn't work with her. Even the friends who owned Lorraine's old restaurant, refused her, stating they were afraid if customers found out, their business would suffer.

Finally, she used a local lgbt network and the owners of a small privately owned dollar store near the college agreed to hire her, but told her they would monitor customer complaints, and if her presence negatively affected their customer base, they would have to let her go. They also asked her to dress ultra-conservatively and do her best not to provoke their clientele, and she dejectedly agreed.

She shared the terms of the hire with Lorraine, and for the next month, Lorraine discreetly recorded the affect the special terms had on Colleen, and knew they needed a night together.

Lorraine walked to her preferred seat on the sofa closest to the loveseat as Colleen watched TV, and placed her tea on the table between them. "Have you ever had champagne?"

The question broke Colleen's focus. "No. Why?"

"I'm making a special dinner for the two of us, and I'm buying us champagne for the occasion. You've been working hard at both your new job and school, and I'm proud of you and think the reward of a fancy dinner with some nice champagne is called for."

"You don't have to go through any trouble. Everything I'm doing is because of your kindness. I should be making you a fancy dinner."

Lorraine softly pointed a finger at her. "You no longer have the time, young lady. You always have studying to do, and I have too much time again, with all the work you now have to do. And I know exactly what I'm making. Let me know what night's best for you this weekend, and the two of us will have some girl time together."

"I could use a night to unwind, and Cody's working Friday night. Does that work?"

Lorraine patted Colleen's hand as it rested on the arm of the loveseat. "Friday works perfectly."

The night arrived and Lorraine set the family room coffee table with a table cloth and candles for the occasion, then lit the fire Colleen had built the night before. Setting the fireplace was one of the chores Colleen had adopted as hers.

Colleen finally joined her for the evening and they sat comfortably, then Lorraine raised her glass after Colleen placed the bottle back in the ice bucket. "To the relationship I was sure would develop, and to my pleasure, has."

Colleen sipped after gently touching Lorraine's glass. "Oh my. That's not anything like anything else." She rubbed her nose.

Lorraine smiled. "No it isn't, is it?"

Colleen sipped and rubbed her nose a second time. "I like this."

Lorraine laughed softly. "So do I, and it's been a while since I had any. We need to have it more, don't you think?"

"Sure." Colleen followed Lorraine's lead and sat back. "Dinner smells fantastic. What did you make?"

"A casserole. I learned over the years, when I cook dinner for someone, I want to be in the family room enjoying them, and making something that goes in one dish and only needs transferring from the stove to the table, works best. I want to spend tonight relaxing with you and not cooking. ...Just one of the silly things time teaches."

"I never thought of that."

"Because life experience hasn't taught you the lesson yet. Many times, even simple lessons aren't learned until life teaches them to you."

"I don't know why but I still think you've learned a lot of lessons other people haven't." Colleen sipped her champagne. "This is like liquid candy. Even the tall skinny glasses are elegant."

Lorraine laughed, then touched the rim of her glass. "Be careful though. It'll punch you and you won't know until it's too late. But the one way you can control its effect right from the beginning is to watch my glass. I've learned to pace my enjoyment of this, and you can use my experience or learn by your own experience, which means you're throwing up my beautiful casserole before the morning comes." Lorraine chuckled. "I'll hold your hair back, but I'm laughing at you the whole time you're in pain."

Colleen glanced at Lorraine's glass, stopped her hand half way to her glass, and rested it on her lap.

Lorraine met her eyes. "You're adorable."

"I love learning from you."

"What a wonderful thing to say."

Lorraine broke the next momentary silence. "Do you trust me?" Lorraine reached for her drink and smiled warmly as she watched Colleen reach for hers; quietly recognizing the imitation as a high compliment.

"Of course"

"I apologize. I didn't mean that as simply as it sounded. Do you trust me enough to believe my experiences might benefit you, and do you trust your instinct enough to understand my years have come with more than just age?"

"Yes."

"You know we're going to play our game, right?"

"I love our game." Colleen grinned. "I'm learning you always teach me when we play."

Lorraine felt her smile widen. This child had all the outer signs of not fitting society's unwritten uniform code, yet she had inner beauty exuding from every aspect of her being, and a willingness to learn lessons, those three times her age couldn't be bothered learning. She lowered her chin and raised her eyes. "You know you can also initiate the game."

"I know, but sometimes I can't put my confusion into words."

Lorraine sighed and nodded softly. "I understand." She paused a moment. "Can you understand I already love you like a granddaughter?"

"You won't be upset by my answer?" Colleen sat straight.

"We'll come back to the original question in a moment, but I need to share a thought on that question."

"Sure."

"I don't see anything you say to me, positive or negative, as a personal attack on me. I look at life differently than you can at your age, and I know you want to tell me only positive things and what you think I want to hear, but the assumption isn't correct. I want to hear your bare soul speak to me, when it would rather tell me the truth, so please understand you don't ever have to apologize for sharing what you think or feel." Lorraine reached for her hand. "And I know; even a change in how you share things is something you'll need to re-learn." She tilted her head in confirmation. "Understand I know that too."

Colleen's eyes narrowed. "How did you learn all these different ways of thinking?"

"Would you dear?" Lorraine motioned gently toward the champagne bottle next to Colleen, then touched her glass. "Through pain, fear, and heartache. Difficulty alone teaches wisdom, and the being you are in this life has set you up for amazing potential. True awareness only comes through great difficulty, and these brilliant awful lessons will be an immeasurable gift to your immortal being. They'll be overwhelming, and sometimes devastating as you learn them. Some you will never recover from. But they'll be your most precious treasure after they're learned."

She watched Colleen's eyes widen. "But that's a complicated lesson I'll spread over time. I have a more current and pressing question I hope you'll answer from your soul. ...Can you understand I love you?"

Colleen breathed deep and hesitated. "To be honest with you, no. I mean, things you just shared show me you're different than any adult I know, but my own parents couldn't love me, so between you and me, I don't see how anyone else …how anyone less close to me than my own parents, could love me. So …no." She took another deep breath. "And I'm scared to think otherwise."

"Dropping your guard enough to accept someone's love is scary, especially if your heart has been broken by those you thought you didn't have to qualify for. It's even hard to love yourself, believe it or not. No one knows our faults as intimately as we know our own." Lorraine lifted her glass and sipped. "But you do deserve your own love, in spite of everyone else. …And I do love you."

"Why?"

"Because I see love as a choice that cannot be topped. In this instance, the opposite choice is hate, though not by timeless definition. The actual opposite is indifference, but not for this discussion. There are definitely times when indifference would be a welcomed alternative to hate." Lorraine paused a moment. "Love or hate are both choices, don't you think?"

"Yeah, but sometimes it's hard not to choose hate, don't you think?"

"I have a secret that will help you make the wiser choice, and will also help your interactions with the people you meet at work. The customers you've met at your new job have taken their toll on you, haven't they?"

Colleen lowered her eyes.

"Being shunned …not accepted, is a form of hate, and it hurts, doesn't it."

"Yeah."

"I'm going to repeat things that helped you before and add to them." Lorraine felt the need to lighten the mood, but a deeper need to teach the child. "I'm sorry sometimes it sounds like I'm some kind of teacher. That's not how I see myself. I've just been through things that'll help you, and like an older friend or sister, I want to help you." She lifted her drink and held it so Colleen would drink with her.

"Remember our talk after buying your phone?"

"Kind of."

"How I told you the people making a complete judgment of you with a quick glance, had no information whatsoever to go by?"

"Oh yeah."

"Well these are the additional aspects of that concept." She straightened the pillow at her side. "When people look at you strangely, you tend to think something's wrong with you. It's only natural. But do you know the real reason behind their reaction to you?" Lorraine sipped her champagne and lowered the glass carefully. "Why are they reacting to you the way they are?"

Colleen touched her chest over her heart. "I don't know. I mean, I kind of know, but the reason I think it is, doesn't really make sense. That's what's so frustrating."

Lorraine smiled softly. "We're each the center of our own world. You see the world through your eyes only. You measure everything only by your own mind, heart and soul, correct?"

Colleen nodded.

"People aren't sad or angry or quiet, because of you. They're working inside their own thoughts based on their experiences, dealing with their own problems, concerned with their own lives, digesting what and who they meet using what they've been taught. You not only don't have the effect on them you think you have, but since you're the center of your world, you think you have greater influence on strangers than you actually do."

"Their reaction can also be complicated by their level of maturity and also nothing to do with you." Lorraine lifted her empty glass. "Ready for a refill?"

"Sure." She motioned toward the big bottle and Colleen quickly reached for it. "I'll fill them."

Lorraine smiled softly. "Thanks."

Colleen handed Lorraine her full glass. "Dinner smells fantastic."

"Thanks. I call the dish, pasta pie. I take cooked pasta and mix in the sauce and a little cheese, place it in a baking dish and bake till it gets a crust like lasagna. I think it's delicious." She stood and Colleen followed as she went to the oven, opened the door and touched the top. "A few more minutes." Lorraine smiled as their eyes met. "I love the crust."

Colleen waited to follow Lorraine back to the family room and Lorraine sat, then pointed to the remote. "Turn some soft music on?"

As Colleen searched the music channels, Lorraine continued their previous conversation. "So, the first point was; don't care at all what people who don't know you think of you, and the new idea is; you're not as big a concern or influence on people, as you think. They have their own issues occupying their thoughts." She sipped her wine. "Isn't that good news? Oh I like this music."

Lorraine continued, "But you know what one of the neatest things I've noticed is?" She carefully wiped the dew off her cold glass. "Take a notice how older people aren't as angry or frustrated by others. We finally start to accept and let live, but usually when we're almost done living ourselves. We seem to love quicker, easier and deeper then too."

Lorraine reached for her hand. "I understand your age is full of self-consciousness and you rightfully have more than the average person your age, but teach yourself that people really don't affect you as deeply as you're allowing, because people aren't affected *by* you. They turn the corner and as soon as you're out of site, they forget you exist for the concerns in their own heads. Realize that and dismiss them as quickly."

Lorraine lifted her glass. "Okay. Enough serious stuff. Let's spend the rest of the evening eating, drinking, and joking. Want to hear about when Robert and I met?"

Colleen energized. "I'd love to hear about when you were younger."

"Okay. Let me take the casserole out of the oven. It has to sit a few minutes before we slice it."

Colleen stood eagerly. "I'll do it."

Lorraine raised her voice as she lost sight of her. "Then I want to hear how you and Cody met."

# Chapter Sixteen
## Preparation

Stephie and Jake shared their unexpected event with Lorraine, for her recent university connections, and Genna as an alumnus, then used their school connections to secure the small theater classroom in the science building. What initially started as a gathering of information to collectively share a more extensive understanding of lgbt issues with loved ones, had expanded into an extensive presentation from an all-encompassing educational perspective on lgbt life, for whoever wanted to attend.

With Lorraine's gentle suggesting, Doctor Laurian voluntarily sponsored the club, allowing access to university resources.

Lorraine's friends at her old restaurant agreed to cater the event, and friends and family agreed to help in other capacities. The university's Social and Behavioral Sciences department also gave the group a small allowance for their accompanying pamphlet.

Once the specific date and venue were reserved, Lorraine and her grandchildren executed the next step of the club's plan, deciding on a dinner party at Lorraine's. The final guests arrived for the dinner meeting and everyone gathered in Lorraine's family room, with the overflow spreading into adjacent rooms.

Connor stood in the middle of the crowd, greeting people and inhaled with his hand on his stomach. "Something smells fantastic." He tapped Lorraine's shoulder. "Did you invent a new gourmet dish for the occasion?"

Lorraine reached for Colleen and wrapped her arm around her. "Nope. This meal was prepared by the other gourmet cook living here."

Colleen smiled brightly. "We actually worked together. She's already taught me so much about cooking."

"Guys!" Vicky looked at his watch, then raised his arm and pointed to it. "Time for phone calls, so we can drink and eat soon. Everyone alright with that?"

Low grumbles spread throughout the room as people found places to sit in every corner, whether on furniture or the floor. Colleen had drawn the lot for the first phone call, and couldn't trade it off before the time to begin. She nervously sat on the sofa and gave Lorraine one last glance before dialing. "Mom?" She turned the speaker on, but didn't announce anyone's presence and the room sat silently listening.

"Honey. How are you? I've been distraught worrying about you."

Colleen paused and gathered herself as she digested the dissonance. "I'm fine. How are you?" She wanted to get right to the point, but for all the grace she had witnessed from all her adopted parents, knew she had to portray a higher awareness and understanding.

"I'm fine, except I miss my little boy."

Colleen's wide eyes immediately met Lorraine's and Lorraine raised her hand palm out, then motioned her to breathe deep.

"I have some news for you mom. Can you get a piece of paper and a pen, please?"

"Is everything alright? Are you in trouble?"

"Just the opposite mom. Everything is great and I want to invite you or you and dad into my life again. Tell me when you're ready to write."

They heard shuffling through the phone, then a slight pause. "I'm ready."

"There's a presentation at the university on the fourteenth, at seven, in the science building; room nineteen. It's a small theater. Over a hundred people will be there. I'll be there. If you want to have a relationship with me, please be there. If you're not there, I'll understand you'd rather not have me in your life."

"Of course I want you in our lives, but it's almost a month from now. What if we can't come?"

Colleen's voice softened and head lowered. "Then I'll understand how important I am to you."

"Can we get together another time if we can't make it?"

"I love you, but this is the last phone call I make from this phone. I'm mailing it to you. You can cancel the number as soon as you want after this call."

"I can't believe you'd do this to your mother."

"Mom, you've played your *mother* card for years. I'm sorry I have to play my daughter card now. I'd love to rebuild our relationship on love and acceptance. This is the opportunity. I hope and pray you'll be there. I love you. Bye."

She pressed the end button, breathing heavily as she stared at Lorraine, and Lorraine stood and opened her arms. Colleen took the cue and walked dejectedly into her embrace. "That was the hardest thing I ever did."

"I know, dear." Lorraine caressed the back of her hair. "But it's always mentally and emotionally healthier confronting your bullies, than continually cowering to them."

Vicky motioned to Stephie, who had the list with names and numbers drawn. "Who's next?"

One by one, each person needing to call and invite a friend or family member with the support of everyone present, took their turn. Vicky went last, and he didn't have the ability to extend the invitation without breaking down and crying audibly, but with strong support and long hugs, this too passed, and after consolations and congratulations, the party slowly morphed into a celebration of great courage and love.

~~~

Jake could hear the chair roll on the plastic mat in the cubicle to the left and spun his chair toward the corner of his work area. It had become his automatic response over the last few weeks. Aaron grabbed the partition and leaned just enough to expose his head and smile sideways. Jake couldn't help but smile back.

Aaron's eyes darted around, making sure no one else could hear, then refocused. "Wanna get a beer after work?"

"Sure, but let me make sure it doesn't cost me."

"I hear you."

Jake finished the open section of computer code and saved the work before texting Stephie. *Aaron asked me 2 get a beer after work. We got anything?*

*No.. I'll pick up a few xtra hrs 2nite*

*Go home and relax. I dont plan on being late*

*I'll c ..hav fun*

He tapped his desk twice, knowing it would get Aaron's attention without him rising above the partition. "Good to go"

Aaron tapped back twice. "Nice."

As the chatter volume amplified and the increased activity signaled the end of the day, Aaron walked behind him and immediately started tapping his foot at Jake's delay. Jake glanced at him, "Yeah, yeah." then sped up trying to finish his task.

"Can't that wait till tomorrow?"

Jake glanced over. "Five more minutes. But you go. I'll be right there."

"I already know you. You'll be here another hour if I leave." He pulled his chair into the aisle, sat and rested his feet on the edge of a cabinet. "I'll wait."

Jake glanced behind him. "Damn. I don't know if I can perform with the added pressure."

"Pretend I'm Gina, watching you."

"Nice." Jake typed frantically for minutes, then pushed away from the desk. "There."

Aaron popped out of his chair. "Yes!"

Twenty minutes later, they were sitting at the bar. "Draft light beer please."

The bartender rested her hand on her side of the bar top. "Tall or short."

"Tall."

Aaron extended his fingers. "Two." and sat back as she walked away. Jake watched him scan the bar, tapping his fingers impatiently, then spin in his chair and stare out the wall of windows behind them. "Now this is the way to unwind from our tedious torture."

Jake watched the server top the second glass. "But the torture pays for these beers." They both reached for their glass as soon as the server placed them.

"Good point, but the place is boring and I need some excitement." He squinted at the basketball game on the TV, then smacked the edge of the bar top. "I got it. We should join a guy's indoor soccer league or beer-league softball team or something."

"No thanks." Jake placed his beer on the coaster. "I have enough going on in my life."

"Like what? Tell me what you do that's interesting and maybe I'll join you."

"You'd definitely be welcomed, but I'm not sure you'd want to."

"Try me."

Jake could feel his uncontrollable grin appear as he turned in his seat. "I belong to an lgbt club. I'm one of the people who kind of run it."

"Really." Aaron's eyes narrowed. "But your girl is Stephanie, right?"

Jake felt his uncontrollable grin grow. "Yeah."

Aaron leaned closer and lowered his voice. "You bi or something?"

Jake smiled. "Something. I don't really like categories for people at all. It's complicated. Stephie's a transgender girl."

"Wow. The picture on your desk is her, right?"

"Yeah."

"Wow. I woulda never guessed. She's hot." He lifted his beer. "Congratulations." He looked around and smiled sneakily. "I never told anyone I think so, but a lot of them are hot. ...But don't tell Kristen I said that. She probably wouldn't understand."

Jake inhaled and patted his shoulder. "Not a problem."

"You said something weird though. You called her a girl. She's a girl to you?"

"Yeah, but like I said ...it's complicated. But I don't mind what you label me. I am who I am and I love who I love."

Aaron leaned both arms on the bar and tilted his head toward Jake. "Everyone says they're guys, but they sure don't register as guys to me either. I mean, I don't like guys, but I'd absolutely do more than a few of the girls I've seen in that category."

"So would more heterosexual men than you think." He watched Aaron's eyes follow two young women walking behind their bar seats.

Aaron leaned closer as he focused on Jake. "Why do they call guys who are attracted to them, gay then?"

"Only the clueless do. People who study psychology don't."

"Really." Aaron loosened his tie. "Now I feel better, liking them. Damn. I didn't know that. I do know they damn sure look like girls. Even the ones that ain't so cute." He squinted. "...That's fucked up."

Jake smiled as he registered the honesty and connection Aaron offered. "If you come to a few meetings, there's all kinds of things you're going to learn that you thought wrong or never knew."

"Okay. I wanna join."

Jake's eyes widened, "Okay. Wow." then he exhaled. "I was worried about telling you ...or anyone in the office. This is a relief ...in fact, it's pretty great. I hate worrying what people's reactions will be."

Aaron patted him on the back. "Dude. It's all good. I actually support lgbt. My parents would probably be confused ...hell, Kristen may even have a problem. But I don't ...at all." He lifted his beer and paused. "Do any people who are straight but just support lgbt belong to your club? Is it a club?" He drank a mouthful then met Jake's eyes. "You should have straight people in your club too."

"Anybody's welcome but nobody's ever offered before."

"Did you ever invite them?"

He eyed Aaron curiously. "No. I never thought... You'd join our club?"

"Hell yeah." Aaron offered a confirming grin. "You're fucking normal, and the assholes who don't think so need to know straight people support you too. I think a lot of straight people support lgbt."

Jake lifted his beer. "Damn Aaron, I wanted to tell you but I wasn't sure I could."

Aaron swirled the remaining beer in his glass. "I don't blame you. There's a lot of assholes who would fuck with you or even cost you shit." He looked around then back at Jake. "Fuck 'em all."

Aaron waved discreetly to one of the servers behind the bar, then glanced at Jake. "You want another, right?"

Jake grinned. "Yeah, we can have a few."

"Definitely." He pushed his glass closer to the far edge of the bar top then turned his chair and faced Jake. "How often do you meet? What do you do?"

"Right now, we're getting ready to do the strangest thing."

"Fill me in, my friend. Fill me in."

Jake shared their presentation idea and how it originated as a way to help friends with unaccepting parents share their normality as a group instead of alone, then morphed into this production at the university for anyone interested, and Aaron's enthusiasm increased. "I could definitely get into that. Can I be part of it? I love shit like that."

"Sure. Are you sure?"

"Yeah I'm sure. I'm telling you. I completely support your cause and I need something to do beside work."

"Okay. You're in." Jake sipped his new beer. "Can I ask a favor though?"

Aaron nodded. "Sure. What?"

"Can you not share everything about this …and me at work quite yet? I don't want to lose this job and I'm not sure how everyone in the place would take the news."

"See? That's the kind of shit that needs to fucking stop. You're already better than two thirds of the people in there, and that would be fucking wrong." Aaron took a large gulp of his drink. "You have my word, but *that's* why I want to help. That's bullshit."

"I agree." Jake sighed as he lifted his beer. "The problem is; it's reality."

~~~

Vicky called Colleen, who called Stephie. After they agreed the proposal was an excellent idea, they formed a plan of attack. Colleen was responsible for Lorraine, Stephie had the Harrisons, and Vicky, the Blairs.

Vicky waited for Stephie's word that all was a go on her and Colleen's end, then sprung into action. He dialed Genna. "Hi."

"Hi Vick. How are you?"

"Good …well not so good."

"Why? What's wrong?"

He sung his next sentence. "Whatcha doin' for Thanksgiving?"

"Oh my god it's around the corner isn't it."

He playfully admonished her. "Why yes it is. And three of your four children are tired of waiting for you parents to get your act together and tell us what the plans are, so we made plans without you."

"Without us?"

"Yes." He paused for effect. "Oh, you're invited. We just made the plans without you."

"Vicky, you have a way with words."

"Yeah? Well I thought I was going to miss this coming family Thanksgiving. So I started this."

"Oh god, Vicky. I'm sorry, but normally it's understood. We have Thanksgiving. I forgot we have new family members who don't know the invitation is forever permanent. My fault and I apologize. You have a Thanksgiving invitation …every holiday invitation for the rest of your life. And I'm very sorry."

"Will you relax, girl? Geesh! You'd think I was actually upset or something." His voice calmed. "I'm not mad. I'm just playing. I figured I could remedy the situation just like I did. I'm sorry for making you feel bad."

"No. I'm wrong."

"Well don't do it again, hear me? …How's that?"

She laughed. "I promise. So what's the *to-do*?"

"Colleen, Stephie and I are hosting Thanksgiving at Lorraine's." He paused. "We're doing all the cooking, but all guests will be in charge of the beverages and maybe a desert. Oh, we're looking for a free bird somewhere along the line, in case one of you gets one from work or something. We haven't worked out all the details yet. Guests will be welcome from the start of football on. Wear stretch pants."

Genna laughed. "That sounds fantastic. Who else is invited?"

"Tell your …other half. I almost said *better* half, please forgive me. Oh. Just the Harrisons, Jonathan, Colleen and Cody. Oh, and Stephie and Jake of course."

"He's a Harrison."

"Yeah, but he's a different kind of Harrison. It's complicated."

She laughed again. "I'm sure it is."

"Okay then. See you then?"

"Of course sweetheart. Thanks for the invitation."

"Oh, no problem. Love you."

"I love you too."

The three hosts were in constant contact, making sure no details were left unattended. Colleen claimed responsibility for the turkey since she lived where it would cook, but confessed she was scared, so Lorraine helped more than Colleen wanted her to, but they both loved cooking together. The three also volunteered Jake, Cody, and Jonathan for clean-up and trash duty.

Stephie and Vicky called the four parents continually, making sure everything was as experience would expect, and during those secondary calls, decided they should all have a family breakfast the next morning, with the grandkids staying overnight so they could finish cleaning up from the holiday and prepare breakfast too.

When Thanksgiving morning came, Stephie popped awake and hurried to the shower. She figured she'd let Jake sleep as long as she could, and woke him before blow drying her hair. She kissed him as she shook him softly. "Come on. Get in the shower. I have a turkey dinner to cook with our brother and sister."

When they arrived, Jake unloaded the car as Stephie hurried inside. "Happy Thanksgiving!" She kissed everyone then pointed to Vicky. "Look at you …all domesticated." He had an apron on, as did Colleen and Lorraine. "Where's mine?"

Jake followed with a casserole in hand and laid it on the table. "Turkey smells great. Is it sample time yet?" He went to the stove and opened the door for a peek.

"Don't you dare touch that."

Colleen was in a creative zone, and coordinating everyone else in the kitchen. She heard Lorraine say "I'll do that." to Vicky, and faced them, raising the wood spoon in her hand and pointing it at her newly adopted grandmother. "You're not allowed to make anything, lift anything but your wine glass, or clean anything. Do you hear me?"

Lorraine giggled and raised her hands. "Are you throwing me out of my own kitchen?"

"Hell no! We absolutely need your supervision."

Lorraine reached for her wine. "You make me want to open another restaurant. I'd hire you in a minute and place you in charge of my kitchen."

Everyone wandered in and out of the kitchen until dinner was ready. The cooks started drinking too early, and the pre-dinner celebration met everyone's expectations.

Lorraine stood in the opening between the family room and kitchen without disturbing anyone's concentration on the game. "Who's carving?"

Connor glanced up from the TV, "Jake" then motioned to him. "Your job now."

Jake straightened in his chair. "Wow. Am I a grown-up now?"

Chris pointed to the kitchen and smiled without taking his eyes off the TV. "Don't get carried away. Go carve. No bleeding."

Dinner was a feast and the conversation took a respite until Connor placed his fork next to his plate and started clapping softly. "This is absolutely excellent. Well done ladies…" Nodding once at each daughter. "…and sir." Nodding at Vicky as he continued to clap, and everyone joined in, clapping and offering praise.

"To my sisters." Vicky raised his glass.

Everyone toasted while Stephie held her glass out to Colleen. "You can cook, girl. And cooking together was a blast, wasn't it?"

Colleen's eyes glistened as she lightly blushed. "I …it was crazy …hectic …scary …and wow. I never had such a good time working so hard." She glanced around the table, then at everyone. "Everything's alright?"

Everyone affirmed but Cody praised loudest. "It's delicious! Can you pass me everything again?" She brightened noticeably as his approval registered.

Lorraine leaned back as she quietly cherished the gathering and silently, secretly, said another prayer of thanks.

A few hours later, Colleen took a break from organizing desert with Stephie, and walked into the family room during halftime of the late game. She stood in front of the TV and softly caught everyone's attention. All eyes watched her fold her hands in front of her and look slowly around the room. "I can't believe what happened here today. I can't believe how you all made me feel. I walked around here today laughing and happy; not self-conscious at all. Colleen, the girl in me walked around here laughing and happy, and none of you thought anything of it. You looked past me when I walked in front of the TV while the game was on. You had no reaction when I sat in Cody's arm and next to any one of you. None of that ever happened in my life. And I never felt so accepted." She started crying. "I can't believe who you people are. I really can't."

All three mothers rose instantly as Stephie stepped into the family room.

Vicky blurted. "Something's wrong with them, isn't there?"

Colleen laughed as she wiped her eyes and hugged the other women. "I can't believe the day I had."

"You know you're standing in front of the TV and the game's about to start." Chris had his hand out pointing to the TV.

"You're an ass." Morgan smirked at him as she extended her arms toward her, and the rest of the room snickered as Colleen walked into them. She whispered in her ear, "Now, you're officially a member of the family. Chris is picking on you just like he does everyone else."

~~~

Vicky opened the bathroom door and saw Colleen shutting her bedroom door as slowly as she could, trying not to disturb Cody. He waited for her to finish, then whispered, "What are you doing up this early?"

"I'm kinda looking forward to seeing everyone."

"I don't think anyone else is awake yet."

"That's alright. I'll make coffee." She hugged and kissed him good morning. "Besides …you're up, and that's perfect for me."

He kissed her forehead. "You're so pretty."

She followed him down the stairs. "I feel like I'm in some old Christmas movie or something."

"Oh, we should all have a night and watch them together." He snickered. "…Just to hear Chris's commentary, if nothing else."

One by one everyone rose to the smell of brewing coffee and frying bacon, and joined the others around the kitchen table. Eventually, Genna opened the front door and yelled "Hi." and Morgan, Connor, and Chris's arrival made enough commotion to wake the last two late sleepers.

Morning greetings circled the kitchen table, then Chris stood at a side counter, removing bottles from the two bags he carried in. He handed Connor champagne to open as he shook the tomato juice. "Who wants a bloody Mary or mimosa?"

Requests were made and the party resumed.

Morgan moved next to Colleen at the stove as she cooked bacon and set her mimosa on the counter. "Give me that."

Colleen's mouth dropped as she took the tongs from her.

"You did enough cooking yesterday, and the food was fantastic. Now go sit down and enjoy the afterglow of your success." She smiled at Colleen, then motioned to Genna. "Shall we show them how breakfast is done?"

Genna grinned as she waited patiently next to Chris. "Absolutely. As soon as I get my bloody Mary."

They worked like a team as everyone else pulled chairs from the dining room and sat around the crowded kitchen table.

"When are we going bridesmaid dress shopping again?" Colleen glanced at the ladies around the table.

Stephie eyed her. "Should we wait until after the holidays? There'll probably be some good sales."

Genna turned from the toaster. "Yeah, but things might be picked over by then."

Connor poured tomato juice into his beer.

"What the hell are you doing?" Jake pointed at his glass.

Connor laughed. "It's delicious. I can't drink bloody Mary's." He rubbed his stomach. "They'll give me agita all day."

"There are sales right before Christmas. I think we could still get a deal if we look."

"I like the black ones with the flowers. Just a regular dress we can wear anywhere, after the wedding." Colleen glanced at everyone and shrugged softly. "And I'll always look at it as my bridesmaid dress for your wedding."

Jake lowered his coffee. "I'm almost done typing everyone's contributions for the presentation. I need you all to go over it and tell me what needs fixing."

Stephie shook her head. "Can you talk about anything besides the presentation? I swear you're obsessed."

Jake held his hand out apologetically. "I only want it to be good."

Morgan squeezed between Vicky and Stephie and slid her plate on the table.

"How many pages is it now?" Jon glanced at Jake then pointed to Connor's glass. "Can I try that?"

"Jake's trademark grin appeared. "Over twenty five."

Cody and Stephie spoke at the same time. "It'll be great." "You're an idiot."

Connor finished pouring, "Sure. It's delicious." and held his glass out to Jon.

Jake's head spun to Stephie. "I don't see anyone else volunteering to coordinate everything."

She motioned dismissal of his sentence. "Yeah, like you'd give up control."

Lorraine sat and watched in silence as her family interacted. There were at least three conversations going and more than three people were in more than two of them. She sat quietly at peace, reminiscing when she and Robert were young; and the two and three day New Year's Eve parties they used to host for the entire extended family, and the breakfasts the next mornings. To her, the next mornings were better than the party the night before; the commotion of a house full of people waking. The love the next morning was always so strong it could be seen.

Chris playfully fighting Colleen to fix her a drink, caught her vision and brought her back to the present, and the accompanying teasing warmed her soul. Another morning after, breakfast party. New loved ones mixed perfectly with old loved ones. New faces caring for each other; no difference whether blood or sworn family.

336

What an accidental twist of fate. She knew she would reap benefits from the arrangement she made with Colleen, but she had no idea the offer would be this satisfying, or that Vicky and Colleen had so much love in them. Oh how she missed this. She shook her head unnoticeably as she realized how much.

Jake motioned to Colleen and Cody. "We're meeting everyone who's helping us distribute presentation posters, at our apartment around noon tomorrow."

"We'll be there."

"Anyone want more coffee?" Genna poured herself another cup, then paused and looked around. "Okay, who wants what for Christmas?"

Four *nothing*'s came almost in unison.

"Stop. You're all getting something, but are there any requests before we have to figure gifts out on our own?"

Vicky raised his hand chest high. "I know what I want more than anything." Everyone quieted and he looked around. "Can we do this for Christmas? This is what I want. This can be my present."

Morgan lowered her drink. "Is Christmas over our house this year?"

Stephie confirmed with a nod. "Yep. And Christmas eve is at the Blair's this year."

Morgan clasped her hands together and held them to her chest. "Okay. Sleep over at our house for day after breakfast."

Genna pushed her sandwich plate away. "We have bedrooms right next door too."

Vicky clapped softly like only he could. "Yay."

Stephie's eyes narrowed. "We're all still having Christmas eve, right?"

Vicky straightened in his seat. "What's Christmas eve?"

"We always have Christmas eve over the other house."

Connor raised his fists straight up. "Three day party!"

Chris laughed. "Everyone bring your own booze, but I'll buy the pink champagne."

Morgan reached past Genna and smacked him on his shoulder. "Is there ever a time when you're not an ass?"

Genna noticed Lorraine hadn't stopped smiling since they all came in. "What do you want for Christmas, mother?"

"Yeah grandma. What do you want?"

"I want one of the bedrooms Christmas night."

"Oh you don't have a choice. You're coming. But you're not driving." Stephie pointed to Jake. "We'll come get you and take you home."

Colleen motioned with her hand. "I can drive us over."

"Perfect. That's settled." Stephie folded her hands and faced Lorraine. "But what gift do you want Nana?"

She thought for a few moments. "I want pictures of all of you like Stephie and Jake gave us the other year, with your partners, and all of you together. I want them for the wall in the family room."

Stephie excitedly straightened in her seat. "We can do that."

"Give us ones too." Connor pointed back and forth to Genna.

Morgan motioned with her hand. "Hey, don't leave us out."

The gathering moved to the family room and snacks were set out. A pot of tomato sauce replaced the breakfast pans as the younger gentlemen cleaned up, and the party continued until the sun faded from the sky.

~~~

Morgan removed her coat from the closet and walked toward Chris. "We're going to lunch after, so you're fending for yourself."

Chris leaned toward her, from his corner of the sofa and kissed her. "I figured. I'll probably have an early dinner at Logan's."

She gave him a smirk. "I figured."

"I may see if somebody feels like going." He reached for the TV remote. "Or not."

"I figured." She checked her handbag for her phone and glasses. "Love you."

"Be careful."

"You too."

She paused in the kitchen and placed her coat over the back of the kitchen chair, then reached in her purse, found her phone and started typing. *Walking out the door.*

She hit send, and almost immediately heard the honk from the shared driveway, "See ya." then walked out the side door and headed toward Genna's car.

Genna's car window lowered. "Hi."

"Hi." She hurried to the passenger side. "When's the last time we went out alone together?"

"Damn, Morgan. I don't know. Why don't we go out alone together, more?"

She laughed, motioning to her side door. "Because we're always dragging our *better halves* with us."

"I know." Genna giggled. "We need to tell them we're going clothes shopping more often. That'll get us a free pass out the door alone."

"Amen." Morgan buckled in. "Where we headed?"

Genna pulled onto the road. "I was thinking the mall. Vicky said we could use his employee discount if we find something there. Sound like a starting place?"

"I like their clothes." She adjusted herself in the seat, then sat comfortably back. "Sounds like a plan."

An hour later, each had an armful of dresses heading to the fitting room. Genna took a plastic number card as she walked behind Morgan. "You're right. This is fun."

Morgan finished first and waited for Genna in the aisle outside the dressing room, then scanned the department store as she approached. "Shall we wander the mall to the other end?"

Genna patted her hand bag. "Sure."

After another few hours shopping, Genna scanned the racks of dresses in view. "I'm not interested in making any final decisions today."

"Me either, and I'm getting tired."

"Me too." They walked out the little boutique and Genna hesitated, then casually turned in the direction of the car.

Morgan took her arm. "Where you feel like going for lunch?"

Genna offered a quirky grin. "A glass of wine."

Morgan giggled and shook her head at the comedic response. "That's a given."

Genna pressed the key fob when they approached the car, as Morgan hesitated and pointed across the expansive parking lot. "How about there?"

Genna examined the building. "Oh, I could go some chips and a margarita."

Morgan laughed. "Or two?"

Genna opened the trunk and threw their only shopping bag in. "One." She shut the trunk, then glanced at Morgan. "...at a time at least."

Morgan placed her hand over her heart. "Don't scare me like that! I thought you were going to stop at one."

Genna made a strange sound. "Yeah, like that's ever gonna happen."

They left the car and walked across the lot, and as they walked, Morgan took Genna's arm. "I adore how close our families are."

Genna glanced at her. "So do I. You Chris and Jake welcomed us from our first day next to you." Her enthusiasm increased, "Do you remember our babies meeting each other? ...I fell in love with him, instantly."

Morgan whispered as they entered the restaurant and stood waiting for the hostess. "And I'll never forget Steven looking up at me with those gigantic eyes, when he came over for lunch the day you moved in."

"Two?" The hostess grabbed two menus.

Morgan pointed to the right. "Let's sit in the bar area."

Genna glanced at the area, then turned to the hostess. "May we have a booth in the bar area?"

The young lady graciously smiled. "Follow me."

Genna waited for Morgan to get situated, then sat across from her. "And my love for him has grown since that first day."

Morgan's expression changed. "I feel guilty about something and I feel I have to share."

"Can I get you ladies anything to drink?" A server placed a plastic bowl of chips and two small salsa bowls on the table.

Morgan sat back. "Regular margaritas please."

Genna added. "Large. The big ones."

Genna reached around the chip bowl, for Morgan's hand as the server walked away. "What do you think you need to confess?"

Morgan hesitated; dipping a chip slowly. "I was mad about Jake and Stephie, when I first found out."

She scrunched her face waiting for Genna's negative reaction but Genna offered no sign of any emotion as she reached for a chip and dip it. "How do you feel now?"

"No. I'm talking about when I first found out, and I hate that I felt like that."

The server politely interrupted and placed their drinks.

Genna stirred and sipped. "So how do you feel now?"

"I'm fine. Better than fine. They've taught me so much about them."

"Then why are you worried about how you used to feel? Aren't you allowed to change?"

"Yeah, but I can't believe I was one of those assholes who knew all about how wrong their lifestyle is, even though I never read a single word about the entire issue, all because I was told to believe a certain way."

"Who you were?" Genna shrugged. "What does that have anything to do with who you are?"

"I know, but sometimes I'm still mad at myself for not being as accepting as I now know I should've been."

"God, Morgan." She shook her head. "I can't tell you how much, who you were before, counts for nothing. Cut yourself a break. You had reasons for the way you felt, and then you learned more and changed your opinion." She reached for Morgan. "That's the only thing that counts."

"Did you notice though? Could you tell?"

Genna's eyes narrowed. "No, but I don't understand. Why does it matter? I see how you are right now …how genuine your love is. So stop beating yourself up. Forgive yourself." She sipped her drink and grinned. "But if you feel you need to, there is something you can do to make it up to me."

Morgan straightened. "What?"

"Drive home after I have a few more of these. These things are delicious!"

~~~

Chris sat fidgeting with the remote, unable to get comfortable. Being alone with a free afternoon always sounded better than it actually was. His first thought was Logan's, but didn't feel like going alone, then pictured going with Morgan and the irony wasn't lost. She had always been his drinking buddy but he also realized she had truly become his best friend.

*Jake.* Maybe Jake felt like a beer with his old man. The few times they had a beer together were definitely enjoyable, but he had his own life now, and the last thing he wanted to do was make the kid uncomfortable declining a last minute invite. Then it struck him. For all the times they had been out together with the wives, and for as long as they lived next door to each other, he couldn't remember ever having a beer alone with Connor.

He grabbed his phone from the end table and dialed. "Hey."

"What's going on?"

"I was thinking. How 'bout we take a cue from the ladies and find a watering hole together?"

"Sure. What the hell. We're practically related now. I guess I can be seen with you."

Chris smiled at the sarcasm. "Thanks. What time?"

"I don't care. I got nothing planned."

"You ready now or do you need time?"

"I'm ready."

"Good. Meet me at the truck."

They both appeared on their outside kitchen landings, and Connor extended his hand as he crossed the driveway divide. "Where we headed?"

Chris did a double-take. "Um, where do you want to go?"

Connor smiled. "I'm only fuckin' wit' you. We can go to Logan's"

Chris stopped walking and stood straight. "Suppose I don't want to go to Logan's"

Connor patted his shoulder. "Yeah, right."

"No. I don't know what I feel like."

Connor eyed him and raised an eyebrow. "Well I have an idea." He pointed to his side door. "I'd rather order pizza or sandwiches, watch a game or three, and drink my own beer. This way we can get stupid without having to drive." His enthusiasm rose. "I have a bunch of different bottles of excellent beer I bet you never tried. What'da you say?"

Chris paused. "You're right. We don't have to go somewhere else to be stupid. We can be stupid right here."

"Exactly." Connor tapped him on the arm. "C'mon. Let's go raid my basement fridge for some exotic ones."

"But if I don't like your shit, I'm drinking mine."

"Of course."

Chris joked, "My definition of exotic is adding a lime slice."

Connor nodded and smiled. "I know." He opened his side door and held it for Chris. "You like peanut butter?"

"Yeah, but I'm pretty sure not in beer."

"Chocolate and peanut butter?"

"Are we talking beer?"

"How about root beer or coffee?"

"Root beer beer?"

Chris followed him to the basement. "You like lime. Ever try orange, or a beer that's half lemonade? Oh, I have a raspberry and a cherry wheat you'll like." Connor opened the fridge. "You don't know what you've been missing, my friend."

"I want to try the peanut butter." Chris's voice rose. "Then the root beer …maybe the raspberry."

Connor moved bottles and handed the selected to Chris. "Are we bringing all these over my house?"

"Yeah. What the hell."

They each took a handful of beers next door and after loading Chris's fridge, Connor started pouring him a chocolate peanut butter stout.

"I'll drink it out of the bottle."

Connor laughed as he waited for the head to settle before pouring more. "No you won't. This ain't your crap."

"Hey. You drink my crap."

"And out of the bottle too. What's your point?" Connor grinned.

"...Just saying."

Connor carefully poured his glass. "Will you let me teach you something?"

"Man... I gotta be related to you?" Chris waited patiently as the beer settled.

Connor carefully poured more, "Yeah. Your son is my son. And my daughter's your daughter." He raised the beer and smiled. "It's why I'm trying to teach you some culture."

"Wise ass. Give me my pretend beer."

Connor handed it to him. "Be careful. This pretend beer has about three times the alcohol of your piss yellow real stuff."

Chris brought it to his mouth. "Damn. That's liquid candy."

"Don't you dare tell me you like it." Connor opened a different bottle.

"Man. The after-taste ...this is wild."

Connor topped his glass. "I'm warning you. Go easy."

"What are you drinking?"

"A cherry wheat."

Chris pointed to Connor's bottle. "I like cherry."

"You can try mine. I'll let you try them all" Connor finished pouring his and lifted it. "Salute"

"Mazeltov." Chris clinked his glass.

"L'chayim." Connor licked his upper lip after taking a mouthful. "Let's order dinner before we get bombed."

"Sure."

Connor spent the afternoon introducing Chris to new beers and dinner came as they relaxed, joked and watched three different games on TV.

Connor interrupted a relaxing silence. "I've wanted to say something to you for a while."

Chris smiled. "What?"

"I need to tell you..." He paused and grinned. "How you treated my child when you first met her. How you just flat out showed you were thrilled to meet Stephanie, opened her up like I've never seen. I think she would have been crushed if you didn't do what you did." He rose from the loveseat enough to extend his hand and reach Chris's. "Thank you."

Chris shook his hand. "My feelings for your child are genuine. I love her like I loved him. I'm honored you acknowledged it, but my love for her doesn't need acknowledging. I love the child."

Connor sat back with a wide grin. "I know you didn't need acknowledging. I just had to say it." He raised his glass toward Chris. "It's a pleasure being your family."

"We are." Chris's smile grew as he lifted his half empty glass and stared at it. "These fucking fake candy ass beers are starting to kick my ass."

"Told you."

They sat relaxing, eating and drinking until Connor received a text from Genna. "The ladies are on their way, and I have the perfect beer for their arrival." Connor wobbled toward the kitchen and came back with two bottles of hard root beer. "If they ask …we're drinking root beer and we have the bottles to prove it." He wiped his forehead. "I think I need a nap."

"Oh, this one we can drink out of the bottle?" Chris held it up and read the label. "I can't like this fancy shit. Too much thinking involved."

"Will you stop already. …You know you had fun."

"Yeah yeah."

Connor shook his head at Chris's playful sarcasm.

# Chapter Seventeen
## Purgation

The stream of people entering the back of the mini-theater made a few of the club members more nervous than expected but they were all feeling a myriad of emotions; from elated so many people cared about them and the subject, to scared to death with stage fright, and each club member either consoled or playfully tormented their friends for the emotions being displayed.

Ciera tested the sound system. "Welcome everyone. We're starting in roughly ten minutes. Please come in and have a seat, preferably down close, especially if you plan to participate, which we encourage."

Jake finally gathered everyone in the hall to the left of the stage, for one last group talk. "Guys …stop thinking this is some kind of performance for a school grade. This is for our families. We're not trying to impress the college. Hell, we're not trying to impress anybody. And I don't give a fuck if you faint before a word comes out of your mouth. Because I'm so fucking psyched I'll do the whole presentation if you let me. So if you can't, no worries, but let me share; don't think of you while you're doing your thing. Think of every other person in our group and speak for them …they need you. They need you to explain how they should be loved …like you love them. This isn't about you. This is about everyone standing around you right now. This is about every person like us, in the entire world …including those not born yet. And if you get overwhelmed because you're thinking about you and your every word and move …look at the rest of us. Do you love someone in this group and have strength for beyond the strength you have for you? …I know I damn sure do." He scanned all the eyes looking into his. "So let's nail this." He motioned and they all started back in. "One last thing; there's a pizza party after. Right here. Food's already ordered and it's for everyone. If you have family here; invite them. I already know we bought way too much."

A song started on cue as club members moved in and out the open side door and began organizing. Some of the group stayed in the side hall going over their notes and practicing, as Graham Nash's voice filled the background. *"We can change the world. Rearrange the world. It's dying …if you believe in justice. It's dying …if you believe in freedom. It's dying..."* Others stood in awe inside the side entrance and to the side of the steps surrounding the tiered seating of the small theater. Some held hands and gathered together at the back of the stage, under the large white screen, as others searched for an inconspicuous place to be alone.

"Welcome everyone. We're going to start in a minute. Thanks for coming. Please have a seat, down closer if you plan on participating. We hope you will."

Leslie waved and whispered as loudly as she could. "Come on everybody. Get on stage."

Everyone hurried next to each other in a line.

"Welcome!" Adriana raised her hand as she began. "I'm Adriana and we're all going to step forward, maybe do something crazy, yell our names, then step back."

"I'm Sean." "I'm Zelma." "I'm Cecilia." Each quickly yelled their names, and curtsied or bowed.

Dawn jumped and waved jokingly. "I'm Dawn. Hi mom!"

Everyone laughed.

Giana and Kyleigh danced a few steps of the waltz together. "I'm Kyleigh and this is Giana."

"I'm Giana and this is Kyleigh."

Polite claps came from the crowd.

Anthony waved a handful of folded papers. "Do all of you have the program Desmond and Mick are handing out as you came in tonight? Raise your hand if you need one."

Dawn spoke as people walked up each isle giving programs out. "And now ...I'd like to introduce Jacob Harrison."

Jake walked to center stage, to light applause and waved. "Hi everyone. Thanks for coming." He paused as he slowly walked across the stage. "We have some interesting perspectives on lgbt, to share with you, but we're not interested in changing your minds tonight. We want to open them instead. When your minds are open to the information we'll share, some of you might come to understand there's more information available on this subject than previously thought, and that often leads to personal re-evaluations which hopefully lead to people thinking differently ...and that's all we hope for."

He continued his soft pace along the stage. "We hope some of you will eventually see certain things with a greater awareness, but we understand; change is slow. Anthropologically – change is gradual and slow. The introduction of new information takes time and the ideas are rarely adopted in full, over previous beliefs. Often, new paradigms are founded on the melding of new concepts with established social standards already set in the history of a culture. Christianity, for example is different on different continents, because existing beliefs melded with the basic teaching, making modified versions of the religion."

He stepped back as Kaden continued pacing on the path Jake had established. "We also adopt information without verification.

This isn't a shortcoming. It's life. We're taught certain things when we're too young to question them, by people we feel are our biggest protectors and have our best interests at heart. Many of you believe certain things because you're 'Catholic' or 'Muslim'; not because you've weighed the information and accept it because it measured up to the scrutiny of your examination."

Michaela walked forward and Kaden made a left toward the group behind. "We hope, because of your love for us, you'll re-examine some of the information you've adopted without investigation. We've studied the information we're going to share tonight, because it's relevant and important in our lives. The information isn't skewed or twisted. If the information wasn't accurate and verifiable, tonight would be as big a waste of our time as it would be for you, and personally, we're at the age where we'd rather be dancing and drinking than standing up here fighting our worse fear to help you understand who we are. Yes, public speaking is on the psychological fear chart as a fear *worse than death*."

Vicky stepped forward. "Hi everyone." He waved demurely and his new family clapped and laughed softly.

Morgan yelled, "We love you!"

Vicky straightened, then covered his heart with his hand, "I love you too." then inhaled as he focused on the rest of the audience. "The information we share tonight is available through email." He pointed to the large white-board behind him as the address appeared. "Please either text this email into your phone or send an email to that address and we'll forward you the entire program information, along with all the internet links supporting the discussion."

Vicky stepped back and Stephie stepped forward. "You're also going to enjoy some of the educational methods many of us have learned over the last few years, since many of us are either in college or just graduating, and the first example of this is the start of the discussion; we're starting with questions." She paused a moment before explaining. "We want you to ask us questions you want answers to. We want them to be bold. We plan on getting things out in the open tonight. We're more used to strong questions than you think. We ask ourselves strong questions constantly, since we were old enough to know we were different. See ...we've been told explicitly; everything from *there's something wrong with us*, to *we're condemned to death*. ...We can handle rough questions."

Stephie stepped back and Kyleigh stepped forward. "As we try to share the information, our discussion will take on an ancient scientific argument; nature versus nurture, and will be broken down into the two categories, which can be loosely titled, The outer world, or the sociology of lgbt and the inner world, the psychology of lgbt, and then into sub-categories in each; culture, history, religion, and geography. The Psychology category, or personal cause effect, will delve into four of the five aspects of inner existence; physical, mental, spiritual, and emotional. And these topic sub-categories will constantly cross during the discussion. There'll be an all-encompassing aspect as the conclusion; we hope will tie everything into a unique bow, no pun intended." She smiled and held out her hands. "See? We can laugh at ourselves."

Anthony stepped forward. "This information was never meant to be presented this way. We created this show because many of us here have family who don't understand or approve of our lifestyle, and we all seem to fail when we try to defend ourselves alone. None of us individually knew there was so much information available, and we found we can explain everything better as a group. All of us know more than any one of us."

Giana walked forward as Anthony finished and headed to the back. "Don't hesitate to interrupt us and add thoughts. Communicate with us. This isn't a play, it's a learning experience. Butt in. That's what family does. Shout out. Interrupt us. Complain, question and disagree out loud. And don't hesitate to ask for more explanation, but don't for a second doubt the information we present. We extensively researched, and painstakingly and thoroughly confirmed, and every statement and fact is documented and available for the asking."

Cody stepped toward the audience. "We hope we have fun discussing this. This subject is our passion, so a few of us will get passionate …and frustrated, loud, excited, and sad. We love and care for you, which is why we did this for you. We hope you love and care for us and why you're here tonight."

Jake stepped forward. "Hi again. We're going to start with Religion. I can imagine you can all imagine why. If there's a more powerful or vocal institution presumably against lgbt, I'm not aware of it. When I realized who I am and heard I was condemned to eternal hell for being who I am, I ran to the information sources immediately to verify my fate. I didn't assume the popular opinion. I couldn't leave my eternal damnation to someone else's declaration. This was my eternity we're talking about, so I searched and read. I took courses in college. I studied and analyzed and then read and searched more …and I found enlightening information.

How many of you have a complete opinion of who and what lgbt is and what their fate in existence is? Show of hands please. It's alright. Everyone has opinions. We're not here to judge. We instead want to have a friendly discussion and get things out in the open. This subject needs an open dialogue, don't you think? Please, show hands.

Okay …now how many think the fate of anyone lgbt is eternal hell? Hands please?

If I can guess, I'd say the percentage is exactly what the percent of society is. Excellent.

Of those people who raised your hands verifying our fate as doomed; how many have that opinion because of religious beliefs?

Okay ..most of you. Excellent. This is good, believe it or not." He smiled. "...Because I've done the homework on this opinion. Like I said I almost had a heart attack when I realized who I was and how that meant being condemned to eternal hell. It's enough to scare the shit out of a person, to be honest."

He inhaled. "The first thing I did was source and read the condemning excerpts everyone references. Then, using a method I learned in college which helps eliminate all information with ulterior proclivities, I found illuminating explanations and interpretations. Does anyone know the passages supposedly speaking against lgbt lifestyle?"

Someone called out, "Saddam and Gomorrah."

Chelsea typed the words and they appeared on the large screen.

"Any others?" Jake paused and scanned the room.

No one offered another.

"I'll fill in the others for you. They are; Corinthians, Timothy, Leviticus, Romans and Genesis. Even zealous religious people have adopted the latest Saddam and Gomorrah interpretation that the story is about greed, excess and corruption, and nothing to do with lgbt lifestyle, which, to anyone paying attention, gives concern considering how the previous belief was so strong, it led to a certain sex act being named for one of the cities. Zealous thoughtless interpretations are a peculiar thing, aren't they?"

Bible passages appeared on the large screen at the back of the stage.

1 Cor 6:9  1 Tim 1:10  Lev 18:22  Rom 1:27  Gen 19

"I'm not going to bore you with the specific breakdown of each passage and its argument. The complexity is too intricate and conceptual for you to fully grasp through lecture anyway. Many thanks to Doctor Benjamin Bloom for the taxonomy confirming that statement." He paused. "You'd all be asleep in five minutes. But there are two things I'd like to say regarding these passages; one, the document available to you through email, has the extensive discussion in intricate detail, laid out in understandable english, and is free for you to enjoy at whatever level of digestion you feel comfortable. I spent roughly two years accumulating the information. The document is thorough.

And two; the original concepts were written anywhere from two thousand to almost three thousand years ago by people who not only didn't know there was a universe around us, but actually thought this fourteen and a half billion year ongoing creation was completed in six days, compounded by the idea they weren't intelligent enough to invent indoor plumbing or toilet paper, then manipulated unfettered, by organizations with enough secret agendas to fill manuscripts that would make the original book look like a Sunday reader." He laughed and looked around with his arms out, then sighed and continued.

"One such wisdom section, Leviticus, has been interpreted to rail against lgbt rather clearly …but it also rails against eating shrimp, bacon, pork ribs, and hot dogs …and better than that, declares cutting the edges of your beard hair a condemning sin. But the best of this supposed tirade is the condemnation of those who wear multi-fabric blend clothing." He waved his finger. "Please don't condemn me for being gay, using Leviticus, if you're clean shaven. Because if that's my hell ticket, guess who I'll be flirting with for eternity."

He paused to calm his breathing. "Five Leviticus condemnations. Four are ignored as if written by a five year old and one is one of the six time tested timeless people condemning paradigms. I wouldn't think of arguing the legitimacy of the ten commandments, but if you're going to insist wearing cotton polyester underwear is a sin, then please forgive me. I can't take you seriously" He inhaled. "…And if you're not going to hold to all five, then I'm afraid your argument isn't worth…" He tilted his head and held out his arms.

"If someone living today wrote the *wisdom* found in that passage, we'd laugh in their face and not give them another thought. Not that we're currently much more advanced. We're still far more accepting of two men holding guns, than we are of two men holding hands.

But to give you a little taste of what I've researched extensively, one of the things the document discusses, is how the operational words *malakoi* and *arsenkoitai* in Corinthians actually translate from the original Greek text. *Malakoi* translates to weak, as in spineless or gutless men and not weak as in effeminate or feminine men. And spineless and gutless men have taken what should be a rallying point for the oppressed, and made the passage an argument for bullying the oppressed.

Arsenkoitai wasn't retranslated to mean homosexual until the mid-nineteen hundreds and the word *homosexual* didn't appear in the Bible until nineteen forty six. And psychology proves the re-translation was influenced by the society of the time. The opposite is argued psychologically impossible; you can't take a human out of the influence of her or his society. It's an existential theory developed in part by Rollo May. And this theory also pertains to the original authors. They did not transcend time and place. They were instead, mired in their time and place, like everyone else who has ever existed on the face of the earth."

He faced the audience. "All I'm trying to share is; there's more depth to this subject than a casual browser would ever know without examination. Please don't have a closed opinion if your depth of knowledge doesn't include in-depth investigation."

He waved, then walked toward the back of the stage.

Haley stepped forward. "Hi everyone!" She waved, bent over at the waist, and then straightened. "This is one of my fears so I'm sharing my passion as I conquer my fear. My passion is stronger than my fear."

She screamed, "Aaahhhh!" then placed her hand on her chest. "There. ...Better. ...I have history and geography. And the history of lgbt is as old as chronicled human history." She pointed to the large screen which had changed to a colorful world map with lines pointing to locations around the world at one end, and the other pointing to paragraphs headed by names and dates of societies, bordering the edge of the picture.

"LGBT is recorded in every culture with a documented history." She ran the laser pointer over the entire map, then stopped the light on Greece. "In some cultures such as ancient Greece, lgbt were part of the ruling class; mainly the senate. Plato even spoke of a third gender in his diaries and referred to those people as part of original human nature; confirmed by one ancient Greek statue which shows a gorgeous reclining well-endowed female with very obvious male genitalia."

"The people in Siberia identified seven genders in addition to male and female." The red laser light moved down. "In China, from one BCE to the seventeenth century A D, homosexuality was considered a sign of cultural elitism and has been documented as early as the Qing, Han and Tang dynasties. Korea, Nepal, India..."

She moved the pointer quickly. "Twenty fourth century BCE Egypt shows tombs with pictures of same sex couples. Africa, Angola, Nigeria, Mexico... Mayan cultures recorded, recognized and accepted lgbt lifestyles."

She lowered the pointer and folded her hands in front of her. "This beautiful map covering highlights of the lgbt cultures from around the world, as recorded in history, is included in the documents we'll send you if you reply to the email."

She paused and breathed noticeably deep. "And on the ground you live, the native people who occupied this land for thousands of years before the great European-American genocide here, revered certain lgbt people as two-spirited; knowing both the male and female aspects of existence, and more in touch with the all gender Great Spirit, than one gender individuals. Great Plains native Americans viewed gender as a spectrum, including transsexual and intersexual people."

She fanned herself with her hand. "To quote a current American leader; LGBT is not a western invention or a new invention; it's a human reality."

She jumped, then pumped her arm in the air. "Nailed it!"

The crowd stood and clapped enthusiastically.

Someone in the group yelled, "Yay Haley, you rule!"

Giana stepped forward. "My contribution is short and sweet, but fascinates me, and I hope will do the same for you. The history of the church and the origin of its current opinion on homosexuality. Before the high middle ages, homosexuals were accepted by the church. It wasn't until the middle of the thirteenth century and Thomas Aquinas's writings that hostility toward homosexuality took root and eventually spread throughout Europe. Twelve centuries of acceptance, influenced by a few medieval leaders, but the church's influence was powerful during that period in history and through their ruling power, their religious hate was eventually incorporated into secular society and legal sanctions developed. Criminal penalties still exist for homosexual acts in many nations. Yet no penalties for the first twelve and a half centuries of modern religion. …Seems we're still suffering and recovering from the dark ages."

Kyleigh stepped forward and jumped around like a cheerleader. "Hi everybody. I'm Kyleigh. I have culture, which I think is the nurture part of the nature nurture argument, and I have to tell you, our culture not only isn't very nurturing, but the parts of our culture swearing they're the ones who love and support, are doing the most hating and condemning. The difference between your words and your actions are enough to really confuse your children, people! Thank goodness some of us have managed to live with that condemnation, long enough to be able to find the reasons for the animosity, and learn to live with it. …But not all of us. The suicide rate for lgbt children and young adults is four times the rate of the rest of society." She raised her head toward the ceiling as her emotions began to overwhelm her. "I miss you Britt." She paused as Giana ran out and hugged her, then stepped back as Kyleigh composed herself. "The suicide rate for lgbt children and young adults is roughly four times the average, and we know people who caved to the idea we're not considered normal." She pointed to all her friends behind her. "We know people whose religious parents refused to accept them in the name of their religion, and they walked in front of a seventy mile an hour tractor trailer." She faced the crowd and peered to the back of the small auditorium. "Is there anyone in here who doesn't think that's as fucked up as humans get? Anyone?" She paced across the stage. "This is not a choice, people. We don't choose to be tormented, alienated, and condemned." She raised her voice to a plea. "Please understand; *just your opinion* comes with a death toll and a body count. No one in their right mind would choose this if it was merely a choice. …Yet I wouldn't be any different, because who I am has taught me more about my world, than billions of straight people will ever learn. I know what love looks like, because I've lived both love and hate. I know what acceptance looks like because I've been accepted and rejected. I know how to measure words versus actions, because I've heard the words and then measured the accompanying actions."

Arianna stepped forward and unfolded a page as Kyleigh bowed and walked to the side of the stage. "I'm going to read something that puts the nurture argument in perspective: A gentleman wrote to an advice columnist. He wrote; 'I recently discovered that my seventeen year old son is gay. We are part of a church group and I fear that if people in the group find out, they'll make fun of me for having a gay child. He won't listen to reason and won't stop being gay, and I feel he's doing this just to get back at me. Please help him make the right choice by not being gay. He won't listen to me. I'm hoping he'll listen to you.' …" She raised the newspaper clipping, then lowered it and continued reading.

"The columnist answered; 'You can teach your son a valuable lesson by changing your own sexuality to show him how easy it is. Try it for the next year. Stop being heterosexual to show your son that a person's sexuality is a choice to be directed by one's parents, the parents' church, and social pressure. I assume my suggestion will evoke a reaction that your sexuality is at the core of your being. The same is true for your son. And he has a right to be accepted by his parents for being exactly who he is.' …"

She folded the paper and placed it in her pocket. "Interesting, don't you think? Organizations telling individuals how they're supposed to act and feel. Social pressure to conform in a country that loves to boast about freedom. …freedom to conform …freedom to shut up, and get in line?"

Her voice calmed. "The history of our attitude is based on our puritan heritage and its influence on our society. People with puritan mindsets were thrown out of Britain four hundred years ago, landed here and became a paradigm altering influence. I'm not suggesting we throw them out too. I'm more accepting of people who are different. Like I said, I've learned lessons many don't ever get. I would like to suggest however, that we recognize the influence of extremism and put it in its place." She bowed quickly then hurried to the small gathering behind her. The gathering opened, and she disappeared inside, to courteous applause.

Shelbie walked forward from the huddle under the large screen. "Hi. I'm Shelbie and I have the medical viewpoint. There is a wide range of inconclusive information, pertaining to the medical and or biological proof of the cause of lgbt sexual orientation. The scientific community is still trying to understand whether sexual orientation can be explained biologically, or scientifically. Conversely, we have extensive biological documentation of gender variation. Incidences are a measurable physiological phenomenon and we have substantiated proof modern medical technology has acutely verifiable measuring techniques. The frequency of intersexual development is one in every hundredth person, with one in every two thousandth having enough ambiguity to make the child's male or female status uncertain. Medical doctors operate immediately on these babies, and a gender is often chosen according to criteria better left for a different discussion.

There are also variations of chromosomal development paired in every combination an $X$ and $Y$ chromosome can be joined and hormonal variations that allow or prevent certain developmental hormones from carrying out their assigned gender development purpose. There's Klinefelter Syndrome, Turner Syndrome, which is an $X0$ combination, Androgen Insensitivity Syndrome, Super males

*XYY* combination and Super Females *XXX*. Gender is far more complicated than pre-modern medicine or biology ever imagined, though some ancient cultures seemed to understand all too impressively.

But for sexual orientation, evidence is less than conclusive. There are studies suggesting the complexity of mitigating factors is beyond our current medical and biological comprehension. This doesn't mean there isn't medical and biological explanation. It means we haven't identified those biological indicators yet.

Medical science isn't as developed as many think. We're still learning about the inner human, like we're still learning about our universe. We didn't know there were other galaxies until nineteen thirty. We've just discovered gene coding. We thought our medical and biological scientists had identified a gene source, but as of now, they haven't found conclusive evidence of a cause." She paused. "But please don't let the inconclusiveness of the medical and biological fields make you think there aren't biological explanations. Like pre-nineteen thirty galaxies, we haven't discovered them yet, but that doesn't mean they're not there, and the rest of the information is more than enough to weigh."

"Deviation from the typical, sexually or genderally is not a flaw …it's only a wider parameter of existence than we're accepting. Natural human parameters include a range of normality we insist on not recognizing or discussing as if discussion would lower our opinion of ourselves, and that flaw alone is one of our great human limitations." Shelbie waved and stepped back.

Stephie stepped forward. "Hi everyone. I'm Stephanie. I have the first part of the nature argument; the psychology of the argument. And I've chosen the mental slash intellectual aspect of the inner being."

She scanned the audience. "See, I wasn't always Stephanie. Let me rephrase that. Intellectually …mentally …I was always Stephanie or a version thereof, though physically, I was born Steven." She paused and inhaled. "I was born to the most loving understanding parents a person could ever hope for. My grandmother is wise and caring. My second set of parents love me beyond my wildest dreams, yet I was scared to tell any of them who I am. I was afraid. I spent months …years hiding in my room, sometimes waiting to grow past …sometimes praying I could grow past the feeling inside me. I would stare at the mirror and cry because my mind told me my eyes were seeing something my body wasn't.

My mind refused to let me not be on guard. I couldn't be happy. Something was wrong and I knew it. I just didn't know what. I was young. Too young to know how to word what I was feeling, to parents who never ever did anything but love me beyond anything I could hope. But I knew."

"Do you know why I didn't share my inner confusion?" She inhaled deep enough for the entire room to see. "Because I didn't want to disappoint my perfect parents …my perfect grandmother …my perfect second parents. I wanted to be everything I thought they wanted me to be. I wanted to be everything I thought they thought I was. I fought myself. I even tormented and tortured myself. How dare I feel feminine. How dare I need to be a girl."

She stood there for a moment, in silence. "But I did …because I am."

She lowered her head. "I can't imagine whether I'd be here or not, if all the grown-ups in my life weren't as perfectly, unconditionally loving as they were. I can't say I would have been able to endure that, since I was barely able to endure my differences, as they were. I can't say I would have chosen to continue living."

She wiped her eyes. "I recently adopted a brother and a sister. Neither of them had the advantage I had. Both were abandoned, and it scares me to think how less my life would be if I didn't have them. And it amazes me; their real families chose not to enjoy two of the most kind and caring people I've ever met. Intellectually, I can't process those things. Intellectually, those things confuse me."

She took another deep breath. "Almost everyone I've talked to who fits into the lgbt spectrum, knew they were different, years before they shared their identity or came to peace with it. I know a person who hid what his unconditionally loving father knew for thirty years. Thirty years to one of the most impressive fathers I've ever known. And he was accepted completely by his father, when he finally revealed. His mother on the other hand, didn't want family members to know. Her son never acknowledged his mother's issues, but that doesn't mean they didn't cut him. Can any of you understand the intellectual turmoil? The inner confusion? …Unless you've lived the experience …probably not."

Vick stepped forward. "Hi again everyone. I'm Vicky …Victor. I chose to do emotional because I have a really high emotional level. I have a very high happy nature and a very low sad nature. I define myself as *emotional*. I remember being more loving than the rest of my family. I remember being more extroverted …more likely to bounce around …to dance …to pretend out loud." He inhaled slowly. "I was different. …It wasn't okay. Many things passed as my personality developed and I became aware why I am like I am, but my flamboyant extroverted personality didn't allow me to hide who I am," He motioned to Stephanie without pointing her out. "…unlike my dear dear sister. But when I shared unashamedly who I was, it cost me my family. I was forced to leave without a place to go and lived on the street for a time. My parents weren't religious, but our nationality is as unaccepting of people like me, as some unwavering religious are. My biological grandmother wants nothing to do with me."

Vicky's voice turned monotone. "I went into survival instinct. I didn't think of being happy. I didn't dare act flamboyant. I gave up part of my soul and happiness …my inner being …to survive. I often did whatever necessary to survive. And I survived. I gave away part of my emotional self to survive …but I survived."

"But I often wonder what my life would have been like if I was accepted and supported. It's something I wonder about more than I'd like. …But I'm still me. I'm still the person I used to be. I can change the outside a little, as necessary; it's now a survival technique. But the emotional inside and all the accompanying reasons never changed. But is who I am really bad? Certain people in my life now, tell me they love the inner me. Certain people in my life now, *show* me they love who I am, so why couldn't the people who brought me into this world? Why couldn't they see the same thing, those who love me now, see?"

His voice turned solemn "I didn't do any homework for this. I don't have any fancy facts about people like me. I've gone right past that part of existence to a point where, I have people who love me, and I love them, and if you want to be one of those people, I have room. I have room for a stadium of you, and I'll stand with you for the rest of our lives if you feel like being one. And if you don't want to, I'll look for the next person who wants my love. I overflow with love. I love overflowing with love, and I wouldn't change me for the world."

He wiped his eyes. "I love you, those who love me and are sitting in this crowd. I love you with all my heart, for no other reason than you love me …differences and all." A moment of silence came over the audience as he stepped back, and then cheers erupted from two separate corners of the gathering.

Jake stepped forward and waited for the crowd to finish acknowledging Vicky. "Hi. I begged for this part of the presentation too, because this specific subtopic is the other side of the religion discussion, and the last piece of the inner psychological aspect of humans; the spiritual."

"Many will get nervous when someone separates religious and spiritual. The religious are often told, when someone purposely separates the two, run from the argument as if demons were about to speak. Relax and instead of worrying about demons, decipher the words as if they stand completely on their merit alone." He waved his notes without looking at them. "Measure the words as if the author is anonymous. If the words make sense and cannot be disputed or refuted, then acknowledge them …even live up to them. If the words aren't valid, dismiss them …easy as that."

"Psychologically, we're unique beings, but there seems to be one single concept which strikes us all to our core. Love. Let me clarify. True love. *Unconditional love.* The concept goes hand in hand with forgiveness, but we need to separate the two for this discussion or I'll lose many of you on the singular message." He paused. "About the only thing we all have in common, is our reaction to what we deem as *unconditional love.* When we think God is unconditional love, we have strength to endure horrific things. When we believe someone loves us unconditionally, we contemplate dropping our most reserved guards. But only for a love we believe won't be affected by conditions …any condition. God speaks of love more than any other concept in the Bible. Many of us claim; *God is love.* I'm now going to offer the argument, God is perfect love."

Jake began slowly pacing across the front of the stage. "If a person believes in God the Creator, then his minimum age is measurable. The universe is roughly fourteen and a half billion earth years old. And as Creator, He must be the initial force or the opposite side of the big bang, since every action has an equal and opposite reaction. That makes Him pretty old, and if He's that old, then why wouldn't you assume He's learned a few things along the way? Let's assume you do think He's learned along the way, and you can comprehend that any being with an inclination toward perfection, which has been in existence that long and can create things like universes, must have arrived at the goal."

Jake paused. "God is perfect. And documentation states; He has no problem with us calling Him *father*. A*bba* father is the exact phrase. *Abba* translates to *daddy*. He creates universes and loves us so much He wants us to call Him, *Daddy*. Now, I'd like you to contemplate *perfect*. What if He's so perfect He loves everything He creates and creates only things He loves? He's God, remember. He can create anything He wants, any way He wants. If you were God and could create anything you wanted, could you be bothered creating things you hate? Would you create anything just so it would disgust you and you could destroy it later? You would get no satisfaction from destroying anything. Nothing can challenge you."

He stopped pacing and stood facing the audience. "This is where I choose to separate religion and spirituality. Religion doesn't teach love, let alone perfect love. Neither dominant religion is preaching unconditional love. Neither is teaching acceptance and tolerance. Just the opposite, actually."

He paused. "How could they rationalize hating in the name of perfect love? How could they say they know and represent God, when they preach hate and exclusion? My syllogistic argument is; When you're supposedly at your judgment, would you hope God asks you: *Why did you love?* Or: *Why did you hate?* If He's perfect love, I know which question means I win and which question I may have trouble with, even before I answer. And if you think your hate is excused, please read the story where He talks about separating the sheep from the wolves. He states the wolves as saying; *but we know you and you know us,* and He tells them; *Go away. I do not recognize you.*"

He stood silent for a moment, breathing noticeably. "And this is where I separate religious wisdom from spiritual wisdom; Because of our imperfect view of His perfection, some will state, He made us perfectly. No. Instead, He made us exactly like He wanted to make us. God is perfect, but we are not. The nature of human is imperfect and one of our most perplexing imperfections is the inability of some humans to separate God's perfection and our imperfection, recognize ourselves and others for what we are …then accept ourselves and each other."

Jake lowered his head and breathed like he had just exerted himself, and the audience began clapping softly.

Cody stepped forward, and waited for the gathering to end their appreciation. "Homosexuality was once included in the psychology bible, the DSM; the Diagnostic and Statistical Manual of Mental Disorders, as a disorder …but no longer is. The DSM classification reflected untested assumptions based on once-prevalent social norms, to quote a source. The fact lgbt lifestyles were once included says a lot about how society influences even the intellectual sciences.

Since the seventies, the behavioral and social sciences and the global health and mental health professionals have come to believe lgbt is a healthy variation of human gender and sexual orientation. Nature has created masculine and feminine males and masculine and feminine females …and every combination within.

The psychological science seems to have now done enough additional research to come to conclusions, societies way older and more primitive than ours believed centuries earlier. They just aren't very skillful at sharing the *new* information. Or certain groups don't want to hear the facts, though we can't seem to figure out why."

Aaron walked slowly to the front edge of the stage. "I hope you'll evaluate at least some of the information we shared tonight. But before your evaluation is complete, please consider hesitating to offer an opinion against things you haven't studied fully. Your beliefs and exclusionary actions have more of a negative effect on others, than you realize."

Colleen stepped from the group of friends, but not as far forward as the other presenters. "Some of this information may at times have been uncomfortable. Some of our lives have at times, been uncomfortable. This may at times have been a level of information you had not experienced before. Many of us have had misinformation affect us in ways you may not have noticed. We believe we addressed things many of us needed to address, and we're hoping we've shared things you haven't considered before. We really did do this out of love." She glanced in the direction of her parents. "We really did."

Leslie stepped beside her and squeezed her hand then eyed the gathering. "We will live our lives. We will live full lives. We wish to live openly alongside you and intertwined within the rest of our community, as caring friends and neighbors, but we will, with regret, do it against your will if need be. Regrettably, this isn't our choice. We choose acceptance and brotherhood. But the choice is more yours than ours."

As she spoke, one by one, each person on stage slowly joined her, and as she finished, the friends had formed a line on stage. Then one by one, they stepped forward.

"We are not a fad."

"Our lifestyle is not a choice."

"We are not the result of some modern twist on laziness or rebellion."

"We are not limited to this time."

"…or this place."

"In cultures past, we were accepted."

"In cultures past, we ruled."

"In other cultures we were condemned, persecuted and killed."

"Throughout history, there's been no rhyme or reason which way society thinks."

"But we've permeated every society."

"And made contributions to every society we've permeated."

"Then continued to exist, long after the collapse of every society."

"Many think we're different, and to many, different is scary."

"But we're not different than anyone else."

"And we don't exist in spite of God's wishes."

"We exist *because* God wishes."

"In spite of all the hate."

"All the ridicule."

"All the atrocities."

"We don't know why the Creator made us."

"But He did."

A pause amplified the silence.

"We don't want to be considered special."

"We don't want to be above anyone else."

"We don't want to be below anyone else."

"We want to be equal."

The line bowed at the audience and the audience stood and clapped. A few loud whistles and different shouts added to the appreciation, as Connor and Chris wheeled carts stacked with pizza boxes, down the side aisle.

James called out over the speaker system, from the screen operating desk to the side of the stage. Everyone's welcome to come down to the stage for an informal meet and greet. There's free pizza and soda.

Jake climbed the first step, plopped in the third padded theater seat and spread his arms and legs. Stephie spotted him, snuck behind him and wrapped her arms around his neck. She kissed the side of his head and whispered. "You're my hero."

He shut his eyes and didn't move. "And you're mine, sweetheart."

"You alright?"

"Emotionally spent. I'm passionate about this shit; you know that, but my fixation drains me."

She glanced up and spotted Lorraine walking toward Vicky with her arms extended, then patted Jake's shoulder. "Come on. Time to greet your new admirers. You can collapse later."

She waited for him to stand and held out her hand, then walked him to friends and their families as everyone hugged and congratulated the participants.

She recognized Colleen's mother from the police station, and immediately scanned the people close to her, looking for her father, then changed directions and pulled Jake toward Colleen in case she needed support. She watched Colleen's mom hug her, as she heard her mom reply. "He sat through the whole thing. He just needs time."

Her mother looked up as Stephie approached, then lowered her gaze.

"Hi ma'am." Stephie extended her hand. "Thank you for coming."

Her mom met her eyes, then glanced at Jake standing behind. She tentatively shook Stephie's hand, then her other hand raised and caressed Colleen's cheek. She nodded once slowly, dropped her eyes, and walked to the auditorium exit.

Stephie sighed and pulled Colleen into her arms as she watched her mother walk away. "Change takes time." She leaned away and lovingly brushed Colleen's hair back with her hand. "Change takes time."

Vicky suddenly appeared bigger than life. "Hi. You guys were incredible. You guys are great. Why don't you have any pizza? Want me to bring you a box? There's a ton!"

Lorraine suddenly appeared and hugged each grandchild. "My children are amazing. You've made me very proud. I'm completely impressed with all of you."

A lady approached as Lorraine finished her hugs. "Hi Lorraine."

"Hi Arlene. These are my grandchildren." She pointed to each. "Vicky, Stephie, Colleen and Jake. Everyone, this is Doctor Laurian, who helped me when I shared my desire to learn more about Stephie, and then helped facilitate the execution of this event. She was more instrumental in the logistics, than you know." She reached her hand out for Arlene's. "I'm grateful for all your caring kindness."

"I'm honored to have been even a small part of what I witnessed." Arlene smiled as she refocused on the four. "I cannot express how impressed I am with what I saw tonight. My doctoral dissertation wasn't as impressive." She shook each of their hands. "May I ask who coordinated this? Who organized this presentation?"

Jake waved at everyone on stage "All of us…" as Vicky, Stephie and Colleen all pointed to him. "Jake." "He did."

He watched the three disagree with him as the sentence began and refocused. "Oh bullshit. This was a perfectly shared joint effort by everyone."

Vicky led the three responses and his two sisters confirmed. "Him." "Definitely." "I agree."

Doctor Laurian's eyes narrowed as she observed Jake. "You look familiar. Were you in one of my classes?"

Jake felt his father's hand caress his shoulder from behind and he quickly acknowledged. "Yes ma'am. You're brilliant. A little overwhelming, but brilliant."

"If I remember correctly; you held your own. And I see some of the information we discussed, stuck well. Relevant psychological information becomes part of your soul, doesn't it?"

He nodded. "My heart and soul."

She motioned to the lady and gentleman waiting patiently next to her. "This is Doctor Galloway, Head of the Social Sciences Department and Doctor Egan, a sociologist and avid proponent of lgbt equality."

Doctor Galloway extended her hand. "Will you kindly share your sources and may we use some of your facts, for our ongoing studies?"

Jake's chest expanded as his breathing deepened. "We'd be honored."

Morgan hugged Jake from behind and he turned, kissed and hugged her.

Doctor Laurian excused herself. "I'd like to talk to you further, before you leave?"

Jake met her eyes. "I'd be honored, professor." Then reached for his mother and hugged her tighter.

She stood in front of him shaking her head. "You're so mature. What happened to my baby?"

He shook Chris and Connor's hands, then hugged and kissed Genna as he answered her. "I'm still your baby."

She reached up and caressed his cheek. "You'll always be my baby, but you keep letting me know you're a man now. I'm so proud of you."

"Thanks mom." His father's plate of pizza caught his eye. "I'm starving. Be right back."

Jake spotted his academic advisor and excused himself from the friends surrounding the food. "Ms. Tanner."

She turned as she heard her name, and extended her hand, "Megan. Please, I'm just Megan." then pointed to the screen. "The presentation was impressive."

"I can't believe you came, Megan. I didn't know you knew about it. Thank you." He extended his hand and she gracefully took it.

"Thank you for sharing. I pay attention to these things. Presentations like this help me be the counselor I need to be."

He smiled. "I remember you telling me that two years ago. Thanks for coming."

"It's my pleasure. I'll be sending you an email for the information."

Doctor Laurian approached with a plate, as Jake, Stephie, Colleen and Vicky stood together eating. "Good pizza."

Vicky instantly replied with a mouthful. "It is."

"So, who's currently a student here?" She made eye contact with all four.

Stephie straightened. "Jake and I finished our undergrad degrees last May."

"Congratulations." She faced Stephie. "What was your major?"

"Finance. I'm already enrolled in the MBA program."

"Excellent."

She glanced at Jake. "And your major?"

"Computer Sciences."

Stephie immediately added, "But his real love is psychology."

Doctor Laurian smiled as her eyes focused on his. "Any interest in an advanced degree?"

His brows rose. "Man, I swore I was done college when I finished my bachelor's degree." He animated mock exhaustion then smiled appreciatively. "Please don't do that to me. I just finished."

She smiled, enjoying his multitude of psychological responses. "What if a portion of the cost is paid for by a fellowship?"

His eyes widened further. "You're peaking my interest. Psychology is my passion."

She handed him a card. "You can contact me anytime in the future, but your aptitude and passion intrigue me, and I'd like to at least leave you an option for further consideration; how's that?"

"I'll enjoy considering it. The subject is fascinating."

She eyed him curiously as she digested his words. "Why didn't you pursue a degree in psychology as an undergrad?"

"The cost of my future wife, family and house." He reached for Stephie's hand.

Doctor Laurian smiled. "Touché."

~~~

Colleen sat on her bed, staring out the bedroom window at the bright Friday morning. She had Fridays off from school, on the advice of her sister, and luckily had the day off from work too. *I wonder what Vicky's doing?* She knew she had spent the evening with him only a week before, but as part of a crowd, and sometimes crowds get in the way of the level of personal contact she now craved. She dialed her adopted brother.

"Hi little sister. What's going on?"

"I miss hanging out, just you and me. Can I come over? We can maybe go holiday shopping or I can cook you dinner or something?"

His voice lightened. "No problem. I don't feel like going in today. I think I'll call out. Oh, maybe we can go to lunch."

His acceptance of her initial suggestion raised her enthusiasm, "I don't care what we do." then as suddenly, the realization of the accompanying social implication registered. "Whatever you want."

"Can you come over in an hour? I'll make you breakfast."

"Yeah, but let me cook when I get there. I'll make you something I haven't made in a while."

His voice rose excitedly. "I love when you say that. My stomach just grumbled. It misses your cooking."

An hour later, she knocked on his front door and stood there excitedly. She missed being alone with him in his apartment. This was her first safe haven after running away, and the loving welcome was still fresh in her mind. The door swung wide and his smile appeared wider. "Hi honey!"

She could feel her heart react to his words. They also produced a soft sigh. "Hi Vick."

She wrapped her arms around his neck and kissed him as his hug lifted her off her feet. He spun and dropped her inside. "It's great to see you. We haven't had a day alone in a while."

"I know. I'm excited." She headed right to the kitchen with the small grocery bag in her hand. "You hungry?"

He placed his hands on his hips. "I was just getting my girlish figure back."

"You're not eating?" Her brows rose.

He playfully admonished her. "Who said that? All I said was I was just getting my girlish figure back. Nobody told you to stop doing what you're doing."

He studied the items as she emptied the small grocery bag. "Where'd you buy this stuff?"

Her eyes widened. "The market."

He twisted his head. "Any issues?"

"No. Both of them stepped back when they saw me."

He registered her answer without a reply. "Want a soda while you cook?"

"Sure."

She split her attention between the two small frying pans as she prepared the flour tortillas. "I can't stop thinking about your presentation. I thought I had it rough. I never knew."

"You did have it rough, honey. Your arm? And Cody told me about the gigantic bruises you had on your thigh, the night we rescued you. And that's only the recent stuff?"

"He saw that?" She frowned, then exhaled. "I didn't think he saw that."

He didn't reply.

She broke another short pause. "Your parents didn't show up?"

"Yeah they did."

The quickness and tone of his answer made her question herself. "Your parents were there?"

"Yeah." He nodded in affirmation and repeated. "Yes they were."

She placed the two wrapped sandwiches on the breakfast counter. "Why didn't you tell us? Why didn't you introduce us? We could have supported you."

His voice lightened. "My parents ate pizza with us."

She looked down, disheartened. "Very funny."

"I'm not trying to be funny. I'm being serious. My family is who loves me. Blood means nothing, especially to me. You heard enough of my story. They threw me out, not caring if I survived. That ain't family. My new family is my family. You're my family."

She scrunched her nose at him. "Do you know Stephanie tried to contact your mom ...birth mother, to invite her again?"

An instant smile appeared on his face, as his eyes narrowed. "She proves my point. She loves me enough to try to make my life like hers. She wants me to have everything she has." He sat at the counter, and stared as if he had entered a trance. "But she doesn't understand some of the things I've been through, which is good. I'm glad she's never experienced some of the things we have. I'm glad you haven't experienced some of the things I have. I thank God for it, actually. I adore her; caring beyond expectation. But I have a family that means more to me than anyone knows. You called me and told me you missed me and needed to see me ...cook for me." He offered her an adamant smirk. "My family was there; every one of them."

They ate in silence as his words had more of an effect on both of them, than he wished. He hated when he did that. He worked hard to be positive, especially around people who cared for him, but sometimes the product of his past experiences proved too strong to quell; the wounds too permanent to always keep completely hidden.

He decided to change the mood and purposefully animated. "What are we getting Stephie and Jake for their wedding? Should we just give them money? Money is what I'd want."

She reached for his empty sandwich wrapping and crumpled it with hers. "I know that's normal, and we can give them some money too, but I want to give them something they can always have and know the gift was their wedding present from us."

"Good thinking. Stephie's definitely sentimental." He downed the rest of his soda. "She'll appreciate that."

"Lift your arms." She wiped the counter under him. "My mom has this stupid crystal cake plate, and she told me this story about when she opened it, she ripped her aunt and uncle for not giving money. Then she told me as the years passed, every time she uses it she thinks about it as a wedding gift and the gift became special to her. I always liked the story."

He made a silly face. "We're getting her a crystal cake plate?"

"Why do guys do that?"

He playfully leaned back as if her response offended him. "I think like a guy?"

She playfully pushed his shoulder. "Not always, but you sure just did. And it's not impressive."

He waved his hand at her. "Well excuse me."

She hugged him and kissed his cheek as he started walking toward the sofa. "You're forgiven."

He sighed. "Then you pick something out. Whatever you want. You know I'm with you."

"Want to do it today?" Her demeanor brightened.

"Sure. Do you want to go out or shop for something online?"

"Online is probably easier." She glanced at his eyes, then pretended to look away casually.

He watched her breathing increase. He knew there were days she didn't feel comfortable in public. "Let me get my computer."

# Chapter Eighteen
## Adjudication

The three mothers knew they were delaying the inevitable, and finally decided it was time to hear the rejection they all knew was coming. Plans had been made and the appointed day had arrived. Genna arrived at Lorraine's house a little before eleven. Their appointment with the Monsignor was in half an hour. Morgan opened the passenger door, ready to go knock for her, when Lorraine appeared at her front door. Morgan moved to the back seat instead.

"Good morning." Both greeted her with a kiss as she sat inside.

The car was silent as Genna drove to the small church complex, and they parked in the lot behind the church and to the side of the matching gray and black stone house.

Morgan scanned the small complex. "This is quaint."

Lorraine softly nodded. "Yes, the buildings are." Her insinuation produced another silence as they entered the white wood framed glass vestibule leaning conspicuously against the large dark stones.

"Hi. May I help you?" The soft-spoken lady stopped typing and greeted them.

Lorraine portrayed equal grace. "Yes, I have an appointment with Monsignor, please."

"Your first name?"

"Lorraine."

The woman stood. "I'll inform him you're here."

Lorraine moved to the two small seats filling the opposite corner of the small vestibule, and Genna and Morgan pointed simultaneously at the remaining seat before both decided to stand.

Moments later, an old white wood door, covered in decades of paint, swung open and a stately gentleman filled the opening. "Hi Lorraine. It's a pleasure to see you. Please come in."

The lady who greeted them followed, carrying one of the two reception area chairs.

Morgan turned as the lady placed it behind her. "Thank you."

"Oh you're welcome." She peered around Morgan, to the monsignor. "Shall I shut the door?"

"Yes, Lyn. Thank you."

They exchanged polite greetings, then he focused on Lorraine. "How can I help you today, Lorraine?"

"We've come to share special news and request you to preside over the ceremony. Our children are getting married."

"Congratulations. It would be my pleasure to perform the ceremony." He opened his calendar. "What's the requested date?"

"If only life was that simple, Gary."

"I'm sure we can work through any special circumstances. You've been a notable patron for quite a long time."

Lorraine smiled. "Let's measure your words."

He leaned forward without further reply.

"The bride is my granddaughter Stephanie. You've met my grandchild many times. Do you remember?"

"I thought you only had a grandson." He looked at her curiously, then inhaled deeply.

"She's marrying a beautiful young man." She gracefully motioned to Morgan. "Morgan's son Jacob."

He sat back carefully. "Lorraine, you know we can't condone such a union."

Genna intervened with her softest voice, "Humans like her have existed in every corner of the world since the beginning of humans. Why can't you recognize that? Have you ever studied the subject and objectively evaluated the available information?"

He met Genna's purposeful eyes. "I'm sorry. My view has nothing to do with the church's stance. The church condemns such unions. My hands are tied."

Genna sat forward. "Monsignor, I've noted the church's continued efforts to prevent human progress for as long as it has existed. GOD says, love all and judge no one, yet the church continues to judge and condemn. I'm starting to think your organization's concern with God's wishes, need revisiting."

"I'm not saying we're perfect, but I would disagree with you."

Lorraine raised her hand gently, and Genna paused, breathing deeply. Lorraine smiled gracefully. "Dear Monsignor, the continuing attitude of your organization toward the lgbt community has brought me to a regretful conclusion; I can no longer support your organization. I've overlooked your organization's faults for years, waiting patiently for it to mature. I'm getting old, and my patience for your childishness has come to its end. You ask me to choose between God's beautiful children and your antiquated edicts, and the choice is all too clear, I'm afraid. My late husband and I refused to support those who opposed us and your organization is the only entity on the wrong side of that demarcation we supported without examination, for a misdirected love of a God you swear to but continually fail to represent."

"Our religion has now decided I take notice of its actions, and I've noticed I'm standing on the opposite side of a line you've drawn against my children, for contrived, antiquated, and childish reasons. We'll find another church or chapel, and our children will have a magnificent ceremony, in front of a God you should reintroduce yourself to. I would have rather the wedding be in the house I've worshipped for decades, but I'll always honor my children before honoring their oppressors."

He remained as calm as she. "I don't view us as adversaries, and I wish you would reconsider. I don't want to see you lose your good standing with God over this single matter."

She folded her hands on her lap. "I'm only throwing away my good standing with your sociopolitical organization. My relationship with God has never been better or stronger. I can now see Him and commune with Him without your organization's intercession."

She waited for his response, then continued after disappointing silence. "I've lived through more than a few new Pontiffs waiting for change, only to be disappointed. The latest stepped in to quell rampant corruption and instead of acting like a true leader and making earth-changing decisions and declarations, he chose to ladle soup. If he was actually a leader, he would have delegated ten subordinates to ladle ten times more soup, while he made decisions that would have set the world in the correct direction for decades. I once ran a business and know all too well the difference between leadership and public relations."

She stood as she eyed her family. "Let's find a cute independent chapel for our children's ceremony and use Jacob's wise words as we acknowledge and pray to that beautiful Being without an intercessor concealing agendas incongruent with love." She faced the monsignor and spoke with a softer tone. "You should speak to my grandson Jacob. He knows of a perfect all-loving all-forgiving God that would make you relinquish your antiquated one in minutes. Call me when you're ready to question dogmatic paradigms, and I'll enjoy watching him dazzle you."

He stood as Genna and Morgan stood, and extended his hand. "Lorraine, we're very grateful for your kindness through the years."

"Monsignor, if you were, your actions would reflect your words. Please forgive me for such a blunt rebuttal, but your words today have been disappointing and I'm worried your concern is more for my contributions than my participation."

"I'm sorry you feel that way."

"And I'm sorry your actions are less than their potential. May God have mercy on your acceptance of your organization's decrees and may He not judge you as you allow it to judge others." She offered him a courteous nod, then led Morgan and Genna from the office.

They walked out into a magnificently beautiful afternoon and less than ten steps from the door, Genna could no longer contain herself. "Mother! I've never heard you talk like that in my life."

Lorraine shook her head softly. "My teaching method for you, when you were a child, is different from my reaction to adults who should've learned lessons they seem to reject. I have patience for one, and the other …little tolerance."

Genna reached for her hand. "You were brilliant."

Lorraine glanced at her. "Oh cara. It makes me sad when I have to teach people who should already know the information. I'm never happy confronting someone. It drains me and I'm always less for it."

Morgan opened Lorraine's passenger door. "Well I can't believe how you spoke of Jacob."

Lorraine caressed Morgan's cheek. "There wasn't a word that wasn't true."

She sat in the passenger seat and buckled herself in. "Now let's go to a willing church. I'll give you the directions to my first choice. It's an exit south on the highway, near that gigantic hotel."

Morgan tapped the back of Lorraine's seat. "Oh, I know it."

Genna turned toward the highway. "You found an lgbt friendly church?"

"I found more than one. It's just a shame some are so discreet about their acceptance."

"They know though?" Morgan leaned forward.

Lorraine smiled. "Yeah."

Genna glanced toward her. "I'll start looking for a minister, immediately."

"I received my ordination certification about a month ago." Lorraine's eyes moved from Genna to Morgan, as her smile grew.

Morgan's voice amplified. "You're going to be the residing minister?"

"Yeah I am! I'm marrying my granddaughter and grandson."

"Oh my god, mom."

"But don't tell them. I want it to be a surprise."

Morgan sat forward. "When did you decide to be the residing minister?"

Genna added, "Why?"

"I like controlling the outcome of certain situations when the opportunity arises. If I control the outcome, I increase the odds it'll turn out like I want." She grinned and turned from Morgan to Genna. "When I realized we had to count on a stranger we didn't meet yet."

Lorraine chuckled softly. "Redundancy is the key to preparedness and preparedness is the key to success." She pointed playfully. "Don't tell them, hear me?"

"Excuse my French…" Morgan squeezed the inside corner of each front seat as she pulled herself forward. "…but you're fucking amazing!"

"Not a problem, dear. I worked a kitchen for years. I know French well." She leaned back and chuckled. "…Been known to drop whole conversations in the art. Oh, and thank you for the compliment."

~~~

Jake turned the car onto the highway toward their parents' houses and Stephie sat back and sighed contentedly. She loved Christmas, but for a completely different reason than she did twenty years ago. To her amazement, the gifts meant nothing now. They were cute and fun, but mostly all they did was offer a token for what year the family celebration took place. She remembered one year when the temperature was so warm, they played out back during the day. Both sets of parents came out, sat in the yard and they all watched the sun go down. That Christmas was the most special. It was the first one the two families joined for the holiday and both families have shared Christmas together ever since.

She remembered another; the laughs at Chris's expense as Morgan playfully ripped him for buying the wrong champagne; some sweet pink variety, and his playful exasperated responses; making fun of her for finishing them just the same. Certain gifts were memorable too. Gifts worth more than their monetary value; the framed pictures Stephie and Jake gave everyone, now hanging in all three houses. She imagined she would remember this one for the new family members included, and noted the joy she felt having Vicky and Colleen as part of their holidays.

He shut off the car in front of his parents' house and she caught herself smiling at the thought of future memories the next few days would produce. "You need help with anything in the trunk?"

"No sweetheart. You get the food. I can handle everything else."

She hurried, throwing an overnight bag over her shoulder then carefully lifting the breakfast casserole that was her contribution to the extended overnight invitation. She knocked on the side door with her toes as she held the casserole with both hands.

Genna opened the door. "Since when do you knock and not just... Oh. Let me take that."

"Thanks. Hi mom."

"Hi sweetheart. I'm just setting the table. Where's Jake?"

"Getting the rest of our stuff. Is Morgan here?"

"No. She's getting ready for tomorrow, but we've been texting."

They shared casual news as they worked together over the next few hours and remained focused until Stephie dropped the last two filled snack baskets on the holiday tablecloth covering the temporary folding table in the family room.

Genna smiled as her eyes shifted from the table to Stephie. "Well done."

Stephie smiled. "We ready?"

"I think so."

She motioned toward the kitchen door. "Mind if I go across the drives and see if Morgan needs any help?"

"Not at all. Tell her I said hi."

She skipped across the driveway, knocked on the side door and cracked it open. "Mom?"

"Oh hi, love."

"I came over to see if you need any help."

"I don't need help, but you can sit and visit. I have things under control."

Stephie recalled a quick flashback from a few years before and the first time she worked alone with Morgan. The memory appeared vividly and without effort. She peered into the large mixing bowl on the counter in front of Morgan, after they kissed. "What are you doing?"

"Making the apple sausage stuffing for the crown roast tomorrow."

"Oh that sounds delicious."

"Check out the roast in the fridge."

Stephie opened the refrigerator. "It's gigantic and beautiful."

"Thanks, and I'm worried it isn't big enough. Our family is growing."

The thought made Stephie smile. "It is …and it's fun, isn't it?"

"I can't believe how much fun it is. Where's Jake?"

"He'll be over. He's probably helping Connor."

Morgan shook her head. "Men. He can't come over and give his mother a kiss first …like my daughter did?"

"You're too funny. Do you need me to peel potatoes or carrots or anything?"

"Nah. We'll finish dinner tomorrow. I'm only doing this because the roast needs to be in the oven, early."

Stephie looked around. "Is Chris here?"

Morgan motioned with her head, as she mixed the stuffing. "Firewood."

"I'm gonna say hi." She walked to the back of the house and opened the sliding glass door. "Hi sweetheart."

"Hi Dad."

"Ready for the next few days?" Chris walked the few steps to her and she kissed him.

"Oh yeah. I love living on our own, but part of me misses living here. I miss not seeing all of you every day."

Chris pointed to her and smiled. "Well you're not moving back."

Stephie shook her head and laughed. Chris never let an opportunity to be sarcastic slip by. "...Love you too dad." She smiled as she watched him refocus on the temporary wood stack he was building by the back door as she closed it.

She crossed Jake's path on the driveway between the houses and kissed him. "You're mother's waiting for you."

"Am I already in trouble?"

She continued toward her side door. "Let's just say I'm the good sibling."

She heard his faint "I had to help Connor." at the top of the steps as he opened his side door.

Vicky and Jon arrived last at the Blair house, and everyone greeted them with hugs and kisses as the new version of their family holiday officially started.

"Hi everyone." He kissed Genna. "Where we sleeping?"

"Morgan's. Mom has one room here and Stephie and Jake have the other. You two and Colleen and Cody are across the drive."

"Oh. I get to wake up in the house where family Christmas is? I haven't done that in a while."

Chris shook his head in amazement at the things he realized he had always taken for granted. "We host every other year, so you'll be waking up where Christmas is at least every other year for as long as you want."

His smile brightened. "Thanks."

Chris walked toward him. "No thanks needed. The invite comes automatically now."

Vicky extended his hand and Chris pushed it aside and hugged him, then kissed the side of his head.

Connor waited for the hug to end, then jokingly added. "And every other year you can stay right next door to where Christmas is." He extended his arms sarcastically toward Vicky and Genna smacked the back of his head. "Idiot."

He dropped his chin in reaction. "Ow."

She smiled at Vicky. "You're welcome at our house anytime."

He rubbed his head. "Son of a bitch, I did not see her behind me." He jokingly glared at Vicky. "Why didn't you tell me she was behind me?"

The glowing fire eventually drew everyone into the family room, and everyone found a comfortable place, after mulling around snacking and drinking. Morgan casually motioned toward Stephie in Jake's arm on the sofa while everyone joked and ate. "Are we ready for the big day?" Her question seemed to lower the other chatter.

Stephie met her eyes. "I think so. I mean, you and mom have the chapel and the minister, right?"

Morgan quickly glanced at Genna and she stopped chewing and stared back. She refocused on Stephie. "Yep …All taken care of."

"The hall is booked and the cake ordered." Genna smiled and sat forward. "I remember our wedding day like it was yesterday. We had a great reception. We drank champagne in the limo to the hall and all my bridesmaids were drunk by the time we reached the reception. We had a blast."

Morgan grinned. "Ours was crazy too."

Chris chuckled. "I almost passed out at the alter though. I started hyperventilating and got lightheaded."

"You never told me that." Morgan eyed him strangely.

"I did too."

Morgan made a face at him. "Lightweight."

Colleen smiled softly at Lorraine. "What about yours, Rain? Tell us about your wedding."

Lorraine sat forward. "I have special wedding memories, but better wedding related memories."

Colleen sat on the edge of her chair. "Tell us." She glanced at Vicky then back at Lorraine. "I love your stories."

"Robert and I didn't have much when we got married. We started saving money the year before, when we realized the relationship was serious. We only allowed ourselves the minimum spending money, and in the year, saved enough for a down payment on our first house. He also found a way we could assume the mortgage of a decent house, and sure enough, we found one we liked." She smiled softly. "One he liked anyway. Don't get me wrong, I liked the house too, but I knew it was exactly what he wanted and I loved him."

"But when we were saving, he used to say, 'Do you want a wedding or do you want a marriage?' ...Meaning we could buy a house or a wedding day. The choice was obvious, but it meant we didn't have money for anything more than the simplest wedding. His father died the year before, leaving his mother less than well off and my mother and father couldn't afford to pay either." She straightened in her seat. "So we had our wedding reception in our empty new house. We didn't have furniture so we rented chairs and tables and the caterer worked in our kitchen." She smiled at the memory. "But the choice we made then, is the reason I live in the house I have now. One led to the next and then to the current one. We actually bought it well before our last restaurant was a success."

"We scrounged for spare change for our first Christmas tree. I'll never forget. It was one of the prettiest trees we ever had." Her eyes gleamed as she reminisced. "I'll never forget the time we went to a neighborhood bar with only spare change and each had two beers because it was all the change would buy."

She lowered her head. "Not much of a wedding story, but fantastic memories of the beginning of our marriage."

She rose. "I need more wine."

Vicky, Colleen and Stephie all volunteered.

"You kids are too much, but I'll get it."

Genna fanned her face with her hand. "I just had a sobering flashback of our wedding preparations though. What a pain in the ass."

Connor sat back and laughed. "If you can make it through the wedding prep, the marriage is a piece of cake."

"Speaking of cake..." Morgan smiled as she eyed Stephie. "...what are you doing with the wedding cake?"

Stephie knew exactly what she meant. "Oh, he's wearing it."

Jake leaned back and laughed. "Oh yeah?" He rested his arm on the back of the sofa. "Okay."

"But don't you get any on my mother's and grandmother's gown, hear me?"

He waved a finger at her. "Oh no. There's no rules. You're fair game."

She bounced on the seat as she pointed at him. "No. I'm allowed to get you but you have to be nice to me."

He motioned to his father. "Dad, when we're married, I won't have to be nice to her anymore, will I ...once she's my wife?"

Her heart jumped. He had never called her that before, even with a future tense. She stood and registered the secret pleasure and felt her breathing increase.

"Hell no son, once she's your wife, she's fair game."

"Oh!" She scowled at Chris, then smacked him on his arm.

"Ow!" He flinched and then rubbed his arm as he stood, grabbed her, dipped her backward and kissed her forehead and cheek. Then instead of lifting her to her feet, gently dropped her on the floor.

She sat up and playfully pleaded to Jake. "Are you going to let him do that to me?"

Jake looked away. "I didn't see a thing."

A while later, Connor interrupted the party with his best authoritative voice. "Okay kids. It's midnight. Time for bed so we can all wake at a decent time tomorrow."

Vicky responded. "Aww dad, we're not tired."

Everyone laughed.

Cody waved a finger, referring to both houses, as everyone rose and kissed goodnight. "Where's breakfast tomorrow?"

Genna squinted toward Morgan. "How did we forget that?"

Morgan's brows rose. "I know why I forgot."

Colleen volunteered. "I'll cook, wherever."

"Breakfast at our house too." Chris's sentence sounded commanding, but his hand gesture and eyes were looking for Morgan's approval.

Connor kissed Colleen as he watched Vicky and smiled at his noticeable joy. "We have eggs and stuff we'll bring over tomorrow, but we're making due with what we have. No shopping in a store that won't let their workers have the holiday with their families."

Lorraine nodded. "I agree."

They finished saying goodnight and everyone headed to bed.

~~~

Lorraine quietly left her daughter's house before anyone else woke, crossed the driveways and knocked lightly on the inside kitchen door, making Colleen jump. She hurried from the sizzling bacon, opened the door and whispered, "Merry Christmas, Rain." They kissed tenderly.

Lorraine caressed Colleen's cheek. "Merry Christmas dear."

"What are you doing up?" She moved back to the pan on the stove.

"I had a feeling you would be exactly where you are," Lorraine pointed to the stove. "doing exactly what you're doing."

She noticed the coffee already made, and reached for a cup. "Did you have fun last night?"

"Yeah. Being accepted feels nice."

Lorraine fixed her coffee as Colleen turned from the stove. "Can we play our game real quick?"

Lorraine's voice softened. "Always."

Colleen eyed her curiously. "Why do you accept me?"

Lorraine sat facing her at the table. She could tell she wanted a deeper than casual answer. Their game had progressed to a much deeper level. "Love or hate again. Accept or exclude take the same effort. Why not love and accept?"

Colleen glanced at the bacon, then back to Lorraine. "You don't seem to have many friends your age. Why not?"

Lorraine smiled. "I'm young in my mind so I'm more comfortable around young people. Young people seem to still want to fix what's wrong with the world. Old people lose their fire ...that edge. I haven't. The planet is wonderful, but not operating at full potential. I always try to increase optimality, but when I discuss solutions with older people, they all seem to want to pass on the responsibility instead of being willing to continue making a difference. I don't have much power or influence, but I need to continue fixing what I perceive as wrong. It's my own little purpose." She rested both hands on the table. "Besides, young people are more fun. You make me tired, but alive."

Their heads turned as Chris appeared at the kitchen opening. "Good morning ladies."

Others wandered in and phones beeped with texts back and forth, and it wasn't long before everyone joined together.

Stephie eyed the gathering in the kitchen. "Hey, we have enough people to play touch football."

"Only if nana plays steady quarterback." Jake smiled at her.

"No way. She's a perfect wide receiver." Jonathan wedged his chair between Vicky and Cody.

"Who's getting in the shower first?"

The conversation stayed light and enjoyable the entire lazy morning and when showers and breakfast were done, they all collected their gifts and gathered in the family room.

Stephie held her hand out toward Colleen and Vicky. "Mom handles the coordination, so wait for her."

Vicky and Colleen sat back together.

Genna sat on her knees in the middle of the floor and scanned the room. "Mind if the older adults go first?"

Everyone agreed and gift cards and money envelopes were given out. After *thank you's* were done, the four younger adults gave out their presents, and the parents waited until they were distributed before opening.

"Perfect." Morgan opened and admired the framed group picture, handed it to Chris, then softly eyed all her children. "Thank you."

He stared and smiled. "Nice."

The gifts were as requested; framed pictures of different combinations of the younger adults and another round of kisses and *thank you's* went around the room.

When everyone sat back down, Genna glanced at her children. "Do you have gifts for each other?"

Vicky hopped in his seat. "Yeah."

Genna shook her head. "Go ahead."

Vicky noisily took over, quickly looking at each wrapped item he pulled from the carry-all bag he had placed between his feet, and passing them around. "These are for the guys. I guessed at the sizes, so if they're wrong, you can exchange them."

Everyone watched as the last package went to Jake, then all three guys started ripping paper and as soon as the first package was recognized, everyone started laughing.

Vicky held out his hands and sung his response. "What? ...Everyone needs underwear!"

Stephie giggled, "Is this for both of us or just him?"

"Hey," He waved his arm. "you can wear tighty-whities if you want, but that's TMI ...way too much information right now, girl."

He reached into his Christmas present bag and threw a small wrapped package at her. "But thanks for ruining a well thought out gift."

Stephie ripped the wrapper and held up the inner package. "I spoke too soon. I have my own."

Morgan looked around Jake. "They're not."

Stephie held it so Morgan could get a better view. "...panties 3 pack" She stared in amusement at Vicky. "I love you but you really are strange."

Vicky joked. "What? They were on sale."

Chris sat back chuckling. "I love this family."

"I'm not done. I'm not done." He pulled out other small gifts. "All the ladies get one of these."

"Us too?"

He glanced at Morgan. "Yes. All the ladies."

They waited until everyone had one to open, and Morgan read her hand-written and decorated coupon first. "A free make-up session at the department store of your choice, which includes roughly forty exquisite minutes of pampering from an expert consultant …and free samples." She raised the homemade coupon. "Oh how exciting."

Stephie waved hers. "I used a gift like this for some very special occasions."

Vicky coughed as he raised his hand to his mouth, then Stephie pointed at him and they both giggled.

"Oh."

Both gasped at Jake as he offered the unexpected acknowledgment, then pointed at him and laughed harder.

Chris couldn't ignore the opportunity. "You're community college class trip?"

Connor let out a loud laugh and Morgan whacked Chris on his arm as she watched Jake lower his forehead into his hand.

Genna noticed Jon's curious confusion and answered his unasked question. "They went away together for a weekend when they graduated community college."

Vicky and Stephie laughed harder as Stephie motioned to her. "How did you know?"

Connor acknowledged Cody's amused confusion. "I guess the larger the family, the fewer the secrets?"

Vicky wiped his eyes. "Obviously the worst kept secret …ever."

Stephie eyed Morgan and asked more enthusiastically. "How did you find out?"

Morgan raised her hands. "I don't remember."

Chris pointed at her laughing. "See? *That's* how you lie."

Connor extended his arms. "Come on. A weekend sponsored trip from a community college? Did you think we bought that?"

"Dad! You knew?"

"Let's just say the four of us had to discuss it over more than a few beers, but we managed to figure it out."

Genna redirected the memory. "And the day you came back. God, you two couldn't have been more in love." She smiled at the memory.

"I really thought we pulled it off." Jake grinned at Stephie. "I really did."

Chris shook his head and his voice deepened. "You're not that clever, kid."

Stephie rose from Jake's side and playfully choked Vicky before kissing him. "Thanks for the gift."

He raised his hands. "But I didn't say a word."

She turned her head as she hugged him. "Are you alright with this information, nana?"

"Dearie, my sisters and I had this conversation more than once when we were your age." She wiped the corner of her eye as she laughed. "Do you think you invented this stuff? Think about it. If it wasn't for my generation doing *things* …your generation wouldn't exist."

"Nana!"

They all laughed.

Colleen wiped her eyes. "Oh my god that was fun."

After the remaining presents were opened, Vicky gained everyone's attention. "Thank you for my biggest gift." His eyes widened.

Jon eyed him curiously. "What?"

He had everyone's attention. "This was the best Christmas I've had in years." Then his focus wandered to everyone around the room. "Being together was the best gift this year."

All the ladies rose and gloated over him with hugs and kisses as Chris brought the room back with playful sarcasm. "Kiss-ass."

~~~

The howling wind whipped through the back alleyway behind their apartment, waking Stephie as it announced another unfriendly winter day. She rolled next to Jake and he softly wrapped her in his arm and snuggled against the side of her face. "Let's have a day in bed."

Her heart jumped. "Okay."

She maneuvered, until they were face to face. "Are we making love all day?"

"That and sleeping."

She folded her arms between them and he brought her closer, then slid his spread fingers up the nape of her neck, through her hair. His warm caress made her shiver.

"You like the idea?"

She pressed the side of her face to his. "Of course I do."

His fingers lovingly entangled in her hair as he held her close. "But I need more sleep."

He kissed her forehead and she felt his arm get heavier, registered her own smile, sighed, and blissfully fell back to sleep, wrapped snugly in his arms.

She woke a time later, remembering their plans and her heart immediately resumed its increased pace. She didn't move though. She wanted him to sleep if he needed sleep. She had a conscious desire for him to have whatever he wanted …whatever he needed.

She knew he would fulfill her needs before the day was done. Each time would fulfill more than a few of her needs. She pictured playing and teasing …maybe even acting out a fantasy, and she knew they would also make serious passionate love and another part of her would have her deepest need filled, though the proof of his love always needed replenishing. The assuredness of his deep love only lasted so long, no matter how complete, …how believable. For now though, his warmth gently soothed her and she shut her eyes.

Not too long after, he rustled and woke her in mid thought. "Oh!" She jumped in his arms. "You know where I want to spend our wedding night?"

He laughed, then stretched and yawned. "You're just figuring out where we're spending that night?" He poked her sides.

She tensed excitedly. "You already reserved our hotel room? Oh I love it. I was wondering if we'd ever go back there. Can we call them and see if we can have the same exact room?"

"I already requested it."

"Jake! You're a genius."

He rolled toward her, kissed her, and patted her bottom. "Know what I feel like?"

She moved her head, trying to look into his eyes. "Me?"

He smiled as he nodded. "I feel like a fantasy. Will you wear something sexy?"

She straddled him, then leaned down and tasted his soft tongue. "Can we do a fantasy I want?"

His brows rose and eyes widened. "You have a fantasy you want? Oh wow. What?"

She rested her hands next to his head and stared into his eyes from arm's length. "And I want to have a safe word for this game."

He leaned toward her. "Like what?"

"Apricots."

"Apricots?" He tickled her waist.

"Yeah. I don't think *apricots* is coming up much in our normal sex talk." She nodded with self-approval. "...*apricots*."

His mouth twisted into a quirky grin. "You have a point. If we ever use fruit, apricots aren't in the bowl."

"The next sentence came out in unison. "What's in the bowl, bitch?"

He tickled her as she kissed him. "I love that line."

"Okay, now that *apricots* is our word, what's your fantasy?"

She pulled him over so she could stare up at him. "I want to be able to tell you no. I want to be able to say stop ...and you absolutely not stop. I want to resist you but you keep seducing me. I want you to take me. But this way, you know I really want you to, unless I say *apricots*. You absolutely keep going if I don't say that word. That word means please stop for real." She could feel her heartbeat increase as she watched his growing smile indicate he liked the idea. "And you take me ...make me do things to you as I try to resist your *charms*, until we both explode."

He laughed. "My *charms*?" He refocused and his eyebrows rose. "I like the sound of this game."

"I bought an outfit that'll make you love this game."

"I already love the idea if it's your fantasy. You never requested a fantasy before."

She caressed his face. "Yeah I have. I buy outfits I love wearing to seduce you. I love when we play."

"Yeah but you wear them for me. I love this because it's yours."

"They're all mine as long as I'm your fantasy."

He leaned down to kiss her and she wedged her arm against his shoulder. "No."

Her *no* caught him by surprise, then it struck him. "Oh. Okay."

She squirmed from under him. "I don't want to kiss you."

She went to their closet and removed a hanger covered in white plastic and a pair of high heels, smiled at him, then disappeared into the bathroom. He shut his eyes with the initial thought of a quick nap, but the anticipation of what was to come had his heart racing a little too fast to fall back asleep. It was a while before she reappeared, but when he saw her, he jumped with excitement, and sat against the headboard.

She walked into the room wearing a stunning black French maid outfit with a frilly white petticoat underneath …all short enough to reveal the lace tops of her white fishnet thigh high stockings, and his heart went immediately into overdrive, then his eyes continued down to the frilly white anklets topping her black patent leather high heels. He traced back up with his eyes, fascinated by each sexy nuance and smiled as he noticed the tiny white lace accompaniment sitting on her flowing dark hair. She paused as she watched him stare at her and take a deep breath. "May I dust in here, sir?" She held up a cute duster.

He met her eyes, and his widened. Her darker make-up enhanced her eyes more than normal and he couldn't help but be distracted. He refocused. "Yes, but don't disturb me."

She curtsied. "Of course sir." She moved to where he could see her best, then bent over with straight legs, revealing all of her stockings and most of her matching frilly white ruffled panties, as she began dusting the bottom of her dresser.

He watched for as long as he could stand it; mesmerized by the sight of her as she moved slowly toward him, dusting the bottom of their furniture. He blinked as he broke the trance. "I've been meaning to tell you, you've been missing something."

She twisted toward him without standing, pretending to continue dusting, then stood at attention with her hands folded behind her and chest enticingly pushed out. "I'm terribly sorry sir."

"It's alright, but I need you to take care if it immediately. …You've neglected to dust the picture over the head of the bed." He pointed to the picture above him. "…Please…"

She folded her hands submissively in front of her skirt and lowered her eyes. "I'll wait until you're out of bed, sir."

He tilted his head, fighting his telltale grin. "It needs to be done now."

"But sir." She pointed. "You're still in bed, and I would have to..."

He interrupted her. "Do you work for me, young lady?"

She smiled meekly, "Yes sir." then lowered her head. "Are you getting up?" She met his eyes without raising her chin, and watched his chest expand.

"Not this moment, no." She watched him discreetly reach under the blanket and push the proof of his enjoyment between his thighs.

She hesitated. "But I'm afraid… my uniform. …You'll be able to see underneath," She covered her mouth with her hand. "…and it might make you want to do things."

"Your outfit already makes me want to do things, and I believe you're purposefully enticing me."

She could hear his breathing getting stronger by the moment. "Oh no sir, I wouldn't." She could feel her heart pounding and knew he could see her breathing. She moved closer to the side of the bed and resumed her obedient posture.

"But I'm not asking, young lady."

She watched him lose control of his smile. "Sir?"

He pointed at the picture behind and above his head. "I saw dust on the top edge of this picture and you need to take care of it right now. I'm very disappointed in your failure to notice."

She lowered her head but couldn't hide her smile. "I'm very sorry sir. Please forgive me." She knelt on the bed, slipped off her heels, then stood, using the wall for balance. She hesitated, pretending his position impeded her.

"You'll be able to reach if you place one foot on each side of me."

"But sir, you'll be able to see under my uniform skirt!" She pressed the front of her skirt, and her growing enjoyment, down with her free hand.

"Well it needs to be done young lady, so I don't know what to tell you."

She bowed her head in submission, "Yes sir." then carefully stepped over his shoulder and a rush came over her. He had playfully maneuvered her into a delightfully compromising submissive position ...against her will. She reached up, pretending to dust and felt his hand begin to caress her stocking covered thigh. Her heart jumped with pleasure, but she quickly reached down. "Oh no sir, you mustn't!"

"I'm just steadying you."

"Oh sir ...please don't."

She heard his exhale. "But I can't help it. You're the most beautiful woman I've ever seen."

"Please sir." She pulled his hand off her thigh and pretended to dust. This time he reached further under her petticoat and ran the tips of his fingers under the bottom edge of her panties.

"Sir!" She pressed her skirt down. "I must insist! Please stop."

He slid his hands under her panties, against her resistance. "I can't help it. I want you."

"Sir, you're very very handsome, but I'm forbidden." She removed his hands and pressed her skirt down.

He slid his hands over her stocking covered legs. "But you realize you're a beautiful fantasy, don't you?"

"Oh no sir …I mustn't be. I'm your maid."

"And your outfit is making me need to touch you." He slid his hands further up her thighs.

She squirmed and reached, trying to fend him off. "Then please stop before you're …uncomfortable." She twisted as she continued to straddle him and glanced at his blanket covered hips and legs.

"I'm afraid you've already made me uncomfortable." He slowly moved the blanket to the side, revealing his already full arousal.

"Sir!" She gasped and covered her mouth, then quickly faced the picture as she tried to control her increased breathing. She inhaled deep. "You're very *very* handsome …but we can't, sir. It's strictly against the rules."

"But you can see I need to have you." He softly grabbed her ankles.

Her eyes grew wide as she twisted enough to study his beautiful erection and her voice softened. "But I'll get fired if my supervisor finds out."

"I'll promise not to tell …if you cooperate." He teased. "You do want to, don't you?"

Her next refusal came with more breath than voice "Oh no, sir." and her breathing noticeably increased as she realized he had pinned her feet, leaving her no choice but to remain spread legged over him as the front of her skirt betrayed her words. She tested his resolve and tried to move, and he held her still, making her heart jump with pleasure.

"Where do you think you're going?"

"Please sir, we mustn't." She could feel her own excitement throbbing.

He released one ankle and slid his fingers up her thigh and inside her panties, making her head sway back with pleasure as his fingers sent a jolt of electricity through her. "Why not?"

She exhaled. "Because I'll dream of being your lover and falling in love with you. …And you'll break my heart."

"What if I told you I've been in love with you and I need you. …I need to feel your soft skin. …to taste you …make love to you." He pulled her legs into him and kissed her silky thighs.

Her hand tried to push his head away as her voice changed to a plea. "Please stop before I can't resist anymore."

His voice filled with matching desire. "Please stop resisting." He gently slid his hand inside her frilly panties and felt her exquisite arousal.

"Oh …you're a special girl. How unbelievably sexy." He lowered her panties, then lifted her petticoat enough to enjoy an amazingly erotic view of his playmate and soulmate.

She reached down with one hand and pulled her panties up as she braced herself with the other, but her attempt still left her well exposed. "Oh no. Please don't." Her reluctance all but gone from her voice.

He sat up further as his hands pulled her down, and he held her by her bottom as his head came between her petticoat and the sensual warmth of her excitement.

"Oh sir! No. Please stop." She gave resistance.

He responded with more breath than voice. "I can't, sweetheart. I can't stop. You're fucking gorgeous and my heart feels like it's going to explode." He pulled her down, then opened his mouth and pulled her closer until she was deep inside him.

She lifted a hand off the wall and caressed the back of his head through the sexy skirt and petticoat. "Oh god, Jacob!"

He pushed on her bottom, moving her involuntarily in and out of his mouth, and moaned as he kissed under her excitement, "You're unbelievable." then quickly buried her in his warm wet mouth.

"Oh Jake." She squirmed. "I'm so close."

Her words prompted him to pull her deeper into him, and she lost what little control she had left. "Oh Jacob!"

She tensed as she reached the first overwhelming rush of pleasure and he wrapped his arms around her, holding her fast and accepting her love with heartfelt approval. She bucked uncontrollably as she shared moans of pleasure, spasmed with each lessening jolt, then finally relaxed in his grip.

When he was sure she finished, he pulled her panties down while lifting her leg, then lowered her onto his lap and kissed her passionately and as their kiss broke, she placed her head on his shoulder. "Oh Jacob. I love when you take me. I love you so much."

"I crave you more than you know." He placed his hands on the sides of her face and tilted her head until their mouths met and they kissed passionately again.

His words and kiss thrilled her and she promptly fixed her little skirt and petticoat around her as she straddled him. "Do you like my outfit?"

He placed his hand on the delicate satin and lace covering her chest. "It's incredible."

"Sir!" She fell immediately back into character, trying to remove his hand.

He reached under her pillow with his other hand, revealing their all too familiar thin bottle, as he playfully refused to remove the other from her chest. "Mister Jacob, what do you think we're going to do?"

He opened the lid with only a smile as a response.

"What's that for?"

Without answering, he held her hand as she watched him pour some of the thick clear liquid in her palm, then place her hand on his throbbing excitement.

She slowly moved her hand on him. "Oh, Mister Jacob, you're becoming all slippery." She watched him shut his eyes in pleasure and lose focus on everything but her hand.

"Oh that feels good." He moved against her motions. "Do you like the way that feels?"

"Oh Mister Jacob. Please don't tell anyone how much I love what's in my hand."

"Now, do you know what I want you to do?" He raised his brows eyeing her dominantly.

"Oh mister Jacob, no!"

"But I need to make love to you."

She tilted her head and her voice rose as she playfully questioned his intentions. "Do you really think I'm a special girl?"

"You are." His breathing increased.

"And you want to make love to me?" She moved back enough to feel his slippery warmth on her hidden bare bottom.

Her motions were making him lose focus. "We have to."

She paused. "Oh. ...We shouldn't." She tried to move off him. "I have to continue dusting."

"But you're going to give me a heart attack if we don't." He grinned wide. "How would you explain that?"

"Well.... I can't let that happen," She moved back. "...so maybe just this once." She slid against his slippery excitement, then stopped as her smile widened playfully. "No. You're going to think less of me." She motioned to move off him and slowly squirmed against him as he held her legs in place.

"Please sir. I need to clean your bathroom."

He held her hips and rubbed against her. "I have to have you. ...right now."

She pretended to demurely fight his pressure, "Oh no. Please don't." but slowly pressed against him as she wiggled with objection, until they accomplished what she teasingly pretended to resist, and he instantly held her still.

"Oh mister Jacob ...what did you do?"

The intensity of his breathing, and flushed face had her heart pounding. "Are you okay? Do you like the way that feels?" She remained still, but fixed the petticoat and skirt around them.

He breathed deeper. "It's exquisite."

"Do you like doing this to me?"

He broke character and laughed. "I love it more than anything else we do together. Don't I prove it to you every time?"

She smiled contentedly. "You do." She began moving slowly. "I like what you did to me too."

"You're delicious."

She primped her outfit and straightened as she resumed her role. "So am I your girlfriend now, mister Jacob?" She moved seductively on him.

He held her hips as she moved. "I want to marry you."

"Mister Jacob," She raised her hand to her mouth. "you don't mean that," She stopped moving. "...and you shouldn't say those things just to get a girl to ...you know."

His breathing intensified. "I mean it completely. I need to marry you and make you mine. You're the sexiest person I've ever met."

She sat down slowly, burying him as deep as possible and sensually whispered. "Then I'd be allowed to do what we're doing." He held her hips still and she smiled innocently. "What's wrong mister Jacob?"

She moved slowly and pressed deeply as he held on for another few seconds, then he stopped breathing and his eyes turned bloodshot before letting out a forceful cry of ecstasy. "Uhh!" He pulled her to him and held her open mouth on his as he bucked with the next release. She tenderly embraced his neck and squeezed him, and as he arched his back with the next wave of pleasure, she let her hair cascade around them and surround their joined faces. Each subsequent waive of pleasure causing an ever decreasing thrust inside her, until he softly moaned in her open mouth, and began to calm.

She waited for him to refocus. "I can't believe what we're doing. You don't even know my name." Her glistening eyes staring deep into his soul.

"I do too, Stephanie."

"You know my name?" Her voice rose as she kissed him softly. "That's so sweet." Her eyes widened. "So am I your new girlfriend?"

411

"No."

"No?" Her head shifted back, playfully indignant. "No!?"

He topped her indignancy. "No. We're getting married next Saturday, so you're my fiancé."

"We're getting married?"

He tickled her waist. "Yeah. We're getting married."

Her voice softened. "Do you like that idea?"

"Sweetheart, it's all I've been thinking about for weeks."

"Me too. I'm gonna be your wife, Jake. Your wife!"

He stroked her hair. "Do you like that idea?"

"Oh my god, Jake. Do you have any idea?"

He gently slid his fingers through the sides of her hair, "I do have an idea." then softly pressed her open mouth to his.

She rested in his arms until their breathing calmed, then leaned away from him. "Can I fix your breakfast Mister Jacob?"

"That would be very nice, Stephanie."

"What would you like?"

"Bacon, eggs, pancakes, home fries, toast coffee and juice."

She nodded once. "Cereal it is."

He laughed, then pointed to the furniture. "After breakfast, you need to dust between the back of the dresser and the wall, Miss Stephanie."

She eyed the dresser and smiled. "Do you think I'll be able to reach over the top, Mister Jacob?"

His right eyebrow rose as his telltale grin appeared. "I'm not sure, but I'll help you reach a few inches further than you would by yourself."

"Oh, that would be very nice of you, Mister Jacob."

# Chapter Nineteen
## Manifestation

The week seemed to last forever, interlaced with hours of too much detail to keep structured. But when the night of planned celebration finally arrived, Stephie sat impatiently waiting and checking her phone as Jake quietly enjoyed her discomfort. Finally, the long white limo stopped in the middle of their quaint street and honked. Stephie jumped and hurried to the front picture window, then quickly kissed Jake, "Love you." and ran to the steps leading to their front door.

"Love you too."

"Have fun tonight."

She heard him reply as she reached for the door. "You too. Be careful."

Haley stood by the open back door of the limo with her hand out, as she approached. "Your limo, *madam*."

"Why thank you, fine door holding type person." She bent over and Haley pushed her on top of everyone already in the back seat and her friends attacked her with hugs and kisses as she tried to find a way to sit up. "Hi!"…"Party!" Accompanying screams and yelps filled the cabin.

Vicky yelled, "Male strippers!" and everyone jeered. "No!" "Boo."

One of the girls yelled, "Female strippers!" and received the same response, and louder laughter.

Jake sat for a few minutes, then reached for his phone and dialed. "Hey dad. They picked Stephie up." He hesitated for a second and inhaled. "Can we meet earlier than planned?"

"Sure, son. Everything alright?"

"Yeah. I just want to have a beer with you before everyone else comes."

"No problem, son. Want to head over now?"

"Yeah I do."

"See you in a few."

"Thanks, dad."

Jake knew his father would be inside. Chris lived much closer to Logan's, but he wondered if his father could transport to the place. He never succeeded beating him there. He opened the door and immediately heard his father's patented deep greeting. "Jacob."

He smiled as his name registered, then headed to the bar and his father. "Hi dad."

"Hey son. How are you?"

Jake placed his hand on his father's shoulder as Alicia passed, pointing to him. "Draught light beer." He glanced at Chris as he sat. "Good, Dad. Real good."

"What's new?"

"Nothing. I just wanted to have a beer with you."

His father raised his glass and took a short drink, then glanced up at the TV. "You ready for Saturday?"

Jake nodded. "Yeah. Definitely."

Chris rotated his glass and centered it on the coaster. "Any cold feet?"

Jake turned his head toward him, "Not at all." then lifted the beer as Alicia released it and held it out to his father. "I've been thinking about everything since I'm about to get married, and I'm thinking about having a wife and maybe a baby and being responsible for them and I wanted to tell you, the more I think about it, the more I'm amazed at all the things you do for mom ...me ...for Steven ...for Stephanie and me. I think you're a great dad and I wanted to tell you. I wanted to have a beer with you and tell you."

Chris lifted his beer. "Does that mean you're buying?"

Jake laughed. "Not at all."

Chris playfully frowned, "Shit." then touched his son's glass with his. "And you've become an impressive man. I would have loved you one way or the other, but you've made me proud."

Jake grinned with pleasure. "And I'm proud to be your son."

Chris smiled. "And in two days, we're going to be equals. Men with their own families. I've been done raising you for a while, but this coming milestone means I'm officially done." He rubbed Jake's back. "I love you, son."

"I love you too Dad."

Chris finished his glass and pushed it closer to the far edge of the bar top. "You ready?"

"Very, Dad. I love her with all my heart."

Chris leaned back for an easier view of the TV, then glanced at Jake. "I can tell."

They sat for a moment as Jake finished his glass and pushed it forward. "Have any last minute advice for me before you call me officially done?"

Chris laughed. "Yeah I do, dammit."

He motioned toward Alicia with his hand and watched her acknowledge. "I'll tell you what my father told me." His eyes narrowed as he stared into Jake's eyes. "The only thing a good woman wants is a good man. ...And I'll add a few things of my own." Chris nodded once and smiled. "Make her your queen. Never compromise her. Ever. If and when you have a baby; love that baby unconditionally and more than anything, but don't give her or him authority over your wife. That baby will be the product of your love, not a replacement. But love and choose your child over every other human on the face of the earth, bar no king, pope or demigod. Don't punish. Teach. Children need teaching, not punishing. And love any other child that comes into your life who thinks you're special." He sipped his newly placed beer. "Love who loves you, and be no more than indifferent to those who don't. But most of all; have fun. This place isn't meant to be taken seriously, and you can tell when you do, because life will start overwhelming you. And that overwhelming feeling is life's signal to back off and take a breath." Chris rubbed his back as his grin widened. "And know your father is the wisest man you'll ever know." He grabbed him from the bar stool and kissed the side of his head. "I love you, kid. More than you'll ever understand …until you have a child. Then you'll understand."

Chris caught Alicia's attention as Jake straightened in his chair. "Can we have two cinnamons?"

She didn't hesitate as she headed toward the other end of the bar. "Sure."

"Now let's have fun." He waved a finger in Jake's direction. "Give Connor a call and tell him to get his ass here. The three of us need to drink like family."

The subject switched to sports as the invited few wondered in. "Hey best man."

Cody offered no reply, but blushed as he offered Jake his hand, and Jake smiled at his friend's unsure reaction. When Aaron and Anthony finally arrived, the six moved to a table away from the bar.

"Where's Vicky and Jon?"

Jake held his glass as Aaron filled it from a pitcher. "Vick decided he'd rather party with the ladies, and Jon has fucked up work hours, but may show up around eleven."

Connor held his glass out for Aaron. "Vicky *is* her maid of honor. Person. Person of honor."

They all laughed.

Cody joked. "I don't think he'd have a problem being called *maid of honor* at all."

Chris lifted his beer. "That shit don't bother him." He chuckled, then shook his head. "I love that nut."

"Anyone else coming?" Connor stretched for one of the shots Alicia placed in the middle of the table.

Jake eyed the small group. "Nah. I didn't want anything big. This is enough, don't you think?"

Connor placed the shot next to his beer glass and caressed the back of Jake's head. "I like your style."

Alicia carried trays of drinks and food back and forth as they ate, drank, and laughed for the rest of the night.

~~~

Stephie's eyes popped wide awake and she threw her arm over Jake. He jumped. "Damn."

She ignored him. "This is our last day not married."

"You're an idiot." He stretched his arms over his head and arched back, then pulled her on top of him. "I was sleeping real nice."

"I can't believe we're not sleeping together tonight." She frowned. "This is the first night we'll be apart since we moved in together." Her frown turned to a pout. "I don't like it."

And her pout tickled him. "I'm not much for tradition, but I actually like this one. You need to be at your mom's when you wake up, so you, her, and my mom can do all the things women do with

417

their moms, girlfriends, and best friends, on their wedding morning." He kissed her. "And all those things will be happy memories for the rest of your life."

He yawned. "Is Vicky doing your make-up?"

"You know it." Her head shifted back. "Hey! Are you saying I don't do a good job?"

"No, you idiot. I was thinking he'd like doing your make-up on your wedding day." He tickled her sides. "You're tough."

She straddled him and fought to control his hands as he kept poking her sides and tickling her. "If you don't knock it off I'm going to be a widow before I'm a bride."

He rested his hands flat on the bed by his head and she held them down. "I bought a beautiful dress for when we go to the hotel, after the reception. You're gonna love it."

His eyes widened. "You're bringing the wedding gown to the hotel too, aren't you?" He couldn't hide his uncontrollable grin.

She raised off him, then landed on his stomach. "Now, you're an idiot."

"Ugh. …Idiot nothing. I'm not going through all this trouble for nothing. I need to do you in your wedding gown."

She energized. "As your bride?"

"Definitely."

"Okay!"

He grinned as his eyes widened. "You're gonna be good and sore Sunday."

She bounced on his hips. "And I'm draining you of all your fluids, so drink lots of water." She leaned forward and tenderly kissed him. When the kiss ended, she sat straight. "And tomorrow, you're officially mine for the rest of your life."

He moved her to his side, "Like I wasn't when we were ten." then climbed out of bed and headed to the bathroom.

The day was long and lazy, with intermittent moments of panic as she thought of things to check on and worry about. Dinner was casual and they cleaned up together. "What time you leaving?"

She turned from the sink. "Do I have to?"

He smiled. "Yeah ...you have to."

"How about I drive over tomorrow morning?"

"And break both your mothers' hearts?" He stared at her with the strangest grin.

She sneered. "I hate when you're right. From tomorrow on, I'm always right and you always apologize for forgetting when you do ...hear me?"

He hugged her and lifted her off the floor. "Yes, dear. I promise dear." He tickled her waist. "I'm sorry dear. I won't ever do it again dear."

She fought his hands, then wrapped her arms around his neck and kissed him. "Are you moving from idiot to ass?"

"Yes dear. I'm sorry dear." He kissed her again.

~~~

She woke as if someone had knocked on the bedroom door, then heard another. "Sweetheart. Time to wake up. Everyone's here and the hairdresser will be here in two and a half hours."

She sat up, "Hi mom. I'm awake."

Stephie scanned her old room. It hadn't been long since she spent a night there alone, but long enough to know it wasn't her room anymore. Every corner held secrets, forever burned in her soul. This was once her hiding place; her fortress for years, but also the place that witnessed more inner conflict than she ever wanted to or could share. And though today was an official parting, she realized Stephanie ...the real Stephanie hadn't spent very long here at all. This was more Steven's than Stephanie's …and it was time to place this room, and all its memories, in the past.

"Get in the shower sweetheart. Time to start your big day."

The light from her window indicating the beautiful day, caught her attention. The sky had been a winter silver for a week, and the clear blue color was a nice change, but the weather didn't matter. She took her grandmother's recent words to heart. The wedding was a celebration, but nothing compared to what it represented. She wanted a marriage and family, and the wedding was nothing more than the day her marriage starts.

"I'm up I promise." She sighed, then registered the goosebumps and accompanying elated but uneasy feeling. The emotional intensity of the day would probably overwhelm her, no matter how much she focused on the intellectual perspective. She felt her heartbeat quicken. Today would be like no other.

Her shower was long and steamy and her heart never seemed to slow to normal, but she went through the motions without attention. She had other thoughts racing through her mind. She pictured Jake; wondering what he was doing. Sleeping without him next to her last night was surreal, though she slept well. She slid an oversized cotton sweat suit on, after drying herself and wrapping her hair in a towel, then wandered down the hall toward the voices in the kitchen.

She stepped into the room, immediately producing five joyous greetings. "Hi!"…"Good morning!"…"Happy wedding day!" Everyone stood and shared kisses.

"Are you ready?"

Her eyes widened as she stared at their smiling faces. "Is this really happening? I'm not having some weird dream?"

She flinched, "Ow!" then scowled at Vicky as she rubbed the spot he pinched. "Thanks. Remind me to kick you later."

"Everyone knows a dream can tell you you're not dreaming." He held the tip of his thumb and finger together. "But dreams can't pinch you." He made a pinching motion. "And you're welcome." He grabbed her and kissed her a half dozen times. "This is a wonderful day."

"Not until I have coffee."

As she said it, Colleen placed a full mug in front of her. "Want anything to eat? There's some muffins, doughnuts, and things in the dining room."

"No thanks. I don't think anything will stay down right now."

Morgan shook her head as she lowered her coffee. "Who would have thought twenty years ago, we'd be sitting here doing this?"

Stephie's breathing sped noticeably.

"What's wrong dear?"

"I don't know, mom." She sighed deeper. "Am I allowed to have this?"

Lorraine reached for her hand and offered with a confident voice. "Why not? Almost everyone does."

Her grandmother's words widened her eyes, but she offered no response.

"But what you're feeling is natural. It's an emotional day. I was unbelievably emotional my wedding day." Genna rubbed Stephie's forearm. "You take after me."

Morgan pointed to the magnum of champagne in the ice bucket. "I know what'll calm you."

Stephie placed her hand on her stomach. "Oh god, not yet."

She motioned toward the hall. "Is my gown…"

Genna interrupted her. "Hanging in my room." Her smile widened. "It's beautiful."

Vicky confirmed. "It really is. I can't wait to see you in it."

"I hope it looks okay on me."

"You're going to be beautiful."

"I hope Jake thinks so."

Vicky laughed as he waved his hand at her. "He's so frigging in love, you could show up naked and he'd still think you're beautiful."

Her eyes widened as everyone laughed, then she chuckled and noticeably relaxed.

He sat back and smiled, obviously pleased with himself. "Better."

They joked, teased and rehearsed the day, and the longer they sat peacefully together, the more comfortable she became. "The hairdresser will be here in an hour and a half. Who's left to take a shower?"

Vicky raised his hand. "Me."

"No one else?" Morgan jokingly smirked at him. "As much as you fit in here, you're still a guy. You can be ready in twenty minutes, can't you?"

He leaned playfully in her direction. "You know, just when I start feeling like one of the girls, some cis girl has to ruin it for me."

Morgan's mouth opened. "I didn't mean anything."

Vicky's eyes widened. "Girl …will you relax? I was only giving your gruff back to you." He lowered his voice as he stood. "I can't help it. I'm wound too tight today."

Four women replied in unison. "We know!"

He playfully scowled at everyone. "Okay. I'm jumping in the shower," He pointed. "then we're opening that gigantic phallic symbol of a bottle over there and drinking its delicious juices."

Genna leaned toward Colleen as he walked out of sight. "Did he just make the champagne bottle dirty?"

She laughed and whispered. "Kinda made my mouth water a little."

Twenty minutes later he reentered the kitchen in a robe and white ankle socks.

Colleen covered her mouth and chuckled as she eyed his feet. "Oh, you look lovely."

He pointed down. "Well I don't have a matching pair of dirty bunny slippers, like the two of you."

Lorraine held out her leg and smiled. "I'll buy you a pair this week."

He sung his response. "Thank you, Nana."

Morgan reached for the magnum. "I'm not waiting any longer. This party needs to get started."

Vicky pointed. "You go girl." then held his hand to the side of his mouth and whispered loudly to everyone. "Look at her use both hands on that thing."

Everyone laughed.

"Well it's big!" She twisted the cork out.

"It sure is!"

She filled five glasses and passed them out. When each had a glass, she raised hers. "To my dear dear daughter on her happiest day."

"Hear hear."

Colleen met Stephie's eyes after the toast. "Can I fix you a muffin or something?"

"I'll get it. Sit."

"No. I want to do it for you."

Stephie inhaled, trying to relax. "You're sweet and that'd be great."

Stephie sat and listened to her two mothers talk about seating at the reception, when Colleen slid the plate in front of her. She glanced at her new sister. "Thank you."

Colleen motioned toward the plate. "I added some eggs and bacon, just in case the muffin makes you hungry."

"So what's the hairdressing order?"

"Does it matter?"

Jake plopped on the sofa, then stood and began pacing. He raised his head and rubbed the back of his neck, then reached across the coffee table for his phone, pressed a few buttons and waited. "Dad?"

"Hey son. What time you coming over?"

"I don't know. Are you busy?"

"Nope. Just sitting here, relaxing."

"Is Connor with you?"

"Yeah. We're taking it easy."

"Good. I'm not doing so good at the relaxing thing over here. Mind if I come over early?"

"Not at all, son. Come on over."

"Okay. On my way." He motioned to end the call, then hesitated. "Oh. Text mom and tell her I'll be next door so Stephie doesn't come out …or gives me warning not to."

Chris chuckled. "See how much trouble it is marrying the girl next door?"

Jake hesitated. It wasn't anything but fantastic in his mind, but he knew his father was just trying to ease tension. "See you in a bit, dad."

"Careful driving. Pay attention."

"I will."

He hit the *end* button, then immediately hit two more and began texting. *Hi sweetheart. You doing ok?*

Vicky grabbed Stephie's beeping phone faster than she reacted, and read the name on the screen, then glimpsed at the mothers as he held the phone away. "Is she allowed to talk to him before the wedding?"

"Give me that. Is that Jacob?" She reached across him to his extended arm.

Her phone beeped again in his hand. *I'm going to my mom and dad's house. Don't go out the side door for like half an hour.*

Genna snickered. "Yes, she's allowed to text him."

Stephie reached further for her phone. "Give me that!"

He held his hand away, then stood and moved a step back. "But isn't it like seven years bad luck or something?"

Her voice rose anxiously as she reached a third time. "Is it him?"

His eyes brightened. "You want me to text him?"

"No." She grinned and held out her hand. "I don't trust you."

He covered his smile. "Oh! I've never been so insulted." His brows rose. "I'm devastated."

Her eyes narrowed. "You look it."

He smirked as he held the phone toward her. "I'm only trying to take care of you."

She brightened, "Well stop before I kill you." then reached for her phone and read the messages standing in front of him.

She quickly typed. *Yes. They stole my phone! Love you!*

Vicky quickly glanced at everyone else, nodding and pointing at her, "Are you all hearing this?" then refocused on Stephie. "You don't love me no more?"

She lowered the phone and stared into his eyes. "I don't love you no less."

He hugged her waist and lifted her. "Say you love me. …Say it."

"You love me." She laughed as she fought his hands. "Stop."

He lifted her high enough he had to look up at her. "Say please."

"Pain in the ass."

He didn't let go. "You know I'm just fooling around to ease tension, don't you?"

She hugged him around his neck and glared into his eyes. "Have you not been playfully torturing me since we became friends?"

His eyes widened. "I like to think I have."

Her voice softened. "Isn't that what older brothers do to their sisters?"

He grinned. "I like to think so."

"Then do you understand you better not stop, and you better stop asking me if it's alright. Do you hear me?" She kissed him before he could answer.

"Yes ma'am." He lowered her softly.

"What do I have to do …legally adopt you?"

Lorraine raised her head. "Now that's an idea."

His eyes welled as he released her "Okay." His breathing quickened. "It's an emotional day." He fanned himself. "Let's get through one ordeal at a time. Is it time for make-up yet, anyone?"

Genna whispered as she watched him leave the room. "He's adorable."

Lorraine sighed. "He really is."

Colleen and Stephie smiled and nodded to each other. "Yep."

The doorbell rang a half hour later and Colleen raised her arm toward Stephie. "You're not allowed near a door."

"Oh my god. Jake's probably next door, isn't he." She ran around Colleen to a front window. "Is our car here?"

"Someone please let the poor woman in?"

"I got it." Vicky opened the door. "Hi Katie. Great to see you."

"Hi Vick. You too. Can you help me with this?" She stepped back and let him grab her rolling cart filled with hairdressing tools.

"Hi everybody." She waved.

Return greetings followed. "Hi Katie."…"Nice to meet you."

"Where am I setting up?"

Genna shook her hand. "Follow us." She led the small parade to her bedroom, and the arrangement of dining room chairs and small folding trays she had Connor set up before he left.

Katie examined the make-shift work area. "Perfect."

Morgan gestured to Genna. "Shall we move the party in here?"

Vicky didn't wait for a reply. "I'll go get the champagne." He came back with the bottle and his make-up box.

They joked and gabbed as they took turns getting their hair done, and Vicky set up a temporary make-up area as Colleen and Lorraine relaxed on the bed, waiting their turn.

Genna whispered something about the ceremony to Morgan and it caught Stephie's attention. She eyed her mom curiously. "Is the minister a man or a woman?"

Lorraine answered, "Woman."

Stephie faced her nervously. "Does she know it's an lgbt wedding?"

Lorraine answered without a hint of emotion. "Yeah. And she thinks everyone's equal and she knows it doesn't matter at all to God. It's one of the reasons I chose her."

Genna stared discreetly at Morgan.

"You chose her?" Stephie's eyes widened.

"Yes." Lorraine looked resolutely into her granddaughter's eyes.

Stephie inhaled deeply and let out a long calm breath. "That makes me relieved. I'm glad you chose her."

Morgan and Genna watched Lorraine break the smallest smile.

The young hairdresser stepped back as the others admired Morgan's hair. "I love it."…"You look very pretty."

Then they all acknowledged the bride. "Your turn."…"It's time."…"You're last."

Stephie sat in the designated chair. "Jake and I decided; even though Cody's Jake's best man, we want you both to walk with your guys. They can switch places at the altar."

"Oh, excellent idea."

Katie softly interrupted. "How do you want your hair?"

Stephie raised her hands to the sides of her hair. "I want it pulled back on the sides but down in the back with some in front here."

Genna interrupted, "You're not wearing your hair up?"

Stephie inhaled as she eyed her mother. "No. Jake asked for it this way."

Colleen and Vicky voiced support. "Perfect." … "Be his everything, girl."

A short time later, Katie hesitated before wrapping up. "Is everyone happy? Do you need me to do anything else?"

"I think we're good, dear. Thank you very much."

She glanced around the room, making sure, then started packing things away.

Vicky finished Colleen's make-up moments later, then paused and breathed deep. "I need to ask something I hope isn't too selfish."

Genna and Lorraine both stopped talking and watched him. "What, sweetheart?"

"Would it be too much to ask if I could do Stephie's make-up in private?"

Stephie immediately enthusiastically agreed. "Could we?"

Genna looked at Morgan, then at Lorraine. "Sure. You can be alone with your best man ...person of honor."

Lorraine smiled, "That's an excellent idea." She motioned toward the door. "We'll take the party back to the kitchen for a bit."

Vicky and Stephie both echoed appreciation. "Thank you."

Stephie shut the door softly after everyone else left, then met Vicky's gaze. "You have no idea how I wanted you to do my make-up alone ...like we've always done. I need this."

She walked to him and hugged him dearly. "You've been such an important part of my life. I love you."

He slid his arms around her and kissed her forehead. "Aww sweetie, you mean so much to me. I love you too." He motioned her to sit. "I can't believe I'm doing your make-up for your wedding. Ha! It's almost as significant as making you up for your big V."

She smacked him on his leg as he moved beside her. "I was thinking the same thing."

He raised his hand to his mouth. "Oh my god that was funny. You were so nervous ...so adorable."

"Jake reserved the same hotel room for our wedding night."

"Ahhh ...too funny! Well you must have done something right that night. You got him to marry you."

He giggled as he reached in his make-up box. "If that room could talk."

He watched her smile as he removed a container from the box, then tenderly touched her forehead and each cheek as he began. "And now I'm doing your make-up for your wedding. ...my little sister's wedding. ...I'll never forget this."

His concentration intensified as he worked his art, meticulously attending to every detail.

She broke the silence. "I could go to sleep when you do this to me."

He straightened. "Wow. I was in a zone."

"I know." She met his eyes. "So ...do you have any advice for your little sister?"

He smiled, "Yeah." then breathed deep and exhaled softly. "Yeah I do."

He searched for a small applicator. "Shut your eyes."

She did as told and raised her chin, trying to anticipate his needs.

"You know I've been through things I don't want to share with you."

She whispered. "I know."

"And you know the reason I don't want to share isn't for me, but for you." He manipulated the color he applied with the lightest touches of his thumb as his fingers caressed her jaw.

"But I can handle what you need to tell me."

"I know you can. But I don't want you to think that's what your world is. My hope for you is to have as close to what I dreamed of having as possible, and I want to do my part."

He continued the application, then the meticulous manipulation with his fingers, wiping them after each step. "I want you to have more than me. I don't even want you to know what I've seen ...where I've been."

"I know more about what's out there than you think."

"I know you do. But there's a difference between reading about things and experiencing them, and I hope ...even pray you're one of the people who doesn't experience those heartaches."

His thumbs gently caressed her eyelids and she felt his love.

"What I'm trying to say is; there will be people who will choose to be against you ...you and Jake ...for the rest of your lives. ...Don't engage them individually. I know sometimes it's hard, but they feed on hate. Don't engage them. Walk away always. They don't affect you more than a level of momentary irritation. But you can't win the confrontation. You can never win the confrontation, do you understand?"

Her brows rose though she didn't open her eyes. "I think so."

He moved his focus to her cheeks and chin. "What I'm trying to say is; you're beautiful. You're beautiful inside and out, but your inside is beautiful in a tender way, and I don't want that harmed ...or lost. Protect the tenderness you have, because it feeds others more than you realize. I watch it feed Jake. Your soft heart draws the three mothers in. I even see it feed Chris and Connor, though I think a lot of your tenderness comes from your father."

He brushed her face lightly ...slowly. "And know I love you. ...And I'm honored to be your brother, even just in spirit."

She whispered. "Stop. I'm going to cry."

He stopped working on her and she opened her eyes and caught him wiping the tears from his. He raised his right arm and blotted his eyes on his sleeve. "Sorry ...emotional day."

He jumped and startled her. "Happy. Today is a happy day. …Unbelievably happy day! No more tears except tears of joy!"

A twisted smile appeared through her perfect make-up "Are you going to cry at the altar?"

"You know it girl. I plan on blubbering through the entire ceremony."

She mocked him. "Wonderful."

He stepped back and jokingly stared at her. "Hope you weren't expecting anything else."

She inhaled deeply. "I wouldn't trade you for anything."

She stood and they hugged tight. "I love you little sister."

And she whispered in his ear. "I love you big brother."

They separated and a strange smile grew on his face. "Time for your gown, girl."

She felt her heart beat in response, but offered none to him. He opened the bedroom door, "Time for her gown!" then heard the instant commotion from the kitchen, and Morgan's voice. "We're coming!"

After much fuss, the ladies managed to dress her without damaging her make-up or hair, then finished primping her as Vicky slipped her heels on.

~~~

Jake exited his old bedroom dressed in his tux and stopped at the entrance of the family room. Both fathers sat dressed in their matching black tuxes, relaxed as could be, and neither budged as he appeared. His eyes narrowed. "Aren't either of you the least bit nervous?"

Connor glanced at Chris, then smiled at Jake. "Hell no. We already did this. Your turn. You be nervous."

Jake smirked, "Thanks …dad." then looked around and waved his arm. "Shall we?"

Chris leaned his head back. "Are we going right there or do you want to stop at Logan's first?"

Jake playfully shook his head. "I'm going to pretend I didn't hear that."

Chris held his arms out after he stood. "What. It's only a suggestion."

Both fathers lifted their jackets off the empty chair, then Chris motioned toward the bedroom. "Go get a hangar for your jacket, for the car ride."

He ran back to his room and met them at the side door. Chris patted his pockets, "Keys …phone …wallet …balls." then looked at Jake. "I got everything."

"Wait." Connor straightened. "Who has the rings?"

Jake motioned in panic then felt his pocket and relaxed. "Got 'em."

His father stood at the door without moving. "Got the other four?"

Jake patted himself and smiled. "Yeah, dad."

Chris motioned them through the door. "Then we're good to go."

~~~

Lorraine waited until most of the guests were seated and Jake was standing in front of the altar before entering the chapel from a side door by the podium. She appeared elegant in a long flowered dress, and the white satin sash cascading down from around her neck gave all indication she would be more than a casual observer. She portrayed a gentle yet comprehensive authority.

Jake noticed her motion as she approached and did a double-take. "Hi." His face brightened. "Are you marrying us?"

He stepped up the two steps between them, then hugged and kissed her. "Oh my god, this couldn't be any better. Thank you." He inhaled in amazement. "Wow. Stephie's going to jump for joy!"

She held his hand after their kiss. "At first, I was doing this for the two of you so there'd be no issues with the ceremony, but the anticipation of seeing you and her together, standing in front of me, being married by me is giving me immeasurable joy."

The organ began playing and everyone stood and turned toward the small crowd gathering in the vestibule between the two sets of doors at the back of the chapel. Most clicked phones and cameras, as six year old CJ and four year old Chrissy began walking toward the altar. He moved slowly, balancing the white ring-bearer's pillow resting in his arms as she intermittently picked a single red rose petal from her basket and dropped it daintily in the isle.

Soft claps and cheers filled the room as they made it to the altar, then everyone looked back as Dawn and Aaron made their way up the center aisle. Colleen and Cody began walking on cue, followed by Vicky and Jon some twenty feet behind.

Everyone watched as they greeted Jake, and took their place along the front, then all turned as the organ changed songs. Goosebumps crossed Jake's neck and shoulders as Stephanie suddenly appeared behind the second set of doors and his chest expanded as he stared. His lifelong soulmate never looked more elegant …more beautiful …more amazing.

She extended her lace covered arm as Connor stepped next to her and placed it in his. Then as if in slow motion, she gazed in his direction, and the goosebumps ran their course once again.

She looked stunning. And her white lace bodice gown was breathtaking. Every motion she made exuded a grace he had never registered before. Her hair cascaded over her soft lace covered shoulders and the thin gown below the lace bodice seemed to glide around her. He met her eyes and lost all thought of everything around him. His bride overwhelmed him, and even from a distance, her eyes left him awe-struck.

He leaned back, trying to breath. The most beautiful woman he had ever envisioned was about to join him for the rest of their lives. She stopped momentarily, twenty feet from the altar and mouthed, Nana? Her eyes widened and her smile lit her face. Jake glanced at Lorraine, fully registering the joy his loving bride exuded as she realized who would be marrying them.

She stepped close, but before greeting him, passed her bouquet to Vicky then turned and kissed her father. Connor then took her hand, shook Jake's, and placed her hand in his, and as she faced him, their eyes met and he felt the air leave his lungs. "Hi sweetheart." He inhaled fully. "You're breathtaking."

She smiled. "I'm so nervous."

They turned forward and her smile grew as she whispered. "Nana. Oh my god, you're marrying us? Oh my god." Her eyes widened. "This is the best thing ever!"

Vicky whispered loudly from behind. "I know!"

Lorraine smiled delightedly and whispered back. "It's the best thing I ever did."

Lorraine's eyes lifted over Stephanie's head as she raised her hands slowly. "Let us begin." She paused for a moment. "Good afternoon everyone."

Soft replies followed.

"We are gathered here today to celebrate the union of Stephanie Blair and Jacob Harrison in marriage. To those who wish to honor and acknowledge the love and friendship this ceremony represents, please offer your silent well-wishes. To those who wish to honor and acknowledge an all-aware spiritual Being, please ask

Her or His favor on this union. And together let's join in the witnessing and participation of one of the most important and beautiful ceremonies known to the society of man."

She hesitated gracefully. "These two beautiful individuals have grown together as best friends since they were five and have already shown countless commitments to each other, through twenty years of life's ups and downs, and wonderfully have decided to make the final and most significant commitment to each other. And I cannot tell you how honored I am to preside over the ceremony signifying their greatest act of love."

Lorraine paused for a moment, before continuing. "Why is this such an important ceremony? I believe it represents love unequaled, and there is no greater emotion, no greater act, no greater force. It is a final commitment and joining of two people who love each other so much, they wish to spend the rest of their lives together, faithfully committed to each other. There is no nobler expression of caring, and because one can break the agreement at any time, continuation is always voluntary; making this a ceremony without equal."

"There have been many attempts throughout history, to explain what love is. Many writers and almost all poets have attempted to express our most important concept with words, and no matter what I've read, the words never seem to fully encompass the concept ...the feeling. But I find the explanation in Corinthians, the most enjoyable word explanation. See if you agree."

She opened the small book in her hands, to a page marked with a thin black satin marker.

"Love is patient, love is kind. It does not envy, it does not boast, it is not proud. It does not dishonor others, it is not self-seeking, it is not easily angered, it keeps no record of wrongs. Love does not delight in evil but rejoices with the truth. It always protects, always trusts, always hopes, always preserves. Love never fails."

She closed the small book and addressed the gathering. "Love is the greatest axiom known to consciousness. Many think it is God's single eternal spiritual rule. Many believe our Creator is the spiritual perfection of this paradigm. I've read where some believe love's unconditional illumination comes eternally connected with the concept of forgiveness; love-forgive divinely interlocked in definition in the spiritual world, and not two separate concepts as they are in our language."

She opened the book to another marked page. "And this is His final command on love. John thirteen, thirty four and thirty five. ...A new command I give you: Love one another. As I have loved you, so you must love one another. By this everyone will know you are my disciples, if you love one another."

She closed the book slowly and raised her head. "Please take a moment, and choose today to recognize all those around you as family. Love and forgive today together, as if we were trying to emulate a perfect loving forgiving Creator ...as if we wished the Creator would recognize us as Her children."

Lorraine paused, allowing contemplation. "We're all brothers and sisters in the family of man, but we also have an additional connection, and the bride and groom have requested a pause in their joining for the acknowledgment of their parents." Lorraine motioned to them, and they walked to Genna and Connor, who rose and exchanged kisses. Stephie whispered between them. "We love you both more than words can explain. Thank you for ...everything."

Genna blotted her eyes. "You're our life, sweetheart. Our love, come alive."

They crossed the aisle and Chris and Morgan stood. They kissed as Jake whispered between them. "Because you are unconditional love, I know how to love. We love you with our souls."

Morgan blotted her eyes and whispered. "You're ruining my make-up."

They both laughed, then he took her hand and they walked back to the altar.

Lorraine held the small black book with both hands. "The bride and groom have prepared proclamations they will now share with each other, with all gathered as witnesses."

Stephanie stared into his eyes as she took his hands. "Oh Jacob. My Jacob." She inhaled deeply. "My love for you hasn't followed a typical course. Most people don't meet their soul mate when they're five. Most soulmates don't experience the opportunity to show their commitment so many times before their marriage. I've already watched you stand beside me, willing to protect and defend me against anyone and everyone. I've already watched you love me beyond any common definition. I'm overwhelmed with how you continually show me I'm unbelievably blessed. I know I'm loved beyond doubt. I've already seen countless examples of your complete love, and I love you with all my heart and soul; almost overwhelmed I have a chance to be your love for the rest of our lives."

Jacob inhaled deeply and held both her hands. "My dearest love. We've already faced more than a lifetime of experiences, and I have a feeling our lives' experiences are far from over. You're my best friend and have been since before I knew I was alive, but as our years together increased, you became more. So much more than words can express. You've never failed to show me a love so deep it reaches the core of my being, and I'll work on returning that genuine joy for the rest of my life. Repeating words my favorite teacher has said to my mother over their years, and never changed. "Only time will show you how deeply I love you. …And I look forward to proving my love for you …for the rest of my life."

Tears trickled down his face as he watched her cry. Vicky stepped toward them, tissues extended in one hand as his other held tissues to his eyes.

Lorraine finished wiping her eyes. "And now, I take great great pleasure in marrying you."

She stepped down the two steps between them. "Join hands."

She opened the small book to another page, then met Jake's eyes. "Do you Jacob Harrison, take Stephanie Blair to be your lawfully wedded wife, promising to love and cherish her from this day forward, through joy and sorrow, for better or for worse, for richer, for poorer, in sickness and in health, until death do you part?"

His eyes widened as he stared into hers. "I do."

"Please place the ring on her finger." Cody handed him the ring and he gently slid it onto her finger.

"And do you Stephanie Blair, take Jacob Harrison to be your lawfully wedded husband, promising to love and cherish him from this day forward, through joy and sorrow, for better or for worse, for richer, for poorer, in sickness and in health, until death do you part?"

She stared deeply into his eyes. "I do."

Please place the ring on his finger. Vicky handed her the ring and her hand trembled as she tried to slide it onto his finger. She finally succeeded, then turned to Lorraine.

Lorraine smiled, then raised her voice as she peered over the gathering. "With great pleasure, I now pronounce you husband and wife! You may kiss your first kiss as a married couple."

He held her tenderly, softly met her mouth with his, and kissed her passionately.

She breathed deep, staring into his eyes as the kiss ended, then whispered softly. "Am I really your wife?"

He leaned closer and whispered. "You're my wife, my partner, my lover, my obsession …my everything."

# EPILOGUE

Danielle heard the commotion as she walked down the stairs, then smiled as she moved closer and recognized the voices. Her two grandmothers were in the kitchen, talking and laughing with her mother.

She stepped into the opening. "Good morning."

"Oh good morning sweetheart."

"Good morning, love." Her closest grandmother caressed her hair as they kissed. "You're beautiful."

"Thanks, grandma."

She kissed her other grandmother. "Hi, nana."

"Hi precious."

…Then glanced at her mother. "Morning mom."

"Hi sweetheart. Want a cup of coffee?"

"I'll get it." She opened the cabinet and removed a mug, then glanced at the table where her grandmothers sat next to each other. "I love when you two visit together." She looked around. "No grandpas?"

"They're with your father, watching your brother play baseball, so we took the opportunity to come visit."

Danielle kissed her mother as she sat next to her at the kitchen table. "Fantastic. What's new?"

"Your engagement is new."

"I can't believe our little girl is old enough to be engaged."

She stared at her ring, moving her hand around for different perspectives, then refocused on Morgan. "Grandma, I'm graduating college this semester."

"I know, I know. But I can still see the baby I used to cuddle with on the sofa, eating snacks and watching cartoons."

Danielle chuckled. "I still watch cartoons."

Her grandmother lowered her coffee mug and smiled. "Me too."

She sipped her coffee. "We should do that again together."

Morgan smiled. "You name the day. I'll buy the snacks."

She turned to her other grandmother. "Then maybe the four of us can go wedding dress shopping together?" She always felt guilty not including both, for whatever tentative plan she made, but they seem to come as a pair; living next to each other.

Genna held her coffee mug with both hands as she met her granddaughter's eyes. "Well that's kind of why we're here this morning."

She straightened in her chair. "Is something wrong?"

Her other grandmother answered. "No, love. Just the opposite. We want to share something with you, we think you'll enjoy."

Genna reached for Morgan's hand. "I'll never forget seeing Stephie…"

Stephie interrupted. "Mom! Don't give it away."

"Sorry dear, but you were beautiful."

Danielle quickly scanned the three of them. "…what's going on?"

Genna eyed Stephie. "Where is it?"

Stephie snickered. "It's been in the same place since you gave it back to me."

Danielle leaned back, placing both hands on the table. "What are you talking about?"

Morgan ignored her and playfully scorned Stephie. "Will you go get it already?"

Stephie stood. "Alright already. Sheesh."

Danielle turned toward the opening as her mother disappeared, then glanced back at her grandmothers. "What's she getting?"

Morgan squeezed Genna's hand.

Moments later Stephie banged into the side of the kitchen opening, with the gigantic white box covered in a living room blanket. "This damn thing is heavy …and awkward."

Genna nodded. "It's bigger than I remember."

"What is it?" Danielle sighed with mock exasperation.

Morgan smiled as Stephie stood the covered box on the table. "You'll see."

Stephie inhaled from the struggle. "We can't open it here. Let's go into the living room."

Danielle's voiced raised with excitement. "Want me to carry it?"

Morgan lightheartedly smacked her hand, "Don't touch that." then lifted the box. "Go."

They all followed her loving command and led her to the living room. Genna lifted the glass bowl off the coffee table and Morgan set it gently in its place.

Danielle pressed on the blanket covered box. "Mom …Grandmas …did you buy me a present?"

"Your great grandmother Lorraine bought this seventy years ago."

"For me?" She sat on the sofa facing it, with her hands noticeably squeezing her thighs.

"Well, not really. Great grandma used it first, then nana …then I used it." Stephie and Genna made eye contact and smiled.

Morgan sat straight. "I can't take it anymore. Can we show her?"

Stephie removed the blanket and revealed the blue words on the white box. *Your Wedding Gown.*

Danielle covered her mouth and gasped. "Oh my god, mom. I thought you said this was ruined and thrown away."

Morgan playfully energized. "We lied."

"And this is the dress all three of you wore?"

"Yes it is."

She met her grandmother's eyes, "Can I wear it?" then looked at her mother. "Do you think it'll fit me?"

Morgan placed her hand on her heart. "Oh god, how I hoped that would be her reaction."

Stephie began unsealing the large box. "You want to?"

"Great grandma wore this?"

"Yep. This was her dress."

She placed her hand on the box as Stephie carefully opened the side, then pointed between her mother and grandmother. "And both of you?"

Genna inhaled, smiled and nodded. "Yep."

Stephie laughed as her eyes gleamed. "Yes! You saw the pictures. Don't you believe us?"

Danielle reached out, almost afraid to touch the gown as Stephie slipped it out of the box. "I just can't believe it, no. This is the wedding gown in all the pictures? …And it wasn't ruined by the cleaners like you always told me?"

She stared at her mother. "You had it stored away the whole time waiting for me to wear it?"

Stephie raised a finger. "Hoping you'd want to wear it." Then her voice turned apologetic. "Sweetheart, the gown is over seventy years old. We were worried it would disintegrate if you played dress-up in it. We had to keep it a secret to preserve it." Stephie's brows rose. "Does that fact make the secret acceptable?"

"Only if I can wear it. Do I get to be the fourth generation to wear it?"

Genna waved her hand, interrupting Stephie and lightheartedly replied, "If you want," then her voice turned solemn. "...but the reason we kept it a secret, becomes the stipulation."

Danielle's head shifted back and she paused as her grandmother's words registered. "I have to lie to my daughter?"

"Yes, to preserve it, don't you think?"

Danielle laughed. "I do! She can't ruin it before her big day."

Genna pointed at her sternly. "And you're forbidden to tell your daughter about this heirloom until she's engaged ...like we just did to you. Do you hear us?"

Danielle glanced back and forth from her two grandmothers to her mother, as the three stared at her with bright smiles. "My daughter?" She thought for a second. "Oh my god, do you think my daughter would want to wear it?"

Morgan interrupted her fantasy. "You promise it's a secret until she's engaged?"

"Grandma, my baby would be the fifth generation. How great would that be?" She stood and lifted the gown by the shoulders and held it against her. "This is awesome!"

The Presentation Addendum…

The Foundation of LGBT Normality

LGBT from a Historical, Psychological, Biological and Religious Perspective:

escarpenter.tumblr.com

www.ingramcontent.com/pod-product-compliance
Lightning Source LLC
Chambersburg PA
CBHW060137260626
47160CB00001B/6